# THE FATAL TOUCH

**CONOR FITZGERALD** has lived in Ireland, the UK, the United States and Italy. He has worked as an arts editor, produced a current affairs journal for foreign embassies and founded a successful translation company. He is married with two children and lives in Rome. *The Fatal Touch* is his second book.

By the same author

*The Dogs of Rome*

# THE FATAL TOUCH

AN ALEC BLUME NOVEL

## CONOR FITZGERALD

BLOOMSBURY

LONDON · BERLIN · NEW YORK · SYDNEY

First published in Great Britain 2011
This paperback edition published 2012

Copyright © 2011 by Conor Fitzgerald

Bloomsbury Publishing Plc
36 Soho Square
London W1D 3QY

www.bloomsbury.com

Bloomsbury Publishing, London, Berlin, New York and Sydney
A CIP catalogue record for this book is available from the British Library

ISBN 978 1 4088 2173 2

10 9 8 7 6 5 4 3 2 1

Typeset by Hewer Text UK Ltd, Edinburgh
Printed in Great Britain by Clays Limited, St Ives plc

MIX
Paper from
responsible sources
FSC® C018072

For my father, Seamus F. Deane

# 1

IN THE PHOTO on his desk, Antonio was smiling straight at the camera and holding up a gold medal with a blue plaque on which was written Manager of the Year.

He was struggling to replicate the smile now as he looked across his desk at a Chinese couple and two cops—one bored, the other hostile. The bored one, sitting farthest away, blended in with the gray wall. He looked like a spoiled priest and barely spoke. The hostile one seemed at first glance like he might be a great thinker or poet, thanks to his high forehead and early onset baldness.

"Tell those two fucking Jap monkeys that if they can't be bothered to come down to the police station to report a mugging, we're hardly going to give the loss of a Nikon camera top investigative priority. They're lucky we bothered turning up at all. No reported crime, no investigation," said the poet.

Antonio held up his hand. "Please, Agente ..."

The policeman slapped the insignia on his shoulder angrily.

"I'm sorry, I don't know what rank those three Vs make you."

"Assistente Capo."

"Please, you're upsetting my guests."

"What, they understand me all of a sudden?"

"Your tone. Also, they are not Japanese. They are Chinese."

"That makes some sort of difference?"

Antonio smiled his whitest smile at the Chinese couple, who shrank back in their seats. He handed two neatly typed sheets of paper to the policeman with the big forehead, and said, "This is a statement declaring the time and place of the mugging, and detailing the items stolen. The description of the assailant isn't up to much, but they do mention he had a pointy knife."

"Oh, a pointy one?" The policeman tossed the papers back onto the desk. "If they want these to be valid, they need to go down to the station and report it."

It had taken Antonio two hours of cajoling and smiling and bowing and persuading, followed by an hour of painstaking translation of Sino-English into Italian. In the end, he had simply written up most of the report for them, as he had done before for others. He suspected the Chinese couple, or the husband at least, of exaggerating their losses. It was now eleven o'clock at night. It would be nice, he thought, if a hole opened in the floor and the policemen and the Chinese guests dropped with a scream into a fiery pit. Then he could insert himself between sharply folded hotel sheets and sleep.

The first mugging of a guest had occurred a year and a half ago. Tonight's made twenty-three, which meant the rate was more than one a month. He had even prepared a template for mugging reports and insurance claims on his office computer. The hotel was gaining a reputation as being in a bad area, which it wasn't. HQ had sent round a memo warning all employees to refrain from using the word "unlucky" in connection with the estab-lishment. Bookings were down, and he had had to lay off three members of staff. His name was being associated with misfortune. Guests that get mugged go away unhappy, tell their friends, write letters, and, in one case, put all the details up on a very popular blog. Embassies had been informed. He was not manager of the year at the last award ceremony.

"My job is on the line," he said.

"Not our problem," said the cop.

"I thought muggings were a problem for the police," said Antonio. "By the way, what's your name?"

The great expanse of head turned red, and the cop stood up. "What sort of an asshole question is that?" he roared.

Antonio beamed at the Chinese couple and made a reassuring gesture with his left hand to indicate that all was dandy, and this is precisely what he wanted to happen.

"Just a friendly inquiry. I can't call you Assistente Capo all the time."

"So call me Capo. And don't bother us with this sort of shit." He picked up the report and flung it back across the table, but the pages wafted gently down in front of the Chinese man who said some word several times over, then reached for a pen, and scored out two of the items from the list of stolen goods.

Antonio breathed through his nose, and tried to enjoy his pearl gray suit and white shirt. Lone women in the hotel liked him. He had not made a million by age thirty, but expected to by the time he was forty. At least he was not a cop. When this streak of bad luck ran out, he would be snatched into the upper echelons of the hotel chain. Within two years he would have an MBA. He spoke fluent English, a language he loathed, Spanish, a language he loved, French, some German, a smattering of Japanese, and some Chinese, which had turned out to be far easier than he had dared to hope.

He turned to the Chinese couple, and spoke to them in English, throwing in a few Chinese honorifics that seemed to leave them cold. He promised them that everything was under control. The police were this very minute trawling the streets of Trastevere looking for the man who robbed them. They would not be billed the full amount for their room. The hotel would do all it could to make the rest of their stay as pleasant as possible.

As they left the room, the Chinese tourists gave him a look of disbelief that he had seen on the faces of the Korean, Japanese, Spanish, English, French, German, and American guests. It seemed humans had a universal expression to denote disgust with hotel managers.

He placed the failed mugging report in his drawer, and turned to the two policemen, giving them his best boyish grin and a what-can-you-do-with-these-people shrug.

"I am sorry about that. Can I get you anything to drink?"

The forehead creased and two gimlet eyes fixed themselves on him. "We don't drink on duty."

"Sorry, I wasn't thinking. Well, if you ever want, you know, refreshments, and by that I mean snacks, sandwiches, whatever, don't hesitate to pop in. Just mention my name, uh—*Capo*."

"Assistente Capo Rospo, and this here is Agente Davide Di Ricci."

Antonio longed to denounce the two troglodytes for dereliction of duty. But he would bide his time. He'd begin with security video footage of them eating and drinking for free. Then he'd gather more evidence and turn his staff into a stream of witnesses. Someday, he promised himself, when he was in charge of the entire Hudson & Martinetti Hotel chain in Italy, this fucker with the unfeasible head would receive a career-ending summons out of the blue. He smiled at him again, and said, "I really appreciate your being here."

The door to his office burst open. Rospo was on his feet, pistol half drawn.

Two young German tourists, a woman and a younger man, almost a boy, heads lolling, staggering in, and collapsed into the chairs just vacated by the Chinese couple. The woman seemed helpless with laughter. A smell of smoke and beer now joined the smell of policeman sweat and Chinese garlic that had already polluted his pristine office.

"*Wir haben eine Leiche gefunden! Einen Landstreicher,*" said the woman, then theatrically shushed the man who had not spoken yet, pointed to the policemen, and said, "*Schon? Italienische Gründlichkeit,*" and giggled.

The man, who had drunk enough to make his eyes shine rather than dull, pulled out one of the free tourist maps from the lobby, and showed it to Antonio and, speaking English, said, "I have circled the place. I think it is right. The police have been very fast to arrive here."

"I hate drunken northerners. What are these two fucking clowns saying?" demanded Assistente Capo Rospo.

"They seem to be saying they have found a dead body," said Antonio.

# 2

IT WAS NOT easy to explain the difference between wanting somebody dead and wanting a dead somebody. Homicide cops understood at once, but to people in the outside world, it came across as the sort of nice distinction a psychopath might make.

On balance, Inspector Caterina Mattiola was pleased to be woken in her warm bed in the early hours of the morning to be told that a man had been found dead on the streets of Trastevere, and that her presence was requested.

Since transferring from Section Two, Immigration Affairs to Section Three, Homicide, of the Squadra Mobile, she had done only administrative work. She was good at it, better than any of the men, but she knew what happened to women who became indispensable at a single thankless task.

She had taken a big risk several days ago and gone to her boss, Commissioner Blume, and asked to be detailed to investigative work. Visiting her parents later that same week, she made an effort to tell her father about what she had done. At no point had her boss promised anything, but she still felt as if she had made some sort of breakthrough. She wondered whether her father agreed. Or was she being too optimistic?

Sitting there across the table watching him chew on the last of his food, his head tilted back, and knife and fork grasped tightly in his fist like they were two ends of a handlebar on an invisible bicycle that he was having difficulty steering, she suddenly wondered if he had understood her at all.

"When was this?" he said eventually.

"When was what?" said her mother, swooping in from the kitchen bearing an aluminum coffeepot and two small white cups with fat lips. "What are you saying, Arnaldo?"

She circled around the table and placed a cup in front of both of them. "The sugar's in the kitchen, but I left it there because I know neither of you takes it. Be careful, Arnaldo, or you'll burn your hand again. I'd leave it for a moment till it stops hissing. Don't pour it yet. None for me, of course. I don't drink coffee since my op."

Her husband waited for her to complete the circuit of the table, gathering speed as she came onto the straight stretch leading back toward the kitchen. When she had gone, he unclasped his fists and put his silverware down on the table. "When was this?"

"Three days ago," said Caterina. "On Tuesday. Since then, nothing. But there haven't been any cases."

"No murders in Rome?"

"Some muggings, probably the work of one person. No murders in our district, though. The weekend begins now. That's always a good time for killing," she said.

"We can only hope," said her father. He drank his coffee, then eyed the bottom of the cup to make sure it was all gone. "If you do get assigned to a murder investigation," he said, "you won't say anything to your mother, will you? She still thinks you process passports."

"Right," said Caterina. She kissed him on his forehead, the least wrinkled and tragic part of his face, and stood up. At the front door, she hitched her shoulder bag across her chest, lifted a heavy plastic bag full of fruit that her mother had left for her despite her pleas that she had more fruit than she knew what to do with, and left.

She rubbed her eyes and refocused on the present. She was to report directly to the scene. She tried to remember what address the dispatcher had given, but although it had been less than a minute ago, it had merged into the dream she had been having about colored fountains and fighting babies. Elia was beside her. He was nine, now. Too old to sleep with his mother.

She sat up quickly before sleep could catch her again.

She phoned her parents, to tell them to come to look after Elia. Her mother said she would be over immediately and expected Caterina to wait.

Caterina was already dressed in yesterday's clothes. If this was going to become a habit, she'd shower in the evenings and set out fresh clothes every night.

"I can't wait. I have to go now. It's an emergency call."

"What if he wakes up alone in an empty house?"

"I told him it might happen. I'll phone him. He knows you'll be here."

"I'll be there right now. I want you to wait. You have to. What sort of mother ..."

"I need to hang up, mamma. I'll probably see you at the gate on my way out."

"I don't see what could possibly be so urgent ..."

Caterina hung up, finished dressing quickly, kissed Elia, snug in the bed and smelling like a warm loaf of bread. She slung a leather satchel across her body, pulled the front door of the apartment closed, but did not lock it from the outside. Her mother always complained about this, saying gypsies could easily kick down the door, get in, and steal her only grandchild away.

Caterina had tried to address this particular phobia, but it was just one of many. "Gypsies don't steal children, mother. That's an urban myth. They have more than enough of their own."

"And you a policewoman."

"Which is why I am not locking my child in for any reason."

She made it all the way to her car without meeting her mother. She did her best to suppress a faint buzzing of anxiety like a trapped black insect bouncing lightly against the inside of her breast. She hated it, the feeling of her mother's fretfulness and fear insinuating its way into her own personality.

She got in the car and phoned the dispatcher to get the address again. Piazza de' Renzi in Trastevere. Near work and far from home.

Caterina drove through the center and crossed the Tiber at Ponte Vittorio Emanuele II, wondering if she had chosen the fastest route. She followed the curve of the river, building up speed on the empty road. Then she turned right, and parked her car in the middle of Piazza Trilussa, to the annoyance or amusement, it was hard to tell, of a group of down-and-outs surrounded by beer bottles, and walked through two dark lanes to Piazza de' Renzi. Out of the shadows stepped an Agente so young he seemed like a child who had dressed up as a policeman. He examined her ID card and wrote down her name. A few more steps brought her into the little piazza where she found four uniformed policemen, the coroner's wagon, a five-strong team of technicians in a pool of halogen at the far side of the piazza, and the medical examiner already at the scene. Even from this distance, she recognized Rospo's oddly shaped head. The other one was what's-his-name—Di Ricci.

She saw no sign of Blume or any other detectives, and was not sure what her next move should be. Between a little magnolia tree and a clutter of small cars, she could just make out something dark on the ground, its presence revealed mainly through the contrast it made with the legs of the technicians as they moved back and forth in their white jumpsuits, and she realized she had been called in late.

She took out her notebook from her shoulder bag and began taking basic notes. The piazza was a trapezoid, shorter at the far end where the body lay. She had come up Vicolo de' Renzi, to her left and fronting the murder scene was a restaurant, Cassetta Trastevere. To her right, turning neatly out of the piazza almost before it had begun, was another lane, its name a mystery. The corner of the piazza opposite her was closed, a tall pink building meeting a lower orange one. Two policemen from another district stood in the shadows talking quietly. One was heavy-set, jowly, and bald, and seemed to be giving instructions to the other, who was average build but with an oversized chin and a protruding lower lip, a mouth made for catching raindrops.

Caterina needed to know something before she dealt with Rospo, so she asked, "Who found the body?"

The bald policeman paused slightly, looking her up and down before nodding in the direction of Rospo and Di Ricci.

"Those two geniuses over there," he said. "Talk to the guy with the big shiny head."

Caterina went over to Rospo, who let his eyes travel up and down her while he adjusted his scrotum in his gray pants. "Well, well. Look who's here."

"Did you find the body?" asked Caterina.

Rospo raised his hands. "Guilty."

Caterina could not think of what to say next. She had a feeling Di Ricci was clowning behind her back. Probably masturbatory movements, thrusting his pelvis, cupping his hands to indicate breasts. Rospo was definitely amused by something.

She spun round in time to catch Di Ricci in mid mime. The man was almost forty. "You," she said, "go over to those two in the shadows, then take up positions at the entrances to this piazza. You can stand guard behind us, where the two lanes almost converge." She pointed to the left. "Don't let anyone through, except for the detectives when they arrive."

Di Ricci did not move. He said, "We're dealing with a dead tramp. A tramp fell down, banged his head, and died."

Rospo said, "Sovrintendente Grattapaglia gives the deployment orders."

"Is he here?" asked Caterina.

"No, but he's on his way. Then things will get organized."

"Who called in the body?"

"I did," said Rospo. "Pair of Huns saw him lying in the street, went straight back to the hotel to tell the manager. That's how they must report crimes in Germany. See a dead body, find the nearest hotel manager. Fucking Germans . . ." he spat.

"Has the victim been identified?"

"Sure."

"By who?"

"Me again," said Rospo. "It's not the first time I've seen this guy, English tramp. Been living here for years. He paints, gets drunk. Sometimes gets into fights, though he must be about seventy. You'd almost admire that. People round here have complained about him for years, pissing into doorways, singing songs in the street."

"Tramp?"

"Artist, if you prefer. Anyhow, soon as I saw who it was, I told the German to fuck off back to his hotel, then Di Ricci and me tried to lift him up and get him to walk home. We dragged him for a few meters, but then I immediately realized he was inert and pretty cold, so we put him down again, called dispatch, and requested a crew."

"You dragged a dead body several meters from its original position?" asked Caterina.

Rospo shrugged. "We'd picked him up off the ground twenty times before. Who was to know he was dead this time? Anyhow, we put him back. This sort of shit happens all the time."

"So those two technicians there are looking at where the body was, originally?" She pointed at two men standing a few meters apart from the others, staring at a piece of empty ground.

"More or less there, maybe a bit to the left, a bit behind that spot," said Rospo.

"You don't feel like going over and telling them to take a step or two back to where you actually found the body?"

"I can't be so precise. Besides, they've probably already looked there. Nothing to see."

Caterina walked over and stood outside the circle of technicians, none of whom acknowledged her. The victim was lying flat on his back on the ground, like he wanted to look at the stars. He had a short white beard, neater than seemed right for a tramp. His hair was white and curly, all of it bunched in curls at the back of his head. The moonlight through the magnolia leaves cast a strange pattern on the upturned face. Caterina moved slightly, but the pattern remained the same, and she realized the man's left cheek was wrinkled and scarred. It looked like an old burn. She bet he had grown the beard in a vain effort to hide it. She felt the muscles in her neck tense and a shudder pass through her and turned around to see Rospo.

"I found him more or less here." He knelt down on the ground, as if looking for something, stood up, brushed dirt off his knee, and nodded. "Yes, no, wait. It was maybe a bit further over. Fuck it. Let's just say it was here."

"Then what did you do?"

"While the ambulance was on its way, I felt for a pulse and found none. The EMTs reached the scene twenty minutes later and pronounced suspicious death, and a forensic team was called in. The suspected cause of death is blunt head trauma."

Caterina looked over to see if the uniformed policemen had sealed off the entrances to the piazza like she said. They had not. Then, to her immense relief, she saw Commissioner Blume and Inspector Panebianco walking over toward her. Blume was carrying a bag, which he dropped on the ground next to her. He unzipped it, pulled out a pair of latex gloves, and snapped them on. Panebianco did the same, and then they waited for her. Feeling self-conscious, Caterina plucked out two gloves from the box and pulled them on, taking twice as long as Blume.

Blume nodded at Rospo, then turned his head downwards at his bag, and pointed at a roll of crime scene tape with his toe. Rospo picked it up, and Blume shook his head in sharp dismissal, saying, "What the hell? You need to be told everything?"

Rospo was gone. Blume asked Caterina to start writing down anything and everything she saw. But first, he wanted her to get the names of the policemen called to the scene and everyone present.

Then he asked her if anything had been added to the scene since she arrived or if anyone had touched the body. But as she began her complicated response he stopped her.

"It's OK. I know about Rospo's body-lifting efforts already. I just wanted to see if you did."

"You were testing me?" A thought occurred to her. "You're not really just arriving now, are you?"

"No. I got here a while ago."

"You didn't seal the area off," said Caterina, annoyed at being played like this.

"I did. You didn't check. The exclusionary cordon you wanted was fine, but I chose to close off Vicolo del Moro. No access there means no access to any entrance to the piazza. One roadblock instead of two. Less manpower. We'll narrow the area later, when people start waking up and going to work."

"I see," said Caterina.

Blume pointed to a pile of cobblestones and sand piled up against the wall of a bar, and said, "Use the tape and ring it around those stones afterwards. They might want looking at."

"OK," said Caterina.

Blume clapped his hands together. "So, are you having fun, Inspector?"

"I am glad to be here, if that's what you mean," said Caterina.

"If I had meant that, I would have asked if you were glad to be here," said Blume. "Don't you think this is fun?"

Caterina thought of her son waking up to her absence, the dead tramp with the white beard a few meters away, the scorn she had seen in the policemen's eyes when she tried to give them orders. "No. I wouldn't say fun, exactly, more ..." She stopped, realizing that Blume did not really want to stand there listening to her trying to give shape to her thoughts.

Blume confirmed her suspicion by getting down to business. "So Rospo and his partner moved the body. Well, that's a good start. I suppose we'll begin with the assumption this is yet another mugging. Certainly, it's another foreigner ..." He stooped and she realized it was up to her to continue.

"The victim—" began Caterina.

11

"He may not even be a victim," interrupted Blume. "Unless you broaden the category to include victims of misfortune or stupidity, in which case we are all victims."

"He was just a tramp, banged his head; then died from exposure," said Caterina. "I saw some scenes pretty similar to this with illegal immigrants."

"Just a tramp, eh?"

"I didn't mean that a tramp is less important," said Caterina.

"It was not a moral reprimand, Inspector. It's just you never know where a corpse is going to lead you. Murder cases can be short or long. Go have a look at those cobblestones, I'll call you over in a minute. Oh, and do a sketch, would you? Of, you know ..." he swept his hand around. "This place. It's a nice little piazza. Sort of like an arena, isn't it? Or a Greek theater. Or something."

Caterina took some crime scene tape and went over to the pile of cobblestones, and stared at them blankly, looking for their significance. Inspector Panebianco, who had not said hello, was standing beside Blume and taking copious notes.

She looked at the notebook in her hand, and, without removing her latex gloves, rapidly sketched the piazza, including the two trees, the restaurant, a bar, a potted sacred fig, the cars parked in herringbone formation in the middle of the piazza; she counted the cars, counted the bolted-down tables and potted plants outside the restaurant, and counted the windows of the buildings overlooking the scene. The cornice along the roof of the tall pink building was a strange white, and she realized the sun was about to clear the rooftops behind. She would have to phone Elia soon, make sure he was OK. As she counted the windows, a pair of brown shutters swung open and a head bobbed out, then back in again. When it reappeared, it was in the company of two more. The three heads gave a friendly nod to the shutter to the left as it opened and another head appeared.

She looked at the cairn of cobblestones, neatly piled there as if for a well-organized riot later that afternoon. She picked one from the top, turned it over, and glared at its gray underside. Was she supposed to be looking for blood, matted hair, bone fragments? Maybe the killer used a cobblestone to batter the victim, but what sort of killer would then put the weapon back in the pile, ready for discovery? Throw it into the river, sure; dump it in a garbage container, maybe, or even just roll it under a parked car.

If the Commissioner was testing her endurance or obedience, she was not going to fail. She checked thirty of the elongated cubes forming the top of the pile, putting aside two with strange chipping on their sides. The idea that a killer had restacked a neat pile after bludgeoning his victim to death in the middle of a piazza surrounded by sixty windows and doors was ridiculous.

The photographer was taking shots of a spot on the ground. He seemed to be moving slowly, but Caterina realized that in the minute or so she watched him, he had taken at least half a dozen separate pictures, all of them close-ups. They were setting up a sort of tent structure around the body, which was largely obscured from overhead by the magnolia tree and from street view by the parked cars, but more and more brown shutters were opening and more heads were looking out. The sun struck the upper stories of the pink building in front, and the halogen lights of the technicians suddenly seemed sickly and yellowish. More uniformed officers had arrived, and the entrances to the piazza were properly sealed off now. The technicians were packing up, and Panebianco was nowhere to be seen.

The Commissioner called her name, inviting her over. She braced herself. She was not afraid of seeing a dead body, but it would be the first she would look at as a murder investigator.

# 3

"HIS SKULL IS caved in from behind," said Blume as she reached him. He bent down and lightly stroked the curly white hair at the back of the prostrate figure. "You can feel the concave indent here." He cupped his hand slightly, making his fingers disappear. "Want to feel?"

"No thanks," said Caterina.

"Not for fun," said Blume. "Put your hand there. Touch the damage. You need to know."

She bent down, pushing her satchel behind her back, put her hand at the back of the dead man's white head, wrinkling her nose against the powerful smell of alcohol, urine, and something else.

"Deeper," ordered Blume. "That's the foramen magnum, where you have your fingers now, which is the natural hollow for the spinal column. Move your fingers up to the occiput . . . There!" he said as Caterina shuddered, closed her eyes, and almost lost her balance. "You've found it. It's almost as if the foramen magnum just continued higher up into the skull than it should, but if you put your index finger in it now you can feel the circular edges. It's like a divot from a bad golf shot."

Caterina completed the examination, then stood up, and ripped off her latex glove. Smiling, Blume took the glove and held out a new one for her, which he seemed to have ready in his hand.

"You need to keep them on while we're here," he said.

"Of course, I don't know why I did that. It was stupid."

"You're doing great. Find any suspicious stones?"

"No. I don't think so. Two, maybe. But unlikely."

"Don't forget to give them to the technicians before they go," said Blume. "But for now, I want you just to stand here. Do you pray?"

"Sometimes."

"Really?" said Blume. "I don't. Nothing out there to pray to. But I find it helps if you just stand as if you were praying. It gives a bit of respect back to the victim and helps empty your mind of noisy thoughts. It's not the same thing as concentrating. Concentration is what we do next."

He stood there, hands behind his back, head bowed, and she did the same, conscious of the risk that this could be a humiliating initiation rite and Rospo might right now be snapping photographs of her solemn, prayerful pose for the office bulletin board.

But she had to believe the Commissioner would not treat her like that. So she stood beside him, and did not turn or raise her head. The corpse staring up at them from the ground showed no visible signs of injury on this side, no blood, no bruises. His arms were at his sides and his legs were placed neatly, but that could have been the solicitude of the two policemen who had let him down gently. Green paper bags, like the ones her mother brought onions home in, had been put over his hands. He was wearing dark pants, with a brown belt, a blue narrow-rib corduroy shirt, and a dark jacket. His shoes were heavy, brown, scuffed, and messy, like Blume's.

Blume's lips seemed to be moving. Maybe he was praying? Hoping it would not earn her a reprimand, she bent down again, and lifted the dead man's arm ever so slightly, then glanced back up at Blume.

"They've done all that stuff," he said, but his tone was approving. "Rigor has set in. We got a body temperature reading that puts the time of death back at more or less when the German tourists say they found him. The magistrate, Bianchi, has already been and gone. He's interviewing the German tourists and then he's signing it over to his colleague, De Santis."

"De Santis who's investigating the muggings?" said Caterina. "So Bianchi is treating this as a mugging gone wrong and transferring the case just like that?"

"I am not privy to the workings of his fine legal mind," said Blume. "But rarely have I seen a man less keen to take on a new case."

She stood up and felt the soothing warmth of a beam of sunlight on the nape of her neck, as the sun cleared the building behind. The victim suddenly looked very white.

"His name was Henry Treacy," said Blume, his voice still hushed. "He was Irish, born in 1949, in a place called Killken—, no Killarney, no that's not it either. Kill-something." He held out an ID card for her to see. "This was in his wallet."

"Wallet?"

"Yes. You forgot to ask Rospo about that and he, of course, didn't vol-unteer the information. It could still be an attempted mugging. Struggle, violence, death, and then the mugger runs off without his loot. But the presence of a wallet does open the way to new possibilities. As does the fact that this guy may well be foreign, but he's no tourist. He's been living here for years. Rospo knew him by sight. Did you notice the burn marks on the left side of his face?"

"Yes," said Caterina. "They look old. I guess he grew the beard to hide the scars."

"Just what I think," said Blume. "He already has a beard in the photo on his ID card which dates from eight years ago. You can just make out the scar there. See?" He showed her the disintegrating ID card.

She read: "Eye color: blue; height: 182 cms." So far it was a description that suited Blume better than the sad shadow lying at her feet. Surely he wasn't that tall? She took the card out of Blume's hand and read the rest of the details: "Nationality: Italian; civil status: single; profession: artist; distinguishing marks: left-handed."

"That's strange," she said.

"What him being Italian but born abroad?" said Blume. "No, that's perfectly normal. Lots of people are born abroad."

"No, the bit about left-handedness. Usually that's for things like a mole, a missing finger, or in his case, scar on left side of face. Visible stuff."

"So he must have felt being left-handed was important to others instead of just to himself," said Blume. "If you ask me, that is just the sort of self-centered bullshit you would expect from an artist. Artists need to be knocked down the social scale again, maybe to about the level of barbers. Same goes for dentists and surgeons and musicians. All hands, no brains. Overpaid for being a bit dexterous. Like soccer players, if you think about it."

"Not a tramp, though," said Caterina, daring to interrupt. She was pleased. She did not want her first body to be a nobody.

Blume said, "He had three euros in coins in his wallet. Not a single banknote."

He paused, and Caterina realized she was meant to contribute. She said, "So he must have spent it."

"You think so? Why not assume someone stole it? If we are

hypothesizing that someone hit him over the back of the head, then it is logical to assume a theft—if assuming on the basis of a hypothesis is a logical way to proceed, which it isn't by the way."

Caterina stayed silent for a moment pretending to understand, then spoke cautiously, watching Blume's face for signs of irritation. "They'd have taken the wallet itself, not just the money inside. And if it was in his pocket, they would have had to remove his wallet, take the money, then put it back, leaving fingerprints. It doesn't work."

"Good. I agree," said Blume. "But of course, the wallet was bagged and taken off by the technical team who will look for fingerprints anyhow. Now, that dimple mark on the back of his skull, what weapon could have caused that?"

Caterina didn't know where to begin.

"I don't know either, but it's more consistent with falling and hitting your head on a protruding cobble while drunk than being hit over the head with a heavy weapon like a bat. Maybe I'm wrong. We'll see from the autopsy. Two receipts were found in his pocket. They give us the name of two bars, one he visited last night, one from a few nights ago. I have two men on that already. Both bars are closed at this time. So we're tracking down the owners, find out who was serving last night. The main thing is to identify who Treacy was with, if anyone. We need to find out who was the last person to see him alive."

Caterina heard the sound of a two-stroke motor ricocheting up the walls of the houses. She waited and a few moments later, a black-and-blue three-wheeled Piaggio Ape van carrying nets of carrots and a thin man appeared, got into animated conversation with a policeman at the closed-off entrance on Via della Pelliccia, then retreated, motor snarling.

"That guy just breached my security cordon," said Blume.

"Maybe he lived in one of the three houses between Via del Moro and here," said Caterina.

"Which is why your idea to close off only this piazza was better than my idea to block off the connecting streets," said Blume. "When you see I'm being stupid, let me know, will you? We need to close off the piazza now."

Caterina realized the city was coming to life. She could hear vehicles moving down Lungotevere Farnesina, rushing while they still could. Shutters had opened, and coffee smells had percolated down to the piazza.

Radios were playing and front doors were opening, and people were trying to step out into the piazza from the surrounding buildings, then stopping as a uniformed policeman yelled at them. Hardly any of them stepped back inside, but their not moving forward and intruding on the crime scene was accepted as a fair compromise.

"It's morning, Inspector," said Blume.

"Good morning, Commissioner," she said. She should phone her son who woke up early, even on Saturdays. Especially on Saturdays.

"This is the beginning of chaos," said Blume. "And I want you to do your best to manage it, Inspector. You have eight uniformed policemen plus yourself. Not me, not Panebianco, nor any of the technicians. We can't help. Sovrintendente Grattapaglia will be here soon. Let him show you the ropes. He's got years of experience at crowd control, setting up the house-to-house interviews, picking out likely witnesses, all that sort of stuff. He's known to be grumpy in the mornings, mind, so don't annoy him. Every civilian you talk to is going to have an unassailable reason for having to traverse the area, so don't talk to them. There are going to be doctors on call, surgeons on their way to save a child's life, politicians with connections on their way to an important vote, a surprising amount of people working for essential services, engineers on their way to rescue old women locked in elevators, teachers giving exams, lawyers with cases, judges with sentences, criminals and rebels who want to compromise the scene on principle. You've got your work cut out for you here. Think you can do it?"

"Yes."

"I bet you the price of breakfast you can't stem the flow for more than twenty-five minutes. But that's all we need, or, better, that's all we can expect to get. You can't close down a place like this for long."

Caterina would have preferred to be invited to do the walk-through with Blume and Panebianco than to be sent off to do sentry duty, but she did as ordered. First she walked in a circle staying close to the fronts of the buildings around the piazza, telling people to step back inside the door-ways, but it was like a game of Whac-a-mole. As soon as she passed, they reappeared. She went over to a group of three policemen standing at the corner of Via della Pelliccia, where they had stretched a piece of crime scene tape across the lane, tying it to a no-entry road sign on one side, and a leg of one of the bar chairs on the other. The bartender, who had put out his chairs and tables, was now inserting a patio umbrella pole into a metal base.

She called out to the nearest policeman, the younger of the two she had seen in the dark, and instructed him to walk counterclockwise around the piazza, making sure people stayed indoors. "Don't talk to any of them, just order them in," she told him. He lingered for some time, on the verge of refusing, but eventually set off at a very leisurely pace. She turned to the barman who had unfolded the vinyl beer umbrella with Tuborg written on it. "That can wait."

The bartender looked skywards, then fitted the umbrella pole into its base. "I know. The sun doesn't reach here until two. But customers like these umbrellas to be up. Makes the place more visible."

"You're setting up your bar in the middle of a crime scene. I said it can wait. Step inside your bar, please, and keep it closed until we say you can open. Is that clear?"

"You want me to send out the two policemen having a cappuccino, then?" said the bartender, and opened the umbrella.

"Yes, I do."

The bartender put his hand against the door jamb and called out, "Agenti, you're wanted."

Di Ricci came out, wiping milk foam from his mouth with the back of his hand. Rospo followed, holding a cornetto pastry. Caterina pointed at him. "You. Go plant yourself twenty meters down Via del Cipresso. Over there." She pointed. "That way you can stop people before they even get to the piazza. Di Ricci, take up position there at the corner of Vicolo de' Renzi."

Rospo softly tore his pastry in two, and inserted half into one side of his mouth, and stood there, cheek bulging and jaw moving, looking at her.

"It's a direct order from Blume," she added.

He shrugged, pushed the other half of the pastry into the other side of his mouth, and moved off.

Caterina had made two rounds, glancing back into the middle of the piazza where Blume and Panebianco were moving up and down in a narrow grid pattern around the area where Rospo said the body had been found. The coroner's unit was zipping up the black body bag, the last technician was taking down a video camera, when she walked into a short man in a gray suit who had gone out of his way to block her path.

"I have diplomatic immunity," said the man in the suit.

He moved sideways to stay in front of her. His accent was funny and he smelled slightly of balsam and moss. He was holding out a plastic-covered card. A miniature elongated silver cross enclosed in a circle was pinned just below the buttonhole of his lapel. "The Embassy of the Kingdom of Spain to the Holy See," he explained. "I need to go to my office now."

Caterina glanced at her watch. It showed 7:12. The coroners had their shiny zinc stretcher propped up beside the black bag, all ready to go.

"I think we have just about finished, Ambasciatore," she said. "Maybe if you waited five more minutes?"

"I have already waited long enough. I have been very patient. And I am not ambassador rank. Yet." So saying, he stepped past her and traversed three meters of crime scene territory. Keeping her hands at her sides, Caterina moved forward to intercept the Spaniard. Finding her in front of him again, he continued to move forward, pushing her breasts with his chest, touching her inner thigh twice with his knee.

Caterina looked behind her and saw other residents from the building, waiting to get out, watching the drama playing out in front of them. Then one or two broke cover, looking left, right, left, as if about to cross a busy street, and walking quickly, leaning into the graffiti-stained walls as if this would stop them from being noticed. Caterina spun around looking for help. Blume was standing in the sun, Panebianco in the shade. She spotted Sovrintendente Grattapaglia, who must have just arrived.

"Wait, please. I'll see what I can do," she told the diplomat. "I'll get the most senior policeman here to talk to you. But in the meantime, will you please return to your place by the front door? I'm sure the Commissioner will escort you personally out of the area."

The Church diplomat snorted, but turned back. The other fugitives had been halted by the policeman at the far end of Via della Pelliccia, and were receiving unsympathetic treatment. Good.

She had no intention of doing anything for the diplomat. All she had to do was make sure he stayed where he was for five minutes, maybe ten. She moved over to Grattapaglia quickly.

"Get over there. Don't let that guy through. He's a troublemaker. Ten minutes. Tell him I've gone to get someone important for him."

Grattapaglia opened his mouth to say something.

"No," said Caterina. "Don't make me repeat myself. The Commissioner put me in charge of this situation, and now I am giving you an order. Mess this up, and you'll be answering to him, not me."

Grattapaglia seemed to be about to say something, then dismissed his thought, or her, as unworthy. He hacked up mucus and swallowed it, then ambled over in the direction of the protesting diplomat.

Voices from the increasingly large group of people gathered at the middle door of the pink building called out their impatience, "*Aho, guardie? How much longer do we have to wait?*"

"*Ehi, annamo.*"

"*Anvedi 'sta ficona che ce fa aspettà.'*"

"*Macché ficona.*"

She went over to them. "Can you people wait five minutes? I promise that's all it will take. Anyone who needs an official note for being late to work can contact me, this is my card." She handed out her business card and three or four hands took one. She added, "Also, if anyone heard or saw anything at around two last night, please call that number."

"Who is it?" asked a woman who was restraining her son from running about by holding onto the schoolbag on his back.

"It's that English drunk," said another.

Caterina singled out the speaker. She was a thin woman made up entirely of wrinkles, and she was standing there in a blue dressing gown, brown stockings, and white hospital clogs.

"How do you know that?" asked Caterina.

"Hah!" said the woman, looking around for approbation and, indeed, getting some. "I was right, see? I live on the fourth floor," said the old woman. "I can see clearly from there. I recognized his white beard. He won't be singing any more loud songs late at night now, will he?"

"Do you know his name?"

"What would I know his name for?"

Caterina took down the triumphant little woman's name, and asked if there was anyone else about who might know the man's name.

"None of my friends," she declared, wagging her finger.

Caterina stepped out of the doorway and looked over at Blume and Panebianco. They were still there, but the coroners were closing the doors on the wagon. It was almost over.

She could call Elia any time now. She reached into her bag for her phone, but before she got to it she heard a commotion to her left.

Grattapaglia had just pulled his nightstick and truncheoned the Spanish diplomat to the ground.

# 4

"SNATCHING HIS DIPLOMAT'S card and throwing it to the ground might have been mistaken for pique, but you ground it under your heel," said Blume. "Classy."

Sovrintendente Grattapaglia smiled broadly. It took him a long time to realize his cheerfulness was not being reciprocated, and Caterina squirmed in her seat, mortified on his behalf, wondering how he had failed to see the anger in Blume's face. Eventually and with defiant slowness, the Sovrintendente allowed his smile to fade, then shrugged, and said, "I didn't know he was a diplomat."

Blume's face showed a mixture of contempt and puzzlement, as if he was coming to accept but still struggling to fathom the depths of Grattapaglia's idiocy. For one who had so casually turned to violence a short while ago, Grattapaglia seemed oddly defenseless now, like a huge child in big trouble. She felt bad for him, and resolved to speak up. "Before the Sovrintendente assaulted . . . I mean, before the incident, that diplomat—"

Grattapaglia jerked his index finger at her, as if in warning. She stopped speaking, trying to understand why he didn't want her backing. Keeping his finger pointed at her, Grattapaglia turned to Blume and said, "You know as well as I do, it's her fucking fault. She shouldn't even have been there if she can't do her job."

Caterina felt her eyes widen and her mouth drop open. She was aware of it, but couldn't help herself.

"I'd like you to explain that to me," said Blume.

"Explain what? It's obvious. She didn't warn me. She just said trouble-maker, like that covered it. If I had known he was an ambassador, you think I'd have done that? I told you she wasn't ready for fieldwork."

Blume mock-reprimanded Caterina. "You didn't think to warn him not to batter a member of the public in front of three dozen hostile witnesses in the middle of a crime scene?"

"So I made a mistake," said Grattapaglia. "But she should have given me a heads-up."

As Blume's face darkened, Grattapaglia adopted a less aggressive tone, somewhere between conciliatory and plaintive. "All I'm saying is she doesn't even lower herself to speak to me."

"You mean she hasn't ever come to you looking for advice?"

"No. Never."

"On what, Salvatore, on how to deal with obstreperous diplomats with direct connections to our administrators?"

Grattapaglia slumped back into his seat, defeated.

The three of them were seated outside a bar on Via Giulia, having crossed the Sisto Bridge. Blume was buying her breakfast because, he insisted, she had won the bet and managed to keep order in the piazza for twenty-five minutes. He was being kind. She had fallen short by ten minutes.

Grattapaglia had ordered peach juice pulp for himself. He now poured the contents of his glass into the cavity behind his bottom teeth, and held the liquid under his tongue as he stared across the table at Caterina.

"Listen, Salvatore," said Blume. "There is no way we can keep your name out of this, or pretend you were never even there, which might have been one solution. You deserve whatever you get. The thing is, I don't. You know this is going to be my discipline problem once that diplomat makes his complaint."

Sovrintendente Grattapaglia swallowed the thick juice and puckered his face as if it had been lemon. "Yes, I see that."

"We'll see what we can do to stop this snowballing," said Blume. "Won't we, Inspector Mattiola? We're going to close ranks on this." He looked at Caterina, who nodded unenthusiastically. She was thinking of Elia. She had called him on the way over the bridge, surreptitiously sliding out her cell phone as Blume and Grattapaglia walked a few paces ahead. Elia reminded her she had promised to watch him play in a five-a-side against San Gaspare del Bufalo that morning, the only team they had a chance of beating in the under-10 tournament.

"Will you be back on time to take me there?" he asked.

"No, darling, I won't. I'll be there this afternoon, though. For your swimming."

"Shall I ask Grandma to drive me, then?"

"Yes, ask her. Score lots of goals."

"I'm a defender. I don't score goals."

"Oh, well, defenders attack sometimes, don't they?"

"If they're really good. I'm not."

"Sure you are. I'll phone Grandma during the game to see how you're doing."

Now Grattapaglia was telling Blume, "I was a bit on edge, you know the way it is. That guy, I don't know, he got under my skin. The way he looked at me. He had this annoying lisp."

"He is Spanish, Salvatore. They all lisp." Blume paused, and closed his eyes like he was suffering from a mild pain. "OK, this is what we're going to do: anyone comes looking specifically for you, we're handing you over. Take the discipline, the suspension, or whatever it is. Anyone comes looking for an unidentified aggressive cop, then maybe we play dumb for as long as we can, but only if you give us a good reason. The other day, I told Caterina here to take on some of your paperwork. She did so, right?"

"Some of it, yes," said Grattapaglia. "Not all that much."

"I'm glad she didn't. Because now it's your turn. Caterina here is going to be busy with this case. She won't have time for unrelated paperwork. You'll do it for her. After-hours, without overtime. I also want you to write up a second report for the incident with the Spaniard. Don't file it. Don't talk about it. Give it directly to me. Clear? And stop throwing dagger looks at her."

Grattapaglia moved his gaze from Caterina and stared with hatred at the sparrows hopping and bobbing among crumbs at the next table.

"Now I need you to organize a decent house-to-house."

Grattapaglia stood up, not looking at either of them.

"One last thing," said Blume. "Get the bill. And get me another cappuccino while you're about it. Inspector?"

"Nothing for me, thanks," said Caterina.

"He's paying, remember." Blume gave her a quick wink and an almost imperceptible jerk of the head in Grattapaglia's direction, encouraging her.

"No, I don't want anything," she said.

"Get me a Danish, too, Salvatore. Get a few take-away pastries and coffees for Picasso-face, Di Ricci, and the others. They'll appreciate it. Tell them they're from me."

"Who's Picasso-face?" asked Caterina.

"Rospo, of course."

When Grattapaglia had gone, Blume leaned back and turned his face up to the sun. "I need a job that allows me to drink coffee, eat pastries, and soak up the morning warmth. A job without people like Grattapaglia. I'd keep the dead bodies and crime victims, though. I wouldn't have any perspective on life without them. So, what's your impression so far?"

"It's hard to know. There were a lot of distractions. I didn't get a chance to examine the scene much," said Caterina.

"That was my decision, Inspector. You need to know how to handle all the peripheral elements, all the distractions, the mistakes, onlookers, traffic, Spaniards with attitude, people like Grattapaglia. It's hard. The technicians do most of the detail work, because they don't have the distractions of all the other stuff. But if you don't have the distractions, then you don't have the big picture, which is what you need to solve a case. The big picture, by the way, is that there's often no picture. All the background stuff you dig up is composed mostly of chaos and irrelevance. You need to look at it all the same. Most of it is a big waste of time. Like most people's lives, really. All I can tell you is just try not to make any case even more complicated by introducing too many of your own interpretations. Did you sketch the scene like I asked?"

Thankful to have something to show for herself at last, Caterina pulled the notebook out of her bag, handed it to Blume who opened it up to the sketch, which she had developed in pencil and ink over two pages. He looked at it in silence for some time, tilting the notebook left and right every so often, nodding his head.

"Did you go to art school?" he said after a while.

Caterina felt a tingling around her throat and knew she was in danger of blushing. "No. I was good in school, but ..."

Blume interrupted, "Let me tell you something, you've definitely got natural talent, a good hand ..." He snapped the notebook shut. "But it's useless for our purposes."

Caterina's smile weakened.

"As art, it's excellent," said Blume. "But that's not our business. Imagine this sketch has just come to your desk. You think, ah, here's a helpful thing for the investigation, you open it and you find ..."

"No measurements. I forgot to put in the measurements," said Caterina. "I was going to but I got distracted."

"The measurements are basically the only things that count. Those and the fact that you were there and made them, which is the purpose of the sketch. The photos and the rulers and measuring tape and the video camera capture all the rest. When I do it, I turn everything into rectangles or, if it's a car, a triangle with circles. Symbols rather than pictures, see?"

He pulled out his own notebook and showed her an assembly of boxes, lines, and squiggles, made even less intelligible by arrows coming out of the boxes pointing to numbers. "The camera killed representational art," said Blume. "It's easy to forget stuff, and it's easy to forget yourself. That is one reason you need to go easy on someone like Grattapaglia. Another reason is that you mustn't make enemies in the department. Enemies above you are bad enough, enemies below are worse. You'll find that out. So you are going to have to make up with Grattapaglia somehow or other. Maybe you could admit you should have told him the Spaniard was a diplomat."

"I do admit it, Commissioner."

"No, not to me. To him. Everything with me is hunky-dory."

"It doesn't feel that way."

"Well, it is. Who did you phone on the bridge?"

Caterina hesitated. She was sure Blume had not seen her make the call to Elia. She had kept her eye on his back all the time. She had hit speed dial, spoke for, what, twenty seconds at most, and Blume had not turned around once.

"How do you know I phoned someone?"

"You deliberately fell back by pretending to be interested in a journal of civil service examinations at the newsstand, and so I figured you wanted privacy to make a call. When you caught up, I saw you were a little distracted. And I've noticed you hook your hair over the back of your right ear when you're using a phone. Your hair was still pushed back when you sat down here."

Caterina brought her hand up to her ear.

"No. It's fallen back in place now," said Blume. "Here's the thing: I like to know who my investigators are talking to while we're at work."

"My son."

"Oh, right. I didn't know you had a son. Or maybe I did, but I'd forgotten. I didn't know you were married either. Or are you?"

"I was. My son's just turned nine. I don't like people knowing. It's hard enough being a woman and getting taken seriously, but being a single mother, well, you can imagine."

"Well, no. I can hardly imagine being a single mother, can I? You should have reminded me the other day when you came in asking for fieldwork."

"Would knowing that have influenced your decision?"

"I don't know," said Blume. "I'd like to think not. But let's do a test. Tell me what we have so far. Give me a hypothesis. Go on."

Caterina cleared her throat and said, "Well, not much ..."

"Good start," said Blume. "Never forget the law of parsimony, Inspector. Whichever theory needs fewest assumptions is the best."

"The tourist mugger, hearing him singing in English, decided to rob him. A struggle ensued, the mugger hit him over the head. Or pushed him down."

"That's short enough," said Blume. "Most reports of the mugger speak of one man acting alone, which is a bit odd since they usually work in twos or threes. That's not a core issue now, but keep it in mind all the same. More importantly, the reports all mention him having an unusual thin knife, like a stiletto or something. So if he is going to kill, why not use that?"

"He hasn't used it yet," said Caterina.

"There's always a first time," said Blume.

"Except, this wasn't it, obviously," said Caterina, surprising herself as she heard annoyance creeping into her voice. "Seeing as he wasn't stabbed."

"So let's rule out that hypothesis and think of one even likelier and simpler," said Blume. "Like this: The man had been drinking. He was in his early seventies ..."

"Wait ..." She double-checked her arithmetic. "He was in his early sixties. Not his seventies."

"Yeah?" Blume looked skeptical, then spent some time counting on his fingers. "You're right. Jesus, that's terrible."

"What's terrible?"

"It's not so long till I'm that age."

"You've still got a fair bit to go," said Caterina, smiling at him.

"I don't drink. I suppose that's a plus," said Blume. "I gave it up eighteen months ago, don't even miss it. Alcohol intoxication lessens muscular protective reflexes, and makes the brain more vulnerable to concussive trauma. This is Treacy I'm talking about now, by the way. So, the old fellow falls down, bangs the back of his head, manages to get up, and struggle on for a few meters, perhaps on his knees. He crawls a bit, but his brain is hemorrhaging, so he lays the side of his face on the street, pisses his pants, and dies a drunkard's death. End of story."

"Oh," said Caterina. "This isn't going to be my first murder investigation, is it?"

"I doubt it. The magistrate has lost interest already. Expect a lot of disappointment in this work," said Blume.

# 5

As THEY RECROSSED the pedestrian bridge to the piazza, Blume's phone rang.

"Excellent. Well done, Linda." He turned to Caterina, "She's the young blond ..."

"Yes, I know her," said Caterina.

"Linda's just done her first piece of investigative work and got us an address for Treacy."

"You mean she looked it up in a telephone book?"

"She did, bless her. Now as for the address, it's just a three-minute walk from here. Treacy had almost made it home."

They reached Blume's car, which sat in the middle of Via della Pelliccia, a blue light flashing justification for the disruption. Now he went over to it, removed a bag from the trunk, took off his jacket, which looked too small when it was on him but huge as he held it in his hand, then his V-neck, which, she noticed, was pocked with moth holes. He folded them with more difficulty than care, then opened the back door of the car, and tossed them in.

"You missed the seat," said Caterina as he slammed the car door shut.

He strapped the bag over his shoulder. "Never mind."

They walked back to the piazza, open again to its residents. The small police tent in the middle lent the piazza an air of slight gaiety, as if someone had set up a food stall, though the festive effect was spoiled by the presence of a blue van of the Mortuary Police.

"Those bastards take their own sweet time," said Blume. "The body went in the back forty minutes ago."

Blume went over and seemed to get into a vicious argument with one of the men inside the van, but when he came back he was laughing.

"It won't start. The battery's flat. He says it happens all the time. Nice to see the police aren't the only ones with vehicles that don't work."

"Is that so funny?" she asked.

"No. Just something the driver said about the guy lying in the back enjoying the air-conditioning, while he had to sit there ... never mind, there's Grattapaglia."

Grattapaglia came out of the pink building to the left accompanied by two policemen. They watched him send them to the next building, then he came over.

"Nothing, no witnesses, most people at work. Six officers are going around all the local bars to see if there were any incidents, arguments."

"You and Inspector Mattiola here can do a bit of door-to-door, then come back here to me in about a quarter of an hour or whenever you see the van leave."

Blume went over to Inspector Rosario Panebianco who had been maintaining the scene, watching the forensic teams, and re-examining the area.

"Anything else here?"

Panebianco tutted dismissively. "Nothing, Commissioner. Surely this is just an accident scene? That's what *I* feel at least."

"Yes," said Blume, "but there's the question of the mugger. Maybe this was a mugging that went wrong."

"He had his wallet."

"He might have put up a fight and the mugger fled without taking it. The victim is foreign, like the mugger's preferred targets. For the Questura and the press, we need to be careful how we treat foreigners."

"Dear me, has anyone ever mentioned that to Grattapaglia?"

"Don't even talk about that," said Blume. "Just to be clear: you found nothing new here?"

"Nothing. No real evidence of a crime."

Blume watched as the last of the forensics team packed away their stuff. A thin man in cotton blue coveralls came walking around the corner. Tucked under his long arm as if it weighed nothing was a gray Magneti Marelli battery. He gave a cheery wave to the driver of the mortuary van, as if they were old friends. Two patrolmen busied themselves taking down the tent, the electrician went to work under the hood of the van, passersby cast curious glances. Ten minutes later, the mortuary wagon drove off, the electrician sitting squeezed in between the driver and his companion, the three of them chatting and smoking. With its departure, the only sign that anything had happened at all was the unusual number of policemen coming in and out of the buildings around Blume and the broken strands of police tape fluttering at the corners of the piazza.

A few more minutes passed and Inspector Mattiola and Sovrintendente Grattapaglia came out of the building to his right.

"How many people did you two manage to talk to?" asked Blume.

"Two," said Grattapaglia.

"Five," said Caterina.

"So which is it," said Blume. "Five or two?"

"Seven," said Grattapaglia.

"Ah," said Blume. "You split up."

"It was quicker that way," said Caterina.

"Sure." Blume lifted his bag onto his shoulder. "Treacy lived a few minutes from here. We're going to check his house, see what we can find."

Grattapaglia stepped forward, "I'll take that bag for you."

"No, it's not heavy – also, you're staying here. Continue coordinating the house-to-house interviews, watch this area, note who comes by."

Grattapaglia stepped back without a word.

Blume nodded to Caterina. "Inspector, shall we go?"

# 6

BLUME SPOKE AS he walked down the lane, "We still have to treat a death from unknown causes as if it was a murder. Because it could be a murder. And to do this properly, we have to convince ourselves that it *is* a murder, which means ignoring all my experience which says it isn't. Are you following?"

"I wish you had not humiliated Grattapaglia like that in front of me," said Caterina. "You were the one who said I had to start getting on better with people."

"Too bad. You blew your chance. I detailed you and him to go door-to-door together, and you didn't."

"So you're punishing me too, by angering him all the more?"

"Sort of. You need to learn to handle this sort of petty stuff. I don't know what it was like in Immigration Affairs, but it seems to me you must have been surrounded by selfless superior beings such as the rest of the force can only dream of."

Caterina increased her pace to keep up as Blume hurried down Via Benedetta. She caught up with him as they reached Piazza della Malva. "Most of my old colleagues were petty bastards, too. Was he married?"

"Treacy? Not according to his ID card, but he could have been living with someone. We'll see now. You know, I've been turning that name over in my mind. It's familiar to me. He was an artist, according to his ID card."

"A painter?" asked Caterina.

"I guess so. It's bad enough putting down 'artist' as your profession, but it's almost justifiable if you're a painter."

"Or a musician."

"Yeah, a musician might do that, but it would not be justifiable. As long as he was not a writer or a photographer, I'll forgive him his pretention."

Blume waited till a small knot of American students outside the John

Cabot University had passed, then turned on to Via Corsini. Caterina wandered over to the first house on the short terrace to check the number. "Which house?" she asked.

"Number 15. Down the far end, probably," said Blume.

Only one side of the street had buildings on it. The other was flanked by railings that fenced in the overgrown courtyard of Villa Corsini. The last house was number 14.

In front of them was the entrance to the Botanical Gardens, to their left was the Podogora barracks of the Carabinieri.

"Where the hell is number 15?" asked Blume.

"We could ask the Carabinieri for directions," said Caterina.

"That would look good, wouldn't it?" said Blume. "Phone lovely Linda and get a confirmation of the house number."

He stood at the front gate of the Botanical Gardens and found himself looking directly at a dark-suited park keeper with a full beard, who sat in his white booth gazing down the strangely rustic street with a proprietorial air, like some Sicilian *gabellotto*. Blume folded his arms, nodded, and was ignored. He decided to let it go and drifted over to the side of the street out of the man's line of vision, and found himself before a green wooden door that seemed to be a side entrance into the gardens. A square marble slab was attached to the wall beside the door, the number 15 chiseled into it, off-white against white. Below it was an intercom with a clear plastic button and a single name: Henry Treacy.

By the time Caterina arrived to say they had confirmed the address, Blume had pressed the intercom button three times.

"Nobody there," he said after a while. He put his bag on the ground and stood back, looking up to the top of the wall as if he had half a mind to scale it. "This looks like a side door into the Botanical Gardens," he said. "Did Treacy live in a flower bed or something? We need to go around to the other side."

The guard in the white box watched carefully as they came through the main entrance. Blume took a few steps to the right, but he could already see there was nothing there but wall.

"Hey!"

Blume stopped and put down his bag which was beginning to weigh. He waited for Caterina to flash a police ID card and send the guard reluctantly back to his post.

Together they stepped over a red-and-white plastic chain that looped around a square of manicured lawn bordered by outsized yellow daisies.

Caterina looked at the wall, then back at Blume, and shrugged. He went over to the wall, folded back a deep curtain of ivy, slapped the dusky ocher wall behind, then clapped the dust off his hands. "This is the perimeter wall," he said. "The green door on the other side was more or less at this point here, which means there must be two walls and a narrow passageway between them. And they must lead to that garden lodge there." He pointed to a small two-story house with a red tile roof to their left. "We could get in from this side, or go back and enter through that green door. I have some picklocks in the tactical bag."

A few minutes later, Blume was working at the tumbler lock on the door. "Almost have it," he said after five minutes. "I'm a bit out of practice."

Eventually, he pulled out a crowbar from the same bag, stuck it into the wood frame next to the strike plate, and hurled his body against the door. The wood of the door jamb was so damp and spongy that the only noise it made as it gave way was a squeak and a sigh.

Directly in front of them was the wall they had been looking at from inside the Botanical Gardens. Blume pushed the door half closed against its splintered frame, and turned right into a passageway that was not quite wide enough for two people to walk abreast. Both sides were covered in ivy and wet moss. The passage was about ten yards long and led up to another door, this one a little sturdier. No longer keen to hone his lock-picking skills, Blume slammed the crowbar under the lock mechanism, jerked it around roughly till he felt it reach deeper in, then started wrenching it back and forth. After several attempts he motioned Caterina over.

"On the count of three," he said, steadying his hands on the bar in preparation. When he reached three, they pushed against the door, but their timing was slightly off. They did it again, and the door burst open so easily that they almost fell over each other.

The sudden brightness in the room into which they now entered was disorientating. They stood there blinking for a few moments, Caterina trying to understand how the inside of a house could have so much light. As her eyes adjusted, she realized they were standing below a sloping glass roof. Ficus, bamboo, dracena plants, and small trees she could not identify grew from wide-bodied blue glazed urns sitting on a terracotta floor. "We've just broken into one of the botanical hothouses."

"No," said Blume. "This is part of the house. A sort of add-on green-house used as a workroom. Hot in here."

He bent down, rummaged in his bag, and came up with a box of latex gloves, and wiggled his fingers like an important surgeon as he put them on.

The glass room contained wickerwork chairs with yellow cushions, a ceramic-topped table with a demitasse coffee cup on it. Blume noticed some bookshelves and, in the far left corner, a high, long work desk, like he remembered from science lessons in school, except this was made from mahogany. A leather-bound folio-size volume lay beneath three quarto volumes, also leather bound. Beside them sat an ebony box, open to reveal five rows of silver-topped jars, filled with colored powders. Three crystal jars held dozens of paintbrushes.

Blume peered at the top book, but the lettering on the cover was too faded for him to make out the title. He opened it; the text was in Latin.

In the corner of the greenhouse, next to the bead curtain, stood a squat cast-iron wood-fired stove, on top of which sat a tall copper stockpot and beside it a double boiler.

A clacking noise made him turn around as Caterina pushed aside a bamboo bead curtain covering what must have once been the back door to the building. She stepped inside.

"There's a kitchen here," said Caterina's voice. "And another stove."

Blume followed Caterina in. The light was less intense and the white-washed walls, the gray marble washstand, and the heavy brass taps made the room feel cool. A pastry-board lay half across a large rectangular ivory marble table, on which three boxes of eggs and an earthenware jug of what appeared to be milk sat. An ice-cube tray filled with black liquid shimmered slightly in response to the impact of Blume's footsteps as he moved around the table, taking it in. A zinc box contained herbs, flakes of charcoal, dried leaves, and a collection of gnarled woody fruits of some sort. In here was another stove, only this was modern, boxy, made from burnished gunmetal steel.

He opened the refrigerator. "A lot of eggs. Milk, cheese," he announced.

The milk smelled old. "Beer. Garlic, feta cheese, some withered greens. A single man's refrigerator." The cold green bottles of beer clinked invitingly as he closed the refrigerator. Tuborg and Peroni. He used to drink both. He felt thirsty. There was no real need for him not to drink. It wasn't as if he had had a problem. Apart from the weight thing, but not drinking hadn't helped much there. He'd think about it later.

The next room, the living room, was lit by two dirty-paned windows. Blume immediately noticed three easels. One was folded and propped in the corner. One was gripping a pristine white board holding red-tinted paper with the first gray lines of what looked like a foot.

Stacked behind the third easel was a collection of paintings and drawings of different sizes, some framed, some mounted on matt boards, some loose. Blume estimated they numbered around thirty, and began to leaf through them. The furniture was old and uncomfortable. The settee was stuffed with horsehair, the chairs hardbacked and spindly, the walls and window frames had the yellow and gray patina of ancient paint. The front door was made of heavy wood and held in place by rusted strap hinges. The grit and cobwebs showed it had not been opened in years. The greenhouse where they had come in was the only functioning entrance. The walls of this room were covered with framed pictures. Some were paintings, but many were sketches, mostly unfinished.

"No TV," said Caterina, "and the furniture is decrepit."

"You don't like it?"

"I love it. Who wouldn't? I'm just trying to make myself feel better that I rent a small apartment and it takes me an hour to get to the station, while an unemployed foreign drunk gets to live in the Botanical Gardens in the center of town. Or does that sound resentful?"

"Want to buy mine?" said Blume. "It's near San Giovanni."

"You're selling?"

"I might have to. The man in the apartment below me is suing for €85,000 in damages."

"What happened?"

"Plumbing problems in my bathroom. Leaked into his apartment. You don't need the details."

"Yeah, but €85,000 in damages. He's obviously exploiting the situation," said Caterina.

"Two things. First, he's a lawyer. Second, he doesn't even live there.

That's why the damage got so bad. It looks like the leak had been going on for at least seven months but no one was in there to notice. He didn't discover it until he opened up the apartment with the idea of renting it. I saw it myself. I don't think he's exaggerating, to be honest. The effect was very unpleasant. Getting it fixed cost me just a couple of hundred. But I may have to sell my apartment to pay for the damages below."

"I'm sorry to hear that, Commissioner. What about building insurance?"

"Ha-ha."

"Do you have a good lawyer?"

"I don't think I want a lawyer. Just cost more money, and there's not much to contest when you fill your neighbor's apartment with . . . Guercino."

"Guercino?"

"There. The artist. Barbieri was his real name. He was cross-eyed, so they called him Guercino."

Blume was squinting at a pen-and-wash figure. "That's definitely Guercino," he said to himself, surprised at knowing the style of drawing so easily; surprised, too, at hearing his father's labored pronunciation in his head. He remembered his father's effort to get his foreign tongue to make the "tsch" sound of the soft Italian "c," while trying to remain casual and natural about it. To Caterina he said, "And what makes you say he was unemployed?"

"Who?"

"Treacy. Concentrate on where we are, Inspector. You called Treacy an unemployed foreign drunkard."

"The fact he died drunk and the way he was dressed. But if he had this place and these paintings—I don't know what to make of him now."

"A lot of northern Europeans, even if they have money, don't dress as well as they might," said Blume. He remembered his father's habit of wearing socks with his Birkenstock sandals, white legs, checkered shirts. "Americans, too. And don't feel resentful. Treacy lives nowhere now."

"It came out wrong," she said. She watched as he resumed leafing through the canvases and sheets on the table again, this time more slowly. "You're looking at those pictures like they meant something."

"My mother specialized in works such as this. This etching by Fontana . . . If any of these are authentic, the only question is why Treacy didn't live in a grander place than this."

They continued their exploration of the house. A cast-iron spiral staircase in the far corner of the room led up to a single bedroom which gave on to a larger bathroom containing a huge enamel tub with lion-claw feet and a large rosewood medicine cabinet with latticework windows. The ceiling was low and sloping.

Blume opened the cabinet and stood back. "Maybe he ran a pharmacy on the side. No one can be that sick."

"That's not too bad," said Caterina. "My father takes about that many."

"I'm sorry to hear that," said Blume.

"Prescriptions accumulate, and before you know it, you're taking ten, twenty pills a day."

"Then you need to stop taking them," said Blume, "before they mount up. That's what I did. First it was Zantac, then they wanted me to take Zocor. Maybe if they didn't make them sound like the bad guys in a comic book."

"Palonosetron, Venlafaxine, Baclofen," read Caterina. "The man was in pain. I think he had cancer."

"Well, that's different," said Blume. "You should probably take pills then."

She picked up another bottle. "Nexavar." She turned it around. "Doesn't say what it does."

"Bag them," said Blume. "We can look them up, maybe get the labs to check them."

When they returned to the living room downstairs, Caterina started looking more closely at the framed works on the walls.

"He was a collector of some sort as well as an artist?" said Caterina. "He seems to prefer unfinished drawings to paintings."

"Art forgery," said Blume. "The name had been bothering me for a while but I remember now. Treacy. My father mentioned him a few times. Admiringly, if I recall. Not an artist, an art forger."

Caterina tapped a thumbnail against her bottom teeth. "That means corrupt dealers, theft, fencing goods, high prices. There is a possibility of some background to the death. At least we have a category of suspect."

The pictures and the books in his room reminded Blume of his parents and their apartment, the one he still lived in. Their books, reproductions, and papers, most of which he had preserved after their death, remained in their study, but not gathering dust. He kept it clean, spending hours in there himself, like he did as a child, just looking at the pictures in the art books.

He went over to a leather-topped writing desk, picked up some papers, and looked through them. They consisted of bank statements, utility bills, discarded receipts, a few stubs from airplane tickets. He looked at the bank statements, and saw Treacy had a balance of €243,722 in his Unicredit checking account. Not bad. The plane ticket stubs were all for London and Rome. Treacy had made at least two round trips in the last year. The utility bills were modest. An injunction demanding payment for a TV license lay on top of a brochure for holiday homes in Umbria.

"It's legal to copy pictures, you know," he said, dropping the papers back on the desk. "Only the moment a fake is offered for sale as an original does it become a crime, and even then it's hard to prove intent. See this?" Blume pointed to a drawing of a nude male in red and black chalk on what looked like old paper.

"A naked man," said Caterina. "He drew that?"

"It looks like a Pontormo, but it's signed Treacy," said Blume. "Also, it's hanging here in his own room."

"What does that signify?"

"Nothing. Just that he was a very good draftsman."

Blume wandered over to a mahogany bookshelf. The lower shelves had been removed to make room for large volumes, mostly art books and reproductions, but Blume also saw coverless dictionaries, road maps, atlases, and journals piled up.

The upper shelves contained mainly novels. Amis, Arpino, Atwood, Banville, Barnes, Beckett, Brontë. An organized man. A man of leisure. A foolscap-size notebook with a marbled cover lay open on the writing desk.

"No date on this," said Blume, looking at the spidery script. It was written with black fountain ink.

"Not great penmanship for an artist," said Caterina, coming over. "I can't make out a word."

"He was getting on in years and if he was in pain, it would have an effect."

Marking the open page with his thumb, he turned to the inside cover of the notebook, and saw Treacy had written his name. Below that he had written "Diary," then crossed it out and written "Untitled," which was crossed out and replaced with "Painting my Outward Walls," also crossed out. The final title seemed to be "An (im)practical handbook for . . ." but he had evidently not decided who it was for. Blume returned to the page he had found lying open.

"I can see why it was hard for you to make out," he said. "It's in English."

"I know English," said Caterina. She sounded very offended. "My father was a NATO liaison officer with the army. I studied in English-language schools in Germany, Turkey, and Canada, till I was fifteen, and later I lived in London for four years. Didn't you read my file?"

"Sure I did. I must have forgotten."

"You didn't read it. You didn't know I had a kid, either."

"OK, I didn't read it, then. I just read the reports about you from the immigration department, two recommendations from magistrates, the details of a few cases. I skipped the rest. What you did in your childhood is not relevant."

"How come you know so much about painting?"

"My parents were art historians, and so I used—ah, well done. Very clever. OK, sometimes the past is relevant. But only incidentally. Still, it's good to know you speak English, if we're going to have to read through this guy's papers."

He took the book in his hands and, frowning a little at the poor hand-writing and crossings-out, read:

*"Chemically, Cinnabar is also called Vermilion or cinnabarite is red mercury (II) sulfide (HgS), a common ore of mercury and an essential part of our palette. Make sure your cinnabar really comes from China, as Italian dealers have been known to fake the provenance by using Chinese papers to contain the powder. I got the perfect mix from a monk, of all people, whom I met one day on the bridge of San Francesco in Subiaco . . ."*

Blume stopped reading, as he spotted the spines of two more note-books of the same type among the novels and Giunti art books.

Foolscap-size notebooks. Impossible to find in Italy. He had ones just like them at home. They had belonged to his father, one of whose nostrums to his unlistening son had been never to commit anything to loose-leaf paper. Well, maybe he had been listening despite himself if he remembered it now. Always use a hardback expensive lined notebook, his father had said. He had them sent over from New York, and this in the days before the internet made it easy. Then he had got himself killed in a bank raid and left half a shelf of them, unused and new then, unused and yellowing now.

The notebook on the desk was half full and seemed to be dedicated entirely to technical advice on oils, grinding, canvases. It contained some interesting illustrations in light pencil, including three versions of Dürer's hare and a page of practice signatures, such as Blume used to do when he needed to sign his own lousy school reports in his father's name. The other two notebooks were full of entries, some of which seemed to have double dates, others none.

Every so often, Treacy had whited out the ruled lines and sketched on the page. Most of the sketches were of single body parts. A hand, a foot, the curve of a neck.

Caterina had picked up one of the first notebooks and was staring at it.

"It seems to be a manual for painters," said Blume. "It's full of recipes . . ." he flicked forward a few pages. "How to age paper . . . convincing spots. Freehand composition . . . We're getting to the point where we should wait for instructions from the investigating magistrate. Still, I think we should take the notebooks."

Blume found three plastic bags for the notebooks, packaged them, and was about to drop them into his bag when he noticed Caterina's shoulder bag.

"What's in your bag?"

"This?" said Caterina, giving it a pat and blushing slightly. "Nothing. It's empty. I didn't know what sort of bag would be best for working at a crime scene."

Blume nodded sympathetically. "I've never worked it out either. I often use a bag, sometimes an old flat leather one that belonged to my father. But you can also use one of the official reinforced briefcases, they're bulky, though. So you've nothing in that bag?"

"My wallet, a pen, phone. That's it."

"Here. Drop these notebooks in."

Caterina lifted the flap of her bag, and angled in the notebooks. They were just too big to allow her to close the flap over them.

"Gives you the look of a student," said Blume. "Suits you."

"I'm too old to be a student."

"We need to log the items we remove from here," said Blume.

"Do we need to take these paintings, too? They must be valuable."

"I'm not sure that they are," said Blume. "I need to take another look at them. I think we might put a guard on this place. Someone to stand outside in the sun for hours making sure no one comes in here. Grattapaglia springs to mind."

Blume's phone rang.

"I'm taking this. You call Grattapaglia, order him to come here. You had better tell him where to find the door."

Caterina shook her head. "I don't want to be the one."

"Do it," snapped Blume.

Caterina took out her phone.

"Sorry," Blume said into his phone. "What? Oh, I see. Good, thanks, yes . . ." He pulled out his notebook, and jotted a few notes.

"Treacy part owned a private art gallery called . . ." he checked his notes, "Galleria Orpiment S.n.c. just off Via Giulia. The Rome Chamber of Commerce database has it registered as a limited company. Treacy held fifty percent and a certain John Nightingale the other fifty percent. Apparently the gallery is listed in the Rome business directory as 'specializing in Old Master paintings and drawings,' and 'original reproductions.' By the way, did you get hold of Sovrintendente Grattapaglia?"

"He's on his way," said Caterina. "Two minutes. He was still going door-to-door."

"Good," said Blume. "Actually, Treacy's gallery I just mentioned, it's not on Via Giulia but on a side street named—can you guess?"

Caterina looked around her in search of clues, then shrugged.

"Via in Caterina," said Blume. "Pretty good, huh? Via in Caterina."

"Mine's a common name."

"I'm still waiting to see a Via Alec," said Blume.

"Well, was there ever a Saint Alec?"

"Not yet," said Blume.

"Isn't Alec short for Alexander?" said Caterina.

"Yes. I'm named after a gay mass-murdering Greek. My mother chose it. Your street's about ten minutes on foot from here, so I suppose it's quicker just walking there."

"You say that like it was a problem."

"It's all a bit claustrophobic. You sort of want an investigation to expand, don't you? First, we wait for Grattapaglia. After that, we start following the money."

"What money?"

"The gallery has to do with money." He drummed his fingers against the underside of his chin. "OK, so we've got: gallery, maybe a follow-up on any bartenders who saw Treacy, then a coordination meeting. What time is it?"

Caterina looked at her watch. "It's just after ten o'clock."

"Right," said Blume. "Let's make the meeting for 1:00 this afternoon, no, make it 1:30 so people can have lunch."

"Why don't you have a watch, Commissioner?"

"I hate watches. I never get used to the feel of one. I'm always aware of it being on my wrist."

"But don't you need one?"

"I can use my cell phone. It has a clock. Or I can just ask an insolent female officer to tell me the time."

A raucous rasp sounded from the old Bakelite intercom hanging from the wall next to the bead curtain.

"That'll be Grattapaglia," said Blume. "We'll go to the gallery, leave him standing outside to guard this place."

Grattapaglia was standing in front of the green door, looking up at the wall, when they opened it. He took a step forward as if to enter, but Blume blocked his way with the bag, and said, "Here. Take this. Get someone to bring my car down here, put this in the trunk." He dropped the bag at Grattapaglia's feet and handed him the car keys. Then he leaned back and pulled the green door shut, which sagged a little thanks to his earlier efforts.

"How long do I have to stay here?" demanded Grattapaglia. "If you want me to do house-to-house and then those extra reports and write up this morning's incident . . ."

Blume cut him short with a wave of his hand.

"We are having a meeting of the investigative team after lunch. At least until then." He turned to Caterina who was hanging back trying not to overhear. "Come on, Inspector. Time for a visit to Treacy's gallery."

# 7

CATERINA AND BLUME stood on Via in Caterina, looking at a shiny brass plaque set into the wall, with "Galleria Orpiment, 1° piano" etched into it. The door to the building was half open, and they stepped inside the small courtyard to find themselves before a wide stone staircase whose many shallow marble steps seemed designed to ease the task of climbing and to impress upon the visitor that this was a building with room to spare. Turning around on the landing at the end of the first flight, they were confronted with another, slightly steeper and shorter, leading up the *piano nobile* and the entrance to the gallery, which was marked by a high threshold topped with red marble and a faded coat of arms and the motto *Ingenium superat vires*. The large double-leaved oak door was open and led to a small access area fronted by darkened glass. Blume pressed the intercom and the door clicked open immediately.

Inside the gallery, the ceilings were high and their footfalls clacked and echoed every time they left the overlapping Persian carpets. The hall smelled of polish and lavender, and the cool air felt smooth and heavy against their skin. It was a place conducive to quiet business between people who understood one another. Pictures that looked like they had been overlaid with a veneer of treacle were set in heavy gold frames, but their irregular spacing on the walls stopped them from being too overbearing. They all seemed to feature people with complacent eighteenth-century faces in extravagant clothes, lounging on urns and surrounded by classical ruins.

At the end of the room, behind a clear desk with a flat-screen monitor, but no keyboard in sight, sat a young woman who watched as they entered. Blume noted her perfect shape, so flat, so taut.

He introduced himself and Inspector Mattiola, and the girl introduced herself as Manuela Ludovisi. She was composed enough not to stand up herself, but instead motioned them to sit down. Using the polite pronoun "*Lei*," she offered them tea, coffee, and water before finally accepting that they were declining all beverages.

"Are you alone here?" Blume decided to use the familiar "*tu*" immediately.

She nodded. Beautiful women often had heads the shape of eggs, Blume decided. It allowed them to have oval faces and tapered cheeks.

Blume's cell rang. He flicked it open, and saw Grattapaglia's name. He'd let Grattapaglia stew for another hour or two before letting him go. He cut off the call, turned to the receptionist with a smile, and said, "Sorry about that. Do you know why we are here?"

The girl shut her eyes without scrunching her eyelids, wrinkling her brow, or bringing her hand to her face. It was a study in self-control. She opened her eyes again, and they seemed bluer and brighter than before. Only then did he realize he was looking at eyes full of withheld tears. "Something's happened to Henry," she said. "Is he dead? The policeman who phoned me earlier just told me to stay here till someone came, but he would not tell me anything."

"Yes," said Blume. "He's dead."

She nodded slowly, and the tear in her left eye fell onto her table. None followed. "Where was he found?"

Caterina leaned forward and said, "The policeman who called didn't say?"

"All he said was that someone would be calling round to talk about Henry Treacy and I was to stay put."

"Why did you ask where he was found?" said Caterina with what Blume felt was aggression. "What makes you think he did not die at home?"

"If he died at home how would anyone even know he was missing?" said the girl. "It's only half past ten. I don't think he had a cleaner and I can't think who might have gone to his house."

"Because no one ever went to his house?" asked Blume.

"Apart from Nightingale. That's John Nightingale, his partner here and my boss."

"Where is Nightingale now?"

"I don't know. He was supposed to come back from Florence early this morning, but he didn't pass by here and he's not at home yet. So maybe he stayed there. I tried phoning his house."

"What about his cell phone?" asked Blume.

"He doesn't have one. Neither did Henry."

Caterina pulled her chair closer to the table. "What made you so sure it was Treacy who was dead. Why not your other boss, Nightingale?"

The girl leaned backwards and wrinkled her nose slightly as if she had caught a draft of bad breath from Caterina.

"It had to be Henry. He was sick. He drank. He was the one who hated himself and everyone. You know, the tortured artist."

"You don't like artists?" said Caterina.

"As long as they stay sober and don't mistake their trade for genius, I don't mind them."

Blume nodded sympathetically. "Good attitude," he said.

"Did Henry think of himself as a genius?" asked Caterina.

"Maybe once he did. Not since I knew him. That's where the tortured bit came in. That's why I knew it was him you found dead. And you still haven't told me where."

"Piazza de' Renzi. Know it?" asked Blume.

"No. Is it near his house?"

"Yes," said Blume.

She touched the tiny hollow above her upper lip. "I really need to get home," she said. "I can't just stay here."

"We need you to show us around, I'm afraid," said Blume. "Are there many more rooms?"

"Just two. Both slightly smaller than this. One for Nightingale, one for Treacy."

Caterina shifted in her seat and leaned forward. "Where is home, by the way?"

"Via della Lupa, number 82b."

Caterina wrote it down. "What's the postal code?"

"00186."

"That's very central."

"Yes. I walk to work." The girl's eyelids flickered slightly as she looked at the Inspector. "It helps keep me in shape."

"I walk everywhere, too," said Blume.

"How much is the rent?" asked Caterina.

The girl rolled her blue eyes sideways as if trying to remember. "Around two thousand six, two thousand seven, I think."

Caterina lowered her notebook. "You think, but you don't know?"

"I don't pay it."

"Who does?"

"Galleria Orpiment."

"Galleria Orpiment or one of your employers or both?"

"It's the same thing, isn't it?"

"No."

"John Nightingale, then. He's the one who organizes most things."

"How much do they pay you here?"

The receptionist looked at Blume. "Do I have to answer that?"

Blume nodded. "Yes, you do, I'm afraid. Though I can't see why it should be a problem."

"I feel as if my privacy is being violated."

"Well, perhaps," said Blume. "We're investigative police. Violation of privacy is basically what we do."

Caterina waved her notebook impatiently. "How much?"

"I get €4,700 a month, OK?"

Jesus, thought Blume. That was about what he and Mattiola made between them.

Caterina arched her eyebrows, then asked, "What does your mother do?" She pushed out her hand to ward off the beginning of a protest from the girl. "Everything's relevant. Just answer."

"She works in a bank. She's a teller. But if you were to ask her what she does, she'd say she was an artist."

"There's that unlovely word again. You don't like artists because your mother is one?"

Manuela wetted her lip with the tip of her tongue, and Blume stood up abruptly and wandered off to look at the paintings on the wall.

Caterina slid into his chair, which was closer to Manuela, and said, "But her works don't sell?"

"No, they don't. She can't even give them away."

"And your father?"

"I don't have a father. Just my mother."

"So Ludovisi is her name, your mother's name."

Manuela hesitated. "No. It's my father's name."

"You just said you didn't have a father."

"I don't. My mother gave me his surname to shame him into returning, but he never did."

"And so, your mother's name is …?"

"Angelini. Chiara Angelini."

"Where does she live?"

"Pistoia."

"So you're from Pistoia, too?"

The girl hesitated.

"Just say yes or no, it's not a trick question," said Caterina.

"Yes."

"You went to school there?"

"Yes."

"What was the name of the school?"

"Um … Liceo Classico 'Niccolo' Forteguerri."

"May I see your identity card, please?"

The girl brought up a square black handbag from below the desk, and Blume came over to watch. From the neatly divided contents, she plucked out a compact Fendi wallet and produced a surprisingly battered-looking ID card, which Caterina looked at closely before handing back.

"What's the bank she works in?"

"Carismi."

"Carismi?"

"It's short for Cassa Di Risparmio Di San Miniato."

Blume continued staring at the dull portraits on the walls as Caterina asked the girl more questions about her mother, Pistoia, school, her friends. She took down a few names and addresses, got the girl's cell number. Caterina was doing a good job, so he left her to it, and wandered around the hall, looking at the portraits, glancing back at the two women seated at the desk. There was an undertow of tension and a sort of subliminal tussle going on between them, but they were managing it with composure. He thought of the shouts and obscenities, the threats, spit, slaps, kicks, arrogance, imbecility, intoxication, and noncooperation that characterized so many of the "interviews" between male suspects and tired, stressed-out cops. Watching the girl's face and lips, the way she crooked her elbow as she straightened a bright strand of hair, with Caterina poised and calm, observing her carefully, he felt humans, or some of them, were worth it after all.

The eight portraits showed young men and women dressed in red or blue standing in front of Roman ruins, with idealized landscapes behind them. The faces were photographic, and some were far more handsome than others, but the artist had somehow managed to render each face slightly idiotic. It was something to do with the pursed lips and smirk.

The interview between Caterina and Manuela seemed to be over, and Manuela, with the air of a vindicated adolescent, arose from her seat and came over to him.

"Five of those are by Pompeo Batoni," she said. "Three are by Treacy. And no one can tell the difference without checking the signatures on the back."

She said this with unaffected pride, as if there was nothing untoward in the way that Treacy imitated another painter's work.

"Batoni charged his customers up front. These are all English and German tourists. He'd do their faces in about two or three sessions, then fill in the rest afterwards and have them shipped. He charged extra for details. If you wanted, say, a dog or a broken classical column, it cost you extra," she said.

"Oh," said Blume. He focused on them again. "I don't like them much," he said after a while.

The girl laughed, and Blume smiled knowingly, as if he had always intended his comment to be witty.

"Nobody likes them," she said, then became grave again. "No one except Henry. He loved Batoni. Whenever he came into the gallery, he'd wave at the people in the pictures and shout, 'Good morning, English cretins!' He said Batoni had no pretention as an artist. All the pretention was in the buyer, whose face is in the picture. He spent a lot of money collecting these."

Blume looked around and saw Caterina opening a pair of double doors at the far end of the room. He went across to join her, and Manuela followed. The room they entered had a very similar leather-topped desk and a handsome oak bookcase. It was extremely orderly and had no pictures on the walls. Most of the books seemed to have been bought for decorative purposes.

"This is Nightingale's room," said Manuela. "He never uses it, really. Except to make phone calls."

The other room was bursting at the seams with objects, books, and paintings. Some paintings and books were stacked on the floor. Behind the desk a full-length portrait, done in modern acrylics, showed a young man with a thin face slouched against a broken pillar, his blue eyes looking slightly sideways and half closed as against the smoke from his cigarette, yet gazing out at the viewer. The man held the cigarette between two lips curled like two tildes, his black shirt was open to reveal a smooth chest whose muscles the artist had exaggerated almost to the point of parody. Something about the man was extremely familiar, and Blume found himself staring at the painting for some time.

"I know him from somewhere," said Blume. "But I can't quite remember."

"That's Henry Treacy," said Manuela. "It's a self-portrait from 1966. It's one of the only original works with his signature, and is worth quite a lot. At least, that's what Treacy himself used to say."

The man's dead face he had seen earlier in the day looked nothing like this handsome youth with the curved lips.

Caterina, who had gone to the far side of the desk and was looking with casual interest into a drawer, said, "What do you mean one of the only works with his signature?"

"Treacy stopped painting soon after that portrait," said Manuela. "I mean, he stopped painting as Treacy."

"Who did he become after that?"

The girl gave a sideways glance at Blume as if giving him the opportunity to intervene and explain the obvious. When he did not, she continued, "Henry Treacy became a restorer and a dealer. He was one of the best draftsmen ever, and it is true that he could imitate many great artists. He did five of the Batoni portraits out there, but he did not copy."

"Really?" said Caterina. "Manuela, tell me this: what's the difference between copying and imitating, then?"

"A copy is just a copy, but not the original. Imitation is when you create something new out of something old. That's what Treacy did. He created new things."

"New forgeries, you mean?" said Caterina.

"It's not like that. His work was his own. Everyone copies anyhow."

"Did he tell you that?"

"I'm not sure if he told me it, but I think that was his opinion."

"And yours, too?"

"Inspector, I'm only the receptionist. I'm still learning. You need to talk to Nightingale, not me, about these things."

Blume heard a soft purring sound coming from somewhere.

"That's the intercom," said Caterina. "As you're the receptionist, you had better see who it is."

Blume looked over at Caterina, and for the first time noticed his colleague's clothes. She was wearing a jacket that was slightly too tight under the arms, and he could see fabric pills and some loose threads on her black slacks. "She's very ..." began Blume, but he hadn't prepared a careful adjective.

"She's very beautiful is what you mean, Commissioner. And young." Caterina fiddled at her blouse cuff, which was missing a button. "Do you think we declare the Gallery a secondary scene?"

"That's for the magistrate to decide, and it's not even a confirmed homicide yet. Let's see if this Nightingale turns up."

Blume and Caterina came out of Treacy's office and came face-to-face with a group of eight Carabinieri, all of them wearing white gloves as if for some academy graduation. They were busy taking down the pictures from the wall and putting them into clear plastic boxes. Behind them was Manuela who was holding a piece of paper in her hand, and talking to a man in his late thirties with long curly gray hair that cascaded in ringlets over the upturned collar of his yellow and black waistcoat.

"Who's that?" said Caterina as the man turned around, saw them, and cast a bright-toothed smile in their direction.

"That creature," said Blume, "is Investigating Magistrate Franco Buoncompagno."

"So that's what he looks like," said Caterina.

"You've heard of him?"

"Of course," she said.

The investigating magistrate moved toward Blume and Caterina, and Blume circled away, standing in front of one of the last pictures not to have been removed from the wall as if it were his. If the magistrate noticed, he did not let on, and took Caterina's hand, clasped it briefly between his own, saying, "You must be ...?"

"I must be Inspector Mattiola, Third Section, Squadra Mobile," said Caterina, pulling her hand away.

"Well, I am—You're so pretty, I've forgotten who I am. Just kidding. Breaking the ice, as the fat penguin said. It doesn't do to be too formal. Investigating Magistrate Franco Buoncompagno."

"How do you do," said Caterina.

Blume stepped in front of Caterina and looked over Buoncompagno's head at the young Carabinieri removing the paintings. "What's going on here, Dottore?" said Blume.

A young Carabiniere hovered behind the magistrate, waiting for them to finish before he took the painting on the wall behind. Blume motioned him away with a flick of his hand.

"Commissioner Blume!" said Buoncompagno, his voice full of surprise and delight. "Finally!" he tapped his nose as if revealing a secret. "I called your office. Twice."

"Did you try my cell phone?"

"Of course."

As Blume took out his cell phone and started thumbing through the missed call list, Buoncompagno added, "I didn't call you personally, of course. I have been very busy. I left word in the office that they were to call you."

Blume found three unanswered calls, all from Grattapaglia, and nothing else. "Well, they didn't," he said.

"That was remiss. I'll have some harsh words to say to the staff when I get back. But no matter. We're here now. But you can relax, Commissioner. This is definitely a case for the Carabinieri rather than the police."

"Why the Carabinieri?" said Blume, finally lowering his gaze to look the magistrate in the face.

"Listen to him!" said Buoncompagno to Caterina. "He loves working! I'm glad I give him orders rather than take them. He hates to lose control. He must be a real slave-driver, eh?"

Caterina did not even allow herself a flicker of a smile. She watched as Blume's eyes seemed to scope the magistrate's upper body and face as if selecting a target.

"OK. So we're not so friendly here," said Buoncompagno at last. "No problem, since we're not going to be working together."

"What I want to know is what the Carabinieri are doing here right now, with these paintings," said Blume.

"We are sequestering all the works of art in this gallery. And anything else of use, of course. As part of the investigation into the death of Henry Treacy, the forger. I have just dropped the order on that sex-bomb at the reception desk." He winked at Blume, then said to Caterina, "Not that you are any the less fair."

Caterina moved away from him.

"That's what I get for trying to be chivalrous. As if there was even any comparison between her and . . ."

Blume lunged forward suddenly and Buoncompagno skipped back out of range, and collided with a Carabiniere, who pushed the magistrate away from him before seeming to recognize him. The Carabiniere excused himself, and walked away. Buoncompagno hooked his thumbs onto his jean pockets and looked across a stretch of Persian carpet at Blume. "I see. I want you out of here now. Take your woman inspector with you. I've assigned a proper expert to the case: Colonel Orazio Farinelli."

It took Blume a second or two to understand. "A colonel?"

"Of the Carabinieri. Do you have a problem with that, Commissioner?" Buoncompagno clumped away in his soft leather ankle boots toward the reception desk and the two women. As he arrived, they both moved across the room back toward Blume. Caterina touched his elbow, and said, "I think we should go. All three of us, if possible."

Blume nodded.

Buoncompagno laughed good-naturedly. "Hold on there, you two! Just where do you think you are taking that beautiful young woman? Sweetheart, you don't have to go with them. I'm in charge now."

He leaned over and lightly clasped her arm.

Manuela gently removed her arm from his grasp, and with a sweet smile stepped forwards as if changing sides and going over to the magistrate. She put her hand flat against his chest, in what seemed like a protective gesture, then suddenly pushed the heel into his solar plexus. Buoncompagno staggered back with a gasp.

"Don't you dare touch me again," said Manuela.

"I didn't!" Buoncompagno looked around for witnesses, but the Carabinieri seemed not to have been paying attention.

"I do not feel comfortable leaving a young woman alone in the company of male officers and a male magistrate only," said Caterina. "So she's coming with us."

"You take orders from me," said Buoncompagno. "I am in charge here. And I say she stays."

Blume looked around him, caught the eye of a Carabinieri Maresciallo whom he half knew. The Maresciallo, whose age and experience gave him authority well beyond his modest rank, gave the tiniest of nods in the direction of the door, then called the magistrate over, and led him to the far end of the room.

Blume, Caterina, and Manuela walked out.

When they reached the street outside, Manuela turned to him to say, "Can I go now?" but Blume signaled her to be quiet as he made a phone call. She turned to Caterina and asked the same question.

"Sure," said Caterina, watching Blume's face for a reaction. "Stay available. Call me if you need help." She looked over at Blume for confirmation, but he was too agitated by something he was hearing on his phone to notice.

"I am a fool," he said, apparently forgetting completely about Manuela, and setting off at a fast pace, driving himself between a tourist couple who started after him in outrage. Caterina, weighed down by her bag and the three heavy notebooks inside, had to break into a short trot before she caught him up.

"I ignored Grattapaglia's calls. I stood there like an idiot listening to that whore of a magistrate. Can you guess where he is, the Colonel he appointed, I mean?"

As Blume framed the question, Caterina knew the answer.

"At Treacy's place," she said. "That's why Grattapaglia was calling you."

"Yes, and Grattapaglia's just told me he had to let the Colonel past, the dumb bastard. He's going to pay for this in ways he can't imagine."

Caterina wondered what she would have done in Grattapaglia's place.

"He could have called in others to help," said Blume in reply to her thoughts. "I'm not the only superior officer he knows. I might as well have put a fucking traffic cone in charge."

"Was Magistrate Buoncompagno there, too? At Treacy's house?"

"Apparently so," said Blume, slowing down his pace a little. "Buoncompagno. Can it get worse? By the way, I see you know about him, too. What act of corrupt incompetence did he visit on you?"

"Not on me personally," said Caterina. "He archived an investigation that should have been kept open. We were on the point of breaking a ring smuggling in Romanian girls—this is from before Romania was part of the EU—and he just went and closed down the whole operation. Someone paid him off."

"That's pretty typical," said Blume. "Six years ago, Paoloni—he's not on the force any more, but he was a great cop . . ."

"I arrived a few weeks before Paoloni left," said Caterina. "I remember him."

"Right," said Blume, slowly, not quite believing her.

"You've forgotten that, too. I arrived just after the killing of the young policeman . . . Ferrucci."

"Right," said Blume. "Of course."

"I don't expect you to remember. Obviously you had other things to worry about at the time."

"No, no. I remember," said Blume.

"Now you're trying to be gallant."

"Nope. I remember you. So, you remember Paoloni?"

"Yes."

"I disagreed with some of the things Paoloni did, but he was a friend. Still is. People never really noticed how close we were, because we had different styles, and now, they tend to forget that when they talk to me about him. So try not to make the mistake of criticizing him or his methods when talking to me."

"I didn't say a word against him!"

"Yeah, but you were thinking it, and I'd hate to have an argument with you. You want to compare Paoloni with someone like Buoncompagno. A moral chasm between them."

"I didn't . . ." began Caterina, but Blume plowed on, quickening his pace on the downward slope of the Sisto Bridge as he did so.

"I'll tell you a story about Buoncompagno. Six years ago, Paoloni and I were investigating the killing of an inspector from the Health Institute, a guy called Lazzarini, also worked as a natural scientist for La Sapienza University. He had been looking into dioxin levels in San Marzano tomatoes . . ."

Caterina stopped dead as Blume walked straight into the moving traffic, slapping his palm hard on the hood of a car that honked at him and giving it a kick in the side as it sped off. He still seemed to be telling the story of the San Marzano tomatoes as he reached Piazza Trilussa on the other side. Caterina watched him go, and waited for the pedestrian light to turn green. By the time it had, her Commissioner was already out of sight.

# 8

As he reached the other side of the road, Blume pulled out his phone and called Kristin Holmquist at the American Embassy.

"Alec!"

She sounded warm. He closed his eyes and imagined her standing there with her bright copper hair, her blue jeans, her white blouse, her smell of talc.

"I'm working an interesting case," he said.

"Really? You want to tell me about it first, or shall we just skip to the part where you ask me to do some research for you?"

"Well, you know it's not safe or practical to do this sort of thing by phone, so why don't I just give you a name, and then maybe we can meet for dinner and compare notes," said Blume.

"Get information *and* a date out of me, you mean?"

"I know, it is a terrible role-reversal for you, Kristin . . . ." The scent of ginger and garlic from the Surya Maha Indian restaurant above him gave him an idea. "I'll make dinner. This evening, my place."

"What's the name you're interested in?"

"Colonel Orazio Farinelli, he's a member of the Carabinieri. I know the name from somewhere. He's just strolled in and taken my case away from me."

"How did he manage that?"

"Investigating Magistrate Franco Buoncompagno, also known as the finger puppet. I don't need you to look Buoncompagno up. I know more than enough about him."

"You can never know too much," said Kristin.

"I hate to disagree, but often I find myself knowing far more about people than I want to. Do we have a deal?"

"I'm not sure, Alec. You have not always been as helpful as we had hoped. And when I say 'not always,' I mean 'never.'"

"That's because I don't like sharing info on my cases with an operative in a foreign embassy."

"I'm not an operative, Alec baby. And you can't go round calling your fellow Americans foreigners."

"Well, let's try this thing again. You never made it clear what you wanted me to do for you anyhow, apart from when we were, you know . . ."

"When we were what?"

"Sorry, that was in bad taste."

"It sure was. I distinctly remember explaining it to you in the clearest possible terms. I was looking for someone to keep an ear to the ground here in Rome, help me flesh out my monthly reports to the country team. You are clearly not that person. So, personal feelings and friendship aside, you're calling me now because . . .?"

"A case was taken away from me, I was hoping you might speed up the process of my finding out about this Colonel. If not, I can do it myself."

"I still don't get why you think I'll do this. Or why you think I have access."

"I know you have access. Even I have access if I try hard enough. It's just quicker this way."

"Suppose I helped you, would you consider that as a favor to be returned?"

"Of course. I never said no to what you were proposing. You know me, I love sharing. Love my country, too."

"I don't know, Alec. Maybe."

"Great. That's Farinelli with two 'l's. And 8 o'clock, my place. I'm making pure American tacos and . . ." he tried to think of something appetizing. "Guacamole."

When Blume arrived a few minutes later, Sovrintendente Grattapaglia was standing at the green door, arms folded as if barring entrance to it, and staring at a dark-blue Carabinieri car with a red flash emblem parked a few meters from him.

The driver, a Maresciallo, had positioned the vehicle below a plane tree, and was leaning on the half-open door. As Blume came up beside the car, a small swirl of smoke floated out from the passenger seat behind.

Blume bent down to see inside, shading his eyes like he was saluting the occupants. The windows were slightly tinted, and he could just make out two or maybe three men filling up all the space in the backseat. Someone grabbed his shoulder, but Blume stayed relaxed.

"Take your hand off me," he said. "I am a police commissioner."

The grip eased, but the Carabiniere did not let go completely. Blume straightened up, turned around, and pushed down the Carabiniere's extended arm.

"If you've been on duty in Rome for any length of time, you probably know my face," said Blume. "So there should be no need for me to have to tell you to step back, now."

The Carabiniere took a step backwards, and nodded.

From behind him came the whirring sound of a car window being lowered, and a blue cloud of cigar smoke swirled over Blume's shoulder.

Blume turned around and looked into the car. The backseat was filled to capacity by a single man.

The voice was slightly throaty, soft, and calm, the face creased and brown like a hickory nut. "I imagine you are Commissioner Blume."

Blume had seen people this large when traveling as a boy with his parents through towns in Iowa, Indiana, and Ohio, but everything they wore was elasticized; and he had seen obese Neapolitan criminals with Velcro straps on running shoes they couldn't see, but he had never seen a man with so much bulk dressed in such a nicely cut silk suit.

"And you must be Colonel Farinelli," said Blume.

# 9

"Y OU PUT THE place off limits," said the Colonel. "Good. I like a sealed environment."

"I hope my Sovrintendente extended you every courtesy during your search," said Blume.

"Oh, he did his best to stop us," said Farinelli. He let out a cloud of smoke and nodded from inside it. "But what could he do? The magistrate tried to send him away, but he wouldn't budge. He even insisted on watching us as we gathered evidence."

"What evidence?"

"Why paintings, of course. That's why I have been called in. Art fraud is my special area."

"Murder is mine."

"Yes. I'm sure you'll have a murder to look into sometime soon. What's the average in your district, two, three a month?"

"Are you saying Treacy was not murdered?" said Blume. "Do you have evidence for that?"

"Of course not. That's up to you, Commissioner. It should be clear within a few hours, or tomorrow after the autopsy, no? Meanwhile, I'm looking after this." The Colonel tossed his cigar butt out the door. His suit began to ripple as he began the process of heaving himself across the seat toward the door.

Blume walked away in the direction of Grattapaglia, leaving the task of pulling his boss out of the car to the Maresciallo.

"You did try to stop them, right?" said Blume as he reached Grattapaglia.

"Stop a team of Carabinieri, a colonel, and a magistrate with a search warrant? I did my best."

"OK, OK. I should have answered when you called. Get back to the station now."

Grattapaglia nodded over Blume's shoulder. "Here they are again. And I can see Inspector Mattiola looking a bit lost at the end of the street."

"Take her back with you."

"So it's all working out? She's a big help?"

"Get lost. Write that report on this morning's incident."

Grattapaglia moved away, leaving Blume face-to-face with Colonel Farinelli who was holding two solid white boxes with "Franchi" written on them in blue cursive letters. He caught Blume's glance and raised the boxes slightly. "A break for lunch, Commissioner. That's where I was just now. Do you like Franchi's take-out fare?"

Blume did—who didn't? But he said nothing.

Blume pushed open the green door, which now sagged on its hinges, and stepped into the narrow passageway, imagining the Colonel trapped there like a hog in a rabbit hole.

"I did not enjoy squeezing in there last time," said the Colonel. "If you'd be so kind . . . ." He handed the boxes to Blume.

Blume handed them back, saying, "Get your Maresciallo to carry them."

"Ah, but he's staying here."

"Then carry them yourself."

By the time he reached the door to the greenhouse, the Colonel was breathing heavily and had difficulty ascending the two steps that led inside.

When he had finally made it up, he put down the boxes and placed his hands on the small of his back and pushed his stomach out even further, like he was considering buying the property.

After a while, with his breathing back to normal, the Colonel said, "Treacy has hardly changed this place."

"Treacy?" said Blume. "You knew him?"

"Of course. I knew him well. Or used to. This house must have been the servants' quarters for Villa Corsini."

Blume went through the kitchen and into the next room. The walls were now almost bare, though several paintings had been left. The unframed sketches and paintings he had noticed earlier piled on the desk were gone, and the papers on the desk had been thoroughly searched and many of them lay scattered on the floor. Perhaps the utility bills and bank statements were not vital evidence, but they could be useful, and Blume had intended to take them in. Yet Farinelli and his men had thrown them on the floor. The only reason Blume could see for that was that they had been looking for something else, something specific.

Colonel Farinelli appeared from the kitchen. "What are you looking for? You're not conducting an investigation, you know."

"I'm curious," said Blume.

"What we have here is a natural death. No need for your *squadra mobile*. The dead man was a forger, hence my involvement," said the Colonel. "But I seem to remember, you don't work well with the Carabinieri."

"Usually I work fine with the Carabinieri," said Blume. "Last time I didn't, Buoncompagno was directing that investigation, too. I just want to see a few things for myself before I sign off."

"Come into the kitchen, then," said the Colonel.

Blume returned to the kitchen, where the Colonel had thrown open the fridge.

"You're an Anglo-Saxon," he declared. "So I suppose you're more butter, beer, and milk than wine, oil, and water?"

Blume did not reply, but the Colonel was not waiting either. "Your northern diet is very high in cholesterol. You need to be careful." He pushed the refrigerator door shut. "What did you see in there that might be interesting?"

"A lot of eggs," said Blume.

"Ah, you noticed them, did you?" said the Colonel, clumping his hands together. He wore a large ruby ring on his middle finger.

"Yes," said Blume. "And I thought maybe he was using the eggs for tempera painting, instead of just eating them."

The Colonel tapped the side of his nose. "What made you think of that?"

"I'm investigating the suspicious death of a man who forged paintings for a living. Eggs are used for tempera painting, it's an obvious connection."

"It's not obvious to everyone," said the Colonel, pulling out a green folding wooden chair from below the marble table on which the two boxes now sat beside a honey pot, a bag of sugar, an open carton of milk, a pepper canister, and a bottle of Worcester sauce. "But I suppose you have the right background."

The Colonel lifted the flimsy chair in one hand, looked at it scornfully, then put it down, and dragged a heavy oak stool with paint spots all over it. He brushed the surface with the back of his hand, sat down, stretched out his arm, and pulled the two white boxes across the table. "Your parents were art historians, Commissioner. I was hoping some of their knowledge had rubbed off on you, and it seems it has."

"Did you delve deep, Colonel?"

"A cursory glance, just to see who I would be dealing with. I am very impressed, Commissioner. Really. That was a terrible thing that befell your parents. What made you decide to stay in this awful country afterwards?"

Blume wagged his index finger at the Colonel, warning him off the subject.

"I don't mean to intrude on your private grief," said the Colonel. "Though it can't have been easy. All these years on a police salary? We public servants, risking our lives, grossly underpaid, unrewarded, unrecognized. Policemen fall into arrears on a mortgage, take stupid risks, some even kill themselves out of despair. Some have killed their families. It doesn't take much to get into a hole, especially if the first place you go to is the criminal underworld instead of your colleagues in law enforcement. A house sale falls through, your kid needs braces, some bastard sues you for some trivial mishap. And there we stand, vulnerable, outbid, underpaid, in debt."

He opened a box with a sigh and a sad shake of his head that caused his cheeks to wobble. "Get those two glasses over there, the ones by the sink, would you?"

Blume stayed where he was.

"Go on," said the Colonel. "I had them washed earlier. The corkscrew, too, if you'd be so kind. And some knives, forks, spoons from that drawer."

Blume spread his hands out in an apologetic way, and said: "Sorry, Colonel. You want a valet, call your Maresciallo in."

The Colonel sighed theatrically. "Look, Commissioner, I am a fat man. What is simple for you is difficult for me. I suffer from diabetes. I have gout in my left toe."

"Gout? Nobody gets gout anymore."

"Nowadays they call it metabolic arthritis. It's been getting worse. It comes in the spring, stays for the summer, and is gone by the winter. Like some sort of evil migrating bird."

Blume went over and retrieved the glasses, corkscrew, and silverware, brought them back to the table.

"To the side of the refrigerator there, in the rack, the bottle third from the top—no, the other. That's it," said the Colonel.

Blume brought the bottle of wine over, set it in front of the Colonel who was now lifting things out of one white box.

"The thing is," said the Colonel, "our man was not known for forging tempera paintings, and I found only two in the house. His real specialty was pen, ink, wash, sketches, preparations for prints. He was a great draftsman, but maybe his eye for color was not so good. Maybe you need to be Italian to appreciate the full palette of color."

"Do you?" said Blume. "Well, then maybe he just liked eggs a lot."

"There was a lot of milk in that refrigerator, too," said the Colonel. "Both fresh and sour. Anglo-Saxons always have so much milk."

"The fresh milk tells us Treacy was here recently," said Blume. "Not that it's likely to make much difference."

"Why would he keep sour milk, Commissioner?"

"Milk is used as a fixative for pencil and chalk, which is what you say he mainly used. Sour is as good as fresh for that. Or maybe he made his own soda bread."

"Soda bread? Good stuff that. You use sour milk? You must tell me about that another time," said the Colonel. "Speaking of bread, did you notice the basket with the stale bread in it?"

Blume went over to a wicker basket sitting on the counter, pushed off the top, and produced two pieces of broken dirty bread which he rapped against the counter.

"Rub breadcrumbs over a chalk drawing, and you get an old look," said the Colonel. "Treacy was a bit of a pig, but I don't think he kept dirty bread to eat."

"It's hardly the only way to get a drawing to look old," said Blume.

"You're right again," said the Colonel. "Just one of many techniques."

"So maybe it was just stale bread," said Blume.

"What else did you notice?" asked the Colonel.

"There was gelatin in the fridge, which maybe he used for glues or for preparing paper, something like that."

"I see garlic, potatoes, vinegar. They can all be used, too, can't they?"

The Colonel had dipped his spoon into the pot on the table. He twirled it niftily between his fingers as he pulled it out, opened his mouth, and dropped in a glob of honey.

"Honey is used for pastels," said the Colonel, his voice slow and thick.

"Vinegar, wine, oatmeal," said Blume. "There is an ice-cube tray full of ink over there, and it looks like he used the pastry-board as a drawing board. Under the sink in the greenhouse, I found denatured alcohol, white spirit, benzene, turps. You can smell the turps in here. Also, he was doing something with oils in that double boiler."

"You haven't missed a trick," said the Colonel.

"Yes, I have," said Blume. He walked over to the zinc fruit bowls and scooped up a handful of small acorns, shook them in the hollow of his hand, then let them drop. "Why did he collect dry acorns?" He went to the other bowl and picked up the woody fruits he had examined earlier. "And I don't even know what these are."

"Oak apples," said the Colonel. "Or galls."

"Galls?"

"Houses for insect larvae."

"Sorry. I still don't get it," said Blume.

"I don't know much about the nature side of it," said the Colonel. "These things grow on oaks, maybe on other trees, too. They contain wasp larvae. What you do is pluck them, dry them out in the oven or the sun, then crush them with a pestle; you mix in acorns, too. But I don't know what the proportion is. You mix it with water, maybe other things, and you get iron ink for drawing."

"And that's the end result in the ice-cube tray?" said Blume.

"You don't use your nose enough, Commissioner. Bring your face down to that ink, breathe in, slowly, use your mouth as well as your nose. Open the back of your throat, too. Get the taste."

Blume put his face over the tray and sniffed. "Nothing," he said. "Maybe a bit like a sweaty cheese rind."

"You need to learn to use all your five senses, Commissioner, and never despise smell which is our most basic, our most reptile sense. That is not gall ink. That's cuttlefish ink. You can smell the salt. Damn, I can taste it in the back of my throat from here. Wonderful stuff. It looks black, draws brown. But gall—it burns through paper, but that's good if all the paper you have available is half ruined. Gives you an excuse for all the wear."

The Colonel pointed to the raised brick fireplace where a half-burned log lay in ash. "It's too warm to be lighting fires for comfort," he said. "So we can assume that had another purpose. Mix the soot with rainwater and you've got bistre which, in the end, is going to be the ink he used most."

"Does it have to be rainwater?" asked Blume.

"Definitely. Especially here in Rome. Too much limescale in the tap water, too many salts in the bottled stuff. Besides, it's free. You know who used bistre a lot?"

"Who?"

"Nicolas Poussin," said the Colonel. "And you know when I first met Henry Treacy?"

"Tell me."

"In 1973, when he was accused of trying to sell a fake Poussin landscape. An oil painting. He wasn't so good with oils. Good, but not that good."

Blume did some mental arithmetic.

"I turn sixty-three on November 13, Commissioner. That's what you're trying to work out. Two years ago I moved out of the Carabiniere Art Forgery and Heritage Division in Trastevere and was posted to Madonna del Riposo."

The Colonel picked up a flat painting knife from the table, stabbed it into the top of the second box, and slit it open. He pulled out several flat and several bulky packages and a half loaf of Genzano bread, then set about unfolding and unwrapping each package. The flat ones contained salamis and cured hams, the bulky ones cheese.

The Colonel broke off a triangle of cheese and popped it into his mouth. He shoved the corkscrew into the black bottle before handing it to Blume. "If you'd be so kind, I'm a little breathless?"

Blume pulled out the cork, handed the bottle to the Colonel, who filled up Blume's glass. Blume pushed his glass back to the Colonel, and said, "No thanks."

"But it's a Sassicaia. Not the famous 1985 vintage, more's the pity, but even so."

"I do not drink," said Blume.

The Colonel held the glass by the stem and lifted it up so that the ruby highlights in the dark wine became apparent. "I see," he said. "And this is because you are an alcoholic?"

"No. I just thought I should give it up, that's all," said Blume. "I prefer to keep in shape."

The Colonel placed his nostrils over the rim and inhaled, sipped the wine, paused, pursed his lips, then drained half the glass. "You must be an alcoholic. There is no other reason for not drinking Tuscan wine. I'm disappointed, but I am sure we can still manage to work together. Informally."

He unwrapped a bundle of waxed paper to reveal a pile of sliced ham. He peeled off the top slice with his thick fingers. "This culatello is particularly sweet. Try it."

Blume hesitated, before finally helping himself to a thin slice of meat. It was good.

The Colonel cut a wedge of yellow cheese with a black rind, handed it to Blume, and said, "Gran Bastardo."

"Who?"

"The cheese. That's what it's called. Comes from the Veneto," said the Colonel. "By the way, if you insist on treating this as murder, just remember that Treacy's business partner John Nightingale is the one with the most to gain and the most to lose. Most to gain because maybe he knows where Treacy has hidden his wealth and is now about to help himself, but most to lose because he may have just killed the goose that lays the golden eggs. You know, I can't bear to see you sitting there drinking nothing. There's some mineral water in the fridge, help yourself."

"I don't drink mineral water. Tap water is fine."

The Colonel tore at a hunk of bread. "You're not eating. Here." He pushed over a plastic carton with soft white cheese. "Testa del Morto. Lovely on the bread. Slide a slice of ham over the top, fold, and . . ."

"No thanks."

"Fine. More for me, then." The Colonel chewed for a while, then started fingering around in his mouth. "Always get these strands of flesh . . . stuck between my teeth. I don't suppose you have any toothpicks on you?"

Colonel Farinelli eventually decided the solution to the annoyance in his mouth was to down another glass of wine.

"As I said, I knew Treacy very well, once. I also knew his business partner John Nightingale, though less well. The two of them came to my attention in the 1970s."

The Colonel pushed away his plate, and continued, "Henry Treacy and

John Nightingale were a very effective pair. Treacy specialized in sixteenth-century forgeries. He used to say no artist after 1620 was worth imitating."

"In America, we're taught that's when history starts," said Blume.

"Sounds to me like Treacy was right," said the Colonel. "No, I mustn't do that."

"What?"

"Scoff at other cultures. Especially the Americans. They are the new Romans. Practical, murderous, and efficient. Now I know you insist on being taken for an Italian, but you must admit, it's a strange thing for us Italians to have foreign names in law enforcement, though for some reason we have had a number of half-foreign magistrates, hundreds of half-breed journalists."

"I met three Filipino recruits, recently," said Blume. "Plenty of Croats and Serbs in the force, too. And some German names. It's not as rare as all that."

"I am not happy with these developments, as I'm sure you can imagine."

"Maybe you can tell from my face how fascinated I am by your views on race, Colonel?"

"You need to learn how to give conversations time to mature and expand, Commissioner. Let people have their say, allow them their little foibles and foolish beliefs. Don't always be so direct. No one will want to talk to you or confess to you. All this directness, which, if you don't mind my revisiting the idea, is terribly American, is not conducive to trust. You're an isolated man, Commissioner. Learn how to tune into others' wavelength. We need to be talking, getting to know one another. So I don't like niggers on TV reading me the local news about my ancient city of Rome, what do you care? You listen, silently disagree, we talk. That's how it's done."

Blume shoved himself and his chair back from the table. "If you have something important to say, then do me a favor and start at the end with whatever the important thing is."

"And talk backwards thereafter? Absolutely not. Anyhow, you're still investigating. I can tell from the way your eyes keep roaming around this room, looking for things. So I know you'll be interested in what I already know about Nightingale and Treacy. But before I go any further, did you happen to find any manuscripts, typescripts, memoirs, notebooks, diaries, papers, when you were here earlier?"

"No," said Blume.

"Written in English, possibly? Probably in longhand: I don't think Treacy would have even recognized a computer."

"No."

"That's unfortunate. Have you spoken to Nightingale yet?"

"No," said Blume. "I'm here with you, waiting for you to tell me something."

"Replicating a picture or doing it in the style of an old master is not a crime, but, of course, you know that. The crime comes when it is offered for sale as if authentic, but Treacy never sold the paintings. That was Nightingale."

"Did Nightingale do time?"

"No," said the Colonel. "And I'm glad we're talking like civilized men now. Treacy was caught with faked provenance documents a few times, but he could pretend he was an innocent victim. As for the sale price, Nightingale always feigned a total lack of artistic sensibility. He would ask the buyer to name a price, sometimes even warning about the possibility of forgeries. He allowed buyers to call in experts, if they wanted. If they came back to him and told him it was a fake, which usually they didn't, you know what he would do?"

"Withdraw it from sale?"

"No. He'd apologize, and ask them if they were interested in buying it as a copy or a pastiche instead. Often they said yes, and the painting would go out with just the surname but not the Christian name of the artist, which is the convention used for imitations. The important thing is, it remains legal. Art forgery, dealing, even theft and ownership—all categories that are hard to pin down. Legally speaking, art is a very gray subject."

Without warning, Colonel Orazio Farinelli's face turned the color of a damson plum. It was not until beads of sweat appeared on his forehead that Blume realized what he had taken for an expression of inexplicable rage was the result of the Colonel's efforts to stand up. When the Colonel had made it off his stool, he placed his hands on the table, lowered his head like a penitent until his face and head returned to white. Then he spoke.

"You are absolutely sure you didn't find a manuscript, a diary, anything like that? Or, if you prefer, I could shorten the conversation and ask you where you put the one you found."

Blume opened his hands like a priest blessing the broken bread on the table, then he, too, stood up. "I found nothing of the kind. But I am interested in your insistence on these papers. Perhaps we should look for them together?"

The Colonel said nothing, but walked back into Treacy's living room, where he eased himself into a leather armchair.

Blume cleared some art books off the bulging settee, and settled himself on it, and looked over to where the paintings and sketches had been.

"I see you have been removing things from here."

"True," said the Colonel. "As you can see, I've left that painting with the seaport, classical ruins, ships on the wall. Take it down, pop it out of its frame, have a close look at it."

Blume was interested enough in where this was leading to do the Colonel's bidding. He unhooked the painting, and immediately checked the back where he saw a monogram made up of the letters "HRTR," with the "T" done like a tower.

"I like the way you checked immediately for a signature on the back," said the Colonel. "There's one on the painting itself if you look closely. Anyhow, HRTR stands for Henry Treacy. That's his mark, so he was not going to sell that as an original. Now tell me, does it look like it could have been painted three hundred and thirty years ago?"

"I don't know. The colors are dark. The paint is cracked everywhere. Thousands of tiny squares."

"How does it smell?"

Blume made a skeptical face, but brought his nose down to the canvas. "Dusty, woody, a little sweet. It smells old," he said. "It's very glossy and hard to see this close."

"And seeing as you're that close, can you see any wormholes?"

"Yes," said Blume. "Quite a few, now."

"Look just inside the rim of one of the wormholes. What do you see?"

"I see nothing. What am I looking for?"

"Ink or paint."

Blume moved his head back slightly, and realized he could see the canvas better. Was that the first sign of needing old-man reading glasses?

"I see no ink inside the holes."

"Of course not. If the painting is genuine, there could be none, since the wormholes are supposed to come *after* the composition, so

72

how would color get into them unless it was false—new paint on old canvas, see?"

"Yes."

"And yet, convincing though this may seem, it wasn't good enough for him to market. He liked it enough to sign it. Maybe he used it to show what he could do. Personally, I think he darkened the tone too far. Treacy ran the most incredible risks. His whole left cheek was wrinkled and scarred from burns he gave himself back in the '80s from boiling oil. He tried to create black oil to darken a painting, and mixed it with mastic varnish. Knowing him, he probably did it next to cans of turps and benzene, too."

"Yes. He had a beard that covered most of the scars."

"He grew a beard? My, my," said the Colonel. "It really has been some time since I saw him. I can't picture him with a beard. Always so vain. He even thought his scar was romantic."

Blume looked at the back of the canvas again. "It's got faded stamps, mildew, even some old netting or something, like it came from somewhere else. It's convincing."

"Yet this is one of his rejects," said the Colonel. "I don't suppose you'd be so kind as to pass me that bowl . . ."

Blume passed a bowl of fruit to the Colonel, who plucked out an apple and bit it in half. "Floury, old. A still-life apple," he said. "Disgusting." He finished it with four more bites and balanced the core on the arm of his chair. "Let me tell you what made Henry Treacy special. He had no artistic personality. I don't mean in real life. He had too much in real life. But when it came to painting, he had no personality at all."

The Colonel picked up and tossed the core of his apple toward the fireplace. It missed and came to rest beside the bookshelf, just below the gap left by the removal of two marbled notebooks. The Colonel did not speak for a moment, and Blume felt sure he must be staring at the same empty spot. Then he heard a grunt and a crunch, as the Colonel helped himself to another apple and bit into it.

Keeping his movements leisurely, Blume withdrew his gaze from the empty slot on the shelves, and said, "Is no personality a good or a bad thing?"

"For a forger, it's good." The Colonel took another bite, and swallowed without chewing. "To know without being known." He finished the apple and this time dropped the core back into the bowl, then casually fingered a leopard-skin banana. "To know without being known," he repeated. "It's a good philosophy for policemen and for serious artists, as well as for forgers. It's the opposite for politicians and junk celebrities. They want to be known without knowing."

"And Treacy?"

"I think he began to be attracted by notoriety. So he began to want to be known, which is suicidal if you're a forger."

"Suicidal or the sort of thing that can get you killed?" asked Blume.

"Good point. What you don't want is notoriety or personality. You do not want people to be able to point at a work and say: That's a Treacy."

"So he adopted the personality of the painter he was copying?" said Blume.

"Not the personality. What I mean is he didn't let his own come through. You're an American, so you must have been brought up watching Westerns, right?"

"Westerns are more your generation, Colonel. I was more into *Starsky and Hutch*."

"What's that?"

"*Kojak*, you've heard of *Kojak*?"

"Yes," said the Colonel.

"Well, Starsky and Hutch were . . . Never mind. They were nothing like Kojak. *Rockford Files? Harry O?*"

The Colonel was shaking his head impatiently.

"*Hawaii Five-0*. Jesus, I loved that," said Blume. He thought of Jack Lord as Steve McGarrett, turning around to look straight at the camera, those three strands of hair out of place, an effect that he used to try and imitate in front of the mirror. Jack Lord had a scar on his face, too, come to think of it. He brought his attention back to the Colonel. "You were saying something about Westerns."

"Westerns are always set in the 1880s or 1890s," said the Colonel.

"Well, you're the expert," said Blume. "But the American Old West goes back at least to the Gold Rush, which was 1848."

"I'm not interested in that now," said the Colonel.

"First you start talking about Westerns, now you're not interested."

"You are being obtuse, Commissioner." The Colonel took the banana, peeled it, and examined the fruit and nodded in approval. He pressed half the banana into his mouth, paused, then spoke.

"When you watch a Western, you can always tell when it was made. They try to dress like it was the nineteenth century, but you can clearly see the styles of the 1940s or '50s or '60s in the clothes, in the makeup, the hairstyles. And that's not even counting the colors used in the print. It takes, what, about five seconds for you to recognize the decade in which the film was made, even without seeing an actor. The personality of the period comes through."

"True," said Blume.

"And yet the directors at the time were usually trying to make things look as nineteenth century as possible." He ate the second half of the banana. "It's the same thing with forgers. You keep looking at one of their works, and you get a feel for when it was really painted, not when it was supposed to be. Naturally, this makes it easier to spot forgeries from the past, from the 1940s or 1950s, say. Forgeries made now are harder to spot, not because they're better, but because we are incapable of seeing the style of our own time. We're too close. We watch a Western made in the last few years, it looks more accurate than the ones made in the 1950s. That's the beauty of Henry Treacy's work. It doesn't have a strong personality. Nothing comes through. He's timeless."

The Colonel put the banana skin on the table, struggled, and rose from his chair and walked over to the davenport desk. He opened a drawer that Blume had completely missed earlier and pulled out a rolled-up piece of paper, and, holding it reverently, showed it to Blume. "Beautiful buff paper, but machine-made, so no attempt at passing it off as authentic, but look at the skill."

Blume saw a yellow and gray image of a woman looking down at her foot.

"This is where he excelled. This is what he sold. Of course he used paper from the period."

"Where did he get it?"

"All sort of places. Fly leaves in old books, old paintings or drawings. Old sketchbooks. You saw that Latin missal in the kitchen? That would have made a good source of paper. What do you think it is?"

"A woman hitching up her dress, turning out her foot—it looks unfinished," said Blume. "He didn't do her other foot."

"What we do is we search through the paintings of Raphael, Bronzino, Parmigianino, or Annibale Carracci."

"We?"

"You and I. Let me finish, Commissioner. If we find this woman, or a woman in this pose, or something that reminds us strongly of it, then we would market this work here as a preparatory sketch by the artist. Seventy thousand euros, minus handling expenses and assuming a good outcome after examination by experts. That works out at maybe twenty thousand for you, thirty for me. And that's just this one. Of course, maybe it won't work out so well."

"You just said it was on modern paper and not salable."

"Quite right. This one here is worth almost nothing. But then he did another just like it. On proper paper. My men removed it earlier. And there are eight more forgeries. I would need to look at them closely to make sure they are marketable, but at first glance I was impressed. More than you, obviously, since you left them here with an aggressive and none-too-bright junior officer guarding the scene."

The Colonel pulled a fat aluminum cigar case from his breast pocket. He unsheathed the cigar, sliced the end with a silver cutter, then, with plenty of cheek-puffing and grunts, got it alight. When he had surrounded himself in sweet blue smoke, he said: "Well, are we working together or not?"

Blume decided to allow the question to hang in the air with the cigar smoke while he worked out a strategy.

"Well?" insisted the Colonel.

Blume parried with a question of his own. "What about Treacy's partner, John Nightingale? He must know about the paintings in here."

"A good practical question," said the Colonel, lowering himself back into the seat. "But Nightingale almost certainly knows nothing about these. They did not get on very well. Clash of personalities or nationalities or something along those lines. One reason they had the gallery was to maintain a neutral space where they could meet. Treacy told me that once. I don't think Nightingale was ever in this house."

"You know a lot, Colonel. So you must also know how they worked together. Logic suggests that Nightingale must have known what Treacy was preparing. To organize things ahead of time."

"Logic maybe," said the Colonel. "But that is not how it worked at all.

Like so many Anglo-Saxon fraudsters, they considered themselves essentially upright men forced to compromise with Mediterranean reality. Not only did Treacy not say what he was preparing, I know for a fact that he never even told Nightingale he was making fakes. I had this from both of them, and though I struggled to believe it at first, I think it was true. They liked to pretend that Treacy had somehow come across a valuable painting or, as an alternative, that he had created a pastiche on period canvas and then forgotten to mention this incidental detail to Nightingale. Nightingale always said he could pass a lie-detector test if he had to. It was always possible that Treacy was finding genuine old masters and passing them on."

"Really?" said Blume.

The Colonel smiled behind the swirls of smoke. "Of course not. But good liars tell themselves lies over and over until they believe them. Treacy specialized in 'finding' the plausibly overlooked. Nightingale built up provenance stories."

"Wouldn't Treacy have wanted some real works to copy from and study now and again?"

"I imagine so. It is possible one of these is real. It's a world of bluff and double-bluff, and almost nobody ever gets caught. It's also as close to victimless crime as it's possible to get."

"Aren't the people who buy forgeries victims?" asked Blume.

The Colonel looked slowly to the left, to the right, and then to the left again. He did this a few more times until Blume finally realized that he was shaking his head in ponderous disagreement.

"Do you feel ..." the Colonel hesitated, looking for a term, "*sympathy* for someone who spends a few million on a painting, which they never even learn is false?"

He allowed himself a silent pause as he continued smoking his cigar, making the occasional appreciative popping sound with his lips. He let the ash fall on the arm of the chair, and when the cigar was finally down to a glowing stub, he started on the elaborate sequence of grunts and movements that indicated he was preparing to stand up again. When he finally succeeded, he seemed to fill the room with bulk and smoke as he moved around in search of an ashtray.

"Over there," said Blume, pointing to a lump of heavy crystal on the mantelpiece, but the Colonel allowed the cigar to drop onto the stone flagging on the floor and trod on it.

"Too far," he said.

The smell of the stubbed cigar was like bad breath. The Colonel picked up an orange from the fruit bowl and began peeling it, dropping the thick skin in slabs on the floor beside the cigar. He divided the orange into four segments and ate three before finally saying, "Let me tell you about a clever trick Treacy and Nightingale liked to work. Treacy would do a damned fine work, usually a small portrait, that looked like it might be a—oh, say a Colberti portrait from his period in Italy, then overpaint it with a poor-quality forgery, usually copied directly from an existing work by someone pretty well known—Van Dyck, say."

"I've never heard of Colberti," said Blume.

"That's because I just made up the name," said the Colonel, and popped the quarter orange into his mouth. "Interesting you should spot that." He winced slightly as if the orange was bitter. "It means you know more about art than you are letting on."

"All I said was I had never heard of him," said Blume.

"You were puzzled by an invented name, Commissioner." The Colonel wiped some juice from his lips with the back of his hand. "Now let me finish. Let's say Dosso Dossi instead of the non-existent Colberti. Better?"

"Stop testing and get back to telling, Colonel."

"Well said, Commissioner. Nightingale would place the easily-spotted Van Dyck fake on the market. When a buyer came forward, he would ask him if he was absolutely sure he wanted the work. Affecting great probity, he would sometimes confidentially reveal to the buyer that he had some suspicions about the authenticity of the work. This served three purposes. The first was to cover himself from liability or any possible setup by us. The second was to insure the buyer examined the painting carefully, including what was under it. Once the buyer looked below the surface and found what he thought was an original by an old master hidden beneath, then he would buy the painting at whatever the asking price was and would usually insist that it had passed all his tests for authenticity. Clever, eh?"

"You said three purposes," said Blume. "Coverage from liability, persuading the buyer to look below the surface to get to the 'real' fake below, and the third?"

"Amusement. Delight," said the Colonel. "The glee of watching people get trapped by their own greed."

"And are you immune from the same risk?"

"No. Are you?"

Blume was saved from replying by his phone ringing. He answered it without looking at who was calling, and felt a slight lift as he heard Kristin's voice.

"Alec, that was an interesting name you gave us. Are you alone?"

"No. I'm sitting right in front of him now."

The Colonel nodded approvingly. "Getting some background on me? Good work."

"And now he knows I'm talking about him," Blume said.

Kristin hesitated, then said, "I'll call you back."

"No, tell me now. There must be something interesting that made you call back so soon."

"He's ex-secret service. SISDE as it was then. One of the bad apples from the barrels and barrels of bad apples Italy has been producing for years," said Kristin. "*Deviato* as the press likes to say. He's supposed to be retired. Also he was involved in an interesting way in the investigations into the Moro murder. In a way that involved this embassy. But that's all I'm telling you on the phone."

"Is that your romantic way of confirming dinner this evening?"

Kristin paused before replying. "Yes. We need to talk. You were joking when you said he was sitting in front of you, weren't you?"

"Of course I was," said Blume.

"Alec, you need to be careful of this guy. He used to be at the center of a lot of stuff."

"Used to, but isn't now?"

"Not now, but he'll still have connections. Don't let him know you're on to him."

Blume hung up, danced his fingers back and forth on the armrest as he considered Kristin's warning, then said to the Colonel, "So I hear you were in SISDE."

"I see you have your sources," said the Colonel. "Can I ask who they are?"

"I'm sure you can find out if you're all that interested," said Blume.

"I am interested. But as you have found out this detail, which I was going to tell you about anyhow, I can get straight to the point. Treacy may have written a diary or some notebooks that contain some compromising details, I won't call them facts, regarding activities from a long time ago."

"How long ago?" asked Blume.

"Long, long ago. 1978. There used to be a bar on Via Avicenna in the Marconi district. It was a hangout for monarchists, nationalists, patriots, activists. One regular customer was a certain Tony Chichiarelli. He, too, was a forger. He got killed in 1984. Along with his son, who was a few months old. Now Tony Chichiarelli had a good friend called Luciano Dal Bello, and you may come across this name if you decide to start delving into my past, which I really hope you won't feel the need to do."

The Colonel paused to allow Blume the opportunity to make a promise. When he did not, he continued, "Dal Bello was a criminal, but he was also an important informer, and I was his contact. Now, another person who used to hang out in that bar was Henry Treacy, who we all called Harry. He was also Chichiarelli's friend. I don't know if they worked together as forgers. It doesn't seem likely, since Chichiarelli specialized in handwriting, signatures, checks, false share certificates, all that sort of stuff. But they knew each other. Chichiarelli knew Nightingale, too. Now, does the year 1978 mean anything to you?"

"Argentina won the World Cup. Crystal Gale and the Bee Gees were in the charts. It was the year of Disco Inferno," said Blume.

"In its proper place, there is nothing better than bantering good humor," said the Colonel.

"That wasn't just to annoy you, Colonel. Those were the things that were important to me then. You may remember it as the year Prime Minister Moro was kidnapped, then executed by the Red Brigades in March. Me, I was a kid in another country. Come to think of it, I probably didn't even know about Argentina and the World Cup. I'd have picked that up later. I know the name Chichiarelli. From books and police reports, not experience. He was involved in mysterious ways in the disinformation campaign. Didn't he produce false messages from the Red Brigades, and from that poor bastard?"

"Which poor bastard?" asked the Colonel.

"Aldo Moro," said Blume.

"Ah, him. Yes. That's the sort of thing Chichiarelli did. Not under my instructions, of course."

After a few moments, Blume said, "Well?"

"Well what, Commissioner?"

"I'm waiting for the end of your story."

"There isn't an end. Not a proper one."

"If you handled Chichiarelli, you must know quite a lot about what really happened in the Moro case."

"No one knows anything," said the Colonel. "There are too many centers of power, none of which trusts the other, and too many transversal operators like Chichiarelli. Apart from me and a few others, most of the people from then are now dead—or in Parliament, of course. Now Treacy's dead, too. I just need to see what he wrote. You are *quite* sure you found no notebooks or diaries or anything of the sort?"

Blume shook his head. He did so with vigor and relish, but felt he might have overplayed it.

"It would be a bad idea to lie to me," said the Colonel. "Especially now that we are negotiating a possible joint venture that, let me remind you, involves no victims, no loss to the taxpayer, and no betrayal of colleagues. Let's say the person who would be most upset at the idea of fruitful collaboration without his knowledge is Buoncompagno."

"I could live with that," admitted Blume.

"Good. Also because certain works, smallish, easy enough to transport, have been removed from this house and, I regret, not logged properly. It as if they never existed, or as if they were here when you arrived, and vanished during the search you and your inspector carried out. If they were to appear on the market and, say, Buoncompagno were to get a tip-off, and then the records show that the works were never logged by us or you, but you were in here first without a magistrate giving oversight, well then, unjust though it would be . . ."

"I understand," said Blume. "That will do."

"Excellent, so we have a deal?"

Blume remained silent.

"I am going to interpret that as a reluctant and principled yes," said the Colonel. "Now, I hate to insist, but, in my capacity as your temporary business partner, I find it odd that you're not interested in finding out more about Treacy's papers."

"That's funny," said Blume. "Because I was just about to ask you, in my capacity as a permanent policeman, how you are so certain they exist."

"A word of warning," said the Colonel, sitting forward in his seat. His drooping eyelids gave a soft and tired expression to his face, but, as Blume now saw, he had the eyes of a younger man, and his gaze was sharp and unremitting. Blume stared back, assuming a look of mild interest, waiting for the Colonel to deliver his warning.

"Nobody interrogates me. Is that clear?" said the Colonel. "Nobody. I will not be questioned." He allowed his eyelids to close for a moment, and his voice took on a more jovial tone. "At least not before lunch. Perhaps you will join me?"

Blume stood up.

"It's too early for me, Colonel. But I wish you luck in your hunt for these papers."

"Thank you, though I am pessimistic. We shall be in touch soon, you understand that?"

"I look forward to it," said Blume.

# 10

As BLUME LEFT Treacy's house, a sudden hard bang rang out and echoed blankly against the wall beside him. It took him a full two seconds to recognize it as the noon cannon, fired from the top of the gardens behind him. The sound was martial and startling, quite different from the muffled thud he heard when in his office across the river. The Maresciallo sat in a car directly in front of him, watching. He must have seen him jump and duck as the cannon was fired, but he showed no outward sign of amusement. Blume walked past him as if he had noticed neither the car nor its occupant.

Blume reached the corner of the road where his car was slotted diagonally into the corner. Behind him, American students sat drinking beer outside a cafe. Blume was thinking about having coffee himself, when a woman rose from one of the tables and waved at him. It took him a moment to recognize Caterina. He went over and sat down opposite her. "What are you doing here?"

"I've just had lunch."

"Didn't I tell you to get back to the office?"

"No, you didn't, actually. And my shift's over."

"Well, you need to go back, write up reports, and file ... do you still have those notebooks?"

"Yes," Caterina pulled her bag from under the table.

"You didn't log them in as crime scene evidence?"

"No."

"That's not how it works, Inspector."

"I know. But what with Buoncompagno, the Carabinieri ... I thought you might want to look at them first."

Blume leaned over and took out the notebooks. "Have you looked at them?" He opened the first one at random in the middle. "You know, you're going to have to stop doing that."

"Doing what?" said Caterina.

"Touching the hollow of your throat with your finger when you're embarrassed."

Caterina brought her hand down from her neck and hid it under the table.

"So you were reading them here, looking like a student—no, a teacher, I think we said—drinking Coca-Cola."

"I just wanted to get an idea of what they were."

"And?"

"Two seem to be a sort of diary going right back to the sixties, and one a manual, full of instructions. It's filled with formulas, ingredients, trade names. I was waiting for you, Commissioner. And I haven't really had time to read them. I've been doing other things, too."

"Oh? And what would that be?"

Caterina stroked water beads off her glass and said, "Do you know what my father calls 'Coca-Cola'?" She poked her finger into the glass and spun the remaining shards of ice. "He calls it 'hoha-hola.' He can't pronounce the letter "C," because he's a Tuscan. From a town called Signa, know it?"

"Sure. It's the exit on the A1 that always has a long line, adds thirty minutes to the trip."

"It's famous for other things," said Caterina. "It makes straw hats, for instance."

"Really?" said Blume.

"You almost make it sound as if that's not interesting. I only mention it because of that girl, Manuela, in Treacy's gallery."

"The one you don't like, I picked that up," said Blume.

"No, you're wrong. She has the arrogance of youth, that's all," said Caterina. "I don't think she's a bad person at all. Spoilt and unhappy, maybe. But seeing as you were picking things up, did you notice her accent?"

"Her accent? No, not really. It must have been one of the things I didn't pick up."

"Me neither," said Caterina. "Not at first, because she has no accent we might recognize easily. But she's supposed to be from Pistoia. That's what she told us, right?"

"I see what you're getting at," said Blume. "But young people don't have such pronounced accents as they used to. All the dialects are dying out in Italy. And now that you mention it, her accent wasn't entirely Roman, so maybe it was Tuscan."

"She doesn't have a trace of a Tuscan accent. Not a trace. I know what it sounds like. Maybe Umbria, north Lazio. Somewhere nearby."

"That's more or less Tuscany," said Blume. "What's the difference? Why would she say she was from Tuscany if she wasn't? Only a Tuscan could think that everyone wants to come from Tuscany."

"I don't know why she said it. Also there's no trace of her birth in the records."

"You checked her out?"

"Sure," said Caterina. "I can make phone calls from here." She leaned over to retrieve her bag from in front of Blume, pulled out her notebook, and flicked through it. "According to the APR, three Manuela Ludovisi's have been born in Italy, but the oldest of them is only eight."

"So, she was born abroad," said Blume. "Did you check that out, too?"

"No. I didn't have time," said Caterina. "But I did check school enrollments, ID card records, and driving licenses. Or rather, Rosario did. He helped me from the office. He also downloaded and printed out the photo of her in the Public Records Office. The one in her false ID."

"Inspector Panebianco thought he should do that? I ordered him to get copies of Treacy's ID photo, I'm glad to see he found the time to satisfy your requests, too."

"He obviously thought it was worth pursuing," said Caterina, annoyance creeping into her tone. "He didn't comply immediately, but then he found out some things, and phoned me back and told me he had put a copy of her photo on my desk."

"What sort of things did he find out?"

"Manuela Ludovisi got her first ID card three years ago. Her tax code dates back to the same time. In other words, both her tax code and her ID card date back to a month or two before she got the job at the gallery."

"She needed the tax code for the job," said Blume. "That's OK. Same everywhere in the world. You apply for your social security number, tax code, tax ID, employment book . . ."

"Right. I can see that. But tax codes are assigned at birth. So I'm interested why she got hers only three years ago."

"No," said Blume. "Tax codes are assigned at birth only to people born in Italy. But if you were born abroad, you have to go and get one. I got mine when I was sixteen. Four hours of waiting at Via della Conciliazione, and then I had to go back and have it changed, because they put me down as female."

"You, a female?"

"It's the name, Alec. It must have sounded girly to some bureaucrat."

"Have you got your tax code on you?"

Blume pulled out his wallet and extracted a green-and-white plastic-covered card. "They changed it so I'm not female anymore."

"May I?" said Caterina. Blume flicked the card onto the table between them. "BLMLCA67B09Z404X," she read. "So your birthday is February 9. The Z404 shows you were born in the United States, OK?"

"I know that," said Blume. "I know how to read these things."

Caterina turned her notebook sideways, so Blume could see what she had written there: MMELDV88M57G713L.

"This corresponds to the name Manuela Ludovisi, born in August 1988," she said. "This is the tax code that the gallery registered Manuela under. The G713 sequence corresponds to Pistoia, which is precisely what she said. Everything fits—except her accent and the fact this tax code was issued for the first time three years ago."

Caterina paused to allow Blume to draw the obvious conclusion. But he just sat there looking underwhelmed.

"Either she was born in Pistoia or she was born abroad," said Caterina. "The code tells us it was Pistoia, but the fact she didn't have the code until three years ago tells us it was abroad. So, Commissioner, which is it?"

"Italian public offices are not paragons of efficiency," said Blume. "They probably didn't assign her a code, then she had to get one when she got her first job. And maybe she's got rid of her accent in the past few years. I changed language and for the Public Records Office I also changed sex. So she can change accent. As far as I can see, you just don't like her."

"I think it was more a case of your liking her too much."

"I'm not a teenage boy."

"She is very beautiful. It's hard to see beyond that."

"Just what are you accusing her of, exactly?" asked Blume.

"I'm not accusing her of anything. I'm just wondering if she is who she says she is."

"You mean she's assumed a false identity? What would she do that for?"

Caterina finished the remains of her drink. "I don't know, but she worked for two men who sort of specialized in that kind of thing."

# 11

C ATERINA LEFT THE bar saying she had to pick up her son, Elia. Blume returned to the office, and secured the notebooks in the third drawer of his desk, the only one with a working lock and key. On the table was another memo relating to "concentrated instances of microcriminality prejudicial to the image of Rome in critical zones of cultural heritage."

"Speaking of which," said Inspector Panebianco as Blume showed him the memo before balling it up and lobbing it in an ambitious parabola toward the wastepaper basket, "I think Rospo wants to tell you something."

"You mean he has already told you," said Blume, going over and retrieving the crumbled ball of paper from behind the leg of a chair and firing it at its target from a more reasonable distance. "Spare me an unnecessary meeting with Rospo and tell me yourself."

"You'll be getting a report soon enough. I told him to do a proper one. Last night, several hours before Treacy was found dead, an elderly Asian couple was mugged. They failed to file a proper complaint and it seems that Rospo made an executive decision not to burden us with the disturbing news."

"He wasn't going to tell us at all?" said Blume, picking up the paper again and dropping it into the trash.

"It's hard to say. But now he is. The couple are staying—were staying, since they left a few hours ago ..."

"At the Hotel Noantri," said Blume. "Good place to target. All that brass, high ceilings, smoked glass, fat, slow, wealthy, and elderly guests. Did Rospo think he could get away without mentioning it?"

"He could have, Commissioner. And the point is he did mention it."

Dark-haired, sharp blue eyes, mid-thirties, angular, slim, and fit, Panebianco should have been a ladies' man, but somehow was not. He had a way of looking at people with the air of a grown-up seeing through a child's hopeless lies. Blume was not sure what his idea of fun might be, but whatever it was, it did not seem to accommodate silliness, disrespect, or dubious taste. Blume counted him as one of his most reliable colleagues, but remained a little wary of his mature restraint.

"The department does not need another disciplinary issue," said Panebianco. "Not now, and not an incident involving foreign visitors. We already have a problem with Grattapaglia and the diplomat."

Blume cursed. "Has that started already?"

"Apparently the diplomat got in touch with the Questore directly. He's given us twenty-four hours to resolve the problem. I think they want Grattapaglia's head on a plate, plus one scapegoat. In other words, Grattapaglia alone won't do. They want to discipline a senior officer who was there at the time, which means you, me . . . or Inspector Mattiola."

"You weren't anywhere near Grattapaglia, Rosario. Mattiola is new on the job, so . . ."

"That leaves just you, sir." Panebianco expressed no admiration for Blume's implied sacrifice.

"Speaking of Mattiola," said Panebianco, "she asked me to follow up some ideas she had about that girl at the gallery. Did she mention that to you?"

"Yes," said Blume.

But Panebianco was looking straight at him, waiting for a fuller response, like his father used to do when Blume tried to be monosyllabic about trouble at school. He decided to turn the tables. "What do you make of it?"

"It looks like a simple case of tax evasion," said Panebianco. "We could pass on the details to our colleagues in the Finance Police."

"We could," agreed Blume. "If it served any purpose. They'll just say fine and sit on their hands waiting for a magistrate's order that is unlikely to be issued. Same as us."

"I see there is another aspect that Inspector Mattiola is interested in," continued Panebianco. "She sees a possible connection between false ID papers, if that's what we have here, and the fact that Treacy and his colleague John Nightingale were in the art forgery business."

"You've been looking into that, have you?" said Blume.

"Well, not me so much as a very good friend of mine," Panebianco said. "He works in the Art Forgery and Heritage Division of the Carabinieri."

"Great, another one," muttered Blume to himself.

Panebianco put his hand on his hip and said, "Excuse me?"

"Nothing. Is he someone you trust?"

"Absolutely."

"How is it you know him?" asked Blume.

Panebianco stood back, adjusted his jacket severely. "We play soccer together."

"Oh, five-a-side?" asked Blume hopefully. The whole force seemed to be made up of amateur soccer players. He wished someone would invite him to play. He was good at defense.

"No, proper soccer. A full-sized pitch. We have a league. A lot of players are former semi-professionals. Serie C. So it's pretty serious."

"Full strips and refs and all that?"

"Yes. We have a strip. Green and white. I don't have to wear it, though. I'm the goalkeeper. My friend plays midfield."

"And what does your friend say?"

"It seems Treacy did the art, and it was Nightingale who did the paperwork and placed the paintings. So I asked my friend if this Nightingale produced false bills of sale for paintings, but he didn't know."

"Is that it?"

"I didn't want to inquire further without official cause."

"I see," said Blume. "Do you think I could talk to this friend of yours?" Blume picked up the receiver from a nearby desk phone and held it out in Panebianco's direction. "How about now?" he said. "Phone him from here."

Panebianco took the receiver, but put it down again, saying, "I don't know his number by heart. I need to go back to my desk."

"All right. Patch it through to me in my office," said Blume.

Two minutes later, the phone on Blume's desk rang. "I have him on hold, I'm putting you through," said Panebianco.

"Good," said Blume. "Wait, what's his name?" But Panebianco was gone.

"Hello? Hello?" said a voice. A southerner.

"Hello, this is Commissioner Alec Blume, *squadra mobile*, who am I speaking to?"

"Lieutenant Colonel Faedda," said the voice. Blume placed the accent as Sardinian. He pictured a thin and swarthy young man in full dress uniform sitting at his desk carefully arranging pencils.

"Inspector Panebianco didn't introduce us properly," said Blume.

"He's useless, isn't he?" said the Carabiniere. "You should see him on the pitch. Hopeless. What can I do for you, Commissioner?"

Blume was taken aback by the easy familiarity of the man's tone. He erased the image of the uniform and the pencils, pictured feet on a desk. "I wanted to talk about John Nightingale and Henry Treacy," he said.

"Yes, I've been looking at files all morning," said the Carabiniere. "Not just on Rosario's behalf, of course, since the case has been assigned to us. I'd definitely appreciate any help you could give me."

This conversation was flowing in the wrong direction. "I don't have anything I can give you," said Blume.

"I realize it's early days," said Faedda. "We can wait for the autopsy. Then maybe we can meet, compare notes?"

"That's really for the magistrate to decide," said Blume rather stiffly.

"I hear the magistrate is Buoncompagno."

"Yes," said Blume.

"Buoncompagno is a man who prefers to have his decisions taken for him."

Blume was suspicious of the casual frankness of the statement.

Faedda continued, "Look, a former colleague of mine—from before my time, really—is involved in the case. Colonel Farinelli. Have you met him?"

"I have," said Blume, on his guard.

"Already? Well, then you'll know who's calling the shots, Commissioner. And the Colonel's influence outreaches his rank. Have you spoken to John Nightingale yet?"

"No." Blume felt judged.

"Me neither, and I don't think I will get the chance. But you might. Now, I don't know what you've found out there, but from our records here I can tell you Nightingale's specialization is provenance. He appears to be exceptionally good at it."

"Go on," said Blume, reaching for a pen and a blank sheet of paper, and wrote down the name Faedda.

"Nightingale knows every branch of every minor aristocratic or rich bourgeois family in England, America, Germany, France. When generating a story, he never begins with a purely fictional character. Let's put all this in the past tense since he seems to have been pretty inactive over the past few years. When he purported to be reselling on a painting, he always used the name of someone who really existed as having been a previous owner."

Blume wrote the word "provenance" beneath the picture of the sad dog he had been drawing. "In what way did he use their name?" He started sketching a tree.

"He'd say the person had sat for the painting, commissioned it, ordered it, bought it, sold it, lost it. It didn't matter. The important thing is to establish a connection with someone with reputation, money, or title who died some time ago."

Blume tapped the tip of the pen on the branches of the tree, but the dots looked more like rain than leaves. He'd make it a stormy scene. "Don't the families deny it?"

"I have never seen that happen. A family will go to great lengths to confirm that their ancestors were perspicacious people, ahead of the curve, gifted with good taste, or on friendly terms with famous artists. It's the celebrity culture, Commissioner, and no one is immune."

"I am," thought Blume to himself. He scribbled in some curly storm clouds and wrote "family."

"Another trick that Nightingale used to do was to attribute paintings to great houses, castles, and mansions that were destroyed in one of the wars. If the place no longer exists because the Americans bombed it, who's to say what once hung on its walls?"

Blume put down his pen. "It's more likely that the Germans would have bombed it, no?" he said.

"No, no. The Germans occupied but the Americans did most of the bombing. They still do."

"Yeah, well . . . Did you find all this stuff about Treacy and Nightingale just now?"

Silence.

"Because it doesn't sound like it to me," continued Blume. "It's almost as if you were following this case before it even happened, and that's a bit strange . . . what's your first name, Colonel?"

"Nicu. It's Sardinian."

"Well, Nicu. How come you sound like you've been following the case before it even happened?"

"I am just well informed of the facts. You know, we really should meet soon."

"Yes, I think that would be a good idea," said Blume.

After he hung up, he added some roots to the tree, then balled up the piece of paper, threw it across the room, and, in the absence of spectators, it traveled straight into the trashcan.

First the Colonel sitting in Treacy's living room looking for notebooks he had no reason to know about, and now another Carabiniere who seemed very well informed about Nightingale. Blume took the small key from his pocket and opened the drawer with the notebooks.

Someone tapped lightly on his door. Blume pushed the drawer closed again, locked it, slid the key beneath the green leather writing-pad on his desk, and called, "*Avanti!*"

The door edged open about wide enough for a cat, then an Agente put his head around and seemed to sniff the air before opening the door fully and coming in.

"What?"

"A Mr. John Nightingale is downstairs. I just thought you'd like to know," he said.

# 12

CERTAIN ENGLISHMEN SEEM to expend so much energy on being English that it empties them of natural vigor. If he had not just heard about John Nightingale's skill at faking provenance, Blume would have dismissed the lethargic man in the downstairs waiting area as being slow-witted. Blume put him in his mid-sixties. His hair was gray and tightly curled like a scouring pad used for saucepans. He looked the kind who might be comfortable in corduroy, maybe with patches on the elbows of his jacket, but in fact his clothes, though wrinkled, were sober, silver-gray, and expensive. Blume introduced himself. Nightingale stood up, shook Blume's hand, and smiled by curving the left side of his mouth upwards and the right side downwards. Then he sat down again and said, *"E' tutto vero?"*

"Is what true?" asked Blume, switching straight into English as soon as he heard Nightingale's accent.

"That they found Harry murdered on the street."

"Hahwy?" said Blume, momentarily confused.

"Yes. Harry."

"Harry as in Henry?" said Blume, resisting the temptation to say "Henwy."

Nightingale said, "Yes. Harry. I never called him Henry."

"Henry Treacy. How did you find out?" asked Blume.

"Dear God!" Nightingale widened his eyes. "It *is* true, then."

"How did you find that out?" repeated Blume.

"Emanuela told me. Manuela, rather. My receptionist. Manuela told me, well, let me see, half an hour ago. She told me to come down here and find you or an Inspector Mazzola or some such name. It's good to find someone who speaks English like this. I can't quite place your accent . . . God, you're not Irish are you?"

"No."

"No, you're American. How stupid of me. Harry was Irish, you see."

"I see," said Blume. "I take it you're here to make a voluntary statement?"

"What?"

"A statement to the police. Since no lawyer is present and I am not a magistrate, nothing you say can be used as evidence in court."

"I came to get information, not the other way round. Am I under arrest?"

"No. Absolutely not. A voluntary statement cannot be used as evidence for or against anyone, period. Whatever you tell us now is of no judicial use, but it can certainly help us. You'll want a lawyer if the magistrate calls you in for questioning, but not now. Also, as long as we keep talking English and remain one-to-one, we are speaking off the record, more or less."

"More or less?" Nightingale's eyes suddenly narrowed and seemed to sharpen as his bewildered and exhausted aspect vanished for a second. But then he ran his hands through his hair again and declared, "Actually, I don't care. I just want to help."

He stood up and began to shuffle around the small room, rubbing his hand up his temple to his receding hairline.

Nightingale was wearing sturdy handmade shoes. Blume had often thought that if he had wealth, he would invest in really good handmade shoes. Strong shoes should give a man direction. A person with shoes like that had no right to shuffle about lengthening his A's and turning his R's into W's.

"Stop wandering uselessly about and come up to my office," said Blume, and led the way out of the antechamber. With a mixture of obedience and watchfulness, Nightingale followed him down the hallway toward the two elevators next to the stairs.

The elevator arrived, and Nightingale insisted on ushering Blume in ahead of him.

"Please, just get in, Mr. Nightingale," said Blume.

Damned Brits. His father had not liked them, and Blume, who had never properly considered the matter, seemed to have received prejudice like a fully wrapped gift which he was only now getting around to opening.

As they passed through the operations room, a few heads bobbed up to see who was accompanying Blume. Blume waved Nightingale into his office, closed the door, and went behind his desk. He sat down and leaned back, and nodded at the space midway between the two chairs on the other side of his desk. One was a cheap red molded plastic chair, the other a comfortable low-slung black armchair. Nightingale chose the second with hardly a moment's hesitation, then crossed his legs at the ankles, and waited for Blume to speak.

"So," began Blume. "We were just about to go looking for you. Can you tell me where you've been today?"

"You say Harry has been killed."

"Did I say that?"

"Then Manuela did. Someone must have told me. I can hardly remember. Clearly I am in a state of deep shock. I feel calm now, and lucid, but I daresay it will hit me later on." He tilted his head and repeated his crooked smile. "Inspector ..."

"Commissioner," corrected Blume. "Where were you this morning, Mr. Nightingale?"

"Florence, but, um, I'm afraid ... look, I'm sorry about this. It's the nature of my job. Always read the small print, *caveat emptor*, all that sort of thing, but I'm not sure I quite believe what you just told me downstairs."

"I can't remember," said Blume. "Besides definitely not mentioning that Treacy was killed, what did I say downstairs?"

"You know, about what I say not being used as evidence. I'm awfully sorry if I doubt your word. It comes with my job."

"To trust is good; not to trust is better," said Blume.

"A smashing Italian expression," said Nightingale. "One of my favorites."

"You'll just have to believe me," said Blume.

"I'd love to do that, but I'm afraid the thing is ... I would take your word as a gentleman, of course, but as an Italian public official ..."

"As an Italian public official, what?"

"Well, you know how it works here."

"No," said Blume. "Tell me."

Nightingale uncrossed his legs and straightened in his seat. "All I am saying is that as a public official, you have certain duties and responsibilities that would prevail over any assurances you give me, as is only natural and right."

"This is an interview, not an interrogation. There is no magistrate present, nor any officer taking notes," said Blume.

"I'm afraid I was born diffident."

"I see." Blume got up, and walked over to the narrow bookcase behind his desk. He pulled out a fat purple-and-blue volume, opened it, then presented the volume face down to Nightingale. "*Code of Criminal Procedure*, 17th edition, which is the latest. Here, read Article 350, paragraph 7."

Nightingale looked surprised for a moment, but soon pulled out a collapsible pair of reading glasses from the breast pocket of his jacket. He balanced them on the end of his nose, and turned the book over. Blume watched him mouth some of the words, close his eyes, and reread.

"You are quite right, Commissioner. Mind if I read the entire article?"

"By all means," said Blume.

Nightingale bent down over the book and read again. Then, holding the page with his thumb, he turned back several hundred pages.

"Sorry about this, but you know how it is: this law is pursuant to that one, which refers back to another and so on and so forth. It's all a terrible bore." He continued reading.

Finally Nightingale closed the book, put it on Blume's desk, and said, "Very well. I was in Florence last night and this morning. I think I just said that. I had an appointment with an art dealer there." He put his hand inside his jacket and pulled out a ticket stub. "This is my train ticket. As you can see, it is time stamped at 8:03 p.m. for the outbound journey last night and at 9:35 for the return trip this morning. I reached Termini at half-past eleven, my home at midday, and Manuela phoned me there shortly afterwards. When I got to the gallery, the Carabinieri had already been through the place, but she advised me to come to you people instead."

"Who were you in Florence with?"

"The art dealer's name is Ricasoli. Same as the wine maker. Same family. He was interested in acquiring a Giovanni Benedetto Castiglione that had come into our possession."

"You kept the ticket stub?" said Blume, reaching out and taking it. "Do you always do that?"

"Only when I remember. Travel expenses can be deducted from the gallery's *imponibile*. If you can be bothered to fill out the tax forms afterwards, of course."

"The gallery belongs to you?"

"The business activity and movables. Not the building, sadly. We founded the Galleria Orpiment in 1974, you know. That's a long time ago. I don't know what I am going to do without Harry. I'll have to close. We were thinking of closing it down anyhow."

"Why?"

"Because we're getting old, Commissioner. Some nights I get up just to lean on a sink and count my heartbeats and wait for them to stop. You'll find yourself doing that, too, someday. Or maybe you will be different."

"I want to be straight with you, Mr. Nightingale," said Blume. "For the moment, the *squadra mobile* is on standby while we wait for an autopsy report and definite instructions from the investigating magistrate. In the meantime, a rather important dinosaur from the Carabinieri has come onto the scene. Colonel Orazio Farinelli, former director of the Art Forgery and Heritage Division and, I hear, a former operative with the domestic secret service, back in the days when SISDE went off the rails. He speaks with such familiarity of you and Treacy that I think you must know him."

Nightingale seemed to sink into his chair. He brought his hand up to his brow and seemed to study his fine shoes. By the time he spoke, it was obvious his reply could go only in one direction.

"Yes, I do know Farinelli. I wish I didn't, but I do. We go a long way back. He was a lieutenant when I first encountered him. We're really off the record?"

"Up to a point," said Blume.

"Can I ask you something?"

"Sure. Let's hope I can answer," said Blume.

"Are you working with the Colonel on the investigation?"

"We are both public servants," said Blume.

"Oh."

Blume waited patiently as Nightingale picked his next words carefully. Like so many other suspects, Nightingale was about to fall victim to the delusion that words pronounced slowly somehow gave less away.

"You may hear that Harry and I were not getting on. I just want you to know we never did. Not really. We needed each other and there were many shared experiences, but we were too different. If anything I felt a greater cultural affinity with Farinelli."

"You consider the Colonel a friend?"

"A friend, good God, no!" said Nightingale, immediately forgetting to pick his words with forethought. "Anything but. The Colonel is never a friend. Look, would you mind terribly if I asked you another question."

"Shoot," said Blume.

"Did you and the Colonel find any writings?"

Blume made a show of not understanding.

"Such as manuscripts, papers, typescripts, something along those lines, so to speak?"

"That's an interesting question," said Blume. "Tell me why you asked it."

"Did you find anything? Tell me that first."

"No," said Blume. He saw a slight release of tension around Nightingale's eyes, so out of interest for the effect it would have, he added, "But I can't speak for the Colonel."

Nightingale had relaxed a little when he said he had found nothing, and seemed to relax even more when he suggested the Colonel might have.

Blume said, "I told you that I found nothing. Now it's your turn to tell me why you are asking."

"Yes, well, about a month ago, Harry told me he had been writing his memoirs, but was beginning to be afraid he might not live to see them turned into a book. He also told me he was working on a second book, which had separated itself from his memoirs and was turning into a manual for what he liked to call 'practitioners.' He meant painters, restorers, forgers, some dealers, even canvas and brush manufacturers. Not the galleries or the art historians. I said I could edit them for him if he died and make sure they got published, but he laughed and said he couldn't let me do that because I'd destroy them and he intended to outlive me anyhow ... ha! Sorry if I sound a little callous here.

"I took this as a sort of threat, especially after the kindness of my gesture to edit his work, and we argued. It was a bad argument, too. One of our worst and, as it turns out, our last. I asked him why I would want to destroy his work, and he said because there were parts in it that concerned me. I told him he had a duty to show me what was in his notes. He taunted me, said there was plenty of stuff in there and that people would soon enough find out what sort of a person I am. That was bad enough, because no one likes to have their personal affairs published for all the world to see, but there was another question about which Harry was not even aware, and it had to do with his . . . well, our, line of business."

Nightingale faltered and Blume intervened to reassure him. "His forgeries, is that what you're shy of saying?"

"No, as it happens, I am not shy at all," said Nightingale. "You see, Commissioner, the art world's got different rules. Different principles and behavior. Let's just say for the sake of argument that I were to admit to placing forgeries on the market over the years. In the first place, I would be protected from prosecution for almost all of them by the statute of limitations. But even if I spoke openly of a forgery sold yesterday, almost all the other interested parties and the people involved in the transaction, especially those who invested good money in it, would be so keen to attest to its authenticity that no one would be allowed to believe me. I would have to work really hard to prove that what I sold was not authentic. Very hard indeed. It's not easy to self-incriminate in this line of work."

"Does Henry provide evidence of forgery in his writings?"

"In the writings you did not find?"

"Yes, in those," said Blume.

Nightingale settled himself more comfortably in his armchair. "Back in the 1930s, Commissioner, there was an American collector called Joseph Duveen. Perhaps you've heard of him?"

Blume shook his head.

"Well, this Duveen was a genuine expert, with both an eye and historical knowledge, which is a rare thing indeed. In an article he wrote, Duveen happened to mention that a version of a very famous painting *La Belle Ferronière*, supposedly by Leonardo da Vinci, was a fake. Now, bear in mind that the people who were in the process of selling the 'discovered' work had a quite unbelievable story to begin with. I mean, really—they hardly even tried to make it convincing. But they did insist on its authenticity, and aggressively, to boot. With barefaced . . . *sfacciatezza*—I don't think English even has a word for that sort of attitude—"

"*Chutzpah*," said Blume.

"If you can call that an English word," said Nightingale. "The point is the work was purportedly a second copy made by da Vinci—the artist famous for not even finishing off his own originals, let alone making copies. So when Duveen said fake, you probably think the vendors would have hidden their faces in shame and pulled the work from sale. *Au contraire.* Declaring that Duveen had depreciated their profits, *they* sued *him* for damages, and won. They bankrupted the poor chap. The painting was duly sold and is still attributed, sort of, to da Vinci, even though no one believes that anymore."

"If you are untouchable, I fail to see why you should be worried about what Treacy wrote," said Blume.

"Reputation, Commissioner. As he got on in years, Harry became more and more open about his forging activities, till he was practically shouting it from the rooftops, though it is worth mentioning he did not start doing that until he stopped producing work that was skilled. I did not depend all that much on him. The relationship was the other way around, really. Even if he had been producing magnificent interpretations of grand masters once a month ..."

"Interpretations, huh? I thought you weren't shy of the word forgery."

"Fine, then, forgeries. We could hardly be selling a discovered grand master once a month. There are limits to what the market will accept. I had quite high volumes of trade in areas that did not concern him, including sculpture. But two years ago, Harry even started sending letters to museums around the world, claiming authorship of various paintings. None of them ever purported to take him seriously, though one or two old masters subsequently vanished from display, often 'for cleaning.' Some of Harry's claims were bluffs, and sometimes I thought he was becoming delusional, genuinely believing he was the artificer behind works that he had never touched. The thing is, Harry was bursting to tell the world what he had done, which is not really what one wants to hear."

"So you would not have edited his writings, you would have destroyed them."

Nightingale looked offended. "I would have edited them, not destroyed them. I might have made a lot of cuts. The best editors cut out more than they leave in."

"I see," said Blume. "And so who better to tell about the notebooks than someone who knows the business, knows you and Treacy, and has authority. You contacted Colonel Orazio Farinelli and told him about the notebooks, didn't you? It should have been easy for the Colonel to get them, but maybe he delayed. Maybe he was doing a deal with Henry."

"I can't even begin to fathom what you are trying to say, Commissioner."

"OK, fathom this: when we or the Carabinieri get called out to a scene, our job is not to gather evidence that can be used against a person, but to gather evidence that a crime has been committed in the first place. That's phase one. The law is very clear on this point. Our evidence cannot really be used as part of the prosecution case unless the prosecutor successfully applies for an *incidente probatorio*—I'm afraid I can't translate that for you. It means using the preliminary evidence retroactively if it turns out there is a perpetrator. After our preliminary phase, we report to the investigating magistrate who chooses which force to use and, from then on, it is up to the magistrate to direct inquiries. Of course, we still have the power of initiative and can make suggestions, but all this comes *after* we have declared the existence of a suspected crime. Are you following this?"

"Without any great interest, I'm afraid."

"Keep listening, then. Today we did not get as far as reporting a crime, which is one of the reasons you have little to fear from this conversation we are having. No one from here filed a notification with a magistrate. Our instinct was that this might be a death by misadventure. But seeing as there is also some mad mugger operating in Trastevere, picking on foreign victims, we were going to look at that, too, and incorporate Treacy's death into an ongoing investigation already under the direction of a magistrate. All nice and simple, so far. Yet, a few hours later, a new magistrate and the Carabinieri are investigating. Well, that's fine, too. This sort of thing occasionally happens, especially when we stumble into something that another force is already investigating. The Carabiniere who arrives on the scene is a colonel, no less. Former director of the Art Forgery and Heritage Division. The dead man is a forger. Well, that definitely suggests the existence of a prior investigation, doesn't it? And if there was one, you were at the center of it along with Treacy, but you did not mention it. Perhaps you did not know?"

"If there was an investigation into us, I did not know," said Nightingale.

"By law, you must receive an official notification that you are under investigation. You never got one?"

"No."

"So it seems there is no investigation, or was none until this morning.

But the magistrate, a very flexible man who is susceptible to persuasion from powerful people, says there *is* an investigation. And then I have the pleasure of a chat with the Colonel himself, and it turns out he, Treacy, and you go way back."

"I am still not sure what you are implying," said Nightingale. "Perhaps you might be a little clearer?"

"I find the sudden investigation into a suspicious death that has not yet been declared suspicious to be suspicious."

"Ah, much clearer now. Who says the art of explication—"

Blume cut across him. "Don't test my patience, Mr. Nightingale. The obvious conclusion to this is that you warned the Colonel about the notebooks."

"That's not the only obvious conclusion."

"It's the one I choose to draw," said Blume. "Refute me."

Nightingale spelled out his words with great deliberation: "I did not tell the Colonel about the notebooks."

"That's not a refutation, it's just a denial."

"It's also the truth."

He was lying. Blume was sure. But he was pleased, too. It was as much and more than he had hoped to get out of the interview.

"And now you tell me, Commissioner, how do you know these writings that you say you have not seen are contained in notebooks?"

Blume and Nightingale sat there looking at each other, neither embarrassed at his own discovered lies, both annoyed at the other's. After a while, Blume said, "If I have Treacy's writings, I will soon read them and discover whatever it is you wanted kept quiet. You might as well tell me what it is."

"I just did. His claims and revelations regarding paintings I sold . . ."

"I see," said Blume. "You're hoping that whatever it is, Treacy did not include it. Perhaps someone killed him beforehand?"

Nightingale stood up. "I think next time we speak, I shall have my lawyer with me."

ʇ

# 13

B LUME HAD ENOUGH to form three interesting hypotheses. The first, almost a certainty, was that Treacy had written something neither the Colonel nor Nightingale wanted revealed, which logically implied it was something the Colonel and Nightingale had done together. The second, probable but not certain, was that the Colonel learned of the existence of the notebooks only recently, or he would have moved to seize them earlier. The third hypothesis, possible and far from certain, was that the Colonel had had Treacy killed to keep him quiet. If that was the case, Nightingale should not be feeling too safe either.

Blume pulled the first notebook out of his drawer, but before he had a chance to open it, his desk phone rang.

"The Questore wishes to speak to you," said a secretary at the other end of the line.

This formality, designed to heighten the dignity of office, infuriated Blume beyond what was reasonable. If he wants to speak to me, said Blume's mind in a well-rehearsed and unspoken rant, then all he has to do is phone and start talking, not instruct his unctuous secretary to inform me about his interest in eventually . . .

"Commissioner. You have a serious disciplinary problem in your squad, and your detection and closed case statistics are a disaster."

The bastard could get straight to the point when he wanted. There followed a detailed account of a complaint received from the *secundo secretario* of the Spanish Embassy to the Holy See. In his reply, Blume tried to insinuate a note of surprise into his voice regarding the unaccountable complaint from the Spanish diplomat. But the Questore was having none of it.

"*Nun ci prova', Commissa'*. If you try to make out like you don't know what's happening, it's going to look like incompetence on your part."

"OK," said Blume. "Point taken."

"Give him up, whoever he is, or you'll take the full brunt of this."

"Yes, sir."

"So, who is it?"

"Can't we get some time to work this out, see whether my man needs some backup witnesses or is willing to accept full responsibility?"

"I want to be able to talk about the one bad apple in a squad otherwise made up of upstanding heroes, Blume. I don't want a show of solidarity that implicates the whole fucking force in the thumping of a diplomat. You have until tomorrow morning. You're not too busy to deal with this, I hope?"

Blume made the beginnings of a response, but the Questore said, "No, listen. I don't want to hear that you're busy."

"OK. You won't hear that."

"You are particularly not busy with the dead foreign forger. Leave that to the Carabinieri, please, before you manage to offend another league of nations."

"Just a few loose ends to clear up, then it's straight over to them," promised Blume. "Though it is to be wondered what the basis of the sudden investigation . . ."

"No, it isn't. Nothing is to be wondered at. Hand it over now. You know why I want you to do that? Let me tell you why: It's so you can concentrate your efforts on improving international relations down there. The American visitor your local mugger robbed last month? Turns out his brother-in-law or cousin or someone owns GM Italia and carries clout. Another victim was a NATO negotiator—that makes two assaulted diplomats by the way."

Now was definitely not the time to mention Rospo's failure to file a report on the mugging of a Chinese couple.

"It's not much to ask, is it? I mean, catch a *mugger*. Skim all the scum off the streets, hold them in five adjacent cells. Eventually they'll pick out or kill off whoever got them arrested. Come on, Blume. And let me repeat this: Keep away from the dead forger before you offend the British Embassy, too."

"I think he was Irish," said Blume.

"Are you trying to be funny?"

"No, sir. It's just he was Irish."

"Great. Well, that means your mugger has probably done all the EU by now, including the minor states. So, head on plate of the policeman who beats up diplomats—I am appointing an external investigator today—and catch your mugger. Clear?"

"Very clear."

Blume had only just hung up and was still making obscene gestures at the phone when Panebianco knocked and, without waiting for an invitation, entered. He always did this: it was part of his efficiency, so Blume had decided not to tell him to stop. Still, it was annoying.

Blume slammed the notebook shut. "What?" He picked up a sheet of paper and dropped it on top of the notebook, thus insuring that Panebianco's eye was drawn to it.

"We've got a hit-and-run," said Panebianco.

"You mean the Municipal Police have a hit-and-run," said Blume. "We, on the other hand, have a mugger."

"Yes, except the vehicle was reported missing a few days ago. The owner is abroad, apparently. He's also a small-time crook with a previous for assault. There are two victims and a third in critical condition. It looks like they are non-EU immigrants."

"Oh well, that's all right then," said Blume, regretting it as he said it, because Panebianco never detected irony.

Panebianco said, "One victim is a child, the person in critical condition is also a child."

"Oh," said Blume. Maybe Panebianco was right to have no sense of humor. "Who did you send?"

"There's a patrol car now." I was thinking of going there myself. With Sovrintendente Grattapaglia."

"No. Choose someone else," said Blume. "Grattapaglia can't go. Keep me posted on it."

When Panebianco left, Blume retrieved the other notebooks from his drawer, and glanced through them. He estimated it would take him eight hours to read through them, perhaps a little less. It was hard to tell with handwritten notes. The following day was a Sunday, and provided the hit-and-run did not balloon into a major case and the mugger did not strike again, he might find the time to go through them. Then he could decide what to do. He wondered if the Colonel knew English well; perhaps he would read them with Nightingale by his side. He pictured them, reading the pages, ripping them out, feeding them into the flames.

He would take them home now, get a start on them. He put them into his father's old leather bag, large enough to accommodate art books, and thought of how they had peeped out of Caterina's bag, making her look like a student. A mature student. He wondered what she had studied in college. Probably jurisprudence like him.

Most people who went to British-American schools abroad ended up in highly paid jobs, but not her. She had lived outside Italy, lived in a different language, which gave her a second soul. Who had said that? And then she had ended up a poorly paid servant of the state. Not just a servant of the state but a cop. Part of society's clean-up crew. She must have come home when her father retired. Possibly another colonel.

He made a sudden decision. He left the office, crossed the road to a bookstore with a photocopying machine. Zalib was the name of the place. It was tucked into the bowels of the huge Pamphili gallery. Paoloni, who had never seen the inside of a bookstore, used to refer to it dismissively as the Arab store, convinced Zalib was some sort of Arab surname. The place smelled of cigarettes, photocopy ozone, and damp paper.

It took Mr. Zalib, who turned out to be a laconic Italian called Marco, half an hour to photocopy all the pages, and another twenty minutes to get spiral binding around them. He charged far too little for his work, apologized for the delay, and sent Blume on his way, bag bulging. Treacy had written on both sides of the sheet, and the single-sided photocopied version was more than twice as thick as the originals.

Blume called Caterina, not sure where she would be. It turned out she was at a swimming pool where Elia was just finishing his lesson. Blume got her to give him directions and asked her to wait.

Twenty minutes later, he was sitting in his car on a road so full of waiting vehicles it had turned into a parking lot. He failed to make out Caterina in the midst of all the other mothers, babysitters, and children milling around the gates of the sports center and swarming across the road, but Caterina and her child found him.

She knocked on the glass at the passenger side, but the kid opened the back door and bundled himself and his sports bag into the backseat and tapped Blume on the shoulder.

"Are you a policeman?" he asked.

"Yes," said Blume.

"Not a boyfriend, then?"

Caterina climbed into the passenger seat. "Sorry about this," she said. "Commissioner, this is my son. Elia. Say hello."

"Hello," said Blume.

"No, not you, Commissioner. I meant Elia. Elia, say hello."

"Hello," said Elia.

"Where's your car?" asked Blume.

"I take the bus here. It's quicker than finding parking here and then back home. It's only ten minutes. Elia, darling, we're getting a lift. Put on your seatbelt."

"Seatbelt? In the *back*?"

"It's the law."

"I can't find any seatbelt," said the boy.

"Well, look for it. I'm sure it's there."

"You never make me put on a seatbelt in the back."

"I'm doing so now."

"Are we going to have a crash?"

"You never can tell."

"Can't your friend drive properly?"

"Elia, please."

Blume couldn't find parking either, so he left them outside the apartment building, and came back ten minutes later carrying his load of paper. He found the intercom button with the name Mattiola on it, and got himself buzzed in. It was only when the door to the apartment was opened that he realized this was not Caterina's apartment, but her parents'.

"Sorry, I thought I'd mentioned it," said Caterina. "I live ten minutes away, back toward the swimming baths. I was leaving Elia here because I thought we had work to do."

"We do," said Blume. "But it's voluntary. For you. I just had an idea, since you know English . . . I didn't mean to disrupt."


Ten minutes later, his bulging bag held protectively against his chest, Blume thanked Mrs. Mattiola again for her kindness.

"Don't be silly, Commissioner. More coffee?"

"No thank you, Mrs. Mattiola."

"Another cookie, Commissioner?"

"No, really, not another."

"I can't think of anything else. A yogurt perhaps?"

"No, really ... I ..."

"Mother! He said no."

"I want yogurt!" said Elia.

Caterina's mother went into the kitchen to fetch her grandson a yogurt, and her husband pounced on the opportunity to struggle out of his chair to reach the coffeepot on the table. But she was back with remarkable speed.

"Are you pouring the coffee, Arnaldo?" She handed the yogurt to Elia. "Here, *tesoro*, this is for you," and then returned to her husband. "Careful with that handle. It needs to be tightened. You used to tighten things."

Her husband, who didn't look much like a colonel, sank noiselessly back into his chair.

"This yogurt has bits in it," announced Elia with disgust.

"Just eat the bits, Elia," said Caterina, then softened her tone. "Listen, do you mind staying here until late? I have some work to do with the Commissioner."

"Of course you can leave Elia with us," said her mother.

"Great." Caterina stood up. "We'd better go."

Blume stood up, too.

"So you two are going back to your place now?" said Mrs. Mattiola.

"The office, we're going back to the office," said Caterina.

"Oh. I was under the impression ... Do you need any fruit?"

"I have fruit," said Caterina.

But her mother had thrown the question into the air as a decoy to cover her retreat, and before Caterina had kissed her son and made it to the front door, she was back bearing two bulging blue plastic bags. "These are apples, from the orchard owner himself, he has apples and cabbages out in Santa Severa, sells them at his stall in the market there on Via Catania. You won't get apples like that in the shops. I've thrown in a few carrots, some fennel, and two lettuces, some artichokes, a few new potatoes, and a handful of onions, and some of those brown pears Elia likes. Kaisers. Also those Kinder chocolate bars. They say each bar contains one and a half glasses of full-fat milk. Do you think that's true? That's a lot of milk. He likes to have two at breakfast. That's three glasses, and he dips them into his milk, which makes four. Milk is good for growing children."

Blume offered to help carry the bags, though it was going to be a struggle, what with his own paper load.

"No. Just open the front door," said Caterina. As soon as he did, she shouldered him out into the hallway.

"Lovely meeting you, Commissioner. Drop by again soon."

"A pleasure, Mrs. Mattiola," said Blume.

"Call the elevator," ordered Caterina.

# 14

CATERINA FINISHED STACKING dirty plates in the sink. Her kitchen was usually spotless. Well, not spotless, but not like this either.

Blume gave her the details of his talk with John Nightingale.

"So we need to check through the notebooks to find if there is any reference to something both the Colonel and Nightingale would want to keep quiet. But we don't know if it's there."

"Shall we look through them now?"

"Either that, or we systematically read the notebooks from beginning to end, which is probably the best way, because the devil is so often in the details, isn't it?" said Blume. "If I can, I am going to read them all the way through, but there is a good chance I won't have time. Also, I have specifically been instructed not to investigate. But before I give up, and it may involve handing over these notes, I want a second pair of eyes. You need to be in the background. Unpaid, unrecognized overtime work, basically."

As her father liked to say, you wanted a bicycle, now pedal.

Blume opened the first notebook and read in a declamatory tone: "*As William Wordsworth once remarked, the child is the father of the man.*"

The phone rang.

"Are you going to answer that?"

"It's my mother," said Caterina.

"You can see the caller ID from all the way over there?"

"No, but I can feel it."

When it had stopped ringing, she pulled her hands out of the sink, and Blume returned to frowning at the notebook. "Already I don't like this guy, Treacy," he said.

"The child's the father of the man," said Caterina, repeating the words and then continuing unself-consciously in English. "As in what you do as a child determines how you turn out as an adult. What's wrong with that?"

Her accent sounded slightly English to Blume's ear.

"I don't mind that idea," said Blume. "Or maybe I do. I haven't thought about it. It's that bit about Wordsworth remarking it that annoys me. He didn't remark it, he wrote it."

"You know the poem?" asked Caterina. "I studied it once."

"Of course I don't know the poem," said Blume in an exasperated tone. "I just know Wordsworth was a poet. So he wrote that line. He didn't just once remark it in conversation with Treacy in a bar."

Caterina sat down on the far side of the table, brushed some Weetabix crumbs onto the floor, pushed her straight brown hair back over her ear, took up a pen, and opened a notebook that she had taken from her son's room with a blue robo-something on the cover.

"If you're going to critique each line, Commissioner, this is going to take some time."

"Well, can you read the handwriting?" asked Blume.

Caterina peered at it, shrugged. "It doesn't look too . . ."

"Because I think it's probably easier for me than for you to guess the English words. So if I read a bit and you follow in your copy, you'll get used to the lettering quickly, then you can go on alone."

"That seems like a good idea," said Caterina.

"Great. So we start off like this, then I'll leave the photocopy here, you read it, I'll go home and read it. Then we compare notes sometime next week . . . We'll play it by ear, basically."

"Let's try it, then," said Caterina.

"Good. I appreciate this," said Blume. He opened the first notebook and began to read, struggling over some of the first sentences, but then finding his flow as he familiarized himself with the handwriting.

*"As William Wordsworth once remarked, the child is the father of the man. When I look back down the years, I see a strange nine-year-old boy whom I barely recognize. Yet it was he who decided how my life would be, and all because of his crush on an eight-year-old girl.*

*"The eight-year-old was called Monica, which was a very exotic name for Ireland in the fifties. I first became aware of my love when I was in 'high babies' (which, for the uninitiated, is one year above 'low babies'). She wore an orange dress with a round lace patterned white collar.*

"One day, Miss Woods, our art teacher, set us the task of drawing our favorite objects, as many of them as we saw fit. We had three lessons in which to complete our drawings. If deemed worthy, they would be pinned to the walls for sports day when parents would be allowed to come into the school to watch the children do long jumps that can't have been all that long, and run egg-and-spoon races.

"Miss Woods allowed us only dark colors to begin with, though we were free to use crayons or pencils. She told us we could do the coloring-in during the next two lessons. I observed Monica carefully, noting the objects she chose to draw; I watched the yellow pencil in her beautiful fingers as she glided her hand over the page leaving careful gray outlines. Most of the other children were still using their fists as they sought to keep their waxy red and blue crayons under control.

"During the second lesson, when it seemed Monica had finished outlining her objects and was preparing for the coloring-in phase, I neatly divided my page into four columns and five rows: 20 boxes in all. In the first box, I drew an exact replica of Monica's entire page, in miniature, without missing out a single object. In the second box, I did the same, only this time I colored in the objects in the way I thought she was likely to choose. In the third box I chose a different color scheme and so on until I had exhausted almost every permutation. When Monica did finish, her picture and colors corresponded exactly to my miniature in box 17. It is still my lucky number.

"Monica's favorite objects were: a comb (I had kept it brown or black until version 12, when I thought it might be silver), a golden-brown teddy bear with a green bow, a pair of black dancing shoes, a red-haired Raggedy Ann doll, a giraffe, and a blue windmill with white sails.

"Miss Woods loved my work. Mrs. Walsh, the headmistress, did not, dismissing it in front of the whole class as being rather too '. . .'. I did not understand the big word she used that day, and I can't remember it now.

"But it was clear the bitch did not like it.

"As for Monica, when she realized what I had done, she took her picture down from the wall, ruined it by adding a large and poorly-drawn cat and a purple cabbage tree in the foreground, whereupon she hung it up again.

"I learned three things from that. First, I could draw in another person's style like it was my own; second, women could be unpredictable and vindictive; third, never imitate a living artist. If I had forgotten the first lesson and remembered the other two, I would have made my own life easier.

"My mother never came to school events and so she never saw the picture. Apart from not having any interest in how I was doing, I think she felt uncomfortable with the ethos of the school. It was Protestant. Church of Ireland, to be precise. My mother was born a Catholic, but no longer practicing. She had not lapsed; rather she had been cast out and thrown over when she became pregnant with me by a man whose name she never revealed to anyone, not even me. After failing to reconcile with her own family and most of her neighbors, she adopted a Bohemian guise, and affected not to care. After a while, assisted by some serious afternoon drinking and several rejection letters from publishers not at all interested in her imagist poetry, she really did not care.

"At the age of eleven, I acquired a reluctant stepfather called Manfred Manning. I call him my stepfather but at the time of his appearance he was married to another woman whom he could not divorce, this being Ireland and then being then. He finally chose to leave his first wife when she was diagnosed with cancer of the pancreas. She lasted almost three years, which may be some sort of record, perhaps hanging on to spite them, perhaps hoping he would come home at least for the final part. When she died, Mother and Manfred were holidaying in Edinburgh, a city I have yet to find a reason for visiting.

"After a Protestant primary education, my mother sent me, aged 12, as a boarder to Clongowes Wood College. It seems strange the Jesuits should take in the child of such an immoral woman shacked up with a bigamous Prod, but the reason is simple enough. Manning made a large contribution toward the building of a new wing and my mother lied about everything. She told them she was married, and though admitting her husband was a Protestant, insisted she was bringing me up Catholic. She might even have produced some false paperwork to prove it.

"The summer before I went, she gave me a crash-course in Catholicism, bringing me to mass, and shuffling me up the aisle to communion. Tongue out, eyes downcast, no chewing, it is supposed to be the flesh of Christ. Yes, Henry, it is a revolting concept, but it helps you not to chew. She explained confession to me, too, and warned me to hold back on some issues, notably religious doubt and my paternity. It was expected, she said.

"She told me in some detail about the first communion party I never had, and the gifts of money I never received from relatives I had never met. After a while, I began to remember all these events that had not happened, and I realized how easy it was to paint a fictional past.

"The most surprising thing I learned during my conversion to temporary Catholicism was that God was a soft blue woman. Cabinteely Catholic Church, to which my headscarfed and unrecognizably pious-looking mother took me to *learn the ropes, had a tondo image of Jesus set into the pier to the right of the altar. A red sanctuary lamp hung over the altar and a second tondo image, this one of a gentle-looking person in blue, was set into the left pier. Now, as the Protestants had given me enough instruction about God's three-in-one-person trick but remained tight-lipped about Mary, Mother of God, my interpretation was: Jesus on the right, the Holy Ghost in the middle, and God was the blue-shrouded woman on the left.*

*"I was soon disabused of the notion, but images are stronger than words. God was then and is sometimes even now an azure Bellini-esque woman . . ."*

Blume turned over the page and looked in dismay at a web of crossings-out and insertion marks.

"I can't make this out, but I think I'm going to skip ahead. This is no good to us. You've hardly taken any notes, I see. Are you following?"

Caterina looked down at what she had written.

Blume flicked forward a few pages. "This section seems to come to an end here."

"You may as well read it through."

*"The Jesuits may have designed the myth of the Immaculate Conception, but the Irish chapter of the order was keen to make sure we boys understood this was basically a goddess created for peasants. One problem, explained Fr. Ferchware, was this: If Mary was conceived and born without sin, for that is what Immaculate Conception means, is it not, Treacy? (It is, Father), then she had no need of the salvific intervention of her son, Jesus Christ, did she? Don't try to answer, child, just tell me, the grammatical term for that question.*

*"A trick question, Father.*

*"A rhetorical question, you godless reprobate. I shall continue. So if there was already one perfect person in the world, Jesus Christ could not have been the <u>Universal</u> Savior. We might conclude, therefore, that His universality is imperfect and that He is therefore imperfect and He cannot be God. And what does this demonstrate?*

*"The evident limitations of logic and the frailty of human reasoning in the face of the divine, Father.*

*"Good man, Treacy.*

*"The thing about the Jesuits is they started off their history as a sort of special operations force, often poised to stage a military coup within the Church, but*

ended up teaching geography to schoolchildren. I think that—and chastity—drove most of them mad.

"I was expelled at 16. The immediate or ostensible cause was my poisoning of O'Leary, a gap-toothed red-faced thug who thought he could make my life a misery because I was not so good at rugby. I patiently waited for him one afternoon behind the science wing, opened that very year and contributed to by my stepfather or whatever he was. When O'Leary eventually came by, he was on his own. Looking back with the forgiveness of years, I suppose he was not the worst type of bully. He didn't have a gang; he didn't spend his time looking for me. It was casual, off-handed bullying, made possible by his size. I hit him over the head with a rock as he walked around the corner. He stood there and rubbed his head like a cartoon character doing a double-take, so I hit him again, on the temple, and down he went. I sat on his chest and opened up three paper twists of powder I had taken from the chemistry lab. The first contained tartaric acid, basically sherbet without sugar, and I held his nose and poured it into his gaping mouth. It fizzed, and he choked and I told him it was arsenic. The next packet contained bicarbonate of soda, which I told him was plutonium. While not generally available to Irish schoolchildren, plutonium was such a scary new word back then that I thought its dramatic reach would bridge the credibility gap. The last package contained copper sulphate, which I had taken for the beauty of its color, and this, unfortunately, <u>was</u> toxic, though not deadly.

"I hadn't figured O'Leary for a snitch but the plutonium and arsenic had him worried. Even then, his babbling report might not have been taken too seriously were it not for the black bruise on his temple, his blue tongue, and terrified eyes. Everyone stood ceremoniously on the pebbled driveway as the ambulance drove away with O'Leary inside accompanied by the headmaster.

"As I was packing my bags, Fr. McCarthy came in holding his black 'biffer,' a leather strap weighted with lead. He administered twelve strokes to each hand, aiming also to hit the wrist. He left saying, 'We've all known the truth about you for some time, Treacy.'

"A biffer works on the hands rather like a coronary stroke, managing to impart pain and numbness at once. With my throbbing and fumbling hands, I was unable to complete my packing, still less close my suitcase and bring it downstairs to the front door, and I think it was this more than anything that caused me to become so upset. At any rate, it was Fr. Ferchware who came up and found me, finished packing my suitcase for me and accompanied me to the front door. Before we went out, he told me, 'There'll be a lot of people looking at you,

Henry. You don't want to go out with a face like that.' He took a startlingly white, sharply folded, and perfectly clean handkerchief from his pocket, and handed it to me. 'Dry your eyes, blow your nose.' The handkerchief smelled of lavender and sunshine, the smells of France, Italy, and my future. I filled it with gray snot and salt, the color and taste of Ireland and my past.

" 'Who is coming for me?' I asked. 'Is it my mother?'

" 'No, son, they've sent a taxi.'

"When I was younger, each month was a compact unit containing so many events and changes that they had to be compressed just to fit. But now an entire year can drift by empty of significance. I thought when I started this I might be able to unpack some of those compressed events and examine them in detail, but I find I have forgotten most of them. Life then was brimming, but I still have to pass over years as if they had hardly happened at all.

"After my expulsion from Clongowes, they sent me to the Presentation Brothers in Bray, but I got kicked out of that, too, this time for setting fire to an outhouse. No one saw me, but I was stupid enough to turn up to my next lesson reeking of paraffin and smoke, and was sent to the headmaster's office, from whose window the smoldering heap across the field was still visible. A red fire engine stood in the middle of the field, one fireman dribbling his hose on the black patch of ground, a second fireman watching. The headmaster waved his arm at the window, and declared,

> See you yon dreary plain, forlorn and wild,
> The seat of desolation, void of light,
> Save what the glimmering of these livid flames
> Casts pale and dreadful?

"Then he burst out laughing, and took some time to get himself under control. As he dabbed his watering eyes with the back of his hand, I figured it was probably going to be all right after all if he found it so funny, but then he said, 'I've phoned your house, and nobody is in, so I'm afraid it is up to you to tell them you have been expelled. We are also considering prosecution, and shall certainly be seeking damages. That is all.'

"I ended up in Ballybrack Technical College, and, in between the metalwork, remedial English, and getting beaten up, finally learned something useful: basic carpentry. But after less than a year, I had left that school, too. This time I was not expelled, I merely wandered off and no one seemed to notice.

"One morning, I was sitting on the number 45 bus on my way to Bray when a group of kids, three boys and a girl, in front of me started slashing the rubbery blue seats with penknives. One of them turned around to see if I wanted to make something of it, then nudged his companion. Here comes trouble, I thought. Then the girl turned around and said, 'Henry!' And I looked at her for a while, then finally said, disappointed but also kind of awed, 'Monica!'

"She was going through her anti-authority phase. Cut adrift and allowed to do her own thing. I was the perfect companion.

"In the summer of 1966, a woman called Mrs. Heath, who was connected in some vague way with someone who knew my stepfather, allowed me to use an empty mews in her garden. The deal was that I would do odd jobs, like washing the forty-two windows of her house (each of which had four panes and, of course, two sides, so it was no small task), weed the garden, clean some of the slime from around the pond, cut the grass, run errands. In exchange, I got to live in an empty stone mews without electricity. But it had running water, a bathroom, a permanently damp bed, some black oak furniture, and was effectively my first apartment. It was an unheard-of freedom that rendered me attractive to Monica.

"For a West Brit, Mrs. Heath was a good woman. She encouraged me to paint, and paid for the supplies. When I did something, she would 'air' it in the house, since the mews was too damp. I thought she was ancient, but she was probably only in her thirties. After a few months she trusted me enough not to follow me around the house as I cleaned the windows or carried mahogany chairs and tables from one room to another, for she was always rearranging her life, ready to start afresh.

"One morning, Monica and I found ourselves alone in the drawing room. Mrs. Heath was away for a few hours and had asked me to dust the room. As I was lifting silverware and china trinkets from the mantelpiece, Monica said, 'We should steal something.'

"I turned around to see if she was serious.

" 'Something really valuable. To make it worthwhile. Something that we could sell and then use the money to go somewhere.'

"Her suggestion was to go to London, a city where everything was happening. I was attracted by the idea, too, but did not want to steal from Mrs. Heath. But I knew Monica would be disappointed if I made bourgeois moral objections to her *idea, so I pointed out the practical difficulties of getting a flat, putting down a deposit, finding a job. Since she still lived with her parents and I was the one with the independent life, she deferred to me on these points. But the result was to set Monica thinking along more ambitious lines.*

*"One day when Mrs. Heath had left us alone in her house while she went out to pick some apples, Monica pointed at a large oil painting over the mantelpiece of redcoat soldiers, rearing horses, and an elephant. 'What's that painting?' she asked.*

*" 'Just because it's the biggest doesn't mean it's the best or the most valuable in the room,' I declared, trying to sound more authoritative than I felt in an effort to deflect the conversation from where I knew Monica was going to take it.*

*" 'You don't know who it's by,' said Monica (it was a Francis Hayman but she was right: I did not know that then). 'What about that one over there, the one with the two sad dogs? I like that one.'*

*" 'That's not good art,' I said importantly. 'It's by a man called Landseer. Actually, it's lousy.'*

*" 'Is it now?' said Monica. 'It looks grand to me. But if it's so terrible, you could do one just as good, couldn't you?' She pointed to another frame. 'Look, there are two wee cartoons even I could copy. All them squiggly lines, little men dressed in black.'*

*" 'That's Jack Yeats. I could do him all right.'*

*"She smiled at me. 'Well, we have to start somewhere. How much would that sketch there of your man carrying the turf get us?'*

*" 'I don't know. About twenty-five quid?'*

*" 'At that rate the big one with the dogs must be worth a thousand. D' you think her ladyship'd miss her Yeats if we just took it off the wall?'*

*"I was thinking that if I did a quick copy it might stand in for a day or two without anyone noticing while I copied the original. A plan formed in my mind and I explained it to her, but she found it too elaborate.*

*" 'All that for just twenty-five quid.'*

*" 'That's a decent amount of money. It would pay the deposit on a flat in London, if that's where we're going,' I said."*

Blume suddenly remembered something, and stopped reading. "There's a half blank page here, more crossings-out, and this is not strictly relevant."

Caterina did not say anything until she had finished writing out her last note. Her arm ached and her wrist had seized up like a lobster's claw, but she wanted to go on.

"Does he copy the painting?" she asked.

"Knowing how he spent the rest of his days, I'd say he does. Otherwise, why would he be telling this?"

"Maybe he wanted to talk about Monica. Let me see." She leaned in to look at the notebook. "I don't know how you can read his handwriting so fluently. I'm going to be much slower."

"He uses abbreviations and plus signs for 'and,' and he's not a great speller," said Blume. "Well, you have the photocopies. Don't tell anyone you have them, OK? Read ahead if you want, but maybe skip the early years."

"I think this works, you reading and me taking notes," said Caterina. "You could stay for dinner and we could continue after. Just to finish this first section this evening."

Blume closed the notebook and stood up. "That's very kind. But I've just remembered I have a dinner appointment. It takes me at least half an hour to get home from here, so ..."

Caterina picked up her notes and held them against her chest. "Oh, well, that's not a problem."

"It's just more work, really."

"I don't mind. I'll continue reading by myself after you've gone."

"I mean this dinner. It's work-related."

"Oh, right. Well, so is this," said Caterina.

"Yes. Everything's just work," said Blume.

# 15

H E LOOKED FORWARD to meeting Kristin. Never having officially acknowledged any attachment to each other, they had conducted an on-off relationship, now locked in the "off" position.

At Via degli Umbri, he went a few meters in the wrong direction on a one-way street to stop at a bar with a good selection of wines, and bought a bottle of Mater Matuta from Casale del Giglio. It would probably remain unopened, but Kristin sometimes drank.

He reversed back up the street to Piazza dell'Immacolata and had to bully his way back into the traffic, using the fact that anyone who hit him from the rear would pay the insurance. Eventually he forced a white van to yield. The car behind it blared its horn, and Blume glanced absently in his rear-view mirror to see what sort of fool was driving, but the van hid it from sight. All he could see were a gray Skoda and a blue Lancia farther down the street.

The traffic was snarled up at Porta Maggiore, as always. An ancient green tram seemed to have died from the effort of switching tracks, and the cars had to edge around it, some in front, some behind. Blume went in front, which meant he had to angle the car over a patch of grass and avoid a stone bench that had been covered in graffiti before being cleft in two.

Blume cut diagonally across the flow to get through an arch in the Aurelian fortifications, and made it. The driver he had cut off was too busy texting on his cell to notice. A hairy arm and crooked elbow from the car behind that showed total relaxation. Nor did the blue Lancia behind them seem in any hurry.

Blume found a parking spot reasonably near his apartment block, picked up his bag with the notebooks, the bottle of wine, and walked up Via Orvieto. Where the street intersected Via la Spezia, a blue car was angling itself into a parking space. Blume wondered if he would have time for a shower before Kristin arrived.

Back home, Blume smashed a handful of Calabrian chili peppers under the mortar and tipped the flakes on top of the hamburger, now frying in the pan. He added crushed garlic, chives, stirring with a wooden spoon, yanking the pan off the heat, and shaking the contents about. He added tomato paste to color the meat. He turned on the oven to heat the tortillas, and mixed powdered cumin, cocoa, coriander, and his secret ingredient, mustard powder, which he poured on top of the meat, then turned it down to simmer. The kitchen clock showed ten minutes to 9. He shredded the lettuce, added salt to the chopped tomatoes in the blue bowl, put the tortillas in the oven. Kristin had said 9 o'clock and was never late. They would be ready exactly on time. He shook Tabasco droplets over the mixture. In the living room, the phone started ringing.

It was Kristin.

"Hey there, Alec. Did you set the table yet?"

"Sure. But we're gonna be using our hands for most of this. It's Tex-Mex, Calabrian style. You into that?"

"Great," she said. "But you're going to have to wait. At least an hour later than I said. Something came up."

A sudden high-pitched beeping noise filled the room and, within seconds, Blume felt like it was in his head.

"What's that?" asked Kristin.

"The sound of tortillas burning," said Blume.

Blume took off his shoes, stood on the counter, opened the smoke alarm, took out the battery, and sighed in relief as the noise stopped. He noticed that he had turned on the grill rather than the oven. He switched it off, opened the door, and allowed himself to be enveloped in a black cloud of smoke. He opened the kitchen window, allowing in a blare of traffic noise that was almost as bad as the alarm. He leaned out and took a breath of cool evening air and glanced casually up the street. The blue car sat snug behind a green dumpster.

He threw out the black tortillas and opened two cans of tomatoes and two of borlotti beans, poured them into a casserole and added the meat mixture and a dash of habanero. They would have chili con carne instead. He added some herbs, then looked through his dwindling collection of spices from Castroni, and found a small jar of Sambal Setan, which he added to the pot.

He walked into the living room and took Treacy's notebooks from his bag, and, instead of resuming where he had left off with Caterina, flicked back and forth through the three volumes looking for references to the Colonel. After setting aside the one volume that seemed entirely dedicated to the technical aspects of Treacy's work, and contained sketches and diagrams as well as words, he estimated how long it would have taken the writer to get from his childhood and early adulthood to meeting the Colonel. He focused on the first third of the second volume and, after ten minutes of looking, his eye finally alighted on a promising passage.

As he read it, he wondered if it was sufficiently compromising for the Colonel to want it suppressed. It seemed to consist of yet another half-baked eyewitness account of the circumstances surrounding the murder of Aldo Moro. Did anyone actually care? He doubted it. Treacy, too, seemed to get quickly bored with the subject, ending it after a short paragraph that stood in apparent isolation in the middle of a polemical piece on a dead art historian called Federick Hartt, whose offense seems to have been he claimed a forger could never imitate the *pentimenti*, the redrawings, corrections, and second thoughts of the artist.

Blume gave up. He'd just have to read from start to finish. He returned to the opening chapter, wondering if Caterina was still in her kitchen doing the same, or had taken the photocopy to bed with her, anxious before she slept to find out how things turned out between Henry Treacy and Monica.

*My replica of Jack Yeats' sketch was an instructive experience in several ways, not all of them good.*

*Jack Yeats had an impressionist's eye for color, but he was not a great draftsman. A good one, to be sure, with fine penmanship, but I could see why he eventually chose color and worked with thick swirling and increasingly confused grays and blues in an effort to capture Irish light. The work I was copying, however, was from his youth, a pen and ink wash, with no color. At first, it seemed little better than what you might see by an unknown illustrator in the Saturday Evening Post, except there was a peculiarity to his style that only became interesting as I tried to imitate it. The lines were undulating, often drawn thickly from a heavily inked pen guided by a confident hand. They never overlapped or showed signs of* hesitation. Similarly, even the finest and closest strokes left a distinct white space between them, so that although he covered much of the paper in ink and although the drawings were tiny, he created a sense of space and movement.

Moving in and out of Mrs. Heath's house, sometimes left alone for a few hours, I was able to copy a rough version of the picture onto a piece of paper that I kept folded in my pocket. It was strange to copy a picture line-by-line in frenetic bursts. If I had asked her, Mrs. Heath would of course have let me stand there all day copying it openly. I think she might even have lent me the original, bless her. But I had embarked on a furtive enterprise, and I was interested in seeing it through.

After several days, I had completed my copy. I brought it home and unfolded it on my pine table. It was a complete mess. It was so bad I burst out laughing as I looked at it. It was like a sketch done by a committee, in which each member was allowed to draw a quadrant without reference to what the others were doing. Each time I had copied a piece I seemed to have brought a different style to it. Worse still, the elements in the sketch were completely out of proportion with each other. Being young and histrionic, I burned it there and then when simply throwing it out would have done as well.

And so I learned how _not_ to copy a work. But I also learned that the easiest way to capture an artist's style was to do it freehand, without direct reference to the original. Over the next two days, working from memory in my mews and without so much as a glance at the original on the drawing-room wall, I sketched my own version of Jack Yeats' turf-carriers. The result, though clearly different to the original, also resembled its style very closely. I now had my first proper forgery, though I did not know it at the time. It would go into the frame as a temporary replacement, so that I could borrow the original copy, hold it in my hand, and copy it at my leisure.

The opportunity to do the changeover came one Friday afternoon. Mrs. Heath was having guests and wanted me to help her polish and set out silver and crystal. She brought out some wine, and asked me to open a bottle to test it. I did as I was told, and she instructed me to pour it into a crystal stem glass and drink some. I did, and it tasted OK, though I felt it was very much an old person's drink.

She came over, poured herself a glass, drank it, and spat it straight back out, which I have to say shocked me a bit. Apparently it was "corked." And so was the next bottle and the next and the one after.

"What a bloody nuisance. I need to get some wine. That means driving all the way down to Dalkey," she said. She asked me to polish the serving platters while she was gone.

As soon as I saw her car leave the gate, I grabbed the Yeats and rushed with it back down the garden to my mews. I removed the original, and hid it in a book. In my rush, I lost two staples from the back of the frame and tore the backing paper as well. When I came to put my stop-gap sketch into the frame, it was too big. It was also bright white, and the new ink gleamed. It would be noticed immediately. I rushed into the kitchen and pulled out the rubbish from below the sink. I emptied the contents on the floor and scooped up handfuls of old tea leaves and broken eggshells (being practically all I ate or drank back then). I threw them on my overclean drawing. If I had destroyed it, I would just have put the original back and started again. Or I might have abandoned the idea and led a different life and become a better person.

I left the used tea leaves and eggshells for twenty minutes, wetting them slightly, then carefully brushing them off, first with my hand, then with a thick bristle brush that I had yet to use for painting. It worked, at least by the standards I had then. By now Mrs. Heath would have left the shop in Dalkey and was probably already halfway up Killiney Hill Road. The page was no longer pristine white, and seemed magically aged. Even the wetting of the leaves had slightly warped the paper adding to the effect. I spent around ten minutes trimming the edges, which flattened and lowered the sky and ruined what little balance I had managed to achieve. But it was a tiny work, and even at arm's length it was hard to make out the details. It only had to fill a space for a few days. As long as no one looked at it. I prayed none of the dinner party guests was a connoisseur. I was still tapping in the staples at the back of the frame with the handle of the screwdriver when a crackle of gravel and the sound of a motor told me that Mrs. Heath was back already.

I grabbed the framed drawing and rushed out into the garden, just in time to see her walk into the house. The frame was too large for me to conceal under my shirt. I was convinced that as soon as she walked in she would see it was missing. She called my name. No point in hiding now. "Coming," I called.

She appeared at the front door and called down the garden. Without seeming to notice that I was carrying anything.

"Fetch the crate of wine from the backseat of the car for me, will you? It's far too heavy for me."

In she went again.

I leaned into her car. There was a wooden milk crate containing a dozen *bottles of wine in the back. I dropped the picture on the top, and heaved it in my arms. She was right, it weighed a ton.*

*"In here, Henry. The drawing room."*

*I struggled in. She was staring at the half-set table.*

*"You didn't do as I asked with the silverware," she said. "Did you do anything while I was gone?"*

*I glanced over at the hearth. A bright rectangle of lighter green wallpaper shone where the picture belonged.*

*"I had to go to the toilet," I said. I put down the crate, positioning myself between her and the empty space on the wall, and whipped the picture off the top of the crate as she turned to examine the crystal.*

*"Oh dear. Well, at least you went back to your own place to do that. I say, Henry?" She turned around quickly and I swept the picture behind my back, but as I did so, I realized this was not going to work, so I continued my awkward movement and staggered backwards, kicking at the desk with the two rejected open bottles of wine. One of them fell with a crash on the floor, and Mrs. Heath shrieked something about her Persian rug, and fell to her knees. I hung my false picture on the wall behind, then sank down as if in a dead faint.*

*Mrs. Heath saved her Persian rug, after which she was full of solicitude for me, convinced the strain of carrying the heavy crate had given me a turn. She told me to go and get some rest. She'd call a friend to help her prepare for the evening.*

*When Monica arrived that evening, I told her of my adventures and brought her over to show her the purloined original.*

*"Is that it?" she said, tilting her head sideways to appraise the work. "Can't say I think much of it."*

*"Neither do I," I remember saying.*

*"It should be easy then. Why not make a few copies, while you're at it? We can sell each one as an original. Make far more that way."*

*"We don't have time," I said. "If anyone looks at the replacement I've put on the wall in there, they'll spot it immediately for a fake. The sooner we get it back the better."*

*"Just copy your own copy. Do I have to do all the thinking for the two of us?"*

*Half an hour later, Monica returned to her earlier idea. "If you make a good enough copy, can't you just use that to make another and another?"*

*"I've been thinking about this, Monica," I told her. "We know nothing about the market. There must be all sorts of things they look for that I haven't done*

right. The paper, watermarks, records, and so on. The way I see it is we can sell this only once, but if we don't want to be caught, we have to sell the original, and watch what sort of things they look for. And we'll need a good story for why we have it, and we need to make sure she won't have reported it missing."

I thought Monica was losing interest in the project, but then she did something that was very crass and revealing, but she thought was very clever. After working for a whole week, I had finished, but was not pleased with my handiwork. It looked like a copy of an original. I had solved the problem of the brightness of the paper and the shine of new ink but there was no fluidity to the composition. When I was back in Mrs. Heath's drawing room, looking at the aged stop-gap work that I so despised, I realized with a shock it was the better work. Bad, but still better, because it had been done with a free hand. These lines drawn from memory somehow made up an original work of art, done in the style of Yeats. The one I had copied directly was a lifeless replica. It was then I realized that forgery had nothing to do with replication. It was an art form, a getting into the mind of an artist.

When I got back to the mews that evening, Monica was on the settee looking up the cinema listings in Bray. I glanced at my copy of the Jack Yeats and froze, then walked over to the sink to get a cup of buttermilk to hide my face behind and regain my composure. In the upper left corner of the page, she had added a tiny dot of ink. She may have thought it was invisible, but it may as well have been bright red for the way it drew in the eye. She had placed it in one of the best parts of the picture, where I had succeeded in getting the lines to curve and overlap without touching. Quite apart from her display of aesthetic ignorance was the other question of why she had done it, to which I had only one answer: she did not trust me. She wanted to make sure that I really kept the original, that I didn't give it back to my benefactress.

We saw the film <u>Born Free</u>.

Oh dear God in heaven, how I hated that film and that song. For weeks and weeks Monica hummed it over and over. Even now I can hear Matt Monroe sing "as free as the grass grows." When the lioness Elsa gets released into the wild, Monica wept. "What elsa were they going to do with her?" I said. Apparently that wasn't in the slightest bit funny.

Partly owing to the lack of contraception in Ireland then, partly to my own failure of nerve, Monica never stayed over. Usually a cause of regret, this night I was glad to be alone. I had been improving my forgery skills so rapidly that my copy now seemed to me to be a pathetic failure. My attempt at the artist's signature was not too bad. I had been practicing, and I had discovered for myself a trick. To forge someone's signature, all you need to do is turn it upside down and copy it that way.

My other elementary mistake had been to make a fresh drawing on a clean sheet of paper, and then try to age it. After my experiment with tea as an ageing agent, I arrived at the solution I was to use for the next few years (until I stopped using anything but original period paper), which was to smoke the sheets over burning green wood. Plane wood can also be used, if you can ever get the plane wood to burn, that is. To put some fox-marks on them to give the impression of the beginning of mold and decay, I had dampened both. On one, I sprinkled a little of the Maxwell House that Monica had bought, on the other I had scraped pieces of rust from one of the old nails sticking out from the walls of my mews. As I took them out now, I could see that the one treated with rust was developing naturally by itself and looked far more natural (though I later discovered that the process can be far too destructive and eat holes in the paper). I took this sheet, and treated it on the back with some glue, which would harden within a few days, giving another sign of authenticity should anyone choose to examine it later.

That night I sat up and copied out the pen and ink wash again, working quickly, getting a far better and far more natural flow to it. When I had finished, it was first light. I put down my pens, flexed my aching hand, sat back, and took off my socks, which smelled a bit. I then dabbed one over the drawing I had just done, very gently, making sure I only rubbed where the ink was dry. The effect was to cause almost invisible smudging and splits in some of the ink lines, as when a stripe of iron filings held in place by a magnet is very slightly pricked by one or two misaligned shavings. The result was almost perfection. My next task was to put Mrs. Heath's original back without Monica ever knowing. Better to run the risk of being caught than to steal from a woman who had treated me with nothing but kindness. Better to be a forger than a robber.

As it turned out, I had an opportunity to get back into the drawing room that morning when Mrs. Heath, in a fluttering panic, came across to tell me that there was some animal trapped in the chimney of her drawing room. I put a penknife, some glue, and a small screwdriver in my pocket and went up to the big house. When I got there, a filthy pigeon with no tail was lying in the hearth, flapping uselessly. Cleaned up, some of its wing feathers would be serviceable as quills.

I smashed the pigeon's head with the poker, then pulled the original Jack Yeats from under my shirt, and with great care replaced it in its frame, where I hope it has remained to this day.

*On the way down the garden, I crumpled up my first effort in my fist, threw it into the bin without looking at it. A few hours later, Monica was there, peering at my two fakes, her eye roving up to the ugly ink spot she had made.*

*"They are identical, Henry! Tell me which the original is."*

*"Guess."*

*She pointed artlessly to the one she had altered. This was supposed to be my big test. Her face was an agony of indecision. One part of her wanted me to nod, saying yes, that was the original, and thus confirm her suspicion that the whole world was as faithless as her. Another part of her wanted to believe in truth and people's better instincts. I felt embarrassed for her.*

*"No, no. That's my copy, Monica. This one here is the original."*

*She beamed at me, tears of trust filling her eyes, and said*

The doorbell went. Blume put the notebook on top of the refrigerator and went to answer.

Kristin was wearing a turquoise silk top with three buttons undone and a dark skirt that stopped just above her knees. Her hair was loose and seemed far longer and slightly redder than Blume remembered.

She came in, brushed his two cheeks with her own, then, touching his shoulder and very lightly propelling him forward, brought Blume face-to-face with a young man in his early thirties wearing strong fawn pants and a twill cotton shirt with a closed pocket on each breast. "This is Greg," said Kristin. "Greg, this is Alec."

# 16

"REALLY GOOD TO meet you, Alec," said Greg, taking Blume's hand. He shook it, squeezed it as he let go, and touched Blume on the elbow as he stepped into the living room. "Kristin has told me all about you. Wow. That's some story." His cheeks folded symmetrically when he smiled.

"What story?"

Kristin said, "The story of your life, Alec. Or bits of it."

"You told him that?"

"Just the relevant bits. How an American citizen ends up becoming an Italian police commissioner."

"Why?" said Blume. "Are you planning a how-to book? Step one, go to Italy; step two, get someone to shoot your parents . . ."

"Hey, Alec. Can I use your bathroom?" said Greg.

While Blume was considering this, Kristin gave Greg directions. Then she and Blume went to the kitchen, which still reeked of smoke.

"Who the fuh-" began Blume, but Greg was already back, his eyebrows wrinkled, a cute-quizzical look all over his face.

"Sorry," said Greg. "I got lost. I think I went into your bedroom, Alec."

"You didn't get lost," Kristin assured him. "The bedroom leads on to the bathroom. It's what you might call en suite."

"I don't like walking into other people's bedrooms," said Greg. "There isn't, like, another bathroom I could use?"

"No, there isn't," said Blume.

"Only one bathroom?"

"Does that bother you?" asked Blume.

"No, no, it's cool," said Greg and disappeared again.

The kitchen table was still set for two. Kristin added a placemat, then went to the silverware drawer.

"We only need spoons and bowls. It's chili con carne. The tacos burned."

"I was wondering about the smell," she said. "Can I close the window now?"

Blume shrugged. He blew out a red candle on the table. "That was supposed to get rid of the smell, but it didn't," he said. He filled a pitcher with tap water and put it in the middle of the table, and removed the silver candlestick.

Kristin sat down and Blume returned to the stove, turned off the flame under the chili, which was beginning to stick, and stirred it.

Greg returned, looked around the kitchen appreciatively, and took the chair opposite Kristin. "Alec, this is a really great little place you got yourself here. Hey, where are you going to sit? You want me to get you a chair? Just tell me where to go."

Blume opened his mouth to do so, but Kristin stood up. "I'll get Alec a chair from the living room."

"Thanks," said Blume. "I don't usually have this many visitors."

"I wonder why that might be," said Kristin as she passed him.

"Kristin was telling me you don't drink," said Greg. "I admire that."

Blume slapped the heavy serving spoon into the palm of his hand, enjoying its weight and potential. "It's not all that admirable."

"It says to me you know how to handle personal issues." Greg poured some water into a glass.

"Is that what it says to you?" Blume brought the pot over to the table and ladled out three servings.

Greg raised his glass. "Can I get some ice and lemon slices with this?"

"I don't know," said Blume. "But you're perfectly welcome to try."

Greg smiled and looked around as if for an interpreter.

"There, in the refrigerator," said Blume.

When Kristin came back with the chair, Greg had his head in the freezer and was saying, "How come you don't have ice?"

Kristin put the chair at the head of the table, went over to Greg, ushered him back to the table.

"I've got a lemon in the refrigerator," said Blume.

Kristin yanked at the refrigerator door until it opened with a reluctant sigh, and pulled out a wizened half lemon filled with blue mold, which she held aloft. "This the lemon?"

"Yup, that's him," said Blume.

The three of them sat down. Greg opposite Kristin, Blume at the head. Greg leaned over to pour some water into Kristin's glass and said something as he did so.

"No. First we eat, then we talk," said Kristin. "So what, we use spoons for this?"

"Seems the best way," said Blume. "It's a bit more watery than I usually make it."

He took a spoonful, blew on it, put it into his mouth. Salt, it definitely needed a touch more salt. It didn't need any more chili pepper, though. Definitely not. He could feel the back of his lips, the roof of his mouth reacting to the heat.

At first he loved the sensation of heat streaming down the back of his throat and from there into his sinuses. As he took a second spoonful, Blume realized that the intensity of the afterburn from the first was still sharpening. The inside of his lips began to numb, and the raw burning in his throat became acute. The sides of his tongue suddenly felt blistered and ragged, and his nose had begun to run freely. By now the trail of heat had wound its way down his esophagus and was attacking the top of his stomach. His intestines were already tightening and loosening and tightening again, trying at once to close off the incoming toxin and preparing to expel it as quickly as possible, explosively if necessary. His eyes were leaking and he started sucking in air in an effort to cool his mouth.

Blume reached for the water pitcher at exactly the same time as Greg, who was just a little quicker. With a reverse flick of his wrist, Blume slapped Greg's hand out of the way. He poured a glass and downed it without relinquishing hold of the pitcher, which he held hostage in his other hand off the table. He refilled and drank. It seemed only to aerate and intensify the capsaicin. Kristin had put her hands over her ears, pressed her thumbs against her chin, and appeared to be weeping. He passed her the pitcher and she drank the rest of the water. Greg had already gone over to the kitchen sink and was gulping back glassfuls of water, suddenly unmindful of the absence of ice. Blume's sinuses were streaming freely now, and a sweat had broken out all over his body. He got up from the table and walked quickly to his bedroom and the bathroom, where he splashed his face with water, wiped his nose, sat down on the toilet seat, and clutched his stomach.

Fifteen minutes later, he returned to the kitchen. Greg had his hand pressed against the side of his face like he had a toothache, and Kristin, whose face glistened, had untucked her blouse and opened another button.

"That was pretty intense, Alec," said Kristin.

"Eating bread is supposed to help," said Blume.

"So I've heard," said Kristin, "but you seem to have filled your bread box with bread-shaped rocks."

They left their plates abandoned on the kitchen table and went into the living room. Kristin took the sofa, Blume the armchair and Greg returned to the kitchen for the wooden chair. They sat there like three exhausted swimmers, dripping and breathing heavily for a while, until Kristin, straightening her back and doing up a blouse button, said, "Greg has been here three months. He's a legat, too, like me. He's attached to the cultural affairs section."

"Does he speak Italian?" said Blume, looking at Greg as he asked the question.

"My Italian was graded excellent," said Greg. "That's why they sent me. I also speak Spanish and French."

"As rare as a white fly, aren't you?" said Blume.

"Whatever that means. Look, Alec, eighteen months ago you agreed, as an American citizen, to leverage your particular competencies to contribute to the knowledge base of the embassy, correct?"

Blume looked over at Kristin, but got no sympathy.

"Alec, I was talking to you?" said Greg.

Blume picked up the remote control and turned on the TV where the studio guests were shouting as they watched a slo-mo replay of a disputed offside by Zlatan Ibrahimović.

"Alec, turn off the TV," said Kristin.

"No, wait a moment . . . I want to hear this. Jesus, Roma lost to Siena. Can you believe that? Siena!"

"Alec!" Kristin walked over and turned off the TV. "Come on, this isn't helping."

"Stop wasting my time, then," said Blume. "Let's talk about Colonel Farinelli. You're interested in him, or you and your boy wonder wouldn't be here."

Kristin laughed. "Alec, grow up. Greg has something to tell you. It concerns events that happened before he was born, but he's learned all the details."

"OK, Alec," said Greg. "I'm going to cut right to the chase if that's OK with you: the embassy fears embarrassment." He paused to see if this had any great effect on Blume, then continued: "It's all ancient history, so it's not that important, but it would be nice if Farinelli and this Treacy investigation did not mushroom, and open some old wounds."

"It's not the history that's ancient, it's you that's young," said Blume. "After Moro got killed, Cossiga took the reins of power, then handed over to Andreotti who shared with Craxi who passed it on to Berlusconi, and here we all are happy in the present again."

"That's pretty simplistic," said Greg. "And you left out a lot of prime ministers."

"Simplistic? I'll tell you what's simplistic . . ." began Blume, but Kristin intervened.

"OK, Greg, I'll take it from here," she said. "Alec, have you heard of Richard Gardner?"

"Wasn't he the American ambassador back then? I remember my parents got invited to a few opening nights when he was in charge."

"Right. He was ambassador from 1977 to 1981."

"During the Carter administration," said Greg.

"Thank you for that, Greg," said Blume. "What about him?"

"He wrote a book about his experience here, called *Mission Italy*. It came out a few years ago," said Kristin. "It's a pretty good book. Well written, elegant, polite, learned—a bit like Gardner himself."

"Well, that's nice," said Blume.

"Yes, it is. It reflects well on the embassy, and gives a lucid and straightforward account of US policy in Italy during the Moro kidnapping and murder."

"What was the policy?"

"To be helpful without getting too involved. Hands-off. Our Chief Security Officer, a guy called Arthur Brunetti, wrote a sort of bible on the Red Brigades and the Moro murder. The US administration sent over a guy called Steve Pieczenik, a hostage negotiator; see if he could help the Italian government by speaking with all sides. Turns out he couldn't, so he went home."

"Couldn't what, speak?"

"Maybe. I don't know. He spoke French, Russian. He spent fifty-five days in the company of Cossiga and a few Carabinieri."

"Including Farinelli?"

"Possibly."

"Is Pieczenik still alive?"

"Yes. He's over seventy now. You know Tom Clancy, the writer? Well, Pieczenik is his co-author. He co-writes all those Net Force and Op-Center thrillers."

"How do you spell Pieczenik?"

Kristin spelled out the name. "One of his books is about the Moro kidnapping," she said. "He couldn't get it published with a real publisher . . ."

"If he writes with Tom Clancy, but couldn't get this published, the only reason is someone stopped him."

"He couldn't find a mainstream publisher, so he self-published, and that should be enough to dispel your conspiracy ideas about some agency trying to suppress his revelations. His book is called *Terror Counter Terror*. And it may have lightly fictionalized versions of real people in it."

"This is just a can-of-worms situation?"

"Basically. We far prefer Gardner's and Brunetti's elegant narratives of those years to any other. If Farinelli gets back in the news and starts reminiscing about his days with the forgers Treacy and Chichiarelli, it might force us into a position where we have to issue damage limitation statements. We can do that, but we would prefer not to."

"No problem. I think Colonel Farinelli shares the embassy's opinion that the less said the better."

"As a matter of fact, he does. But a man died last night who may have written a draft of a book that talks about precisely those things the embassy, Farinelli, the government, and most of the opposition parties would prefer to forget about."

"How do you know this?" asked Blume.

"By funny coincidence, not long after you called about the Colonel, the Colonel called about you. He seems convinced you might have these writings in your possession. Do you?"

Greg decided it was his turn. "It's not like we want to suppress anything, we're not . . . Iran or China. But it would be nice if we could see what sort of stuff to expect."

"Prevention is better than cure, even for a minor chill," said Kristin.

"This could mean suppressing publication?" asked Blume.

"No way," said Greg. "That's just not us."

"Who says anyone would want to publish the ravings of a discredited art forger anyhow?" said Kristin. "By the way, it sounds to me like you do have them, Alec."

Blume stood up, went into the kitchen, opened the window, and leaned out, scanning the courtyard gate and the street three floors below. The blue car was still there.

He turned back from the window, picked the notebook off the refrigerator, and returned to his guests.

"Hey, Greg," he said pleasantly, "let me read you a bit from the notebooks, tell me what you think."

He located the passage on Moro he had seen earlier and read it out.

*"In May that year, the two American students J. had been talking to found a leather bag in the back of a taxi. It contained a Beretta pistol, an unopened packet of Muratti cigarettes, the brand that the assassinated Prime Minister used to smoke, eleven 7.65 bullets, the same number as were pumped into Moro's body, an ink-stained golf ball, a key ring and keys, a false driving license, camera flashcubes, a piece of paper, a packet of Paloma tissues, the same make stuffed into the bullet holes on Moro's body, and a map showing the Vigo lake area and several pages in code . . . The two students brought the bag to the Carabinieri barracks of Podogora, and were interviewed by Captain Farinelli. Farinelli never laughed, but even he must have smiled sardonically to see the evidence he and Tony had so carefully planted in the taxi come straight back to his own desk. If those American kids had only brought the evidence to another station, or better still, to the Polizia. Instead, it all came back like a boomerang, and suddenly everyone was suspicious of Farinelli. A lot of people suspected the two American kids were in on the plot, but they weren't."*

Greg looked stunned. "Eleven 7.65 bullets. The same number as were in Moro's body . . . it's all there!" He looked up at Kristin and said, "I don't get the bit about the golf ball, though."

Blume answered for him. "A golf ball from an electric typewriter, not one you hit."

"Oh shit, yeah. I knew that," said Greg.

"You can't be expected to remember everything you learn, Greg," said Blume. "Tell me, did you come here on your own, or were you accompanied by Kristin?"

Kristin arched her eyebrows at him.

"Is this like a jealousy thing?" asked Greg. "Because there's no way . . ."

"Yes or no?" said Blume.

"Of course I came in my own car. Kristin phoned and we agreed to meet here."

Blume held up his hand. "That's fine. That's all I needed to know. Well, that and your cell number."

"What d'you need it for?" Greg sounded worried.

"You'll see. You got mine?" Greg hesitated, and Blume said, "I see you have. Good. Call me."

Greg picked up his phone and a few seconds later Blume's rang in his pocket.

"OK. I'll save that number in a minute."

"Alec, please tell me what you're doing," said Kristin.

Blume pulled the notebook out of Greg's lap. "This is just one," he said. "The other two are in the study."

He went into his parents' study, hid Treacy's notebooks under the horsehair sofa. He pulled down three of his father's blank notebooks, dropped them into a plastic bag he found in the kitchen, and brought them into the living room. He gave Greg a flash of the contents of the bag.

"I don't want to have these anymore," he said. Greg began to pull them out of the bag to look, and Blume said, "No, seriously. I've had enough of this ancient history. As I'm sure you two already know, the Questore has taken me off the case. This is something that is useful for my country, I'm glad to be able to help. But those notebooks are also part of an inquiry I had begun, and—well, let's just say I'd like to see them again someday."

"We appreciate you doing this, Alec," said Greg. "It's very helpful."

"What are you playing at, Alec?" asked Kristin.

"I am being helpful. Is that so hard to understand?"

"Yes, actually. It is," said Kristin.

"Greg," said Blume. "I'm breaking Italian law here, but I'm sure the Colonel won't object if he knows they are in safe hands. But your hands must be safe. These notebooks cannot go missing, is that clear?"

"Sure, I'll look after this."

"No, Greg. I need a solemn promise from you. I want you to take these notebooks and put them in a safe place in the embassy. Right now. It can be your room, but it's got to be in the US Embassy. It's about the most guarded place in the city. Can you do that for me?"

Greg hesitated, sensing a trap but unable to see what it might be.

"As soon as you get there, you can read them, copy them, do what you need to do. But these originals—they have to stay safe. You understand that?"

"Why are you trusting me instead of Kristin? I understand you two are good friends."

"Exactly," said Blume, winking at the young man and lowering his voice. "So if I have to choose which one of you I want to stay here with me this evening . . ."

Greg grinned. "Yeah, I totally get that."

Blume stood close to him, pressing the plastic bag into his hand, urging him to leave. Greg looked for guidance to Kristin, who merely shrugged.

As soon as Greg had left, bag in hand, Kristin said, "I don't know what game you're playing."

"No game," said Blume absently. "Excuse me. That chili. I need to go to the bathroom again."

"I think I'll leave, too."

"At least wait till I'm finished in the bathroom before you do."

Kristin's nose wrinkled. "Do you have to be so explicit?"

"Forthright, you mean. Explicit would involve description . . . give me three minutes."

Blume locked the bathroom door, stood in the bath, opened the window, and peered out. He heard the squeak and clash of the front gate closing, and then Greg came into his line of vision on the sidewalk. Blume pulled out his phone and hit the redial button, then watched as Greg put the bag between his knees to search for his phone.

"It's me," he whispered when Greg answered. "Did I give you all three notebooks?"

He watched as Greg opened the bag, peered in, pulling one of the notebooks out a little.

"Yeah, I got three here."

"Cool," said Blume. "Maybe you should hand them in to the marines at the gate, you know?"

"I can handle it, Alec. It's my job."

"Great." Blume hung up and watched Greg tuck the volumes firmly into his armpit and disappear into the night.

He came out of the bathroom. Kristin had redone her buttons and was looking severely at him. "You're not being cooperative, Alec. It's written all over your face."

"Don't you want to stay?"

"I don't think so. I get the feeling you want me here as some sort of alibi. We can talk again another time. Thanks for the lovely dinner."

She left. Blume went over to his kitchen window, which afforded a more generous view of the street below. Greg was out of sight now. As he watched, Blume saw the blue car pull out of its place, its metallic sheen glinting briefly as it passed a streetlight. Three minutes later, Kristin appeared. She glanced up at the window and he waved.

She did not wave back.


Blume made himself a sweet espresso on the stove and heaped sugar into his small cup. He blew it cold, then gulped it down like a shot of bourbon and kept the cup tilted to allow the sugary sludge at the bottom to slide into his mouth. Then he phoned Greg again.

"Me again. Do they teach you countersurveillance?"

"What's this about?"

"Maybe you are being followed. I wouldn't go home until you're sure. Get the notebooks to the embassy. I'll call you back in five."

"Wait, I . . ."

Blume had a second coffee, with less sugar this time. Five minutes later he phoned again.

"Well?"

"You're right. I am definitely being followed. I don't think they are even trying to hide it."

"They probably are," said Blume. "It's just they're no good at it. Carabinieri. Can't get anything right."

"Is that who they are?"

"That's what I would guess. You had better make the trip from your car to the embassy gates as short as possible."

"I have a permit, I can drive right in," said Greg.

"Well, thank God for that," said Blume.

He opened the first notebook and began to read from where he had left off. Two hours later, he made another pot of coffee. It was not until six in the morning that he finally shut the second book.

# 17

BLUME SLEPT LIKE a baby for four hours. At ten, he went for a run in the park, already filling up with the Sunday crowds. He was still enjoying the ache and stretch of his leg muscles when he reached the station. Saturday nights were the busiest, late Sunday mornings were the quietest. Grattapaglia was standing by the coffee machine in the corridor, stirring sugar into the mini plastic cup that made coffee and everything else the machine dispensed taste like crude oil. Blume touched him on the elbow.

"You're doing the reports?"

"Yes."

"Glad to hear it. But things aren't looking good for you. A special investigator is being appointed tomorrow. He'll take a day or two to get started. You want to keep working right up to the suspension."

Grattapaglia nodded calmly.

Where was all this serene acceptance of the veteran yesterday morning, Blume wondered.

Blume went into his office, the reinvigorating effects of his run already fading. He was about to call Caterina to find out where she had got to with Treacy's notebooks, when the phone on his desk rang. It was the Questore, phoning from home, reminding him of the need to cooperate in the disciplinary action for the policeman who had assaulted the diplomat. Blume gave bland assurances and hung up not quite while his boss was still speaking, but almost.

Kristin phoned him on his cell.

That took longer than I thought, said Blume to himself. He had been expecting her call in the wee hours of the morning.

"I suppose you think that was a very clever thing to do?" she said as he answered.

"More than anything else, it was funny," said Blume, though he heard his own voice say the word "funny" in a flat and unapologetic tone. "When did Greg find out?"

"This morning. I'm the only one he's told, as you can imagine. He wants to kill you now."

"I'd enjoy seeing him try."

"I doubt you'd enjoy it really. Look, Alec, I need to know what you are doing. Not cooperating with the embassy is one thing. We're fine with that, up to a point. But actively working against us . . ."

"I wasn't. I'll cooperate with you. I just need a little time to look into them."

"This giving him blank notebooks was what, a practical joke?" asked Kristin. "*Uno scherzo da prete.*"

"Sure it was."

"What about Greg saying he was being followed and that you tipped him off. That was a joke, too?"

"You can't believe anything Greg tells you after that," said Blume.

"Did you use him as some sort of decoy?"

Blume's phone beeped in his ear to indicate another caller was trying to contact him. He took the phone from his ear and looked at the display. Another unknown number.

". . . waiting for an answer, Alec."

"Look, Kristin, I'll get back to you on this."

"I really think you should."

Whoever had been calling him had given up. His desk phone rang.

"Commissioner Blume." Farinelli's voice sounded softer on the phone, almost girlish. "In the office on a Sunday morning, and what recognition do we public servants get?"

"How can I help you, Colonel?"

"I thought you might be interested to get the autopsy report on Treacy."

"It's ready?"

"Not yet. Tomorrow, afternoon. We could look at it together over lunch. And before you ask: no, I have no idea what to expect in the report."

"Sounds fun, but I'm not sure I can make lunch."

"I am flexible with my mealtimes. Three o'clock is a good time for a snack. So is five. I'm sure you can make time during the working day. You are a commanding officer. Delegate, then call me to find out which restaurant."

"I'll see what I can do, Colonel."

After the call, Blume wandered around the offices, greeting the few people that were around, then decided he would be more productive at home. He chose three files on personnel management that he was supposed to comment on, and dropped them into his bag, knowing in his heart of hearts that they would stay there until he carried them back the following day. As he was about to leave his office, someone knocked on the door. He opened it himself, and was surprised to see Caterina standing there.

She came into his office and stood in the middle of the room, a little awkward all over again.

"Are you on duty today?" he asked.

"Yes. Half day."

"Ah."

"I wanted to ask you something about the case."

"Right. Actually, Caterina, the Treacy investigation is not a priority now. We have this new hit-and-run killing to handle first. Krishnamachari is the name of the victim. And his son. Attempted murder also of daughter. It shouldn't take long since there's no investigative work to speak of. Just liaising with the investigating magistrate, plea-bargaining with lawyers, running a check on phone records, alibis, trying to get others to come forward. We'll have to run this by the DIA, too, since extortion is automatically Mafia-related. But try not to mention the Treacy thing in front of people for now."

"I was mentioning it in front of you, not 'people,'" she said.

He noticed her face was pale, and her eyes so hollow and shadowed from tiredness that it looked like she had bruises. "Are you OK?"

Caterina went across the room and sat down heavily on a broken armchair that Blume had relegated to the corner. "I'm exhausted," she said. "I was reading the notebooks, and I have been thinking about Manuela and Pistoia. I want to ask you a favor. I was thinking of going to Pistoia tomorrow morning. Early. Just to settle this thing in my mind."

"No," said Blume. "We are permanently understaffed, we have the Krishnamachari case, the muggings, and Grattapaglia is going to be suspended. You should know better than to ask for special favors."

"I have the first half of the day off tomorrow."

"Lucky you. You don't want to waste it, then. Spend it with Elia. Look,

I'll make a few calls. We'll work out this mystery about Manuela's tax code."

"If you're going to make some calls, I'd prefer you got in contact with our colleagues in Pistoia to let them know I'm coming. No overtime claims, of course. I'll even pay the train ticket."

"No, keep the receipt. We'll find a way of reimbursing the cost even if . . . Well, we would if you were going, but you're not."

"I know you didn't read up on my background thoroughly, but did you at least read about my biggest success in Immigration Affairs three years ago?"

"The bust of the Croatian human-trafficking ring?" said Blume. "That was good police work. Good teamwork. Of course I read about it."

"Let me tell you how it started," said Caterina. "A team had been watching an apartment, not far from where I live, as it happened, hoping to establish a link between two Croats who lived there and an Albanian arms smuggler, but no contact was made. After three days, they were winding down the surveillance of the house as yielding no hard evidence. We had resigned ourselves to relying on phone interceptions, but they kept switching numbers and the magistrate was tired of issuing decrees to allow us to tap new SIM cards. I was off duty, a few streets from the apartment block they had been watching, on my way to pick up Elia. My eye was drawn to a silver-gray BMW. I can't remember the model, but it had that new look to it, the sort of patina that makes some people want to score it with a key.

"As I passed, I noticed, almost without looking, that the license plate at the back was slightly bent and covered in dead insects, and I walked on a few steps, but I had this feeling, like when something has been moved from where you put it. No, that's not right. It's more like a tiny shock of recognition, except you don't know what you've recognized."

"I know the feeling," said Blume.

"The dirty license plate, slightly bent at the edges, did not belong on a polished BMW. I'm sure you and many others would have spotted it immediately, but for me it was a revelation. A revelation that I might be suited to the job, that I had not fallen victim to the sort of stupidity that comes with hating your work. It was a good feeling. The plate was a DX registration, which corresponded with the age of the car more or less, but I went over and had a look. The edges of the plate were very slightly crumpled inwards, like dog-ears on a book. It's the sort of damage that small bumps, parking, and so on leave on your front license plate, but not on the back. Also, there was no corresponding damage to the bodywork. It looked like an old front license plate had been put on the back. I called in the number then and there. It turns out the plate was registered to a different vehicle belonging to someone in Turin, and that a replacement request, accompanied by a module reporting the theft of the originals, had just been made to the vehicle licensing authority. The surveillance team was there in half an hour, and, well, it was the Albanian. He was visiting the Croats just after the surveillance had been called off. It was the beginning of the takedown of the gang."

Blume nodded. "I get it. You've got some sort of similar feeling about Manuela and her identity and that tax code."

"I know it sounds silly . . ."

"No. You're dead right. It is what we do. The thing is . . ." He made a fist of his hand and knocked it slowly and repeatedly against his chin. "Let me think . . . You're off duty tomorrow morning, so it's not like . . . Look, don't bother mentioning your trip to people here. Just keep the whole notebook thing quiet for a few days, or until we have a bit more breathing space."

"Which means never."

"I don't want them to think I'm wasting personnel, and I've sort of been told not to pursue the Treacy investigation. But you are right to want to follow an instinct. I'll do as you ask. I'll call ahead to Pistoia. When shall I say you'll be there?"

"8:15 tomorrow morning. There's a train leaves Termini at 5:45."

"You've already checked the timetables, I see."

"Yes," said Caterina. She pulled out a printout from her bag. "Actually, I've already bought the ticket."

# 18

A FTER PHONING PISTOIA and telling them about Caterina's imminent arrival and being assured she would receive every courtesy, Blume returned home where he spent the next few hours reading Treacy's third volume, which evidently formed part of a textbook for artists that he was planning to write. Blume found it technical and rather dull, and was pleased to be able to set it aside as irrelevant. Taking notes, he worked his way through the first volume again until dinner. Then he boiled rice, over-salting the water, added oil and parmesan, and ate directly from the pot, as he began rereading the second volume.

Night stole up on him, and he realized he had been enjoying the work more than he had expected. He particularly enjoyed its potential for dis-comfiting the Colonel, John Nightingale and, he had to admit it, Kristin, Greg, and the rest of them at the embassy. Not that she or anyone there had any reason to worry about Treacy's ancient memories, but her job was to anticipate this sort of stuff, to brief and forewarn and minimize the pos-sibility that some journalist might someday ask an official an unexpected question. Fat chance. Investigative journalism had been dead for more than a decade. But giving Kristin the notebooks or even just some details of what was in them was a favor he could do for her, and he liked to be in a position to do her favors.

Before bed, he put Treacy's memoirs in the study, filling the small space left by the three empty notebooks he had given to Greg.

The Monday morning meeting on the Krishnamachari killing was at 10 o'clock in the conference room with its horseshoe-shaped arrangement of desks. When he arrived, there were already eight people in the room, including the magistrate assigned to the case. Blume chose a place in the midst of the ranks, a demotic touch that unsettled some of his superiors, yet failed to connect him to his men. He knew it wasn't working, but he had decided that the principle was sound, and so he stayed there, making the people around him uncomfortable. What he needed was someone like Paoloni to tell him to fuck off back to the top of the table where he belonged.

The meeting began. Inspector Rosario Panebianco stood up, touched his lips to indicate he wanted less noise before speaking. "It was not a hit-and-run accident. It was deliberate," he began. "The victim is . . . let me see how you say this name . . . Krishnamachari, an Indian national, had a store in a district where there is no real Indian community to turn to. An isolated place just off Via Pamphili on a dirty little street called Via Busiri Vici. He was on his own there all day. An easy target. He had two children to support. He came under pressure to pay a *pizzo* of ten percent of turnover, and reported it. This was last year."

Panebianco sat down and nodded at Investigating Magistrate Gestri.

Gestri wore the tense grimace of a man who was traveling fast on a motorbike toward some important fate. His hair was swept back, his chin pointed forward, his cheekbones high, the tendons on his neck stretched forward. He remained seated, one hand gripping the edge of the table.

"We have the files here," he said. He pointed to a short stack of file folders held together by red tape on the table. He clenched a yellow pencil in his teeth, took it out, and examined the bite marks. "Get them. That's essentially my only instruction here. This is a crystal clear, linear exercise. It requires almost no investigative work. I shall concentrate my energy on shattering the understanding between the culprits and those who allowed them to operate."

Gestri released the edge of the table, cracked his knuckles, glared at the papers like he wanted to set them on fire with his eyes, and said, "The extortionists are a repeat offender called Leo Leporelli and his monkey, Giacomo Scariglia. They went back to Krishnamachari, and kept going back, and Krishnamachari kept reporting them to us."

Panebianco stood up again. "Here we have the usual stuff," he said. "They superglued his locks, spray-painted the front, exploded three or four carton bombs at night, smashed the windows, followed Krishnamachari home, followed his wife. This wife has to go to a factory in Pomezia and uses the buses from EUR to get there. So Krishnamachari accompanies his two children on foot to school every morning, picks them up again in the afternoon. Sarjan is eight and Sabina five. This afternoon after school, they're crossing the road at the traffic lights just outside the school, daughter on one side, son on the other, a Pathfinder doing about 55 runs the light, plows into the three of them, continues on its way without slowing. Hundreds of people about, nobody got its registration. But we know who it was. We know this because one of Leporelli's friends reported his Pathfinder stolen a few days before."

"Like they wanted to taunt us," said Rospo from behind Blume.

Blume felt he had been among his men for long enough, and left his seat. He walked over to the table beside Panebianco, and addressed the room. "I don't think it is because they wanted to taunt us, I think it's because, like most criminals, they are morons. They probably think reporting a vehicle stolen covers them."

Panebianco slipped a report over the desk and Blume glanced at it. "Inspector Panebianco and Deputy Inspector La Magra arrived on the scene around thirty-five minutes after the incident." He looked at Panebianco. "Anything to add, Rosario?"

"Well, the son died on the road, twenty meters away from his father. He was still alive on the street when we got there. This is because the ambulance took a long time coming, then the crew spent some time trying to immobilize him, and then, in the end, trying to resuscitate him. He was alive and speaking. Usually the shock stops that, but not this time."

"What about the girl?"

"The daughter's critical. The hospital says she could suffer brain damage, but it's too early to say. They operated last night to relieve the pressure on the skull, but I don't know how it went."

Blume asked, "Is that it?"

"Yes," said Panebianco. "I can't think of anything else—regarding the scene."

"La Magra?"

The Deputy Inspector stood up. The year before La Magra had got married, and invited the whole department to the wedding. Blume happily contributed to the gift. Unsure about what the invitation was supposed to mean, he asked around the office. There was a lot of eye-rolling and shrugging, and muttering about not even knowing the guy. It seemed clear that no one was going, so Blume made a weak excuse and opted out. It was not until about a month later that he realized he was the only person in the department who had not been there. Since then, La Magra had started referring everything through others so as not to deal directly with Blume. He was doing it again now, his gaze fixed steadily on the magistrate who was squinting intensely ahead. But as he listened to the young man, Blume felt the words were intended for him.

"Yeah, well . . . I saw nothing . . . Nothing useful for the investigation. There weren't even skid marks to measure. The bastards didn't brake, they accelerated." He paused, and his gaze flickered toward Blume, who nodded encouragingly. He liked the young man, and kept meaning to congratulate him on getting married.

"A bit later," continued La Magra, "when the medics had given up and put sheets over the two bodies, the mortuary men went in with the body bags." He stopped as if to check that Blume was following the description in his mind's eye. "So, one of the medics goes over to retrieve the sheets from the bodies. He takes the sheet off the father, whose arms are stretched out so wide, one hand had been visible all the time. He pulls at the sheet, takes two corners, and one of the mortuary men comes over to help. He takes the opposite two corners of the sheet and, together, they fold it up. Then the medic goes over to the child, and he picks up the sheet covering him, gives it a quick shake, and snaps it likes this": La Magra mimed the action. "Then he folds it, tucks it under his arm."

La Magra attended to an itching above his eyebrow and shifted his gaze to a space behind Blume's right shoulder. "You see? That second sheet covering him, all it needed was one single fold."

Blume took out a pen and opened his notebook. He did not need to write anything, but La Magra needed a space in which to recompose himself without Blume scrutinizing his face.

"We know it was these guys?" said Blume, pen poised over the page. He glanced up to see Panebianco nod. "Right. Then we'll get the bastards. Like the magistrate said, we don't need too many detectives. You, me, Grattapaglia until . . . well, when Grattapaglia takes some leave of absence, maybe Inspector Mattiola can take his place."

When the meeting was over, Gestri reached over and tapped Blume on the arm.

"Can I have a word? In private?"

"Sure," said Blume. He clapped his hands loudly. "Come on, clear the room. I need to talk to Magistrate Gestri alone in here. Come on, come on!"

When the room was empty, he nodded to the magistrate. "OK, so what is it?"

"That wasn't exactly subtle."

"You mean you don't want anyone to know you're having a private word with me? You should have said."

"No, no. I suppose it's fine like this. I wanted to talk about tactics and explore the possibility of a shortcut. These two extortionists operated with the express consent of a Camorra gang in Ostia. They paid a fee. The gang won't be happy with what's happened, and to make it even less happy, I'm going after their commercial interests, or I'm going to make a big show of it. Can we put out the word that as soon as we have these two the pressure stops? Speed things up a bit. I've been asked to deal with this as fast as possible."

"Sounds like a good plan," said Blume. "But they could turn up dead."

"I don't prosecute corpses, so alive is best."

"OK. I'll see what I can do."

"Do you know someone who can get a message through to the Ostia gang? Preferably through unofficial channels."

"Yes," said Blume. "I do know somebody who's rather good at that sort of thing."

Blume headed back to his office, telling Panebianco to send Rospo in.

Ten minutes later, Rospo arrived, a fug of cigarette smoke coming off him.

"Have you finished your report on the mugging of the Chinese couple?"

"No."

"Why not?"

"I need to talk with Agente Di Ricci, who was on duty with me. He's nowhere to be found right now."

"Just do it. With or without Di Ricci. Meanwhile, I want you to find out if the preliminary autopsy report on Henry Treacy is ready, and if so, go get it. They won't send you a copy. You'll have to tap your vast reserves of charm."

The forehead creased in annoyance. "Which do I do first?"

Blume's phone began to buzz in his pocket. "Both," he said. "Now get out of here. I've got a call."

"Surely Largo Argentina is a handy lunch venue for you? A four-minute walk, and that's at my pace."

It was the Colonel. Blume drummed his fingers on the desk, and thought.

"I'll have Treacy's autopsy report with me by then," said the Colonel.

"I can see that whenever I want."

"True. But we have other arrangements to discuss. An autopsy report will make a difference."

Blume agreed to meet in two hours' time. He spent the next hour catching up on paperwork. He read a report on human resource efficiency mapping, and felt pleased to have got that done. A minute later, he realized he had not taken in a single word.

Shortly after midday, Panebianco knocked, entered, and told him Inspector Mattiola wanted to see him.

"Tell her to come straight in. She should always come straight in, damn it," said Blume.

Panebianco gave him a funny look and left, leaving the door open. Caterina came in and closed it behind her.

"So," said Blume. "How was Pistoia?"

"Great. The locals even sent a car to pick me up at the train station."

"That was a courteous touch," said Blume. "Well, enlighten me."

"I found Manuela's artist mother."

"Where?"

"Working unhappily and inartistically in a bank, Cassa Di Risparmio Di San Miniato SpA, to be precise."

"Exactly as her daughter told us yesterday in the gallery."

"Her daughter told us a pack of lies, but like any good liar, she based it on the truth," said Caterina with evident relish. She sat down in the armchair. "I had the local police take me to the bank, and the guard let me straight in. I had to wait for the manager in his office. He arrived at nine. I asked him if there was anyone called Chiara Angelini who worked in the bank. That's the name Manuela gave us. Chiara Angelini. He said no."

She paused for effect, so to humor her, Blume said, "Wrong bank?"

"No. Right bank, wrong name."

She paused again to let this sink in.

*151*

"Look, just get on with it," said Blume.

Caterina took her time in producing her notebook, and then appeared to have difficulty in finding the right spot. Blume swallowed a sigh, which made his ears pop. Finally, when she judged she had made him wait long enough, she continued:

"The bank manager said he was sure there was no one by that name, and since there were only twenty members of staff and he had been working there for ten years . . . So I asked him to pass round a quiet word that I had come up from Rome as part of an investigation, details of which I could not divulge, but that a girl called Manuela Ludovisi was in serious trouble. He went out and whispered this to the three members of staff there, and five minutes later, Manuela's distraught mother, who is not called Chiara Angelini but rather Angela Solazzi, was sitting in front of me in the manager's office, begging me for information and reassurance."

"So Manuela Ludovisi's mother is called Angela Solazzi," said Blume. "Angelini—Angela. Always good to keep a pseudonym close to the original. I suppose this means Manuela Ludovisi is not really called Manuela Ludovisi, and you were right all along?"

"Yes, I was right. The girl's real name is Emma."

"Emma . . . Manuela, another close match. Emma what?"

"Emma Solazzi. She kept her mother's name after all. But the part about her father being gone seems to be true."

"Solazzi and Ludovisi aren't particularly similar."

"True," said Caterina. "Not that it matters any more given what I found out this morning. I was right about the accent. Angela Solazzi and her daughter Emma moved to Pistoia just a few years ago. Before that, she and Emma, who you still think of as Manuela, lived in a villa near Nettuno. Oh, and the mother says her daughter hates Pistoia, and wanted to move back to near Rome as soon as she could."

"Why all these pointless lies?"

"That's what I wanted to know," said Caterina. "We left the bank—that was her idea and the manager was so relieved to see me go he didn't seem to mind—and went to a park bench, but she began to clam up and become unhelpful. I had to apply pressure."

"What sort of pressure?"

"It's not something I feel good about. In fact, I still feel a bit sick. I scared her about her daughter, as if something bad had happened. She kept asking me for reassurance, and I wouldn't give her anything until I was sure she had told me as much as she could."

"That's a perfectly good strategic ploy," said Blume. "It's legal, too."

"It wasn't moral. And I was using the image of Elia in my own mind to make it more real, so she could see anxiety in me, too. I should have found a better way. But I was in danger of missing the train back, and I needed to work quickly."

"Deadlines make creative geniuses of us all," said Blume.

"She knew Emma had taken up a false identity in Rome for the purposes of getting a job in a gallery. So then I asked her why her daughter would do that, and she wouldn't say. I asked if Emma has a criminal record of some sort, and she got all indignant and righteous, so I told her Emma was about to get a criminal record for giving false testimony to a public official, for possession of false documents, pursuant to Articles 476–80 of the criminal code and all that stuff, which kept her worrying. Then she tells me she was against the idea from the start, because it was always going to lead to trouble. At this point, she suggested we have a drink, though it was not even ten in the morning."

"Sounds like she was nervous," said Blume.

"I think it would not be the first time she had had a morning drink. She must have been very good-looking once, like her daughter, and she's still good-looking now, but slightly bloated, and her eyes have the watery-lazy look that you see in drinkers. We had cappuccinos instead. All she would say was that Emma needed a different identity to work at the gallery. It was never meant to fool public officials, or even the tax authorities, or so she said, and that was more or less it. Except I did miss the train."

Blume looked at his phone clock. "You got back quickly enough."

"The Pistoia police drove me all the way to Florence, saw me on board the Eurostar. They were great."

"Glad to hear it," said Blume. "I'm not sure what it tells us, but it's interesting. Your instinct was right. I apologize for almost getting in your way."

"But I haven't told you the best bit, yet."

"You're enjoying this, aren't you?" said Blume, and she really was. He had never seen her so happy, seen a smile light up her features quite like this.

"I was leaving some coins on the table to pay for my share of the coffees," said Caterina, "and Angela was sort of looking into the middle distance when I had an illumination, or an insight or whatever you want to call it."

"When I hear what it is, I'll decide what to call it," said Blume.

"I said, off the cuff, that we knew John Nightingale was Emma's father. She went deathly pale. Then she asked how I knew."

Caterina stretched out her legs and leaned back, plainly enjoying both the memory and Blume's expression of surprise.

"That was a damned good question," said Blume. "How did you know?"

"I didn't. But the reason I guessed is from another thing that I think will interest you. On the train up, I was leafing through the photocopy of Treacy's notes looking for a mention of Nightingale and the Colonel together, and I found one. And it makes sense that both Nightingale and the Colonel would be anxious to stop Treacy from publishing, if only for this part of his writings."

"You read this bit on the train?" said Blume.

"Yes."

"I have read through the notebooks twice," said Blume. "What's the passage you are referring to?"

"Basically, it's where Nightingale and the Colonel sold forged paintings to a Cosa Nostra boss in Trapani," she said.

"That's toward the beginning of the second volume," he said. "Do you have the photocopy with you now?"

"Yes." Caterina bounced out of her chair and came back a minute later holding the photocopies.

Blume glared at her. "Where were they?"

Caterina's step faltered. "In my desk. Locked."

"You brought them here?"

She nodded.

"And you just said you had them on the train, too. What if you had forgotten them there? What if Panebianco or Rospo or someone had found them in your desk?"

"They were locked in a drawer."

"Fuck it. That's not good enough, Caterina. I asked you to be extra careful."

"So where are the originals, Commissioner?"

"In a safe place," said Blume.

"Here?"

Blume hesitated.

"Or maybe somewhere in your apartment? So which one of us is physically guarding them. Actively looking after the documents? You or me?"

"Sorry," said Blume. "It's more the idea of them being on your desk out there than anything else."

"In my desk, not on it. There's a difference." Caterina sat down again, her face creased. She seemed ten years older than a minute ago. "You could have said thank you for what I achieved this morning. Maybe not thank you, even though you and I both know this is now your private little investigation. How about a 'Well done, Caterina,' something along those lines?"

Blume held up his hands in an exaggerated gesture of surrender. "Sometimes I'm not so good with people. It's something I can't seem to do much about."

"Then you're not a good commander."

In the silence that followed, the loudest noise was the sound of the scratch of Blume's pen as he amended something on his notepad. Caterina sat mutely listening to the heavy slowness of Blume's breath, punctuated by a strange sound that seemed to come from far away but, she realized, was coming from him. He was humming broken bars of some song very softly and intermittently to himself, apparently without being aware of what he was doing. She realized she could look up, since he was bent down, attending to his work. Her photocopy sat unopened on his table.

After a while, she said, "Do you at least want me to show you the piece I am referring to?"

"Well, just to be sure."

She opened the section, which she had marked with a Post-it note.

"The Trapani deal with the Colonel. What made you associate this with Nightingale's being Manuela's father?"

"Emma, not Manuela," corrected Caterina. "The girl's real name is Emma."

"Right."

"My own fears."

"Of?"

"That some criminal event will break into my private life. I often wonder what I would do. And I was also thinking of Emma's generous pay, the apartment, her confident manner. I'd like to see Nightingale."

"I forgot, you didn't meet him the other day."

"No. In fact, I wanted to ask you what he looks like and the color of his eyes."

"Bald. Gray . . . pink. I have no idea. Who notices these things?"

"Emma has blue eyes, fair skin, fair hair," said Caterina. "She looks more northern European than Italian, really. Her mother, Angela, has dark hair, graying now, dark-brown hair, huge brown eyes, and sallow skin. They don't look alike at all. But it's not just that. If Nightingale really did feel under threat from Cosa Nostra, it makes sense for him to hide his daughter's identity. It's what I would do if I knew how. Nightingale does know how. He invents histories. So when I got confirmation that Emma's history was partly made-up, it made me think of him. He creates provenances for works of art. Emma is his work of art. Fear of proxy reprisal seemed an excellent reason for hiding her identity."

"If he was anxious to hide her identity, it doesn't make sense to have her working with him," said Blume. "That puts her right back in danger."

"I know. I thought about that later. But it keeps her close, too."

"So we have Nightingale, Angela, and their daughter Emma," Blume traced an imaginary triangle on his desk. "Mother, father, daughter. You know, more than anything else, it looks to me like some sort of plot to exclude Treacy. So Nightingale did not like or trust Treacy enough to reveal the existence of his daughter."

"Which raises an interesting possibility," said Caterina. "By inviting his daughter to work in the Galleria Orpiment, Nightingale was making a fool of his partner. Or imagine a very pretty woman arrives in the gallery, maybe Treacy thinks he can make a move on her, ignore the gulf of years. She tells her father, or maybe Nightingale sees it happening, gets very angry, confronts his partner, they argue, or he hires someone, or he just comes up behind him at night, flattens him with an iron bar."

"It was an inspired deduction," said Blume.

"A lucky guess. If I had thought about it more, I might have discounted it again."

"It makes Treacy a bit of a bastard for putting them in danger by writing about how they defrauded the Mafia."

"I agree," said Caterina. "I don't think I'd have liked Treacy all that much."

# 19

I am not a thief. It is not part of my identity. I made that choice the day I returned the Jack Yeats to Mrs. Heath. But like any sensible person, I will cave in to pressure.

Nightingale made a couple of stupid moves with some big dealers, and we suddenly found ourselves in trouble with Lieutenant Farinelli who, for the first time, had some real leverage in the form of witnesses and proof of false provenance. Farinelli had contacts up and down the hierarchies of crime, politics, and even the military, which in those days hovered over everything in Italy like a thin mist, best visible from a distance, hard to notice, but still limiting when you were in the middle of it. Farinelli was there in 1969 when the Carabinieri formed the "Unit for the Protection of Artistic Heritage," and was an officer in 1971 when the unit became a fully independent division. Independent as in Farinelli's fiefdom, until, in one of those obscure maneuvers that no one, not even the participants, ever properly understands, a challenge was mounted to his authority. The challenge came from outside, in 1983, when a series of de Chirico works were stolen from the home of Angelica Savinio, the artist's niece, a person I am proud to call my friend.

Giorgio de Chirico, as it happens, had been something of a hero of mine. Not only did he share my belief that the only true art is an imitation of past art, he even liked to put false dates on his works. Sometimes he signed paintings that imitated his style. He forged himself. He encouraged me, was kind to me, and was a man of great integrity.

When the Carabinieri unit arrived to investigate the theft, Farinelli made his usual recommendation, which was to keep the whole thing as quiet as possible. Angelica Savinio was told that the best way to get her paintings back was simply to wait. Then, with any luck, when the thieves made a false move or tried to sell the paintings, Farinelli and his team would pounce.

Then he told her that a lot of stolen art was recovered by means of negotiation.

It was a sort of plea-bargaining system, he explained. The system was to catch one of the dealers trying to fence a stolen work, find out from him about other works, and if he cooperated, not press charges. Maybe he would even be allowed to pass on some small stuff in exchange for the Carabinieri getting the big items. Angelica told me the more Farinelli spoke, the more it seemed her uncle's works were being held to ransom. To get back what was hers, Farinelli seemed to be demanding a kickback.

So she agreed to all he said, then went and did the exact opposite. She went straight to the press. She told everyone. Every newspaper, every TV station. She even called in the foreign press. Her husband spoke English and talked to the British and American newspapers. She kept this publicity campaign going and going, reasoning that de Chirico was so famous that his paintings would be unsalable once word was out that they had been stolen. And she was right. They never got to the market.

This act of defiance was a catalyst, or a signal of something, for Farinelli's power finally began to ebb. First, he got a sideways transfer to headquarters in Piazza Sant'Ignazio, removing him from direct access to some of the recovered works of art and reducing his interaction with the criminal underground. He did not lose much power, and it was only the beginning of the end. But he recognized it as such, and it was in the middle of Savinio's press campaign that he visited me.

Having arm-twisted some pusillanimous magistrate into accusing me of being involved in art theft, he arrived with a warrant to search my home, which he did with more brutality than efficiency, ripping my signed works from the walls, overturning furniture, emptying drawers without even looking at the contents, opening my food press, and sweeping his arm across the bottles, sending them all crashing to the floor. I am pleased to say I remained impassive throughout. Then he started destroying the tools of my trade and I began to lose equanimity. Finally, he took out a paring knife to slash the work on my easel, something on which I had been working for a considerable time, and of which I was not only proud, but extremely fond. The work in question was a restoration of a religious painting by Bassano which had been stolen decades ago and then cut up into smaller pieces, each of which had been sold separately to crooked dealers. With Nightingale's approval and assistance, I had acquired three, perfectly legally, and was completing the missing fourth. The deal was that we would either sell the newly united and completed work (we had not decided whether the missing piece was to be attributed to me or not) or, once I had finished my project, the work would be redivided and sold onwards at a profit.

*So when I saw this overweight, swaggering bully approach my work with a knife, I hurled myself upon him. It was all planned of course, and I was soon hauled off and kicked half senseless by three of his men, but not before I managed to land two very rapid punches to his pudgy face, one of which had produced a satisfying crack from his nose. Evidently he had underestimated my speed.*

*I spent four weeks in Rebibbia, the scariest four weeks of my life. I was charged with resisting arrest, outrage against a public official, and some other minor charges. I sat there waiting for the charges of forgery, fraud, deception, illegal export, and so forth to be brought, and was expecting to be brought face-to-face with Nightingale any moment. Instead, to my amazement, the PM then charged me with possession of illegal substances and dangerous chemicals with the intent to cause injury. I was remanded again on charges relating to bomb-making and terrorism. Looked at in a certain way, said Farinelli, the kerosene, petrol, oils, chemicals, boilers, gas canisters, bleaches, the bottles of nitrocellulose, white spirit, and the plant fertilizers outside, the tins, pots, and cans in my house—they all pointed to one conclusion only. "It's a miracle that cottage of yours has not self-combusted," said Farinelli. I fully expected to go back to Rebibbia. At least if I declared myself a political prisoner, I might gain some respect and protection.*

*Instead I was led out into a small room with* <u>compensato</u> *on the walls. A room from which not much noise could escape. My hands were handcuffed behind a chair and Farinelli came in. I looked in vain for a sign of the black eye or bent nose from my fists, but his face showed no sign of injury. He took out the same sharp little peeling knife with which he had attacked my painting, watching me all the time, smiling. Then he dug his hand into his pocket, and pulled out a peach. He skinned it, then cut off a slim disk, and popped it in his mouth.*

*When he had finished, he said "sticky," and walked out, leaving the wet peelings on the table.*

*A few minutes later he was back.*

*Speaking in a murmur, and nodding as if we had already made a covenant, he told me he could get me out of here immediately, and I did not doubt it for one moment.*

*"I have a proposal that I think will resolve our problems."*

*"Do I have a choice?"*

*"Of course you do. Humans always have a choice."*

*"If I agree, how much longer do I spend in detention?"*

*"The time it takes me to walk behind you and take off your handcuffs."*

*"Does it involve my artistic skills?"*

He nodded.

"Does anyone get hurt?"

"Definitely not."

I agreed.

Farinelli brought me straight back to my place. Leaning against the wall of my living room, plastic wrapped and protected by one of my own bed sheets, were eight plywood packing cases containing as many paintings carefully attached to backboards with foam cushioning. He explained that the works were by de Chirico and Guttuso and I was to copy all eight.

I protested of course, saying I never did direct copies of living artists. Instead of threatening me with jail again, he spoke encouragingly of the proceeds we would reap. But I understood that his motivation was revenge, pure and simple.

He gave me two months.

Colonel Farinelli, as you now are, I don't know if you will be reading this someday. If you are, did you really think marking the backs of each original canvas with a matrix of pinprick points and the dots visible under UV light would escape my notice? You clearly had no idea of the care I invested in my work. Before even considering the painting itself, I examined everything about the canvas, its translucence and sizing, the gesso and the warp and weft of the fibers, the ridges and pits and imperfections and strains. You were no cleverer than Monica and her ignorant blob of ink. One of the very first things I did was to close the shutters of the room and examine the works with a tube of UV light. All it takes is a single purple dot shining in the darkness, and it is clear the canvas has been marked. And Guttuso, Colonel? Do you think I had no moral compass? An artist dedicated to resisting the fascists, the Mafia, and people like you.

I was into the second month on my unwanted commission, splashed with Indian ink as I struggled to imitate the sexy curves of all those thighs in <u>Swimming Party</u>, when it struck me with total clarity that you intended to complete your revenge on Savinio, de Chirico, and Guttuso by selling to exactly the sort of buyer Guttuso despised. I warned John Nightingale about it, and all he did was wave his hands about like a pansy and deny it.

Then, to make your revenge complete, you decided to bring us along to the meeting, all in a hotel room on Via del Tritone, and force us to watch the surrender of the paintings to the Mafia and make sure we were as compromised and hostage to fortune as you. A Sicilian-Canadian Mafia boss. Until that meeting I didn't even know Canada had a Mafia.

Nightingale's job was to give the authenticity and provenance lecture which he delivered like an adolescent with a squeaky voice, as the Colonel watched smiling like a teacher proud of a gifted queer student. The buyer sat there in yellow sunglasses in a room with three other men, and nodded each time a painting was pulled out.

Then suddenly the Colonel introduces me as a leading dealer and expert. He tells the men I am about to show them how to spot a fake, and demonstrate, almost incidentally, why these paintings were originals. I spouted nonsense about craqueleture on old paintings, which had nothing to do with these modern acrylic and ink works, then about technical flaws, cracking in supports, watermarks, and so on, and talked a lot about complementary colors, the importance of light. I got into a sort of riff on de Chirico's use of magic shadow when I happened to glance up and see these two tinted glasses looking straight at me, and I heard myself saying that if he was properly interested in seeing what I was telling him, he needed to take off the fucking yellow glasses.

The room froze. Farinelli's soft fat smirk seemed to turn to marble. The only person still moving in the room was me.

Then the boss lifts the glasses to let me look at his eyes for a moment, then, thankfully, puts them on again, and says, "_Tutt'è bbonu e binirittu. Bel quàtru questo, Prufissùri._ When I take off my glasses, I can't see properly. They are adjusted for sight, do you understand?"

Then he waves his hand around the room at the other guys standing there, and adds, "I've spent my whole life hiding my weaknesses, now they know I can't see properly."

It was not much of a witticism, but everyone laughed, even me, I'm sorry to admit. Then he asked me if I would give him a solemn pledge that the works were authentic. I gave him a solemn pledge, and he put his arm around me again, told me not to worry, that my services had been much appreciated, that he had forgotten all about the glasses incident. The only reason you and your friends here would have to worry, Prufissùri, was if these turned out not to be the originals. But I don't imagine you just stood here for an hour making a joke of a man like me in front of his men.

They took out a suitcase full of used bills, mostly 20,000–lira notes. Then they stood there making sure Nightingale and I got as much as the Colonel, which I had not been expecting, and we were sent our separate ways. Nightingale never mentioned it to me again, and the Colonel never came to claim back the share I got.

*Oh, I almost forgot the proof that they were not originals.*

*Measure the shadow cast by the cube in the foreground of the de Chirico. It will be precisely 2.84 cm, which is 2 mm longer than the original. I'll leave the fun of finding the extra shadow lengths in the other de Chirico works. In each case, I have added between 1 and 2 mm.*

*As for the Guttuso, I sort of drew my inspiration from Monica with her little extra dot, but more than that, I drew my inspiration from Farinelli himself. Shine a bright light on the front of the painting, I recommend using a halogen or a projector lamp. See those tiny pinpricks of light coming out the back? Join them up with a pencil top left, middle, bottom, a bar across, then another tiny point of light. Continue, until you see my initials HT. I like the wordplay. Pinpricks for Mafia pricks. As for the Guttusos, they're back with their rightful owners. Farinelli, Nightingale, and I knowingly sold the Mafia eight fakes. Personally, I feel good about it.*

# 20

"I T'S AN INTERESTING concept, and one that I would never have sub-
scribed to but I am glad they persuaded me," said the Colonel. "Red
currants in what is essentially a carbonara sauce. It ought not to work, and yet,
and yet. The tang of the fruits offsets the smokiness of the bacon and the
creaminess of the egg and parmesan. If I have any complaints it was that it was
too little." He swiped a piece of bread across the center of his plate, leaving a
clean white track, then pulled out a sheaf of papers from a briefcase set on the
empty chair beside him. "Here. It's the preliminary autopsy report."

Blume set aside his glass of water and took the papers.

"You don't need to read it," said the Colonel, placing a piece of pink
bread in his mouth with one hand and reaching into the bread basket with
the other. "It concludes that it cannot be shown that Treacy was deliberately killed, and comes down on the side of unlikely. The death was probably accidental. No murder, which should get rid of any lingering doubts
you had about this being a matter for your squad. The magistrate's not
interested in any murder inquiry. You know Buoncompagno has a personal
backlog of eight hundred and twenty-three cases?"

As the Colonel sponged up more sauce from his plate, Blume scanned
the report.

*Alcohol intoxication is determined to have impaired muscular reflexes and
increased the vulnerability of the brain stem to concussive trauma ... Stretching
of vital nerve cells caused apnea, which is determined as cause of death (see ...*

"Can I offer you some mature ricotta?" asked the Colonel. Blume
shook his head and waved the report at him without looking up.

"To eat alone is to lead the life of a wolf," said the Colonel. "I wish you
would keep me company."

"Uh-huh," said Blume, reading and not really listening. So far the pathologist had not made any arguments against a possible violent attack.

*The examination revealed clear signs of a contercoup type of contusion with damage being concentrated in the frontal and temporal poles, diametrically opposite the impact point in a manner consistent with a backwards fall. The severe lacerations strongly suggest negative suction pressures and contercoup force, increasing the possibility of the injuries described in the foregoing as having being caused by a fall rather than a coup or blow.*

"Its conclusions are not binding and it leaves open plenty of possibilities," said Blume.

The Colonel tipped half a glass of red wine into his mouth. "Did you look at those ethanol readings? It is a miracle he was able to walk at all. His medical records show that he had liver cancer, heart disease, and had already suffered two strokes. His colon wasn't in great shape either. According to this, it was unlikely that he was struck on the head by any blunt object. We are verging on a death by natural causes, though an open verdict is probably the best way to go here. We shall see. Maybe a guilty party will emerge from the woodwork. By the way, you can keep that, it's a copy. One should always make copies of important documents."

Blume drummed his fingers on the table. Apart from one table where two ministerial bag-carriers in bright white shirts and bright silk ties were finishing up, the only people left from the lunchtime crowd were himself and the Colonel. The waiter-owner was in the kitchen talking to the cook.

"It was the wife who made this," said the Colonel.

"Whose wife?"

"Vito's wife in the kitchen. She also made the strozzapreti with giant shrimp and baked ham." The Colonel opened the briefcase beside him. "Now—are you going to keep that report?"

"Yes. I may as well."

The Colonel said, "By the way, a funny thing happened during the autopsy. You go to autopsies?"

"Not as often as I would like," said Blume.

"Personally, I don't mind them. But Buoncompagno. You'd think after all these years as a magistrate he'd be used to it. Anyhow, we get there, and Buoncompagno starts cursing saying he'd forgotten to bring his jar of

Vicks. He tells me he rubs some under his nose to keep the bad smells at bay. Well, as it happens, I have a small tube of camphor ointment I use for my back, so I kindly offered him some. But I neglected to mention how strong it was. This stuff goes right into the muscle. You should have seen Buoncompagno, standing there, eyes flaming red, streaming tears, blowing his nose, the pathologist asking him if—get this—if, if Treacy had been his friend!"

The Colonel's own face was streaming with tears of laughter as he remembered this.

"And the more he rubbed his face, the more it burned. In the end he had to leave." The Colonel began to calm down. "Well, you had to be there, I suppose. But you'd have enjoyed it. I know what you think of Buoncompagno, of course. And you're right. A clown of a man. A weathervane."

He peered into his open briefcase, and said, "Enough. I have already been in contact with some people, and I think we can get a good sum for those seven drawings and two paintings. I think that if we stagger the sales of the paintings we found in his apartment over, say, two years, we can earn three hundred thousand. That's net. The gross will be closer to four hundred and fifty, but then there are the expenses and commissions and the cost of putting clear blue water between ourselves and the sale. Split fifty-fifty gives you one hundred and fifty thousand, payable over two years, that's a bonus of seventy-five thousand this year, same again next. How does that sound?"

"Appetizing," said Blume, and sipped his water.

"You'll see. Once you get into the spending bit, you'll love it. Do you need any help in setting up a bank account? I know someone who operates out of Lugano. You know that thing about the Swiss not paying interest on deposits? Not true. Well, technically it is true, but the bank will open a money market fund for you, which is like having interest on the deposits. We can talk about that later. First income within two months, so you need to set up the account soon. Have you got around twenty-five thousand to open an account?"

"No."

"Never mind. Call this guy." Farinelli gave Blume a business card. "Get the account open soon. We don't want the money to enter Italy at any point."

"Great," said Blume. He pocketed the card.

"Oh, wait. I think I gave you the wrong card. What's the name on that?"

Blume pulled out the card and read it: "Claudio Neri, *Dottore commercialista.*"

"No, that's the right one," said the Colonel. "He's the man you want. This works on the basis of trust, Commissioner. Which is why I am feeling very worried about what happened to Treacy's manuscript. In the form of several notebooks, I believe."

Blume widened his eyes as if in surprise.

"I specifically asked you to give them to me. I presumed you would have them photocopied and read them at your leisure, and it was never my intention to deprive you of that pleasure. But you removed them and said nothing, then tried to hide them from me. Why would you do that?"

Blume considered denial, but it suddenly seemed like so much time-wasting.

"If we are working on a relationship of trust, why did you have me tailed last night?"

"That was after." The Colonel reached over to the next table, and lifted the menu.

"After what?"

"After you lied to me, and after I had Treacy's place taken apart by a team. He was writing a book. I know this. The manuscript is not there. You were in there before me and now you have been seen with manuscripts."

"Maybe these notebooks or manuscripts or whatever they are don't exist except in your mind."

"You handed them over to a functionary from the US Embassy, which was a bad move and narrows my options. I am presuming you copied them first."

"Let me give you another thought to turn over in your mind as you choose dessert. Your men never saw the notebooks in my possession. All they saw was a functionary from the embassy with what seemed like note-books leave my house and head straight for the embassy."

"Am I supposed to think a US government employee agreed to run a decoy for you?"

"Keep your mind open to the possibility, Colonel. The Americans may or may not have Treacy's notebooks. It's fun to keep you guessing."

An apple-shaped man with glossy cheeks approached the table, and the Colonel waved him away impatiently. "Not now, Vito. Thanks to the Commissioner here I have completely lost my appetite. Just bring me a coffee, a vinsanto, and a few cantuccio biscuits."

To Blume he said, "What's your game, here? You want a bigger cut, is that it?"

"Maybe," said Blume. "Remind me why the notebooks are so important."

"Have you read them?"

"Yes. They are interesting. They'll make a good book, someday."

"I told you," said the Colonel. "Treacy is liable to have made discomforting allegations regarding the years 1978 to 1982. It would be useful for me to see these. It's old politics, and no one's very interested any more, but it's still my job to deal with these things, just as younger people than me are dealing with more current matters of national security."

Blume nodded as if in approval. "Exactly. And that is almost word for word the argument put forward by the US Embassy. Old stuff, no one cares but it would be nice not to give it a new airing. Now, as far as I can make out, you and the US Embassy have always been on the same side. Broadly speaking."

The Colonel stared across the table. "Yes, we have. They will be pleased to see the manuscript go unpublished. Meanwhile, there may be some other details that affect me personally that I should like to know about. Perhaps you have already come across them?"

"I couldn't say. Unless you are referring to the Mafia, or the Moro kidnapping, or, let me see . . . actually, you do crop up a lot."

The Colonel's coffee, fortified wine, and almond biscuits arrived. He ripped open two sachets of sugar and poured them into the cup, stirred, and said, "A redacted version. That's what you are planning on giving me." He inserted a biscuit sideways into his mouth. "Sun Tzu tells us that the converted spy must be treated with the utmost liberality," he said. "I thought that's what I was doing with you. But you're not converted, are you? I'll give you seventy percent of what we get from the sale of Treacy's paintings."

"I am not a spy either," said Blume.

"No, maybe not. And another thing, I think you accepted my art deal too readily. If you were that venal, I'd have heard about it. So all I can think is that you are trying to double-cross me."

"On whose behalf?" asked Blume.

"That's the part I can't figure out," said the Colonel, licking his glistening thumb. "*Cui bono?*"

"Maybe I am working for the good of the State," said Blume.

The Colonel laughed good-naturedly. "I don't mind this standoff with you. It's rejuvenating. But let's not make it last any longer than it has to."

"The paintings taken from Treacy's place—where are they now?"

"Merely to demonstrate goodwill, I can tell you they are in storage at the Carabiniere Art Forgery and Heritage Division. As safe as possible. All mixed up with stuff from the gallery and items of evidence necessary for the investigations. A logistical nightmare. It's impossible to keep track of these things. The place is run by kids with computers now. They're no match for the old guard. It's as if I had them in my hand."

Blume stood up. "Thanks for lunch, by the way."

Ten minutes later, Blume was leaning against a bollard next to Bernini's sculpted elephant and thinking about the Colonel and Treacy. The blood, urine, and bile ethanol readings in the autopsy report were that of a serious drunk. Treacy's liver was an inflamed wedge of fat permeated with cytokines. The ethanol reading for his vitreous humor confirmed the rest. He was literally drunk up to the eyeballs.

A group of Japanese tourists gathered around him, pulled out several-thousand-euros' worth of high-tech equipment, and began to photograph the stone elephant.

Blume stood up, immortalizing himself in a dozen Japanese home videos, and walked the 200 meters to his station at Collegio Romano.

On his way back into the office, he bumped into Assistente Capo Rospo. "Did you get the preliminary autopsy report like I asked?"

"No," said Rospo. "I tried. It's not ready. They haven't even done the autopsy yet."

"You're sure about that?"

"As far as I know," said Rospo.

"The mugging report?"

"Almost done."

"Good work, Rospo."

"Yeah, well. Too much stuff to do."

Blume sought out Panebianco and asked if he had seen Caterina.

"She had to go pick up her boy," he said. "You know it must be really difficult being a mother, always having to run off in the middle of the working day."

Blume went into his office and called Caterina on her cell phone. It rang and rang, then was answered with a disconnect.

# 21

ELIA'S CLASS WAS always the last to be released into the courtyard, not because the teacher was too dedicated to heed the bell, but because she was too deaf and distracted to hear it.

School was supposed to be let out at 2:15. At 2:25, Caterina and the other mothers formed several huddles so that they could share their dissatisfaction and lament the passing of the afternoon and their lives. Then all of a sudden the children came tumbling out. The teacher, two years shy of retirement, but still shell-shocked like it was her first day, gave the courtyard trees a vague salute and wandered off.

Half the class formed a quick knot, then scattered like escaping fish to every corner of the yard. Soon they had organized a raucous game kicking a rolled-up wrapper around the concrete. The fatter kids clung onto their parents and demanded food. Caterina turned around looking for Elia, but could not make him out in the chaos. She went back to listening to a mother talking about having to pay for parking outside her own house. The class representative came by collecting money for toilet paper for the school bathrooms.

Elia's friends were called to order and went on their way. The number of players in the ball game began to decrease. The janitor shouted at the remaining ones to stop and at the parents to get out of the yard. Elia was still nowhere to be seen. She called his name, twice. Then a third time, louder. The pools of chatting parents were breaking up, and she started asking around. No, no one had seen him.

Caterina's next heartbeat seemed to cause a sudden change of pressure in her inner ear. For a moment she could not hear properly. Nor think.

*Where is he?* She checked her own memory. Her mother had taken Elia to school that morning, right? Right. Was it this morning she had gone to Pistoia and met Emma's mother? Was that relevant? No. Maybe. Something to think about later, when she had Elia in her arms.

She grabbed a child from Elia's class who was on his way out with his mother and fired questions. Yes, yes, he told her, Elia had been at school today.

She stood still until she could again hear the logical side of her mind underneath the loud bullying panic in her head. Clearly, he had forgotten something and gone back to the classroom to get it. That was it. The stupid, stupid child was always forgetting things. Caterina waited by the door, setting her face to stern for when he appeared. The school yard had almost emptied now, and the hubbub and noise were moving slowly up the street as the children were whisked away to one another's house, the park, dance lessons, catechism.

She went inside and was stopped by a woman with a massive bosom.

"You can't come in."

Caterina explained her case.

"No children are allowed back in after the last bell. If the child forgot something, he can get it tomorrow."

Caterina realized talking to this caretaker woman was merely putting off the thing she dreaded. She pushed her way by, dimly registering some sort of protest, and increased her pace as she reached the stairs. She took the steps two at a time, reached the third floor. It smelled of paper, glue, leather, wood polish, poster paints, shoes, sweat, felt pens, children. He was not in his classroom, and the corridors were empty. One wall was covered in photos of all the children in the school. She knew exactly where Elia was among them. She glimpsed his wavy hair and his brown eyes as she rushed by, heels clacking and echoing as she headed back to the stairwell. Her skin prickled and something icy mushroomed in her solar plexus. As she came back down the stairs, her phone rang. She grabbed it and saw Blume's name. No. She did not need him now.

*Get off the line. Get off the line. I need this line to be free.*

The phone rang on and on. *Fuck off. Fuck off, fuck off. Please, leave my line free.* She flipped the phone open and snapped it shut. There, it had stopped.

She reached the front of the school again. The yard was deserted: the janitor was closing the gates.

Oh, Elia.

Anything but this. Dear God, let nothing have happened to him. Please, God, listen, please—wait, logic. Could he have gone to a friend's house without asking, without the friend's mother telling her?

Her phone rang again. No. This line: it had to be kept free. That was essential. She was not sure why. It just was. But if Blume didn't talk. If he just listened—She flicked it open. "Alec, listen to me! Something terrible—I think . . ."

"I'm not 'Alec,' dear," said her mother's voice. "Are you all right?"

"No. No. You need to get off the line. Oh, Christ."

"Caterina!" her mother's voice was sharp. "What's the matter?"

"Elia . . ."

"Elia's here with me," said her mother.

Caterina made her repeat it. Then again.

"Now tell me, what's going on," said her mother. "Do I need to call someone?"

Every drop of moisture in her body seemed to come suddenly out of her pores, leaving her throat dry. She found it difficult to talk.

"He's there. With you?"

"Of course he is. If you couldn't make it, all you had to do was call me. I don't see why you had to send a car around to pick him up."

"What car?"

"Are you sure you're all right? Your colleagues. They brought him straight here, though I think they might have arrived a bit early at the school, they took him out of his last lesson. Next time, just call me if you can't make it on time."

"Can I talk to him?"

She heard her mother call Elia, and then he was on the line, his voice the clearest, purest, sweetest sound she would ever hear.

"Mamma?"

Caterina felt her legs wobble, so she just sat down in the middle of the yard. The janitor watched uncertainly from the gate, showing his impatience from a distance, but not daring to come over.

"Who took you home? What did I tell you about strangers?"

"They weren't strangers. They were police. Two men."

"Did you know them?"

"No, but they said you had sent them, and they showed me a badge, and . . . it was like the other day when the Commissioner drove us."

"The other day I was with you, Elia. What did they do?"

"They drove me home. Straight here. But they came too early, so the janitor had to call me out of class."

"I'm coming right over, Elia. I need to talk to you about this."

"OK. Can I go to Giacomo's today to play on the Wii?"

"How can you ask that? No, you're not going anywhere today. I'm coming right over."

Caterina rose unsteadily to her feet, and noticed the woman with the bosom watching, making no effort to hide her satisfaction at her distress.

"Did you release a child to the care of two adult males this afternoon?" said Caterina, coming over.

"Certainly not."

"All right. Did a police patrol come by today to pick up a child?"

"Yes, but they were Carabinieri."

"Look, let me tell you something about how easy it is to forge an ID . . ." Caterina stopped as her phone began to ring, the number withheld. As she answered the woman walked away.

"Inspector Mattiola, I hope we didn't have you worried there. It seems there was some sort of mix-up about the pickup time from school."

"Who is this? Who are you? I know your voice, you bastard. I can identify you."

"It's simpler if I identify myself, Inspector, takes the guesswork out of it. Colonel Farinelli. Commissioner Blume and I are working closely together, but I don't think he's being entirely open with either of us. I would like us to meet in, say, an hour, on the corner of Via Catania and Via Bari. There's an office supplies store, which will be handy."

"Handy for what?"

"For photocopying the photocopies of the notebooks Blume left with you. I really don't want him to know about this, so we're going to leave you with the photocopies he made for you, understand? Phone your mother again; tell her you'll be a bit later than planned. Don't phone anyone else. Especially Blume. In fact, the best thing would be for you to turn off your cell phone altogether. They are little better than self-inflicted listening devices."

# 22

WHEN WORKING IN immigration, Caterina had liked to think she would fight harder, give up less easily than some of the people she had to deal with. A lot of immigrants were tough, independent, scary even. But many were weak, exploited, and tormented because they had sold out. Selling yourself is the last option. At the very most, you might buy some time but once that time passes, you belong to someone else.

It was something the dead immigrants smothered in the back of trucks failed to understand. The Chinese girls, those white, dusty moths that never saw the sun, who lived, slept, gave birth, and died in underground factories in Prato, had not figured it out. Caterina wanted to sympathize with them, but in a secret part of her heart she knew she despised them, their stupidity, their flat, alien faces, their total helplessness. They had driven her out of Immigration Affairs into Blume's Squadra Mobile.

And now she was walking down the same road with her eyes wide open. In her case, all it had taken was a single phone call and an implicit threat to her son.

Twenty minutes later, Caterina parked her car in a space reserved for the handicapped and tried to work out what she was really thinking. Was her idea to satisfy the Colonel's demand for now, but lay a trap for him later? Or was this a self-serving lie? Her father would tell her to test the feeling she had in her stomach and believe that. The body does not lie. This was something he used to say, until his own, quietly and painlessly, betrayed him in old age.

Even though she was early, the Maresciallo was already waiting. She saw him give a brief signal as she walked toward him, and the Colonel emerged from a red Alfa Romeo 159. She saw him toss aside a toscano, and she touched her service Beretta. To have him fall dead at her feet, she would need to start firing now, like a hunter taking down an advancing hippopotamus.

When he arrived, he put out a big floury hand with manicured nails. She looked at it with revulsion.

"I see you are still peeved. Never mind. You have the copy? Good. In we go."

There was one other customer, a nervous student type. Farinelli held up a hand and snapped his fingers, then pointed down at Caterina as if she were a glass that needed refilling.

"We need these copied, very quickly. No binding." He pulled out three twenty-euro notes. "Here. I'll pay in advance for speed." He took the pile of papers from Caterina and handed them over the student's head to the man behind the desk, who took them and went straight into the backroom.

"Hey! I was first," ventured the student, addressing himself to the smooth silk back of the Colonel's jacket, causing not a ripple of a movement. He glanced accusingly at Caterina, but the look she flashed back caused him to lower his eyes and then his head.

A few minutes later, the assistant came out with three neat piles of typing paper.

"You sure you don't need these bound or stapled?"

"They're fine like that. Thank you." Farinelli popped them into a briefcase, gave Caterina her original copy back. He caught her arm and propelled her toward the door, saying, "There's a little hotel four doors down. The Hotel Malaga. I know the owner. We can have a drink there, a sandwich if you haven't eaten."

She shook her arm free. "I'm not hungry, and I don't want to be in your company."

"I'm not asking," said the Colonel. "I need to talk to you, put you in the picture. I don't want to see you in a panic like this afternoon. Soon you will be acting with complete serenity, I promise. You'll be happy to know what I am about to tell you."

"Tell me now."

"No. Just four doors down. Follow me."

When they reached the hotel, the Colonel ushered her in first, and Caterina found herself in a ludicrous state of social embarrassment at not knowing where to go. She wanted to kill the Colonel for having threatened her child and was rushing through ideas of how she might be able to do this, yet she felt awkward and, incredibly, apologetic as she led the way. The lobby connected to a breakfast and dining room and to a narrow corridor, surely too narrow for the Colonel. She ignored the person at reception, only registering his presence a few seconds after she had entered the room. She sat down at a polished wood table facing the door. Stainless steel food warmers and steak knives sat on a table to her left, and the walls were sponge-painted yellow and orange. A mirror on the wall made the table seem twice as long. She sat with her back to it, and realized the Colonel would now be able to see all of her, front and back, at once.

If she tried to pull a gun, he would see it coming but he was too large to run, and impossible to miss. As she fired, she would have to tell him why. *This is for threatening Elia. This is so that nothing may ever harm him.* Then two, maybe three crack-thump sounds as the bullets tore into him. She felt sick. The Colonel entered and sat down at the far end of the table.

"I know the owner. We shall be left alone in here. Can I get you something to drink?"

Caterina did not answer. She was wondering how many people she would have to kill before Elia would be safe. The Colonel, that Maresciallo who accompanied him. And others, no doubt. She could never do it. She already knew she was going to accept whatever he proposed if it meant putting her son beyond harm.

Her photocopies sat in front of her on the table. She could not remember carrying them or putting them there. She said, "You kidnapped my son."

"Not at all. He was taken straight to his grandmother's. He was perfectly happy in the car. Chatty, one of my men said. You know, I ordered them to pick him up, drive him straight home. If I had ordered the abduction of a child, they would not have obeyed. They are Carabinieri. Their smiles were genuine and your son was not afraid. He was in safe hands."

"I will kill you if anything ever happens to him. I will kill you if anyone even goes near him again. Is that understood?"

The Colonel bowed his huge head and murmured something, as if he were warning himself off something. His lips were liver-colored, almost the same color as his tanned face. He paused, and looked up and raised his voice a little so that Caterina could hear.

"Negative happiness. That is what I have just given you. Negative happiness is waking up every morning and knowing you have a son and knowing he is safe."

He pulled out a slim white device like an air-conditioning remote control and slid it across the table.

"Here. The buttons on the damned thing are too small. My Maresciallo set it up for me beforehand, for voice activation. He's just fixed it up again, now he tells me all you have to do is press play."

Caterina picked up the device, holding it like it was a turd. It was a digital voice recorder. Buttons on the front, tiny speaker at the back. Manufactured by Olympus.

"I made the recording just an hour ago, at a late lunch with your Commissioner. We were talking business, as you'll hear."

Caterina pressed play, and for the next few minutes, she listened to the lunchtime conversation between the Colonel and Blume. They were talking about selling Treacy's forged paintings.

As she listened to Blume take the name of an offshore accountant, demand a bigger cut from the sale of the paintings, she felt betrayed but detached, too. She was still thinking of Elia.

When the recording was over, she slid the device back across the table. It didn't matter. She did not care what Blume did. Elia was her only concern.

The Colonel peeled his lips back over his front teeth in what was probably intended as a sympathetic smile. "It's disappointing, isn't it? You think you know someone, then *pfft!*" He conjured nothing out of empty hands, "They turn out to be a different person."

Caterina said, "Blume would not threaten a child."

"Are you absolutely sure about that? And, let me remind you: nobody threatened your child. Talk to Elia, you'll see. Don't mention the unusual trip to him today, and he'll forget about it as something unremarkable. Go home full of questions, and you'll frighten him."

"Stop using his name."

Caterina's phone rang.

"Is that Blume?"

Caterina looked at the display. It was her mother. "Yes," she said. "It's him."

"Don't answer."

Caterina placed her cell phone on the table where it rang loudly and rotated slowly as the vibrator shook it. She could tell from his folded arms and air of studied indifference that it was making the Colonel uneasy. Then it stopped.

"I think you had better go back home, or to the office or wherever you're supposed to be. Remember, not a word to Blume, just like he did not breathe a word of his side-agreement to you. In another move that he did not report to you, your Commissioner passed on what were probably Treacy's originals to a third party, so there are now other people involved in this. Let's hope it does not become too complicated."

Her phone started ringing again. This time it was Blume.

# 23

B LUME SNAPPED HIS phone shut, annoyed. His mood had not been
improved by his recent conversation with Grattapaglia, who had just
shrugged and looked unsurprised when Blume told him the report
detailing his misconduct would be forwarded in a few hours.

It was Grattapaglia's shrug that had got to him. It implied that
Grattapaglia had never expected anything different, as if Blume always let
his men down.

Blume started signing off reports to be submitted to the investigating
magistrate, reports in which he was supposed to write down all his decisions and developments in the case, and present them to Buoncompagno,
Farinelli's pawn. The last entry was "case transferred by PM to Carabinieri."

Two knocks, a pause of two beats, and Panebianco walked into the
office.

"You remember my friend Nicu in the Carabinieri?" he said. "The
Lieutenant Colonel in the Art Forgery and Heritage Division?"

"The one you play soccer with," said Blume. "What about him?"

"He wants to meet you."

"I don't have time," said Blume.

"He said that if you said that I was to tell you to make time. Sorry, sir.
He's not usually that arrogant. I asked him what he meant by that, and he
said I was to mention your arrangement with Colonel Farinelli."

Blume looked for signs of warning, knowledge, irony, or contempt in
Panebianco's calm eyes, but got nothing back.

"When does he want this meeting?"

"Now. He'd like you to go over to the division in Trastevere. I'd be
happy to convey any harsh replies you'd like to make."

"No. Thanks, Inspector. I'll deal with it."

*

As he drove past the Ministry of Justice, Blume pulled out his phone and called Beppe Paoloni, now a better friend than he had ever been when they were on the force together. A friendship born from confuted expectations was how Blume described it once. Paoloni's version was that Blume was not as much of a prick as he had thought. When, two years earlier, Blume found out that Paoloni was on the point of assassinating a cop-killer, he had told him to quit the force and Paoloni had complied at once. Blume never reported the incident, which was why, Paoloni explained, he was not a total prick. As for Blume, he was pleasantly surprised at Paoloni's immediate contrition and acquiescence instead, which was not what he had been expecting.

The friendship strengthened when it turned out that quitting was the best and most profitable thing Paoloni ever did. After a very brief stint as a bank guard, he was making a fortune as a private security consultant. As part of the compact they had struck at the time of his resignation, Blume had offloaded a large, unmanageable dog on his friend, and then occasionally popped around to see how the two of them were getting along. Paoloni liked to pretend it was Blume's dog and he would be taking it back some day, and Blume liked to pretend that Paoloni had grown immensely fond of the animal.

"Yes?" Paoloni's voice was wary. He never looked at the caller display.

"It's me, Alec."

"Alec!"

"Am I disturbing something?"

"No. I'm taking your dog for a walk."

"He's not my dog. I gave him to you," said Blume.

"Hey, dog, say hello to your real father." Paoloni must have really put the phone to the animal's mouth or else was doing a good impression of the fast breathy sounds of a big black Cane Corso.

When Blume was sure it was Paoloni on the phone again, he said: "You still haven't given it a name?"

"No. If I did, it wouldn't be a nice name. The beast eats more in two days than I do in a week," said Paoloni. "Most of my grocery bill is dog food."

"He probably smokes less than you, Beppe, so it all balances out. What are you doing now?"

"I'm standing outside a sportswear store waiting for your dog to shit on the doorstep. We've been doing this every afternoon for a month now, ever since the owner refused to take back a Lacoste polo that I bought and was too small. Ahaaaa. There we go."

"Beppe, I could do with a bit of your expert opinion on how to deal with a few things . . ." Blume listened to the sounds of Beppe praising and patting his dog. "You there?"

"Of course I'm here."

"Did you hear about the killing of the Indian storekeeper?"

Paoloni's voice became grave. "I heard about that. They drove a jeep over two kids. Are you looking for leads?"

"We know who it was," said Blume. "I was thinking maybe if I gave you the names, you might help us find them."

"Sure. Give me the names."

"Have you got a pen?"

"A pen? Sure."

"Something to write on?"

"I'll use the dog. Give me the names, Alec."

"Leporelli . . ."

"And Scariglia," finished Paoloni. "What do I need a pen for? What's the deal?"

"They hand themselves in. They have until tomorrow midday. In good time for the TV news."

"OK," said Paoloni. "And why do they do that?"

"The magistrate is Gestri. Remember him? Intense guy. He's closed down a Cineplex in Ostia already, and at least five beach clubs won't be opening for a week. He's going to disrupt Camorra activities until they are delivered up. Simple deal. I think it's in their interest to turn themselves in while they are still breathing. They shouldn't be too hard to locate in the circumstances, and I was hoping you might act as broker."

"What's in it for me?"

"That sense of inner peace you get when you do the right thing."

"I always feel that. What else?"

"You get to tell the Ostia crew the good news that the heat is off, their Cineplex and clubs can open again. You get to say you arranged it. Grateful gangsters: what else could you wish for?"

"You are sure Gestri will call off the police?"

"Of course he will. He can't tie up all that manpower for more than a day or two anyhow, you know that."

"OK," said Paoloni. "I'll see what I can do."

"I've another favor to ask, maybe two. But I'll tell you about them when we meet."

"Your dog simply can't wait to see you," said Paoloni.


The Carabiniere Art Forgery and Heritage Division was located on Via Anicia, next to a Franciscan church. Blume walked up to the high perimeter wall and past a sentry box, flashing his police ID at the three men inside. He was briefly challenged by a young Appuntato manning the door, who stood aside and let him in as soon as he had seen the card. Now a Brigadiere Capo behind a desk stopped him.

Just then a tall, elegant, and strangely white-faced young man appeared on the far side of the turnstiles. "It's OK," he told the Brigadiere at the desk. "Commissioner Blume?"

"You still have to sign in," said the Brigadiere.

Blume signed the logbook and waited for his visitor's badge.

"I need identification, please."

Blume flicked his ID card on the desk.

The Carabiniere carefully wrote down the time, opened a drawer, took out a visitor's badge, and very reluctantly gave it to Blume.

Blume went over to the stile, which refused to turn.

"Sorry about this," said the young Lieutenant Colonel. "You need to swipe the visitor's card."

Blume was through. The young man held out his hand. "Pleased to meet you. I am Nicu Faedda. Let me show you to my office."

Blume was fascinated by how a man with such white skin could have a Sardinian accent. He felt he was in the presence of a comic or an actor reciting the part of a Sard. There was a *Candid Camera* feel to the experience, and it put him on his guard.

"Stairs or elevator? It's the second floor."

"Stairs," said Blume.

Faedda took the first flight of ten steps in three bounds, and stopped on the landing. "Did you know that UNESCO says seventy percent of world art heritage is in Italy?"

"Yes. No. Whatever." Blume reached the landing. "Are you really a Sard?"

"Because I'm tall, is that it?"

"And white," said Blume.

"I have sallow skin. I tan deeply in the summer."

"Do you shrink, too?" asked Blume.

Faedda shook his head and smiled. "These misconceptions we have. I thought all Americans were fat and politically correct, yet here you are." He gained the top of the stairs and opened the first door in the corridor, holding it for Blume. "Did you know that an art theft takes place in Italy on average every two hours, and that fifty-eight percent of what is stolen is never recovered?" he said as Blume walked in.

Faedda sat on a comfortable office chair behind his desk, empty apart from metal knickknacks and plaques with medals, bearing the insignia, symbols of the Carabinieri, feathers, rifles, the burning grenade . . . The Carabinieri certainly love their symbols, thought Blume. The police were satisfied with a themed calendar showing pictures of squad cars and the occasional Italian flag.

"OK then, did you know that our recovery rate has improved by forty-five percent over the past fifteen years?"

Blume sat down. "Are you seeking election?"

"No, no," said Faedda. "I am just telling you that things have improved a lot."

"And you are telling me this because . . ." Blume thought about it. "Because in the past fifteen years methods have improved?"

"There is another reason," said Faedda.

"Because there has been staff turnover in this department and tall dynamic Sards like you have taken over from old-school people like Colonel Farinelli," said Blume.

"Sometimes law enforcement agencies will defend a colleague simply because he is, or was, a colleague, not because he is worth defending," said Faedda. "The Colonel has long exploited that, but his time is almost up. So I would appreciate it if you could tell me, in total confidence, officer to officer: Did the Colonel offer to cut you in on a deal to sell the paintings found in the home and gallery of the art forger Henry Treacy?"

"What makes you think he is even thinking of doing such a thing? And if he is, why would he offer a piece of the action to me?" said Blume.

"Good. Well, that sounds like a no to me," said Faedda.

"A 'no' sounds like an 'n' followed by an 'o,'" said Blume. "That was a question about how you reached such a conclusion."

"You were there. You saw the paintings. It makes sense. As for the Colonel's planning to steal the paintings, I'm basing that idea on his past form."

Blume looked into the unwrinkled and trusting face of the Lieutenant Colonel and said, "You are accusing your commanding officer and me of graft and theft."

"Him, yes. You, no. On the contrary, I think you agreed to participate in an attempt to corner the Colonel. I want to be part of whatever it is you are planning or, if I can put it better, I want to be able to help."

"What makes you so sure? What makes you so sure I wasn't planning something with the Colonel, and that I will leave this office, warn him, and together we will completely fuck you over?"

Faedda frowned slightly. "I asked."

"You asked what?"

"I asked Panebianco about you. What sort of person you were. He said there was no chance you would be corrupted like that."

"Panebianco said that?"

"Sure."

"And that was enough for you?"

"Yes."

Perhaps, Blume thought, the kid was a recent Christian convert or something. All that faith.

Faedda said, "Well, I ran some background checks, too. And I have a friend who ... we checked your finances, going back ten years. And I spoke to a few magistrates and reviewed past cases. I am not sure what makes you tick, Commissioner, but it isn't money. So I thought I would take a risk. Was I right to do so?"

"I ... I have no idea."

"Well, I feel confident," said Faedda. "I hate dishonesty. We Carabinieri are not like that. The force deserves better leaders. The Polizia are lucky ..."

Blume held up a finger to halt Faedda's flow. When he was sure no more flattery was forthcoming, he said, "Do you have any idea how much more powerful Farinelli is than you? Forget about his rank, which is higher than yours anyhow. He can do what he wants, and as for those paintings, I doubt the Colonel put all of them in storage. Maybe none of them are there."

"I hope that is not the case, because it would mean that some men here were accomplices to a fraudulent operation, which . . . Well, these things happen," said Faedda, opening his palms in a gesture of devout acceptance. "The Colonel is famous for his secrecy. He's the sort who used to pull the strings of the people who worked behind the scenes. He operates, or used to, two, three levels down. But he's losing power. His contacts are fading. His former controllers are dying of old age, and some of the men he controlled have moved beyond him, found new masters, got elected to office."

Faedda squinted his left eye in an attempt to make it look like the thought was just coming to him at that moment. "In this case, he's being uncharacteristically straightforward. The Colonel bribes you, maybe plans to pay, maybe plans to expose you as the bad guy, the extortionist, maybe both. Pretty simple."

"I'm a simple kind of guy," said Blume. "I don't recall confirming to you that the Colonel offered to cut me in on a deal."

"But he did, right?"

Blume was not sure what to make of the young man's mixture of candidness and presumption. "Let's say for argument's sake that he did," he said.

"Like I said, Panebianco vouchsafed for you. That will do for me. But I was wondering, do you have something else the Colonel wants?"

Blume shrugged. "Obviously I do."

"What?"

"I have no idea."

"That's fine. I accept that response," said Faedda. "But if you really have no idea, let me suggest money. Or something that is worth a lot of money."

"What about something that gives him power, leverage, or exonerates him. Or something that he wants hidden?"

"Those are all very plausible reasons," said Faedda. "And it could be any one of them, or all of them. But I still think it's money."

Blume, thinking of an interesting section of the memoirs he had read the night before, said, "If it wasn't money to start with, it soon will be."

# 24

BEFORE RETURNING TO his office, Blume passed by his apartment, showered, changed, and picked up the three notebooks. The idea of their remaining unguarded in there made him uneasy. The damned things were becoming a burden to him. There was a safe in the office, but he was not the only one with keys to it. His best bet was to give them to Paoloni to look after.

The phone on the desk was ringing as he entered his office. The Questore or, rather, his smarmy secretary again. It seemed to Blume the Questore had no one else to talk to apart from him. And he always phoned Blume in his office, as if to check he was there.

"I've been having complaints about you," he announced when they were connected. "A magistrate, Buoncompagno, claims that you have been making unauthorized interventions in his investigation into the art forger. I thought I told you to leave that alone."

Blume gestured to the gods of the ceiling with the phone, then brought it back to his ear. "Buoncompagno has been told to say that, sir," said Blume. "It's just a minor jurisdictional dispute with a Carabiniere. Meanwhile, I have been working with Magistrate Antonello Gestri on a double murder."

"You mean the hit-and-run on the Indians?"

"The vehicle was the murder weapon."

"Don't change the subject," said the Questore. "I told you to leave the Treacy case alone."

Blume slid the notebooks into his drawer. "I just had to make sure there was no connection with the muggings, which you said are our priority right now," he said.

"Are you saying there is a connection between Treacy and the muggings?"

"Oh, just that Treacy was a foreigner like the rest of them."

"It seems rather flimsy," said the Questore. "Have you any proof?"

"No," said Blume. "Which is why I need to follow it up."

"Don't follow it too far—unless you think it might help us stop the muggings, will it?"

"You never know, sir," said Blume.

"No, I never do know with you," said the Questore and, finally, hung up.

Panebianco stuck his head around the door. "A Mr. Nightingale, accompanied by Avvocato Feltri, is downstairs. They want to see you."

"Have them sent up."

"Right." Panebianco remained where he was.

"What?" asked Blume in irritation.

"How did your meeting with Faedda go?"

"I don't see . . ." began Blume, but then he remembered Faedda explaining how Panebianco had vouchsafed for him, and he softened his tone. "It went well, thank you. Enlightening."

"Good. I am pleased. I'll have the two men below sent up."

Five minutes later, Nightingale's lawyer, a sleek man whose black hair was so shiny it looked wet, slipped into the seat in front of him. Nightingale, dressed in a rumpled linen suit and looking tired, hot, and lordly, sat down next to his lawyer, who turned to him and, speaking mainly for Blume's benefit, said, "Remember, you are free to stand up and leave the interview at any point. You do not have to answer any questions that you do not want to, and no matter what you say, it cannot be used in evidence against you. A witness may not self-incriminate."

The lawyer then turned to face Blume. "Since some of his voluntary statements will now become inadmissible as evidence, you will not want to ask him too much to do with whatever you are investigating. We are happy to cooperate inasmuch as we are assured that you have not been appointed to investigate the case, and I have it on good authority that scientific evidence will point overwhelmingly to accidental causes, a fact that you acknowledge in this statement that I have prepared and I'd like you to sign."

Blume ignored the proffered document, picked up his desk phone, and called in Caterina from her desk. A few seconds later, she came in, crossed the room without looking at him, and took a plastic chair to his left, near the wall. She had gone back into sulk mode, evidently.

"Please explain in what capacity this Inspector is present," said the lawyer.

"I need to keep an eye on her," said Blume.

"No, we have no time for humor, Commissioner. This is a serious imposition on my client's goodwill and time."

"Inspector Mattiola," said Blume. "Why do you think I invited you in here?"

"So I could see Nightingale for myself."

"If the policewoman is here to satisfy an idle curiosity ..." began the lawyer.

But Caterina, who was indeed looking very closely at Nightingale, continued, "And to tell Mr. Nightingale in person that we know he is Emma Solazzi's father."

In the silence that followed the whirr of a laser printer in the room outside became audible, and the four of them sat still until it, too, stopped. Now they seemed to be listening to broken strands of conversations deeper in the office. A sudden burst of noise from a passing *motorino* below presented itself as a possible topic of discussion.

Finally, Nightingale said, "Avvocato, I think you should leave now."

The lawyer looked affronted. "On the contrary. You need me more than ever. If I have understood this correctly, this implies errors in public records, alimony issues, inheritance ..."

"Yes, there is a lot to it," said Nightingale. "But I really would prefer if this sort of thing were not known or spoken about, even to my trusted lawyer. We can talk about it later. For now I want to speak with the Commissioner and the Inspector alone."

"I advise most strongly against it," said the lawyer, but he had tightened his lips and was already standing in preparation to leave. The experience of being the one person in the room not to be in the know about something had been a humiliation. Blume almost expected him to announce he was no longer representing his client.

Another silence ensued as they waited for the lawyer to gather his papers and wounded dignity and leave the room.

"He didn't know that," said Nightingale, switching into English as soon as the door closed. "I should have told him, but he was Henry's lawyer, too. I've never been comfortable with the idea of client privilege. Priests, doctors, lawyers all claim it for themselves, but they're not particularly *likable* people, now, are they?"

Blume said, "How did Treacy not get suspicious? Wasn't there—I don't know—some way you and Emma interacted, touched, or didn't touch? Treacy picked none of that up? Emma is your child. It must have been hard, not to plant a kiss on the crown of her head now and then. Something like that. I'm not a parent, but," he pointed at Caterina, "she is."

Blume looked over at Caterina. Again, he saw only the side of her face, the rigid outline of her body, her legs out straight, like she was a two-dimensional figure in a three-dimensional space.

She did not answer him or look at him, so he continued alone. "Another thing, you went to great lengths to hide her identity and to keep up the pretence, yet at the same time you didn't."

"I don't understand you," said Nightingale.

"It took Inspector Mattiola less than half a working day to ascertain Emma's identity as your daughter. She became suspicious immediately, thought about it for a while, then ran a basic background check beginning with the tax code. We're talking about a few hours' work to discover your daughter's identity. It's the strange mix of thoroughness and carelessness that has me wondering."

Nightingale seemed to be studying the swirls on his fingertips. Finally, he said, "Let me address your outrage at my lack of paternal feelings first." Nightingale turned toward Caterina as he said this, then getting little response, focused on Blume again. "Before Emma came to the gallery to work with us, I had met her exactly five times."

He held up a fist and splayed his fingers. "I held her in my arms just once, and it was on the day I first saw her. She was three. She was showing me how she could jump higher than anyone, and she landed on a book she had been reading, slipped, and banged her head hard on the side of a low table. I scooped her up and tried to stop her from crying, but she had this huge bruise and Angela, who hadn't seen the incident, seemed to think it was my fault, and maybe it was. So, you see, Commissioner, we really were strangers. And if I hid her identity carelessly, it's because it was well enough hidden already. We did not risk a spontaneous outburst of affection. Emma herself only learned my identity a few weeks before she came to work in the gallery."

"You and Emma's mother had a difficult relationship?"

"You can't call my later contacts with Angela a relationship, really. Our story ended before Emma was born. It's completely my fault. I'm the one who walked away."

Finally Caterina spoke up, using English. "She didn't say anything to you about a daughter until Emma was three?"

"You're English?" asked Nightingale, surprised.

"No. Just answer my question," said Caterina.

"Emma's mother was trying to be sometimes an artist and sometimes a critic, as if they could ever go together, and if they ever could, she was not the person to do it. She became desperate for money, and that was when she swallowed her pride and called me."

Blume eliminated a smirk he felt growing at the side of his mouth by the expedient of rubbing his chin thoughtfully. "So she presented you with this little girl and you ..."

"Look, Commissioner, I know what you're thinking. You're wondering what made me so sure she was mine."

Blume raised his palms in denial of such a thought.

"Well, to start with," said Nightingale, "have you looked at her?"

"Me, looked at Emma? Well, yes ... she's very beautiful."

"Thank you. She is. Can't you see the resemblance?"

Blume looked at the man in front of him. Nightingale had the pale blue eyes of many northern Europeans. Emma's eyes were also blue, he remembered, though hers were almond shaped and had green tints. Her eyes soaked in the light and darkened it, his just reflected it straight back. He had high cheekbones and a triangular face. She had high cheekbones, too, but her face was oval. He remembered it well. There was a difference of sex and forty-something years between them.

Blume decided to be diplomatic. "Yes, I think I do."

"That, of course, is the most obvious thing, and I was always afraid Treacy would notice. Treacy had a sharp eye for detail, though he used it in painting, not in the real world. Also, I saw Emma's birth certificate."

"And that was enough? I mean, of all people to trust a piece of paper, surely you ..."

Nightingale interrupted, "Emma was born six months after I broke up with Angela. When we were together, Angela and I were utterly inseparable. We had been going together for three years, living together for a year and a half, and we were on our way to being married. When we had sex, we took no precautions. We had sex all the time. We were together all the time. We rolled all our strength and all our sweetness up into one ball, and we traveled around the country, around Europe, and farther abroad. We went to India, Sri Lanka, Mexico, Guatemala, California, and New York. And when we had finished traveling, we bought—I bought—a run-down *casale* near Anzio, and we spent all day every day fixing it up."

"You fit this in with what you did at the gallery?"

"Not really. I was—I feel embarrassed even saying this now—I was thinking of giving up the art world and becoming a poet. I thought if we fixed up the house we might take in Dutch and English holidaymakers. You know, long-term, cultured guests. Angela thought she might cook for them, though she was even lousier at cooking than painting . . ."

"Well, if the guests were to be English and Dutch that would hardly be a problem," said Blume. "What ended the idyll?"

"We fell out. Silly stuff but, in the end, serious, too. Toxic little asides from me to her, her to me, like when she told me I had made a travesty of a Tasso poem I was translating, which was bloody annoying coming from a woman who couldn't speak English and, if the truth be told, couldn't paint for toffee. She couldn't judge paintings either, or write a decent essay. Long pretentious sentences full of jargon, dismissive judgments of things she didn't understand, which was most things . . . One day, she gave me a choice: my work or her. So I went back to speculating in the art market. She persisted for three more years, a bit longer, trying to make it as an artist, and then she contacted me, asked me for some money. I'd already left her the house in Anzio, so I told her to get stuffed. That was when she revealed the existence of Emma."

"Did she threaten to sue for maintenance?" asked Blume.

"No. She wasn't like that. She was not greedy for money, though I wasn't sure then. After the house, she asked me for money just this once. It was a decent sum, I suppose. Ninety million lire. This when a middle-range car cost around ten million lire, a small apartment in Rome around two hundred million. She gave up her painting and started working in a bank. I waited for her next demand for money, but it never came. The years went past without any more contact or requests, and, when Emma was about to start secondary school, I phoned up and asked her if I could pay for her education. Angela said public schools in Italy were better than private, so she didn't need it. So I offered to pay for books, holidays, sport clubs—that sort of thing. She said she'd think about it. She phoned me back about a month later and invited me to the house."

"The one near Anzio. She still lived there?"

"Yes. She's in Pistoia now, but that's recent. So I went. It was the second time I met Emma. Angela said she'd be happy to accept my money, and I could choose to give her whatever I deemed fit. But she made one condition, which was that the money should be a fixed sum to be paid at regular intervals. She said she did not want to see the sum going up and down reflecting my mood or opinion of her."

"Why did you conspire to give Emma a false identity?"

"I did not. That is to say, we hid her identity; we did not really create a new one."

"Manuela Ludovisi, whose real name is Emma Solazzi, false tax code, false background . . ."

"Yes, but as you said yourself, it was not deeply done. It was to obscure her identity, not set up a new one forever. We just wanted to hide it from Harry."

"Why?"

"To avoid awkwardness. You see, long ago, before she was with me, Angela was Harry's."

Caterina interrupted. "I beg your pardon? She was his—as in she belonged to him?"

"Yes. Exactly that," he said with irritation. "He owned her. That's what Harry was like. It was he who persuaded her to paint, told her she had talent, when she manifestly did not, drew her into a bohemian way of life, molded her to fit his idea of what he thought his woman should be. Then when he tired of her, he walked away, calling her bourgeois. People still used that as an insult back then. People like Harry, anyhow."

"I don't see the need for the subterfuge all those years later," said Caterina.

"Angela had told Harry she had had her tubes tied. She told *me* that. Maybe she did, maybe she had a reverse op, and maybe Emma is a miraculous birth. Angela used to say she never wanted children, made a sort of philosophy of life out of it. Kids kill off sex in the home, they are little Disney-fixated capitalists, and they kill your youth and replace it with their own. The planet can't take any more, and . . ."

"And yet . . ." said Caterina.

"And yet nothing. I'd just started on the good reasons not to have any," said Nightingale.

"And yet Angela had a child, is what I meant," said Caterina.

"Ah. Yes, quite right. She had a child after all. I think she felt embarrassed about it for a long time, until she finally stopped trying to be an independent, free-floating artist. But there was another reason not to advertise the fact. When Angela and I started going out, Harry, well, he was vile. One day, shortly after we returned from Mexico and I had started working with him again, we invited him down to Anzio for a sort of truce negotiation. He arrived already half pissed, then got viciously, violently, and overwhelmingly drunk like only the bloody Irish can get, and he called her bitch, whore, or 'hoo-er' as he mispronounced it, *puttana*, *troia*, *zoccola*, cunt, and threw a full bottle of wine at her. It hit the wall behind and shattered, and a piece of glass pierced her neck, narrowly missing the jugular. There was blood everywhere, and the hospital called you people, and I was questioned since Angela refused to name Harry. The morning after he claimed not to remember anything. But that was it. Angela cut all ties with him. So you can see why she did not want him coming near her child, or knowing of her existence. Harry and I never again mentioned Angela between us. He did not even know when we eventually broke up."

"Henry Treacy had a mean streak," said Blume.

"A broad stripe of cruelty, more like it."

"He was mean when drunk. What was he like sober?"

"Angry. Confused. Funny. Bad-tempered. Clever. An immensely gifted second-rate artist. Generous. Underhand. It depends what you're looking for. I knew him for so long, I got to see all sides."

Blume said, "Can you explain what you mean by immensely gifted and second-rate."

"He copied others," said Nightingale. "He did it well, but he copied. Also, there were things he couldn't copy. He could draw anything, and that was his great gift, but there were things he could not paint. He was like a prodigiously gifted child."

Blume shook his head. "No. I'm not following you. You're talking as if his limitations were plain to see, when evidently, given the money you made off him . . ."

"And he off me," said Nightingale.

"... which, given the money you both made, was not the case. What was his failing? As a painter or forger, I mean, not as a human."

"He could not paint air," said Nightingale. "Look, as long as we're dealing with Early and Middle Renaissance painting, it was not a problem, because for most of them, color was something that came after composition. But later on, when northern Italian painters started doing pictures where you could see and feel the air, the sunlight, and the shadows, Harry was lost."

"What sort of painters?" asked Blume.

"You know, Titian, Tintoretto, Giorgione, and basically anyone after them who used light in a certain way, or painted directly, Caravaggio or, for that matter, Turner, but also—"

"What about Velázquez?" said Blume. "Could he do a Velázquez?"

"No, I don't believe he could. Why are you asking that, Commissioner?"

"No particular reason," said Blume.

"I am sure you do have a reason," said Nightingale. "And it's probably based on something you read in Harry's writings, because you have read them."

"I'm not in the mood for sharing," said Blume. "Did Henry Treacy hate you?"

"Maybe. But he had mellowed with age. I might have told him about Emma someday."

"Do you think he would have betrayed you?"

"Possibly. I'm not sure. It depends what you mean by betray."

"That's what drove you to Colonel Farinelli, isn't it?" said Blume. "You knew Treacy was writing his memoirs, and there would be details that compromised you. I don't know if you were worried about the whole story or just one episode, I can think of at least one that would have got Farinelli interested. I'm talking about your sale of false paintings to the Cosa Nostra boss."

Nightingale plucked at his pant legs exposing thin vein-colored socks. "False?"

"Yes, they were false. He is quite specific about it in his writings. He even gives instructions on how to prove they were false. I believe you when you say you didn't know, because he's specific about that, too."

"That bastard."

"So he betrayed you twice," said Blume. "Once by swapping real paintings for forged ones, and then once again by writing about it. The stolen paintings went back to their rightful owners. Or so Treacy says. If this were to be published, it could spell a special kind of trouble for you and the Colonel, only I think the Colonel is probably better equipped than you for defending himself from the Mafia," said Blume.

"I could leave this damned country. It is probably not worth their while sending someone abroad after me."

"You'd be surprised," said Blume.

"And you might be surprised to know that the Mafia threat is not my first thought. Only once was I involved in the sale of stolen works, but here you are telling me I was not. In a certain sense, I feel relieved. No doubt I'll get round to worrying about the implications of selling forgeries to the Mafia later—though the danger was surely greatest at the moment of sale. Perhaps the buyer is dead now."

"Don't pin your hopes on that," said Blume. "The Mafia has a corporate memory."

"I see you like to comfort people, Commissioner. So have you read all his writings?"

Blume nodded. "Yes. Three notebooks. Two dedicated to his life, one to technique."

"The Colonel was right about you, then," said Nightingale. "Before this conversation began, I had entertained the very faint hope that Harry might have destroyed his manuscripts. Sadly, that is not the case. The reason I called in the Colonel in the first place was to persuade Harry. Force him, if you will. Harry was bound to compromise the Colonel many times over. I am sure the sale of the stolen paintings, or what we thought were the stolen paintings, is just one of several questionable episodes. Did Harry by any chance speculate as to why I broke the habit of a lifetime and went along with the Colonel that day? Does he even wonder what I felt about dealing with violent criminals?"

"No. He doesn't speculate. He just has you turning up at the sale in the hotel room."

"He never considered that I might have my reasons. That the Colonel might have forced me to act. That's Harry all over. He's always the only victim. It's the Irish in him."

"So what did the Colonel threaten you with?"

"He threatened Angela and Emma," said Nightingale. "Whereas to persuade Harry, all he had to do was threaten Harry. See the difference there?"

"Yes," said Blume. "There are many advantages to being single." He paused. "On the other hand, Henry Treacy only pretended to cave in and swapped the works to save the rightful owners."

"How noble of him."

"So the Colonel knew Emma was your daughter?" asked Blume.

"He knew about Angela. I don't know if he knew who Emma was. He was always very oblique in his threats. He never even mentioned the child directly."

Caterina finally spoke, her voice trembling with emotion. "I don't understand you, Nightingale. After what he did, how could you even think of going to the Colonel to tell him about Treacy's book? How could you do that? No normal person would want the Colonel in his life again."

Nightingale glanced at Blume as if to gauge how seriously he should take Caterina's intervention.

"Answer her."

"You're right, of course. I made a bad mistake. All I can say is that the Colonel has always been there in the background. I'm used to him. And it was a long time ago, and he never did do anything to Emma or Angela, so I guessed he was bluffing."

"Why are you so keen to suppress Treacy's writings? So much so that you invited that evil bastard the Colonel back into your life?" said Caterina.

"Well, if you must know, it's a question of principle. I don't like the idea of Harry writing an autobiography or whatever it was in which I have a leading and probably unflattering role. I value my privacy, regret my mistakes, and I claim my right to a peaceful old age. How dare he write me into his version of the past."

"And so," said Caterina, "you called in the Colonel to dissuade him."

"Yes," said Nightingale. He rubbed his cheek with the side of his hand. "The thing is, I called the Colonel about a month ago, warning him that Harry was writing about the past, some of our dealings, things that might be embarrassing. Farinelli told me he would deal with it, and now Harry is dead."

"Wait," said Blume. "Are you saying the Colonel killed him or had him killed?"

"Hardly," said Nightingale. "And if I were to say such a thing, it would not be to you, Commissioner. There would be no point."

"Why not?"

"Because Colonel Farinelli has bought you off, or perhaps set you up. My lawyer received a recording of a conversation between you and the Colonel in which you are heard agreeing to take a cut from the sale of paintings found in Treacy's house. You, Commissioner, are corrupt, and I am calling my lawyer back in, if you don't mind."

# 25

B LUME'S FIRST INSTINCT was to look at Caterina. She had sat forward in her seat and seemed slightly curious to hear his response. He realized with a shock that the idea was not new to her.

His second instinct was to pick up the nearest object on his desk, which happened to be a copy of the *Code of Criminal Procedure* and pitch it straight at Nightingale's face. Although the man was no more than two meters from him, he missed.

Blume then picked up a massive cut-crystal ashtray that he used as a paperweight.

Caterina jumped out of her seat. "Commissioner!"

Nightingale was already halfway to the door of the office.

"Just kidding," said Blume, and put it down.

Nightingale opened the door and beckoned in his lawyer, escorting him to the seat he had been occupying before. Then he placed himself, still standing, behind the chair.

Caterina came round, picked up the law book. She put it back on Blume's desk.

"You don't believe that, do you?" whispered Blume.

"He taped you in the restaurant talking about selling the pictures," said Caterina. "Not that I care."

"Excuse us, gentlemen," said Blume. "Inspector, outside, now."

Blume closed the office door behind them, and pulled Caterina to one side, keeping his voice low so as not to be heard either from inside the office or from the operations room where he glimpsed Grattapaglia and Rospo and caught sight of Panebianco catching sight of them.

"First thing," said Blume in a hoarse whisper, "you're off this case. I want you to take over from Grattapaglia on the muggings. Whatever he's doing, you take over. Panebianco will give you the background."

"I already know the background," said Caterina. "I've been looking into that case off and on for months, like everyone else."

She turned to go.

"Wait," said Blume. "I haven't finished with you."

Caterina gave a slight shrug and turned around again. "What else is there to say?"

"You gave the Colonel your copy of the notebooks, didn't you?"

Caterina lifted her foot, pliéd it like a ballet dancer, and re-centered herself half a pace farther from him. She lifted her head to be defiant, but avoided his eyes. "Yes. He photocopied it. Did he tell you that himself? I can imagine he likes to gloat."

"Maybe he does," said Blume, "but more than that, he likes to divide, mystify, create distrust. He did not tell me that he got Treacy's notes from you. It's in his interest that I don't know. He probably told you not to tell me, didn't he? Otherwise, why did he photocopy instead of just taking them?"

Caterina nodded slowly, remembering.

"I guessed that now because I trust you. There must be some reason you suddenly cooperated with the Colonel. Even if you gave him access to the writings, I am willing to believe you had good cause, just as you should be willing to believe I am acting in good faith no matter what you hear on a digital recording. And there is only one thing I can imagine making you do that. Elia. Is your son all right now?"

"Yes. I'm sorry," she said.

"If Elia was in danger, you've nothing to be sorry about."

"All I can think about is Elia, and it's clouding my judgment."

"Did he harm the boy?"

"No. Like Nightingale said, he's oblique. Elia's fine. Really."

"And so he shall remain," said Blume. "You're off the case, like I said. That's the first step. I'm going back in there now and I promise you this— are you listening?—I promise I will get the Colonel out of your life."

"I want to talk about this."

"We can do that later. Get back to proper police work now. Make sure everyone knows you're off the Treacy case, which we don't have assigned to us anyhow. That's step one."

Caterina smiled. "I'm sorry. I don't believe you're colluding with the Colonel. I didn't even listen to the tape properly when he played it."

"That's OK."

She leaned forward and touched his elbow. "You won't throw anything at the lawyer, will you?"

"Nothing too heavy," said Blume.

He stepped inside the door and was annoyed to see Nightingale just behind it.

"Eavesdropping?"

"No!"

Blume returned to behind his desk. "*Per l'amor di Dio, si sieda.*"

Nightingale remained standing.

"They say you need to use German or English to command a dog," said Blume. "Let's see if it works: sit, Mr. Nightingale. I won't throw any more objects at you, unless I hear more moral judgments from the mouth of a crooked dealer."

"I never sold a stolen work of art in my life," said Nightingale, switching back into Italian for the benefit of his lawyer. He placed himself at the far end of the room and finally sat in the chair vacated by Caterina.

"So what, you are still a swindler, a con-artist, a fraudster, a forger's assistant, a falsifier. If you don't like any of those names, I've got some more."

"I facilitate happiness and perpetuate good taste," said Nightingale. "That's what I do. And I make money from it. Morally, I have no problems with what I do." He looked over to his lawyer, who was regarding the stained fabric of his chair with fastidious distaste. "Explain it to him, *Avvocato.*"

"If you need a lawyer to explain your ethics, you're probably not going straight to heaven," said Blume.

"What Mr. Nightingale means," said Feltri, smoothing the turbulence out of the air with a stroke of his hand, "is that he helps the buyer feel that his purchase is legitimate, which is the basis of all value in the art world. At the same time, he helps the dealer conclude a profitable transaction and some of that profit trickles down to artists, art hunters, and minor collectors who supply him. You are a policeman, so I hardly need remind you what a confirmation bias is, but let me explain the term, for the sake of Mr. Nightingale. It is simply this: People believe what they want to believe."

"Well put!" said Nightingale from his corner.

Feltri gave a slight bow of acknowledgment. "Once someone gets an idea into his head, he—and I say he advisedly, because women in this respect are a little less susceptible than men—will see only evidence that confirms his belief, and remain blind to anything that contradicts it. I do not say ignore or deliberately overlook contrary evidence, but simply not see it for what it is. I am sure that happens often in your line of work."

"I have heard of such things," said Blume.

"Quite. So you know exactly what I mean. So if Nightingale were to discover a painting of dubious provenance, first he would need to persuade himself of its value. Then he would need to persuade another dealer or a buyer of the same. Once that is done he has no active role in what happens next. The dealers and buyers will consciously and unconsciously gather evidence to confirm what they want to believe. Once you have a true believer, there is often a bandwagon effect, with more and more becoming convinced of the same thesis, until it is established as fact. It is a self-fulfilling process, and the value he attached to it to begin with is often well below the value finally accorded to it by others. It has nothing to do with intelligence either. The more intelligent a buyer is, the more convincing his arguments in favor of the authenticity of the work he has bought."

"And you are here because . . .?"

"Mr. Nightingale has provided you with a great deal of information. Far more than I would have liked. In return, he asks to see the notes Mr. Treacy left. We know they are in your possession, and were illegally removed from Treacy's house."

"Is that all?" said Blume.

"Look, Blume," said Nightingale. "I have told you an awful lot. I don't believe you are the designated investigator, and I am not even sure you have a right to those notes. I think it's my right."

"Almost all of what you told me I found out in Henry's notes," said Blume. "And no, you can't have them. Not yet, at any rate. Tell you what though," he pulled across his notepad and flicked it open. "I took some reader's notes . . . and . . . Here we are . . . see if you can shed some light on this."

"Why should I help you if you won't help me?" said Nightingale.

"No reason," said Blume. "None at all. It's just your lawyer's little speech reminded me of a passage by Henry—Harry, you call him—which ends with a slightly mysterious note. Ah, here it is. Now just before the passage he has made a sort of note, in which he lays down three laws for a forger. I copied them out but I'm not sure I follow them. But they appear again in his third volume, which was evidently the first draft of a handbook for forgers and painters. Avvocato, I am afraid this is in English. I hope you can follow:

*"Basic rules for forgers, interpreters, emulators, admirers, and genuine artists:*
1. *Authentic materials count for more than quality.*
2. *Quality will eventually move general opinion, but it may take time.*
3. *General opinion is more important than authentic materials.*

"Is it me, or is there something a bit circular going on there?" said Blume.

Nightingale shrugged and said, "Harry liked to sound wise. He had almost no education, you know."

For some reason, Blume found himself wanting to defend Treacy, or at least ruffle Nightingale's air of self-satisfaction. On impulse, he pulled the notebooks out of his drawer and placed them on his desk.

Nightingale jumped out of his seat and came over. His lawyer, too, stood up and approached the desk.

"Are those the notebooks?" asked Nightingale.

"These?" said Blume absently. "Yes. They are. Sit down both of you. *Avvocato, si sieda, per favore.* And you, too, Nightingale, sit down."

This time Nightingale chose the chair next to his lawyer, as close to the desk as possible.

Slowly, though he knew where to look, Blume turned over the pages, tapping passages with his finger as if searching for a word. Finally he said, "Ah. Here it is. Allow me to read to you.

*"One of the simplest and best ways of building up provenance and value for a painting was to buy it. This was a trick at which John excelled. I don't think he ever used the same route twice for getting a painting into an auction, so there was no clear pattern—not that this was of any real concern to the auction houses, which often place false bids themselves to push up prices. Nowadays they and dealers do it all the time. They have to, because they have invested in contemporary art which they all secretly know is intrinsically worthless.*

*"We dealt mainly in legitimate art, so John, or someone he was paying to bid*

*on his behalf, was often to be found at auctions buying works. Sometimes he would pay over the odds for a work, and then sell it for less. But not often.*

*"Let's say I had created a 'Corot' landscape, which is the easiest thing in the world, in my opinion . . ."*

Blume looked up startled as Nightingale barked like a seal, "Hah! He could never do a Corot. I told you, he couldn't paint air. Too much weather even in old Corot for Harry. The man is a pathological liar."

"Shall I read on?"

Nightingale muttered something, and when he stopped, Blume continued:

*"Nightingale would bring the painting to a dealer friend who, for a fee, would agree to pass it on to another dealer who, again for a fee, would pass it on to a 'buyer' who would then decide to sell it to the auction house, setting a minimum price. John would turn up and bidding would begin. If there were no takers, one of John's hidden agents would bid against us until they reached a suitable price. Now the painting had a history and a value ascribed to it. There was no legal danger in this, because if the painting was exposed as a fake John came across as victim. But there was a moral danger. If everyone knows you are buying a fake, then you are either a poor swindler or a sorry victim. Swindler is a term you can live with in the art world. Victim, no. No one likes a victim.*

*"I think it's fair to say that the more important a person is, or is supposed to be, the less I shall like him or her. I particularly detest self-important artists, those self-advertising modernists who think they have something to say because they are too ignorant of art history to know it has already been said and done, and vastly better, by others. Worse still, of course, are the Nihilists, the showmen, the charlatans, shit artists like Pietro Mazoni, whom I once had the misfortune to meet at a dinner party. But I was very honored to meet Giorgio de Chirico. This is a man who has recognized the crisis in art. He accepts my argument that since there is nothing more to say and nothing can be better done than it already is, the only solution is to become surreal or to imitate. De Chirico manages both and, to top it all, he forges his own work, signing other people's paintings with his name (only if they ask, of course, for he is a gentleman).*

*"But unlike just about every other surrealist, none of whose works I can bear to look at, let alone honor by emulation, de Chirico is a draftsman. Nobody wins my affection and admiration more than a modern artist who still knows*

*how to draw. His surreal works (which he insists on calling <u>pittura metafisica</u>, even though I think surreal will do just fine) have a command of line, shadow, and perspective like any of the old masters. He's always closer to Mantegna than that mustache-twiddling Spanish showman Dalí. To be sure, he messes about a bit, but he knows how it's done.*

*"Another thing that marks him out from the others is the breadth and depth of his learning. His linguistic skills alone make him exceptional. Italian, Greek, German, French, English, Latin, and, of course, Russian (and what a beautiful Russian wife he has).*

*"A draftsman when he is being surreal, he is a classicist when he's being post-modern (how I hate that term). Like me, he knows that the giants, Titian, Raphael, Rubens, and Velázquez, dwell in the past. Like me, he does freehand riffs on them, but unlike me, he imposes his own style on them. Me, I let their style speak directly through me.*

*"I prefer his 'classical' style. Most of all, I adore his references to Velázquez, his re-elaborations of Velázquez's pictures of Villa Medici, Villa Falconieri. And Velázquez, of course was interpreting great Italian architects, some of them also mad, like Jacopo Zucchi. So when I copy de Chirico, I am drawing on layers and layers of great tradition.*

*"But here's the thing. This is important. Pay attention those who love me. When I painted some works in the style of de Chirico, I found he did not have a style completely his own. He was uncomfortable with himself. He was a modernist, in other words. So my interpretation of de Chirico's Villa Medici is different. I have made slight changes. It could be the same villa; it could be another one that is very similar. An attentive observer should be able to tell. Perhaps I am referring more to Velázquez in this work, which bears my signature and imprint. Some day it will be worth millions. And I am referring to the work itself, my painting, not just what it indicates."*

"None of this makes any bloody sense!" Nightingale exploded. "That bastard couldn't paint Titian, Raphael, Rubens, Velázquez. I just told you that. De Chirico, yes—like Harry said, that was all draftsmanship."

"That's what had me wondering," said Blume. "And what about the last bit about de Chirico, Velázquez? And the 'Pay attention those who love me'?"

"I have no idea what he is on about," said Nightingale. "No one loved him. Not even his own mother, if I recall his drunken confessions, which unfortunately I do. But I have no context to judge the meaning here. You really ought to let me have the notebooks."

"I will," promised Blume. "As soon as I work out one or two things for myself. Meanwhile, to judge from the uncharacteristically agreeable smile on your lawyer's face, I don't think he understood a fucking word of that. Explain it to him on your way out."

# 26

T HE YOUTH DID not say anything, but he sat down as asked.

"What's your name?" she asked.

"Sandro."

"Sandro, I want you to tell me what you know about the muggings of foreign tourists."

"Nothing."

Caterina's feet hurt. Her bra strap was cutting into her side like it was made from bailing wire, and her eyes and nose felt hot, dry, and flaky.

"Your friends will be here soon. It will take twenty minutes at most."

"I know nothing."

"What was this I heard about you seeing something?" she asked, not holding out much hope for a meaningful response. It was probably a setup, Grattapaglia getting his revenge by showing her the sort of stuff he knew she couldn't handle.

His suspension from duty, still her fault evidently, was just hours away. But she did not need him to prove she could not do what he did. She already knew that. She did not have his bulk, swagger, girth, experience, age, his bullying instincts and capacity for sudden violence, his slyness and menace. Maybe Blume was punishing her, too.

Stay there and question this one, Grattapaglia had ordered her; ordered her though she was his superior in rank; I'll round up a few more. Then he abandoned her, against regulations, with a male youth and no supervisors anywhere.

The youth was shaking his stupid shaved head and mumbling something incoherent. What did you have to do to a child to allow him to become like this? Ignore him. That was probably all it took. That and the bad luck of giving birth to him in the first place.

She tried again, probing gently at first, then with more insistence. All she got were monosyllables. After twenty minutes, she had established that Sandro knew nothing about tourist muggings. All he knew is that when a patrol came to move him and his friends off the bridge, he had told the two cops they were cowards, hassling him and his friends but not bothering about rapists.

"What rapist?" asked Caterina automatically, wishing she hadn't bothered.

"Maybe not a rapist. I don't know."

Which was why she shouldn't have bothered asking.

"When was this?"

"On Tuesday, April 4."

The precision seemed uncharacteristic, and caught her attention. "You remember the date?"

"It was three days after my birthday."

"Happy birthday. How old are you?"

"Eighteen."

"An adult now. What time did you see this incident?"

"Around three, four in the morning."

"Where?"

"That piazza with the bar on the corner, you know. Trees. Behind Vicolo del Moro."

"Are you talking about Piazza de' Renzi?"

"I don't remember the name."

"Can you remember the name of a bar or anything?"

Sandro cleaned his nose with the back of his hand. Caterina fished a packet of Kleenex from her bag. "Use a tissue, for Christ's sake, child. Clean your hand."

He wiped his hand across his sleeve and said, "There's a bar with two umbrellas. The bartender's an asshole. I totally tagged the front of his bar."

"You spray-painted his walls? I'm not going to follow up on this, so just say yes or no."

"He caught me doing a throw-up on a wall once. It wasn't even his wall, but he thought he'd intervene. He reported me to the cops, but not before he had tried to blind me spraying the aerosol into my eyes. So we've been targeting his bar."

"Tell me what you saw."

They were interrupted by shouting and curses and trampling feet that announced the arrival of Grattapaglia and three more youths. Two girls, no older than sixteen, and a kid who looked about fifteen.

They all wore tattoos and metal studs and rings on their faces, and as soon as they entered the basement, they seemed to converge on Caterina. They were aggressive, but they crowded her also like kids around a teacher, or greedy toddlers around a mother with candy. Two of them were clutching bottles of beer by the neck.

"You didn't take the drink away?" Caterina asked Grattapaglia, who was standing with one foot against the wall.

"You afraid they'll use the bottles as weapons? These creatures?"

A greatly pierced and abscessed girl walked with a sideways lurch, as if the bottle of Ceres she held in her hand weighed heavily.

Caterina said, "OK. Both of you put your bottles on the floor. Both of you."

She stood patiently as a torrent of abuse flowed toward her, moving back and forth a few steps trying to show it did not bother her, but it did.

When they had stopped cursing her, they looked at each other for new ideas. Then the young boy detached himself from the group, picked up a beer bottle, and dangled it at his side. He went up to Caterina, leaned closer, then belched loudly in her face, opening his mouth wide.

It was the funniest thing they had ever seen.

Grattapaglia took his foot off the wall, stepped forward two paces and, with a lazy, sweeping slow-motion movement of his arm, slapped the kid across the face. He opened his fingers at the last moment to lessen the blow, but the kid still fell sideways as if shot. The beer bottle dropped straight to the floor and cracked and rolled.

The pierced girl came running over, screaming. She knelt down beside him and cradled his face. The other two shuffled around, bumping into each other like blinded animals in a pen, unable to decide whether to stay or go. The girl began to cry, rubbing the back of her hand across her perforated nose.

Caterina was beside Grattapaglia now, her lips drawn back, the tendons on her neck throbbing. "What the fuck was that? The child is about fifteen, younger maybe."

"I hardly touched him. It was a slap, not a punch."

"That's not what you do to a child."

"He's bigger than you," said Grattapaglia.

She looked at the youth whose head the girl was trying to lift and cradle. The scarlet weal on the boy's face showed the white outline of Grattapaglia's fingers.

"I'm going to sue you fuckers," said the boy, pushing the girl away and struggling into a standing position.

"That's likely," said Grattapaglia. "You really look like the sort of person who has a personal lawyer on a retainer."

"My parents will sue for me. When they hear this, they'll sue. My father has contacts. When I tell them, they'll ... they'll ..." He pointed to Caterina. "What's your name? You're going to jail, *puttana*."

Caterina tried to touch the child's face, but he pushed her hand roughly away.

"I'm sorry," she said.

"The fuck you are. I'm suing."

"Stop it," said Caterina. "Nobody's getting sued."

She had had enough. "Sovrintendente, get these kids out of here. Put them back wherever you found them, send them to social services. Just so that you and they get the hell out of my sight. Now!"

"I thought they might have seen something."

"Sandro stays with me," said Caterina. She looked over at his white face. He had put his thumb in his mouth. When he saw her looking, he started biting at the nail, rubbing his teeth, rolling his eyes as if the police exasperated rather than terrified him.

To her surprise, Sovrintendente Grattapaglia did what she asked.

When the clumping up the stairs and babble of voices had died away, she repeated her question. "What did you see?"

"I already said. I saw this old guy try to grab a girl. I saw him do it. Then she lashed out and punched him and ran away. And the old guy fell and didn't get up."

"How do you know he didn't get up?"

"I went over to him. I was going to give him a kicking, and I don't have a problem saying that. But when I got there I could see he was, you know, out of it."

"Do you mean unconscious?"

"Almost. His eyeballs were sort of swimming around and then they floated right up into his head, out of sight. Like this." Sandro rolled his eyes around.

"I don't need the visuals, thanks. Did the man say anything?"

"Yeah. He said, 'Call her back.' Amazing he could say that."

"Is that it?"

"That's all I heard."

"Did he have an accent?"

Sandro scrunched up his face. "Can't say. His voice was all husky and sort of gurgly. Maybe he had an accent. What sort?"

"Forget it." She did not want to start suggesting details to him. "Did you call an ambulance?"

"For a rapist?"

"I see you're quick to condemn, Sandro. Just like those people who look down on you and your friends."

"Someone tried to rape my girlfriend Elvira."

"That was the older girl in here just now? The one with the red hair extension?"

"What's a hair extension?"

"Your girlfriend's string of red hair. It's not her own."

"I thought it was dyed. Yeah, Elvira got attacked once, but didn't report it."

"You said tried. Did she get raped or not?"

"She said no. She said one grabbed her from behind, the other started ripping at her clothes. She said she fought and spat. When she screamed she was HIV positive, they ran off."

"When was this?"

"A few months ago."

"Where?"

"Monte Mario."

"An old guy that time, too?"

Sandro looked puzzled. "No, no. She said two young guys."

A different time, different place, different attacker. "So you were sort of revenging her, even though this was someone else?"

Sandro shrugged. "Old guy molesting a young woman."

"Did you see him attack her?"

"No. He was trying to hold her. An old guy like that."

"How do you know she was a young girl? It was dark, she ran before you arrived."

"She had long silver-blond hair. I heard her voice, which was young,

211

and then when she ran. You can sort of tell someone's age from how they move, you know?"

"What age would you say she was?"

"I don't know. She could have been sixteen, she could have been maybe as old as thirty, but no older."

Caterina made Sandro go back over the events twice more, and then made him do it in reverse chronological order while she checked against her notes. His story did not change. He saw the girl push the old man, then run. The old man lay on the ground. Sandro went over to him but did not help. He did not see anything wrong with his own behavior. He told the story a fourth time, and again mentioned that his original reason for going over to the old man was to kick him, not help him. In not kicking him, Sandro felt he had shown restraint.

"Also, I didn't steal money or anything from him."

"That was good of you, Sandro." Caterina reached into her shoulder bag and pulled out a blow-up of Emma's ID photo.

"Sweet!" said Sandro. "Who's that?"

"You've never seen her?"

"I'd have remembered a face like that. What's this got to do with anything?"

"Nothing," said Caterina. "Just an idea."

Caterina accompanied Sandro back up to his friends, who were seated on the plastic bench at the entrance on the first floor, eating pizza and drinking cans of Coca-Cola.

"I may be in touch." She gave him a half-push, half-caress on the shoulder to propel him down the corridor.

She watched as the sorry little crew gave their Sandro a welcome fit for a returning warrior king. They piled out of the station into the evening air, their energy returned, their spirits temporarily lifted as they were given back the excessive freedom that was killing them.

She went back up to the operations room, where Grattapaglia was beginning to clear his desk.

"Anything?" he asked.

"Not that will help us with the muggings."

He shrugged and turned back to his work.

Caterina said, "Where did they get the pizza and Coca-Cola?"

"From the *pizzeria a taglio* down the road, I suppose," said Grattapaglia.

"You accompanied them, right?"

"Of course. You told me to keep an eye on the scumbags."

"You took them out and brought them back. Did you buy the pizza for them, too?"

"Dumb little fuckers spend all their money on drugs," said Grattapaglia. "Who else was going to pay?"

# 27

For the next half hour, Grattapaglia slammed things on his desk and kicked at chairs, while Caterina stood in front of a large-scale map of Trastevere, pulling out and putting in the pins showing where the muggings had taken place. The map had been on the wall for three months, and the number of pins had gradually expanded.

She had to pass by Assistente Capo Rospo's desk on her way to turn on the overhead lights, and he took the opportunity to say, "Those pins don't mean shit."

"They all converge around two places," said Caterina.

"Yeah, two hotels. Big fucking surprise that, finding tourists in hotels."

"This hotel has more than ..."

She had to stop talking, because Grattapaglia's metal desk drawer refused to slide, and Grattapaglia smashed the side of his heel into it several times, swept the stuff from his desk, and left it on the floor.

"*Ma vaffanculo a tutto!*" Grattapaglia clenched and unclenched his fists, then rubbed his left bicep and whitened.

Rospo was suddenly busy with his work.

Caterina went over to the Sovrintendente. "Let me help you," she said. "Don't let the stress kill you."

"Fuck the stress," said Grattapaglia. "It's being indoors. Last thing I'm going to do here is find out who the damned mugger is. You coming?"

Caterina hesitated. Her shift ended in half an hour.

"Sure," she said. "Just let me call my mom, tell her I'll be late again."

Grattapaglia surprised her by suggesting they go on foot.

"It'll calm me. We catch the mugger, we can call a car."

As they were crossing Ponte Garibaldi, she pulled the blow-up of Emma's ID photo from her shoulder bag and showed it to Grattapaglia.

"The kid who knew nothing about the mugging?" she said. "I think he might have seen her, but he did not identify her."

Grattapaglia looked at the photo carefully. Emma waited for a crude comment, but none was forthcoming. "Who is she?"

Caterina explained. Grattapaglia nodded, "This has nothing at all to do with the muggings."

"I know. I just thought I'd tell you what I was doing down there with that kid. Look, I know you're the one who's going to be doing all the work and all the talking for the next few hours, and I'm basically going to be in your way . . . but I was wondering, could you . . ." she delved back into her shoulder bag and pulled out a photo of Treacy.

Grattapaglia looked at the photo of Treacy in one hand, Emma in the other. "You want me to ask about the girl and Treacy as well as the muggings?" said Grattapaglia.

"As a favor."

They veered right toward the Jewish school, for no other reason than that Grattapaglia seemed to want to shoot the breeze with the four patrolmen guarding the entrance. Caterina waited in the shadows, listening to a stream of guffawing misogyny.

Then they walked to a bar where the bartender greeted Grattapaglia like an old friend and nodded warily at her.

"Wait here," Grattapaglia told Caterina, and he and the bartender disappeared into a back room. Ten minutes later, he reemerged.

They left the bar, Grattapaglia whistling, swaggering slightly as he occupied the absolute center of the street, forcing young people and tourists to move to either side of him.

Caterina realized the price to be paid for asking a favor was she would have to chisel information out of him.

"Did that bartender see Treacy or Emma?"

"Emma. I didn't even know the name," said Grattapaglia. "He knew the Englishman. But he couldn't remember if he had seen him on the night in question."

"Shit, I just remembered something," said Caterina. "Her name would not have been Emma. Use the name Manuela instead."

"Whatever you say. I still don't know who she is."

Caterina explained, and Grattapaglia listened attentively, bending down in a way that reminded her a bit of Blume. Tall men, the two of them. Broad, too, though Grattapaglia was out of shape.

"Now I know who I'm talking about, I might be able to ask better questions. Maybe I should have been told before now. You seem to be in a privileged position with the Commissioner."

Caterina was glad of the dark that hid her face. She changed subject as casually as she could manage. "The bartender you were just talking to, was he working that night?"

"*Porcaccia la misera!* I forgot to ask."

He was jerking her about, but he was also doing what she had asked and so she kept quiet.

He walked on a bit, then said, "Yes, he was working that night. No, he didn't see them."

In the next bar, on Piazza Santa Maria, a bartender in a starched white outfit with gold buttons glanced at the photos and became immediately adamant that Treacy had not been there. About the girl he knew nothing.

"Are you absolutely sure?"

The bartender sprayed blue detergent on the zinc counter and wiped it even cleaner.

"I'm not saying I don't know him. I do. That's why he doesn't come here anymore."

"You won't serve him?"

The bartender touched his toothbrush mustache with his finger, and spoke in soft and confessional tones, throwing an anxious glance at two well-dressed men with briefcases seated at the table outside. "He threw up vomit and blood all over a table of Germans. I don't know what's wrong with him, but a guy that age and that sick should know better than to drink like that. Is he dead?"

"Yes."

"Not surprised," said the bartender, and dried droplets from the sink.

They left the piazza and reached the third bar. A fug of marijuana sat above the fifty or so people sitting outside.

A thin skinhead Roma soccer "Ultra" with blue arms was trying to stare them down.

Grattapaglia led the way toward the farther of the two ancient tin tables to his left, which was occupied by three men, two of whom had hardly taken their eyes off them since they arrived.

Grattapaglia said, "Let's have something here. It's always very informative."

Caterina was not so sure, but she sat down and ordered a granita while Grattapaglia ordered a beer. When the bartender came back, Grattapaglia asked him who had been here on the previous Friday night.

"Can't say," said the bartender, bending down to put the beer and granita on the table. Caterina pulled out the photos but Grattapaglia forestalled her, placing his outsized hand on her arm.

"No. First the muggings. Also, not here. You can't ask Danilo questions in full view of everyone. He could be telling us anything, as far as they're concerned. So the only move open to him is to tell us nothing and make sure they all see him saying nothing. Do you follow?"

"I think so," said Caterina.

"OK." He handed her back the photos. "You keep these. This is your gig, and I want them to understand that. Now, see that Brazilian over there?"

Emma looked and saw a small guy dressed in a Brazil soccer strip wearing a baseball cap.

"Every time we meet that guy, we yank off his cap and throw it away. Then he has to buy one, to hide the fact his head is the size of a pin. He's so sensitive about it." Grattapaglia spluttered into his glass, evidently recalling the last time this fun had taken place.

Beside him sat a sagging fiftyish man with long curling locks of gray hair and an unfinished mustache over dead lips.

"That's Fabio the Failure," said Grattapaglia. "Whenever I'm depressed at still being a sovrintendente at this age, and think I've made a mess of my life, I just think of Fabio, and it cheers me up. In the 1970s, Fabio got a walk-on part in a film and has been living on the glory ever since. Well, the glory, a disability allowance, and a little extra from some casual house-breaking. Uh-oh, what have we here?"

A third person, the one ostentatiously not looking at Grattapaglia and Caterina, sported a tight-fitting T-shirt and large orange glasses with pimp jewelry and ethnic tattoos on his arms. His underpants were hitched up to his stomach, the waistline of his jeans rested halfway down his backside. The other two treated him with the deference due to a prince.

Grattapaglia picked up his beer and walked up to the table, big smile on his face. He looked like he belonged. He waved Caterina over to join him and his friends.

"Weather's changeable, isn't it?" said Grattapaglia. "Hot one minute. Raining the next. Empty the contents of your pockets and place them on the table."

"Go fuck your mother," said the tiny Brazilian, glancing sideways to see if Orange Glasses appreciated how hardassed he could be. Caterina noticed the Brazilian lisped slightly.

Grattapaglia reached out suddenly and snatched the baseball cap off the Brazilian's head, then just as quickly put it back on again.

"Still no hair, Luis?" he said sympathetically, then turned his attention to Orange Glasses who was surveying faraway rooftops with regal indifference. "I don't believe we've been introduced."

No reply.

"Ah, *pardon*," said Grattapaglia, putting a real French accent into the word. "You speak shqiptar, right?"

The gaze moved down from the rooftops and locked on Grattapaglia's face. He had eyes like a carrion crow. Caterina was glad she was not receiving the stare.

Grattapaglia, however, seemed to find the stare funny. After beaming at the face in front of him for a while, he reached over and gently removed the orange glasses, put them on the metal table. She felt the other two shifting outwards, away from the center, and she did the same.

"Hey," said Grattapaglia, "maybe you can help me. I'm looking for Albanian translators. We can hardly cope, all these Albanian pimps and housebreakers. We looked everywhere for an Albanian teacher. Can't seem to find one. My girlfriend here says there's no such thing, says you can't teach Albanians anything. Unless it involves goats."

The Albanian kept his movements measured as he turned and studied Grattapaglia's face, as if previewing a lingering death scene. Then he said, "She's not your girlfriend. You're married. Remember that next time you insult me."

Grattapaglia raised an imaginary glass. "*Gëzuar*, my friend. Danilo!" he roared as the bartender passed. "Sit down here."

The bartender sat down, his eyes wary.

"There have been muggings in our area," said Grattapaglia. "Now I distinctly recall telling people a while ago that these muggings had to stop. But they didn't, did they?"

The Albanian yawned.

"And now it's too late. Stopping is no longer good enough. We need the fucker who's been doing them, and we need him fast."

Caterina looked at the faces of the men around the table. None of them seemed to be taking in a word that Grattapaglia was saying. They had all assumed the expression of commuters on a crowded train. Even the hostility was gone.

"Hear about the Indian guy and his kid got killed?" said Grattapaglia.

It would seem that no one had. But Grattapaglia talked on regardless. "I wouldn't want to be the guys who did that. Dead on Arrival, sometime tomorrow. Just you wait."

"I thought you wanted to talk about the muggings, not the dead Indian and his kid," said Danilo.

"Who says they're not connected?"

"Look, I've got work to do," said Danilo, making as if to get up.

"Hold on, Danilo. Inspector, show the gentlemen the photographs. Now these, you may be interested to learn, have nothing to do with the muggings, or the hit-and-run. We have so much shit on our plate we need you guys to help us eat it."

Caterina put the photos of Treacy and Emma on the table. The Albanian glanced at them for a moment, stood up, picked up his glasses, and wandered off, dead casual, like he had just now thought of it. Grattapaglia did not even look up as he left.

"Well?" Grattapaglia snatched the baseball cap off the Brazilian again, stuffed it in his pocket. "Well, you two?"

"That man is dead," said Fabio the Failure, pointing at Treacy.

"We know that, Fabio. All we want to know is whether he was here on Friday night."

Fabio shrugged. "Yeah. I think so."

"You, Danilo? Did you serve him or her?"

"Hey, I wasn't here Friday," said the Brazilian. Grattapaglia held up a restraining hand. "We're talking, Luis. Can't you see we're talking? Please."

Suddenly the bartender grinned.

"I know her. Who wouldn't remember her? Most of what she orders here she gets on the house, and I still haven't managed to get her to look at me properly. Maybe when she does, she'll like what she sees."

"Those lips round my cock," said the Brazilian.

"Danilo, was she here on Friday night with Treacy?" Grattapaglia looked at Caterina. "That's the main thing we need to know, isn't it?"

Caterina nodded.

"Yes, she was here," said Danilo. "I served them at least five drinks."

"I see, and were they on their own?" said Grattapaglia, leaning back and stretching his arms lazily above his head. Coming out of the posture, he suddenly smashed his elbow into the Brazilian's ear. "You mind your language in front of Inspector Mattiola, Luis." The Brazilian opened his mouth wide in pain, but made little noise. Caterina noticed all his bottom teeth were missing.

Grattapaglia smiled at the bartender. "I asked you, were they on their own?"

"Don't do that here. You'll lose us customers."

"No one noticed," said Grattapaglia. "Luis is too small to see."

"Sometimes she is with one of those university types. But not on Friday night. Manuela and Henry were alone."

Caterina looked at him sharply. "You know their names?"

"Henry practically lived here. As for Manuela, I learned her name the first day I set eyes on her. Ask around, and I bet you wouldn't find one male customer who doesn't know her name. Looks like that get you noticed. I hope she wasn't screwing that old guy. It would be such a waste."

"One last question," said Grattapaglia. "What time did they leave?"

"Closing time. One thirty."

"Hey, I wasn't even here that night," repeated the Brazilian.

"Too bad, Luis. No baseball cap for you, then," said Grattapaglia. "Fabio, were you here—why, what am I saying? Are you ever anywhere else? I think we'll keep this table, now. So you'll have to move."

Before leaving, Fabio spilled beer on his chair, and Luis hacked up mucus and a shining silver glob on to the cobbles. Grattapaglia sat back and seemed to enjoy soaking up the hostility radiating from the customers around him.

"The Albanian saw the photos and let them all know he didn't care what they said. It has nothing to do with their trade, so he'll be fine with it, and Danilo, the bartender, has nothing to worry about, you see. It was the only way to ask. But did you see the way Danilo said the killing of the Indian had nothing to do with the muggings?"

"I noticed that, yes."

"To know that, he must know something. Someone needs to talk to him, and it can't be me, since I'm getting suspended thanks to you."

She let that pass.

"Yeah, so, anyway . . . You should follow that up. Not on your own, of course."

"Right," said Caterina. "Thanks."

"No problem," said Grattapaglia, standing up. "Well, that's my duty done for the day, maybe for the next three months, maybe forever." He touched a slight bulge in his jacket pocket. "Hey, where are you going now?"

Caterina felt a lurch in her stomach like she had just lost her grip on a height. A slight thawing in their relationship and now Grattapaglia thought he could make a move on her?

"Me? I am going home."

"Directly?"

"Yes. Straight home. I'm tired." No, that was worse. Don't make excuses.

"Right," Grattapaglia grinned at her. "You have a son, right?"

"I do have a son. Yes."

Grattapaglia pulled out the bulge from his pocket. "Could he use a baseball cap?"

# 28

Elia was asleep on his feet as she steered him toward the apartment. His grandmother thought it unforgivable that Caterina should insist on dragging him out of bed and back to his own house. But Caterina wanted him at home.

Because he is my son, she told her mother.

As she was opening the front door of their apartment building, a dark figure she had noticed standing at the street corner began to walk quickly toward them.

"Get in," she told Elia. She handed him the house keys. "Here, can you open the front door by yourself?"

"No."

"Take the elevator. Wait for me upstairs . . . Go on!"

Reluctantly the child entered the building and she pulled the front door shut behind him, stood back, and moved her hand down to her weapon, then back again to a more relaxed position as she recognized the tall shape and sloping gait of the man.

"Grattapaglia phoned me to say you were going straight home," said Blume as he arrived. "But you took longer than I expected. You had to pick up Elia."

Caterina stood away from the door. "And now he has the keys, and we're locked out."

"Wait till he's in the apartment, and then ring the intercom," said Blume.

"He can't open the apartment door. He'll be standing in the corridor as I stand here outside. Why didn't you just phone?"

"I wanted to see you in person, and I am a little distrustful of my cell phone. Do you have a neighbor who stays up late?"

"The woman above me, she brings men home sometimes, and they clump about above my head and worse until late. She owes me."

Caterina pressed the intercom button and, after some time, got a very belligerent challenge before the door clicked open.

"She doesn't have a man tonight, I guess," said Blume.

Caterina held the door open with her foot. "You had better come in."

She called the elevator, and they squeezed in together. Caterina pressed the button to the third floor. When they got out, Elia was leaning his head against the front door, with his eyes closed.

"We'll talk in a minute." She put Elia to bed, kissed his forehead, already clammy. She felt his hands. Slightly waxy. Harder than they used to be, bigger, too. His breath was OK. A child in his class had diabetes. Elia didn't, of course. She shouldn't worry.

When she returned to the living room, Blume began speaking as if they had been in mid-conversation, as if it was not half past eleven at night in her apartment after a long and stress-laden day, the day in which her son had briefly disappeared, she had betrayed her own principles . . . She closed her eyes.

"So," said Blume, sounding inappropriately cheerful, "the Colonel has had a copy of the notebooks since this morning."

"Yes, I'm sorry. I should have told you everything at once," said Caterina.

"What you did was justifiable, though I don't think it was right, or wise. I've brought the originals with me. I'm going to put them in a safe place."

Caterina sighed and stood up.

"You're tired. Make some coffee. I'll have some, too."

"You want coffee, you make it," said Caterina.

A few minutes later, she was seated on her sofa. Blume's voice, careless of sleeping child, boomed out from behind the kitchen partition at the far end of the room. "Tell me what you discovered about Emma this evening," he poked his head around the corner and looked in.

Caterina opened her eyes wide. "Grattapaglia was reporting to you on me?"

"I asked him to tell me when you were going home. He volunteered the rest of the information about Emma and Treacy being seen together at the bar. He also told me you seem to have learned something from one of those drop-out kids, but that it could not have had anything to do with the muggings, since you said nothing. Where's the coffeepot?"

"On the stove, straight in front of you. No! Straight in front as in Straight. In. Front. Well done."

She summarized Sandro's brief account of the old man and the young woman in the piazza, as Blume washed the pot and spent some time looking for the garbage can for the coffee grounds.

"If we connect that to the evidence that Emma was with Treacy at the bar beforehand," said Caterina. "We've got the bartender as a witness and, well, there's something else."

"Coffee?"

"Second shelf, left, in a blue box with golden stars on it."

"Got it," called Blume. "What's the other thing?"

"Emma's got one of those BlackBerry phones. It would be easy to track her movements using phone mast triangulation and GPS positioning. We can check whether she was at the bar and whether she was at the piazza when Treacy was killed. We should have checked before now."

"You're right," said Blume. "Except we don't have a magistrate to issue an order to the phone company. The Colonel does."

"But there are ways of getting the information without a magistrate's sanction."

"Sure," said Blume. "As long as we don't try to use it as evidence. But you are right. The Colonel will already have that information."

"I don't feel comfortable with the Colonel knowing this about Emma. I think he'll misuse it."

"Eventually. But I think he is going to be distracted by something else in Treacy's writings. Unless he knew already, which is possible since Treacy was a drunk, and drunkards like to boast, reveal themselves, and then forget . . . How do you turn on this gas? I mean light the gas. I think I turned it on some time ago."

"Press the black button but first . . ."

A blue flame flashed and the thump of the displacement of air was forceful enough to rock the crockery in the cupboards above.

"Found it," said Blume. He spent some time turning the gas knobs in an effort to lower the heat. Then he rubbed his hands, in anticipation of the coffee and in satisfaction at a job well done.

"The fact that the notebooks are in English might slow the Colonel down, but not by much. Somewhere across town, at this very minute, he and the Maresciallo are probably sitting together at a table, reading through the photocopies and discovering what I discovered last night. We need to keep a step ahead."

Blume brought coffee to Caterina, which he had saturated with sugar. He sat in the chair opposite, rapped the marbled cover of the top notebook, and then started leafing through the pages.

"After you left today, I read out a related passage to Nightingale. I wanted to see if what Treacy was talking about made any sense to him, and I am sure it did not."

He gulped back his coffee.

*". . . But of course, my works were never found out. Not once. It is not just that I am good, and I see no point in false modesty here, I am also self-critical and without illusions. If one of my works was not good enough, we never made a play with it. I would study it, see where I went wrong, and then either re-cover the canvas, if it was an antique one, or destroy the work. At any one time, I am not afraid to say, I would have fifteen, twenty unsuccessful works lying about my house . . ."*

Blume stopped. "Sorry, I started a bit early. Though that's interesting there, isn't it? It implies the works we found in his house, the ones I am supposedly trying to sell with the Colonel, aren't worth much."

She watched him leaf forward a few more pages and wondered if reading those few lines had really been a mistake, or he felt she needed more persuading of his honesty. His big foot hit the coffee cup on the floor and sent it spinning away, but he did not notice.

"Right. Here's the bit. He's talking about how he and Nightingale worked together, about how he sourced his materials, especially old canvases, and about the workings of Galleria Orpiment. The year is 1996.

*"Sometimes there would be a genuine bidder in the room, and that was always to be welcomed. If they went over a certain price, enough to cover the expenses incurred by John and enough to reward my labors, then we would let it go.*

*"It so happened one day that I was present at the auction, which was unusual. The bidding was taking place in Christies of Rome, and it was a tedious affair. We were not interested in most of the merchandise, mainly silverware and marble busts of God knows who fashioned by an artist justly forgotten. All legitimate, all very dull.*

*"Then an interesting item came up for sale. I had examined this work in the*

*catalogue before the auction. It was listed as a painting by an 'unknown Spanish artist' c. 1680–81. Of course, only an academic would dare place such a precise, and wrong, date on a work that he has just admitted he cannot identify. The painting was a blurred mess. The layers of varnish applied to it over the years had darkened it so much that when the auctioneers placed it on the display easel, all we could see was a shiny black square. Listed in the catalogue as Portrait of a Lady, it might as well have been titled 'A Study in Bitumen Cracks'.*

"I do not believe in a sixth sense, nor fate nor God, come to that. But I do believe the unconscious mind has enormous processing power and that sometimes it sends a clear signal to our conscious mind. There was something in that painting that I wanted.

"The starting price was low, so I raised my finger, which caught John by surprise. 'We want that?' he asked.

" 'Yes. It's interesting. And I like the old frame.'

" 'Very well. I'll bid for it,' said John.

"After three or four bids, the price had risen to around three million lire or thereabouts, but it was already beyond the price John thought the painting was worth.

" 'Someone's bidding against us,' he said, nodding at a broker across the room. 'Let them have it.'

" 'No. Keep going.'

"The price rose to five million lire, then six. John was getting agitated. It was not the sum itself, which translated into about three thousand pounds, but the fact it was unplanned bidding and he did not feel in control.

" 'Keep going,' I whispered.

"The room, sensing that something might be going on, became tenser and a new bidder joined in. The price, moving in increments of 250 thousand, climbed up to seven million, and the new bidder dropped out. At seven and a half million, the price of a secondhand Fiat, the painting was mine.

"I brought it directly home, placed it in my lean-to greenhouse, which, with the permission of my kind Pamphili landlords, I had added to the side of my house. It has just enough wood in its frame to be counted as a temporary structure, and thus no planning permission was needed. The conservatory is full of natural sunlight, which is far more powerful and penetrating than any artificial light in an auction room. I stood and stared at my acquisition for some time. It was like trying to see the bottom of a barrel of tar. I took out a bottle of acetone and wetted some cotton balls, allowing it to drip down between my fingers and evaporate *leaving the unmistakable scent of pear drops in the air, which I inhaled greedily as I tried to calm the manic energy I felt coursing through my muscles and nerves. With my hand trembling, I took a second wad of cotton and soaked it in turpentine (to act as a restrainer, if the acetone was too destructive), which gives off the best smell in the world. It had a good calming effect.*

*"Beginning in the bottom left, where mildew and damp had attacked the canvas, I applied the solvent, and watched as the black turned green. I worked at the painting for the entire day until the evening sun became too orange for me to be able to judge what I was doing. I went to bed, slept fitfully for a few hours, and was back at work at first light which being weak and gray tends to make one err on the side of caution, which is precisely how you want to be when working first thing in the early morning surrounded by the fumes of turpentine and acetone. At the end of the day I had a painting that was covered in green. Now, rather than frowning into a barrel of oil, I was smiling into a pond of slime.*

*"By evening, the green had turned to gray, and I was beginning to be sure of what I had here. I was nervous and had to force myself to eat. But I was focused and my hand no longer trembled.*

*"Another full day passed between swabbing and restraining. The closer I got the more frequently I changed the cotton balls so as not to confuse the colors, dropping one after the other on the floor, where they lay like dark-stained field dressings in a war hospital. Still I kept going, realizing on the third morning that I had not had a drink for two days.*

*"I could see the face that was emerging, and it made my heart beat and the blood in my chest sparkle with recognition and love in the way that no real person has ever done. The last time I had seen this beautiful young woman, she was pulling aside a curtain and peering down at a spinning wheel in the Prado Museum of Madrid. Even in the painting in the Prado, she is painted with indistinct, almost impressionistic strokes that convey movement and energy, and here the touch was even lighter. She was also poised in a slightly different position. It was a study for a later work, of that there could be no doubt, but it was a study done by the hand of Signor Diego Rodriguez de Silva y Velázquez. There is no mistaking the touch of that hand."*

They sat in their separate silences for a few moments. Caterina had eased off her shoes and swung her legs up onto the sofa, and buried one foot beneath a cushion.

"He found a Velázquez," said Caterina, allowing a note of doubt to creep into her voice. "Do you believe him?"

"Do I believe the story of how he found it? Possibly. Nightingale might remember the auction, but then again he might not if he never knew the significance of the find. Do I believe the story at all? I don't know. It might all be made up."

"Even if everything is true," said Caterina, "can we trust Treacy's identification of the Velázquez? He might have forged one. All these writings might be a long and elaborate hoax. Or he might be mistaken."

"Another thing," said Blume. "He doesn't say where it is. I need to reread the notebooks, or at least the second one. It's full of hints and allusions, and toward the end it reads more like a letter than an autobiography. He didn't date all the entries, but the latest ones were written last year. It reads like he knew he was dying. Stuff about each heartbeat is the bleeding away of his life, the soul's dark cottage."

"The painting is probably in his house. If it is, the Colonel will find it."

"I don't think it's in his house," said Blume, turning over pages. "I don't think he left it there. Later on—here we are—he seems to be telling Angela where it is. It's more like a letter of repentance. I think Nightingale's stories about how nasty Treacy was to her must be true."

*"I have stored that Velázquez where it belongs, Angela, and I want you to have it. It is legitimately come by, and I want you to use these notes and my story as part of the process of establishing provenance because, unfortunately, it will take some time before you are believed. I have not seen the painting these past years, but that has not been nearly as difficult as not seeing you.*

*"Do you remember meeting Francis Bacon? You might not, since at the time you did not know who he was. In Italy, nobody did in those days, and even now, he's regarded with that wearied tolerance that Italians maintain for experimental northerners. I saw him in London in 1972. I would like to say we met, but that would be overstating the case. But John introduced us in 1976.*

*"He was interested in me for a while. To begin with, we were Irish. Well, as he himself added, 'sort of Irish.' He was Irish in the way Mrs. Heath was Irish, which is to say English with a house in Ireland. People still think it's a shame so many big houses were razed by the IRA in the 1920s, but I find it hard not to sympathize with all that burning, even if it involved the loss of artworks.*

*"Although I was the younger man, as our conversation and acquaintanceship*

*progressed, my deference began to falter. The man had so many things wrong with him, and I am not talking about his sexual proclivities, though they disgusted me. Him with his big round head and his knobbly nose. No, that was not the problem. The problem is, was, that he could not draw.*

*"He could not draw. And he saw nothing wrong with admitting it. He wore it as a badge of honour. Like his sexual proclivities. Francis Bacon and his sausage.*

*"Nor could he prepare a canvas properly. He knew nothing about priming and then, once again making a 'virtue' of necessity, took to painting on unprimed canvas. He produced these ropy thread-encrusted bumpy works, all of which seemed to be based on Munch's Scream. He seemed to have no respect for the Old Masters, yet felt he had something new to say, which, in the end, are the two things I dislike most in contemporary art.*

*"But, I need to be fair to the man, because he allowed me, an unknown, aggressive, younger man, to criticize him. He said he was not imitating Munch, and pointed out that the man in Munch's painting was not screaming, but blocking his ears against a world that was screaming at him. He also reassured me that he did respect the Old Masters, one in particular, Velázquez, and, specifically, Velázquez's portrait of Pope Innocent X, the famously irascible Giambattista Pamphili, ancestor to the very family that had treated me so kindly over the years, allowing me to live on their property, now, sadly, owned and mismanaged by the Comune di Roma. Velázquez's work, he said, was the perfect portrait. He had been painting variations on the theme of that one work for years, and expected to continue for more years to come.*

*"I told him I knew the Doria Pamphilis, my benefactors, friends, and landlords, and promised I could arrange, next time he was in Rome, a private viewing of the Velázquez work, but—and this is how I know his respect for the Old Masters was less genuine than mine—he said he did not want to see the actual painting. He preferred to work from photographs.*

*"In being so bloody-minded and strange and annoying, Bacon, who wasn't a bad drinker either, was, in fact, sort of Irish after all. And he inspired me to look at that Velázquez portrait of Pope Innocent X until I, too, became obsessed with it and the painter. In 1982, the year Spain went into the European Community (and out of its own World Cup, thanks to Northern Ireland), I spent three months in Madrid, going every day to the Prado to look at <u>Las Meninas</u>, the <u>Forge of Vulcan</u>, and the portrait of Philip IV, especially the last. I immersed myself in the life of Velázquez. I even learned Spanish, though this is not very*

*hard to do if you already speak Italian. I made a point of seeing the rest of his work in New York, London, Vienna, and, God help us, that bloody awful swamp city Washington. What fascinated me, I suppose, was that I knew from the very start that I could not do Velázquez. I made a go at <u>Los Borrachos</u>, just to see. Ironically, I used photographs. The result was unpresentable. I could not do Velázquez, but I think it's safe to say no one alive could know him better than me. Although I failed to capture his style, I knew precisely how it should be. It's like when you fail to speak a language or mimic a voice properly. You can hear the accent, intonation, and characteristics of the voice in your head, but can't get your own voice to make the right sounds.*

*"All it took was the hint of a form of a woman peering in from the left in an unknown painting for me to get a fluttering of excitement followed by a jolt of recognition that almost stopped my heart. I swear, seeing the unmistakable line and chromatic touch of the artist in the painting on my easel almost killed me, even though I was the one who had sensed something in the canvas and had uncovered it. I had sought him out, but was shocked to find him.*

"The next half page," said Blume, "has a diagonal line drawn through it. Just one line, which suggests to me he was not convinced that he wanted to cancel these thoughts:

*"Angela, I began these memoirs and my handbook on how to emulate the Old Masters with the intention of getting them published, and I would appreciate it if you could get someone to finish and correct them for me if I don't finish in time, which seems likely. Don't ever give the only copy to John. In fact, keep that bastard away from this.*

*"A year at most, the doctor told me the other day. My doctor is a man who likes to hedge his bets. Like all doctors, he knows nothing. The Men Who Guess. All these years, they get away with guessing and then prescribing. Like economists, art critics, but worse. When the patient dies, they shrug. He gave me a year, as if the earth's circuit of the sun had anything to do with the pace of my body's self-destruction. I am writing this in the spring. One year later it will be spring again, so I hope he's wrong. I don't want to die when everything else is coming into life. I don't want to die before then either, of course. I really don't want to die. I need to resolve so many things first. And then, I want to have time to enjoy living with things resolved. Does anyone get to enjoy all that?*

*"Angela, I'm sorry. I know it sounds self-serving but you need to accept this.*

*You need to forgive people before they die, because being angry with the dead is the most frustrating and useless thing you will ever experience, and I know what I am talking about. Once they are gone, you can't get at them, you can't ask, you can't do anything except rage inside yourself. I'll tell you something: if there is an afterlife, it'll be full of the recently deceased picking fights with the earlier dead.*

*"Peace I leave with you, my peace I give unto you.*

*"Everything I have I leave to you. But I have already given you the most valuable thing I ever had. It is there before you, it is in these words, it is in our hearts and our memories. Remember the parties with Gustav the self-effacing Swedish archaeologist, who also happened to be a king? Remember the day we sat on the bench looking at the fighting putti in the open-air theatre convinced we had the whole garden to ourselves? And you kissed me, and one thing led to another, in there among the yew trees, after I played that trick and suddenly this mad Englishwoman was there, looking at us, asking what we thought we were doing. She would not accept that I lived in the garden, a guest of and friend of Pogson and his wife, Princess Pamphili. 'Babs' Johnson. Mad auld bat in a big straw hat. She set her dogs on me. She wrote under a penname. Georgina Masson and wrote the best guide to Rome there ever has been. Remember that?*

*"Look at that painting. Use your artist's eye and your lover's heart. Then you'll understand. Maybe you'll want to edit this bit out of the published work.*

"There's a blank page here, which he sized with gesso, as if he was planning to draw on it. The next few pages are blank, too, and then another bit, which I was thinking of reading out to Nightingale this afternoon, because it would have been interesting to see how he reacted.

*"The doubters will be legion, A. Trust me.*

*"John Nightingale and I were successful because we were indirect and invisible. Over the years, the works I did gathered more credibility and provenance, acquiring value and legitimacy like so many snowballs rolling downhill, always building momentum and growing larger the farther they got from us. I have seen my own paintings on display in some of the leading museums of the world. I shall give a list of the museums and the works in the appendix, but do not expect the museums to accept my claims.*

*"The time lapse between our sending a work out to seek its fortunes in the big bad world of art and its appearance as a completely provenanced and*

*documented Old Master's work in a top museum is around 20 years. Meanwhile, I have refined my techniques even further, so if you are reading this 20 years hence and a museum has just announced the purchase of a long-lost Italian Old Master, pause to consider and perhaps to smile.*

*"The prices fetched by some of my own works made us green with envy sometimes, but that is how it worked. The nearer a work was to us, the less it was worth, and the more suspicion attached to it. For, yes, of course, we were suspect. Many dealers knew, the Carabinieri knew, the auction houses, art historians, and museums knew. But they never knew enough, and most of our dealings were in authentic works.*

*"And here is where the irony begins. In recent years I have become more and more open about what I have done, the artists I have emulated, the paintings and drawings I have invented—and I invent, I do not copy. No more than I steal. But because I have become known, and because I am so good, and because I have been honest enough to talk about these things, I am the last person in the world who can announce the discovery of a long-lost Velázquez and be believed. If experts really were experts, they would know immediately that it is genuine, but they are not, and it is going to take them some time. To be sure, Nightingale could get it on to the market, but at a fraction of its price, and he'd steal the money from you, Angela. There are less than 120 Velázquez works surviving. Adding one to the repertory is big news. I had a painting worth tens of millions sitting in my kitchen, and I couldn't think of how to sell it.*

*"Knowing I could not rely on Nightingale, I began to look into the provenance myself, and found it was excellent. The painting had been in the possession of Adam Brookes, a private collector who ran a Chicago commodities brokerage that was doing pretty well until World War II, but went bust. He in turn seemed to have bought the painting from Joseph Duveen in 1918, which, I am afraid, like 1946, is one of those years that raises suspicions. After the European wars, an awful lot of plundered art changed hands, and it is a known favorite trick of people like John to pull up dubious records from just that time, when all was confusion. In any case, it appears that the painting was owned by Count Johann Ludwig von Wallmoden-Gimborn, the illegitimate son of George II of Britain. It stayed in royal hands until George V, that ignorant bollocks who was on the throne when Ireland struck for independence in 1916.*

*"In finding all this out, I enlisted John's help without letting him know what I was doing. I simply said I wanted to see how he set about his business and I learned what books to look up, how to consult catalogs, how to make deceptive phone calls and send innocent-sounding letters purporting to be from*

*students, travelers, guidebook authors, heritage groups, art appreciation societies, and the like.*

*"I would have told John, I would have enlisted his help, and together we would have shared the vast proceeds had he not treated me in the most ignoble fashion. I was still reeling from what I had discovered, certain yet hesitant to utter it aloud, when I learned that John and Angela had betrayed me. If John is reading this someday, he will be surprised to learn that I found out so soon, but I did.*

*"A few days later, I revisited our gallery, and John asked me about the painting.*

*" 'Oh that,' I said. 'Nothing. It was a good frame. I washed the entire thing clean with solvent. I'll make good use of the empty canvas.'*

*" 'Wasn't that a bit expensive for a worn canvas and frame?'*

*"Oh no, not at all, John."*

*"Fuck you, John. John Bull."*

"What does that mean: bull?" asked Caterina.

"Bull?" said Blume. "It's short for bullshit. *Frottole, panzane, cazzate.*"

"They didn't like each other much," she said.

"No," said Blume.

She pushed her feet farther under the cushions, and wished she could follow with her whole body. Tiredness rang in her ears, and for a moment a mistimed inhalation of air through her nose caused the back of her throat to make a snore, and she jerked her head up. Blume still sat there in the armchair. What was the etiquette for telling her commanding officer to go home, to let her sleep? It wasn't just a question of etiquette. She didn't want to hurt his feelings, either. But still he sat there, like a big dog. Maybe if she threw a stick out the window, he'd go bounding enthusiastically down the stairs. But she wanted him there, too, protecting her and Elia as they slept. If only he'd send her to bed, tell her he would be keeping vigil.

"I'll be going in a minute," said Blume. "I am meeting someone, but I don't know where until he phones me."

Caterina swung her feet onto the floor and shivered and yawned. She was too tired to be disappointed or even worried.

"Who?"

"Paoloni. You said you remembered him. He's surprised everyone, himself included, by becoming a successful 'security consultant.' I'm going to give him the notebooks for safekeeping, and then maybe we'll throw out your photocopies, too, put this behind us."

"Paoloni's the person to trust?"

"Yes," said Blume. "He is. Also, I think he can help me make sure the Colonel doesn't bother you again."

Caterina forgot to be tired for a moment. "How will he do that?"

"I don't know. We shall see," said Blume. "Also, I think he might be able to speed up the resolution of the murder of Krishnamachari and his son."

Blume's phone went, and she shivered again. Blume spoke a few words and stood up to go. She forced herself to stand up too.

After he had left, she gathered up the pile of Treacy's notes, her eye falling on the scrawled "*Fuck you, John*." And yet they must have been friends once. She flipped back to the beginning, past the days in Ireland, which she had read. There was the arrival in London with Monica. John's name appeared for the first time in the next pages. She took them to bed, undressed, got into red cotton pajamas that were the most comfortable things in the world, switched on her bedside lamp. The dictionary was in the next room, where it could stay. She could look up any unknown words tomorrow.

*Monica and I arrived in London and I managed to sell my poor forgery to a failing dealer ready to try anything. He gave me twelve pounds for it, which got us into a squalid bedsit on Queensway. I had brought some but not enough of my painting tools with me, but could not afford to buy any more. The dole kept us going, just. After a month, Monica found a job at the cosmetics department of Selfridges. After one week in the job, she had been asked out eight times. She accepted the eighth invitation. I found out and raged at her, and told her she had a choice: Forget about going out with customers, or forget about me. She interpreted this quite literally, so that six months later, when our paths happened to cross on Hampstead Heath, she was unable to remember me at all, and therefore saw no reason to stop and introduce me to the buck-toothed haw-haw Englishman in the chalk-stripe business suit, who was recounting what must have been one of the most amusing stories ever told for the way it made her laugh.*

*After Monica had left me, I was lonelier but freer, and without her pressure to find a job, I was able to wander as much as I liked through the city streets.*

This is how I discovered Ramsauer's art shop in Cecil Court. Nowadays, London is all spruced up and stressfully tidy (a risk that Rome does not run), but back then, streets were dirtier and rents affordable. The shop now is an ordinary rectangular place with minimalist furnishings and pointless books of utter bollocks (mostly "art photography" as if such a thing existed) for the perennially bored. Then the rectangular plan was divided into a grid of tight corridors whose walls were made of antiques, easels, army surplus stocks, paintings, vases ready to topple over. I wandered through the place, free to steal any of the tiny silver, china, and polished wood ornaments that I chose, or perhaps an eighteenth-century letter-writing set. But I am not a thief. Only when I had explored every corridor, though not every object, did the owner appear from a basement area. He nodded to me, asked me if I needed any help and, when I said I was just looking, disappeared again.

On my third visit, I spotted an interesting painting that looked to me like a work by Coello. Of course it was not, but it almost might have been. The subject was a Spanish nobleman. Mold had eaten away at the painting so much that the face seemed to have decayed and exploded outwards in a burst of gray and green, like something from the <u>Night of the Living Dead</u>.

Interested also in the monogram on the back of the canvas, which seemed to suggest the painting had belonged to Lord Mountbatten, I brought it up to the end of the shop, waited patiently for Ramsauer to appear, and asked him how much he wanted for it. Two guineas, he said. "But see this chalk mark? That means it has already been sold."

"Who to?" It seems like an impertinent question, but so far I was the only person I had ever seen enter the shop, and I wondered why the buyer had left a chalk mark on it rather than take it home, since it was not a very large painting. Ramsauer explained that the buyer had not had the money on him at the time, but was coming back.

"When?" I asked defiantly. I was conceiving a dislike for this buyer already.

"Later today, sometime tomorrow, or by next Thursday at the latest." The old bastard didn't have a clue, of course, but he didn't really care. The only thing that mattered was honoring his own chalk mark. I wanted to offer more for the painting, but Ramsauer would not have accepted and I did not have it anyhow. Besides, it was not all that great a bargain considering the state of the work.

As it turned out, the buyer was a young man of about my own age, who did not look as if he had that much to spend either. I saw him the following Wednesday (not Thursday, then) pick up the painting and bring it to old Ramsauer and pay for it.

I went over and demanded to know what he intended to do with it. He looked at me in astonishment, and clutched his painting tighter.

"Are you an artist?" I wanted to know.

"No."

"What do you want with that, then? It's ruined."

"It's my business what I want with it, Paddy."

I could have given him a clout there and then, but if he fell over he would have broken about a thousand objects.

"Take that back."

"What?"

"You called me Paddy. Call me that again and you'll need to put a toothbrush up your arse to clean your teeth."

He put the painting on the counter and said, "Paddy."

His eye tooth cut my knuckle when I hit him. He staggered backwards.

"Jesus. Mind the vase behind you," I said. "It's a bell krater."

He obediently moved away from it, and I hit him on the nose.

He cupped his nose between his hands and shouted, "Fucking hell! That hurt! I am calling the police!" He was outraged, as if I had just made a terrible mistake. Then he added, his voice nasal and his eyes watering, "It's not an original krater, is it?"

"Course not," I said. I picked up the painting.

I walked out of the shop, then stood and waited for the young man to come out after me.

"Here, give it back. I won't call the police, and I won't say Paddy anymore."

I handed over the painting. "I could restore it for you," I offered. "For a fee."

"I can restore it myself, thanks."

"With what? The canvas is blooming. How do you get rid of that mold?"

"Freeze it."

His reply stopped me dead. I was expecting him to say Dettol disinfectant and sunlight, which is what most people would have done back then. In fact, it's a better method than freezing. But in those days freezers were a bit exotic.

"That's clever," I said.

"I'm clever," he said. "Well, if your name's not Paddy—and it had better not be after that—what are you called?"

"Henry. Henry Treacy."

He put out his hand. "Well, Harry. How about you buy me a drink at the Lamb and Flag?"

236

*"Henry, not Harry. You have a problem with names. What's yours?"*

*"John Nightingale."*

*He carried the blasted painting with ghastly precision . . . we drank pale ale and I said . . . In those days they had fires in the hearths of London and overflowing ashtrays . . . One is never as lonely as when . . .*

The manuscript fell with a thump on the floor, and Caterina opened her eyes wide for a moment, turned off the bedside lamp. What was that thump? Manuscript, same sound as the gas made when he lit it. Waited for hours, then lit it. Poor Blume. Propped up like a zinc coffin, the bed tilted pleasantly back.

# 29

"N O. IT'S HALF past one in the morning, Beppe. I don't want to go to a McDonald's," said Blume, looking into his rear-view mirror for the tenth time.

Paoloni's voice sounded both metallic and intimate as it came over the earpiece: "Some American you are. Do you want to meet?"

"Of course."

"Do you want to know if you're being followed or not?"

"I don't think I am," said Blume.

"Do you want to know for sure?"

Blume sounded his horn at an oncoming car he felt was driving too close to his side of the road, raised a finger as the other car flashed its lights, and swerved toward the bastard to force him over. "I suppose so."

"You know the McDonald's at the Agip station on Via Aurelia? Go there. You'll be coming from Piazza Irnerio. So call me as you get to the piazza. Don't bring the phone up to your ear or they'll get suspicious, especially if they've tapped your service phone. You start making calls without them hearing anything, they'll know you know. Use hands-free."

"I'm already using a Bluetooth earpiece," said Blume.

Paoloni asked Blume for his car make, color, and license, and they estimated meeting in half an hour.

A kilometer before the rendezvous, Blume called again.

Paoloni answered after half a ring. "I'm about 300 meters behind you. No sign of anyone. Now, just as you reach the turnoff for the Euronics warehouse on your right, hit your brakes twice."

"OK, I'm there . . . now." Blume tapped his brake pedal twice as he passed it.

"I see you. OK, you're not going to turn into McDonald's, though I am. Go straight past the forecourt, don't even slow down. Go on to the next overpass, which is a mile ahead or a bit less. Use it to reverse direction and start heading back into the city. After the road sign marking the city limits, take the entrance road and another overpass to reverse direction again to get to the McDonald's you're now passing. I'll be waiting for you."

Fifteen minutes later, Blume pulled into the McDonald's parking lot. Five vehicles were parked as close to the door as possible; one, a white Audi Q5, was parked near the exit. That would be Paoloni.

Blume parked near the entrance and waited. Five minutes later the Audi drew up alongside him and Paoloni disembarked. Blume picked up the notebooks, climbed out of his car, and proffered his hand, but Paoloni punched him on the shoulder instead, saying, "None of the next thirty or so cars behind you reappeared on the ramp bringing you back here. Only two other cars took that entrance road and over-pass in the five minutes after you. When you reversed direction down the Via Aurelia, they might have called it off. If they're good, they won't have sent a car onto the second overpass to follow you. If you had a tail, you've lost it for now, though they might pick you up again afterwards. I am assuming they exist, because it might just be that you've finally cracked. I'm starving. You can tell me who the bad guys are over a Big Mac."

The harsh white light of McDonald's did no favors to Paoloni, but all things considered, he was looking better than he had during his last days in the police force. He had put on a bit of weight in his face, and seemed to have developed a liking for sunlamps, for his skin was a bright glowing orange rather than the jaundiced yellow Blume remembered. Getting out of the police also seemed to have liberated his inner bling. Chains dangled from his wrists and he had taken to wearing rings on his thumbs and a flat silver link chain around his neck. He had sculpted his hair so that it stood like a bristly gray cube on his head. He was wearing a white sleeveless hooded training top, and his tattooed arms showed signs of weight training. The gym look was completed by Capri shorts with untied strings that dangled down his bare calves.

"You're looking well," said Blume.

"Thanks. Business is good. I should have left the force years ago."

Blume stood behind a pot-bellied man in flip-flops who was speaking Russian on his phone. Paoloni placed himself in front of the Russian, who paused his conversation, said a few words, and hung up. A man in a porter's uniform finished his order. Paoloni stepped up to the till, and the Russian followed and tapped him on the shoulder.

"I am in front of you." He jerked a thumb behind him. The girl behind the counter glanced backwards in search of support from the kitchens.

Paoloni looked the Russian up and down, then gave him a light back-handed swat on the stomach, and wagged his finger.

"You've eaten at McDonald's before, haven't you?" He allowed the Russian to go in front of him, stood beside Blume, and said, "What are you having?"

"Anything that doesn't begin with a 'Mc,' I think."

Paoloni looked at the overhead menu. "Coca-Cola or Fanta?"

"Coca-Cola, please."

As they took their seat next to a plate glass window, Paoloni said, "These people who you imagine are following you? You don't think they want to shoot you too? Because we're sitting like two goldfish in a lighted bowl here." He flicked open his hamburger box, poured the French fries into the top flap, and ripped open two packets of ketchup.

Blume sipped his Coke and shook his head. "Uh-uh. I don't think that's going to happen."

Paoloni caught a sliding disk of gray meat between his fingers and deftly reinserted it with ketchupy fingers into his bun. "OK, but first things first. Leporelli, Scariglia: it's all arranged. I even met the two scum-bags myself, and they are very keen to turn themselves in. Magistrate Gesti really annoyed the Ostia gang. Those two clowns will pay the price once they get to prison."

"That is well beyond my scope of competence," said Blume. "Where are they now?"

"Somewhere in Casetta Mattei."

"They are not going to resist arrest or try to flee or anything?"

"That wouldn't make sense."

"What they did doesn't make sense," said Blume. "Why are criminals usually so stupid? Even the relatively clever ones seem to choose retards as associates."

"It's because they cannot advertise to get good people," said Paoloni, with the air of a man who had spent some time considering the question. "So they have to depend on blood relations, which is no guarantee of excellence, or else on people they have always known from the neighborhood. But if they're still living in the same neighborhood, chances are they're not too bright."

"Speaking of people who aren't that bright, you hear about the hole Grattapaglia's dug for himself?"

"I heard that. He was unlucky. Of course, it's very funny, too. A diplomat of all people. Can you make him the solver of some big case, make him look good? It's all I can think of."

"The thing they care most about now is the mugger who targets tourists and foreigners," said Blume. "And we're not getting anywhere with that. You haven't got anything, have you?"

Paoloni licked a dollop of ketchup off a finger, then wiped the remaining orange stain onto the Formica of the tabletop. "Nope. Zilch. The only thing I can tell you is no one, and I mean no one, knows who this mugger is."

"An outsider of some sort?"

"That's the impression I get," said Paoloni. "Definitely someone without a record. Works alone, too, which is weird—more a rapist's profile. Now, tell me about these imaginary beings who are following you and why."

Blume began with the Treacy investigation, skipping over most of the details and focusing on his meeting with Colonel Farinelli.

"Heard the name. Never met him, though," said Paoloni. "Go on."

Blume told Paoloni everything he thought was important. When he came to the part about the Colonel recording the two of them discussing the sale of the paintings, Paoloni interrupted him. "Were you thinking about it? You can tell me, you know."

"I know I can," said Blume. He swirled the ice cubes in his cup, then looked at the window, which the darkness outside and the brightness inside had turned into a mirror. "If I could use the paintings to catch the Colonel, then somehow still sell them, get a little extra, I don't know. How bad would that be, given the context we work in? But thanks to Treacy's notes, now I know they are probably worth little or not enough to justify the risk. So the temptation isn't there anymore."

Paoloni nodded understandingly and stood up. "I think I'll have some McNuggets and a cheeseburger," he said.

He was back a minute later saying, "The girl behind the counter says she'll call me when the food's ready. You'd think she'd bring it over. Doesn't seem like she has much else on her hands, and she could definitely do with the exercise. I got a Happy Meal. Tell me more about Treacy and his notebooks."

"I can do better than that," said Blume. "Here. These are the notebooks themselves." He slid them across the table.

Paoloni sucked a finger, and gingerly opened one and peered inside. "It's written in . . .?"

"English," said Blume. "I told you."

"Could be Arabic. You're not expecting me to read these?"

"No. I want to leave them with you for safekeeping."

"You told me the Colonel already has a copy. What's the point?"

"I don't want to be caught with them," said Blume.

"So don't get caught."

"I don't want them. They feel unlucky."

"Alec! I'd never have guessed you were superstitious."

"I'm not."

"So you think the notebooks are jinxed, and that's why you want me to have them?"

"I don't believe in jinxes. I just don't want them around for a while."

"Fine, but your dog is more likely to read them before I do. So you'd better tell me a bit about what's in them."

Blume started talking about Treacy's early life.

Paoloni was called for his Happy Meal and McNuggets. When he got back, he unwrapped his hamburger, flicked open the chicken box, and waved a magnanimous hand at the shining brown lumps inside.

"No thanks," said Blume.

Paoloni bit into his hamburger. "You could eat this food even if you had no teeth," he said. He wiped his mouth with the back of his hand, then the back of his hand on the underside of the table, and said, "What the fuck do I care about Treacy's early life? What do you care about it? Why were you even reading that?" He removed two slices of pickle. "What's the basic structure?"

"Two volumes are autobiographical. A third is full of technical stuff about painting and forgeries, fixatives, different brushes, a history of pigments, papermaking, famous painters, styles, grounds, canvases, woodwork."

"Sounds fascinating. You say he's from Holland?"

"Ireland."

"Yeah, well, one of those islands. Something's made you get lost in the story of this guy's life. I don't know what it is. Seeing him dead or something. But you're not working effectively. And another thing, who's the chick you're supposed to be studying these notebooks with?"

"Inspector Mattiola. She came in just before you quit."

"Yeah, I think I got her. Brown hair, straight. Nice tits. Looks at you like this." Paoloni popped a chicken chunk in his mouth, bent his head, and then raised it to give Blume a horrible leer.

"Not like that, no."

"You know what I mean, puts her head down a bit, then looks at you from under her eyebrows, like she's judging you. Good legs. Getting on a bit, though. So, what's with you and her?"

"Nothing."

"You just go to her house and read her bedtime stories, huh?"

"I think she's got instinct," said Blume.

"What makes you say that?"

Blume told him about Caterina's trip to Pistoia that morning and her discoveries about Emma and Nightingale.

"You keep adding bits," Paoloni complained. "Is that it, you've told me everything now?"

"More or less," said Blume. He decided to hold back on the Velázquez angle for now.

"OK, but something's still missing here, Alec. The Colonel's stringing you along, just as you're doing to him, but you both know the paintings aren't worth all that much. The Colonel says he wants the notebooks because of what it says about what—Gladio agents, the CIA Stay Behind operation in the 1970s, his past dealings with Treacy—all that secret agent stuff. I don't believe it. No one cares about that shit. Andreotti is a life senator, Cossiga got made a life senator, Berlusconi's in power, there are seventy convicted criminals sitting in Parliament. No one gives a damn."

"I forgot. There's also this thing about the Colonel and Nightingale selling stuff to the Mafia."

Paoloni turned and addressed the four empty bucket seats to his right. "Now he tells me."

As Blume explained, Paoloni methodically shredded the food cartons on the table. Then, scooping them onto the tray, he placed the tray on the table next to them, crumpled his straw into his cup, and sucked his teeth.

"Except, it's still bullshit, Alec. Maybe the Colonel found out about the notebooks through Nightingale, but if his main concern was about some minor Sicilian Don finding out he was swindled fifteen years ago, and the Colonel knows you've read the notebooks, then he'd have come to you, spoken to you about it, tried to buy or force your silence. But he didn't do that. I don't think he cares too much. The way you have told me this suggests the Colonel wanted to see what was in the notebooks, and he has some good reasons for not wanting them to go completely public. But he doesn't seem all that worried that you have read them. It may have started out like that, but now it's basically the other way around. *You* are more concerned about what *he* might find in them. There's something else, isn't there?"

Blume watched the Russian sleepwalk in their direction wondering whether he was going to come to their table or walk right on by. The Russian could be a hit man. This could be a hit. No reason it should be, but it could be.

"I think he is looking for something else in there," said Paoloni. "And I think that whatever it is, you have found it."

The flip-flopped Russian walked right out.

Paoloni said, "You don't want to tell me."

Blume said nothing.

"Hey, Alec, we're good friends, right?"

"Yes, we are."

"Then it's cool. Friends don't have to tell their friends stuff if they don't want to. A friend is not someone who doubts, hassles, probes, questions, and disbelieves you: that's what wives are for. There's a lot of stuff I don't tell you."

"Christ knows I'm glad you don't," said Blume.

"See? Friendship is all about not sharing," said Paoloni. He floated his hand in the air, and Blume slapped it. "Maybe you'll tell me later, huh?"

"Tell you what?" said Blume.

"That's my man."

# 30

A FTER FOUR HOURS' sleep, Blume stood under the shower listening to his cell phone ringing. When he had dried himself, mopped up the floor, and made his bed, he picked the phone up and pressed the callback button.

It was Inspector Rospo, who spoke in a tired voice with an undertow of insolence. He told Blume that at five in the morning Leporelli and Scariglia, accompanied by a lawyer, had presented themselves at the Corviale station and confessed to an accidental hit-and-run. The only thing greater than their panic at the time was their remorse now, according to their lawyer. They had agreed that Scariglia was the driver.

Already, it was no longer a police concern. From here on it was the prosecutor versus the lawyer. On past form, the prosecutor was not one to let them get away with it.

Rospo said he was ready for reassignment. The purpose of his phone call seemed to be to impress upon Blume the extent of his wasted effort. Blume told him to put himself at the disposition of Inspector Mattiola for the mugging investigation, and hung up.

Blume rinsed the floor cloth and decided to do the bedroom and hallway floors, too. He sprinkled pink alcohol down the hallway and mopped his way backwards into the sink, then set about washing and putting away the plates and saucepans from his Mexican failure. He wrung all the dirty water from the floor cloth into the washbasin then wiped the limescale and dirt from the aluminum using white vinegar. When the counters, steel furnishings, and fridge were shining, he opened the window to air and dry his house and to check if anyone was watching him. The higgledy-piggledy parked market vans below shone innocently back at him in the morning sun. He scrubbed his coffeepot till it gleamed, then made himself a good cup of Illy coffee, and sat down. The sunlight illuminated an annoying smudge on the window.

His phone rang again.

"Commissioner Blume?"

It was what's-his-name, the Lieutenant Colonel from the Carabinieri Art Forgeries and Heritage Division. In his effort to remember the name, Blume failed to register what the man had said.

"What? Who?"

"Lieutenant Colonel Nicu Faedda."

"Yes, I knew that. What do you want?"

Faedda transmitted an offended silence down the line.

Blume tapped the side of his phone with his thumb. One tap a millimeter or so to the left on the red button would close the conversation.

"I am calling you as an act of courtesy."

Touchy formal bastard. Especially for one so young. It must be part of being Sard.

"Several hours ago, the paintings that the Colonel deposited in the storeroom were removed," said Faedda.

"Removed by who? Colonel Farinelli?"

"Not personally. It's not important who moved them. It was a Carabiniere who may have been acting in good faith and was certainly acting under orders. This is something that need not concern you and will someday be the subject of an internal inquiry."

"How?" asked Blume, but he already knew the answer. Similar things had happened more than once with police evidence. All it took was someone with authorization to enter the storeroom.

"I think it was during the removal of a group of recovered Roman bas-reliefs which—it's not important. They've gone, and they disappeared less than a day after you and I met. I believe the Colonel must have learned of our meeting."

Finally it dawned on Blume that there was an implied accusation behind the information.

"You think I told the Colonel? You think I have something to do with this?"

Significant silence. Blume counted one beat, two beats, three, and just as the Carabiniere officer drew breath and began to speak, he hung up.

The market on Via Orvieto was already crammed with elderly women buying fish and prodding at vegetables. Although a shadow of what it was when Blume first arrived here as a child with his parents, it still reached down to the end of the street, which remained closed to traffic. You could park there the night before, but once the market opened you would be trapped until lunchtime. The only place to watch his apartment, therefore, was at the corner of Via La Spezia. Blume walked up to the bar on the corner, passing by a metallic green Ford Mondeo in which a man was studying something. As he sipped a cappuccino, Blume watched the man in the car suck a pen and make a mark in his book.

Blume went to the stall near his gate and bought himself a shiny sea bass. He could bake it in salt, boil three potatoes. Boil and fry them, maybe. The fishmonger asked if Blume wanted him to clean the fish. Blume nodded. Did anyone ever say no? Did any of the old women clean the fish themselves for the pleasure of it, or could you use the insides, like giblets?

The fish had good fine bright eyes and sparkling scales. It would keep two days. Three at a pinch. He took it up to his apartment, placed it in the fridge, straightened the sofa cushions, ran a Pledge grab-it cloth over the piano and television, then left.

The man in the Mondeo was still there.

# 31

W HEN BLUME WALKED into Paoloni's apartment, the Cane Corso bounced like a huge happy ball into his arms, almost knocking him down.

Blume had not been in the house for a while, but despite Paoloni's improved circumstances, little had changed. Paoloni had evidently chosen to invest his money in technology rather than furniture. The marmalade-colored settee was the same as before, and the pizzeria chair on which Blume sat spent most of its life folded in a corner with the others. The room was dominated by a massive TV. Two new laptops sat on the table.

Blume sat down and the dog came over and put its big black face in his lap. He ran his thumb slightly against the nap of the short hairs at the base of the beast's skull. Two years had passed since he dumped the dog on Paoloni and gone to the USA to be with Kristin. He had met her, slept with her, talked with her and then they had both come back on separate flights to Italy. She went back to being a legate in the embassy, he to being a policeman in the Squadra Mobile of Rome. They still met. Their relationship had humor and life, but no future.

Paoloni stubbed out a cigarette in a square black ashtray in the middle of the table that bore the inscription: "With the compliments of the Jolly Hotel Cagliari." Blume remembered that convention. Three days being taught how to build up crime maps and geographic profiling. It hadn't been a bad course. And by happy coincidence they had been able to see Roma play Cagliari on the Sunday.

Blume told him about the man outside his building. "He's definitely a Carabiniere. I think they're only watching my place, not following me. Can you call someone, get them to check outside now. I know, it's the second time I've asked you to do this."

Paoloni seemed delighted, and immediately made a phone call.

"My cousin," he explained. "He's started working for me. Thirty-five an hour tax-free. He's good at it, enjoys the work, and I trust him like a brother. Though not with money."

Blume looked at his watch. He needed to get into the office.

"So how long will it take this cousin of yours?"

"He lives across the way. It'll take him about fifteen minutes to see if anyone is watching us here."

"Then he'll go keep an eye on the guy who's supposed to be watching me?"

"Yeah," said Paoloni. "Unless you have a better idea."

Blume felt he should, but none came to him.

Blume's phone rang. It was Panebianco, who seemed to think it was OK to ask Blume where he was.

"That's what I ask you," said Blume. "Not vice versa."

"Sorry, Commissioner. It's what the Questore wanted to know. Then he told me to get in contact with you and tell you."

"Tell me what?"

"There was another mugging. It happened last night at around three."

"Any more details?"

"The victim was not injured."

"Another foreigner?"

"Yes. Inspector Mattiola is working a new angle. She says something she learned last night with Grattapaglia made her rethink the cases."

"I'll be there as soon as I can," said Blume.

Fifteen minutes later, Paoloni's cousin called in to report, as Blume had imagined, that no one had followed him. He thanked Paoloni and left.

Just as he was pulling into the station, Paoloni called again to tell him the guy outside Blume's house was still there, still watching and playing Sudoku. "More Sudoku than watching."

"He may as well play Sudoku, seeing as he knows I'm not there," said Blume. "Tell your cousin not to waste his time."

"Let me handle this, Alec. My cousin's entire life until now has been a waste of time."

When he arrived at the station, Caterina was at the far end of the room, placing pins on a map of Trastevere. Grattapaglia sat nearby arms folded, face homicidal. His first meeting with the investigator was in the afternoon.

"Try to smile during the interview, Sovrintendente," said Blume.

Grattapaglia bared his teeth and tightened his arms. He looked like a man trying to crush himself to death.

"Seriously. We'll get you out of this. Just don't intimidate or antagonize the investigator. Go out for a walk. Go on. I know it relaxes you. Have a drink, too, if it helps. Try to get some perspective on this."

Grattapaglia did not move.

"It wasn't really a suggestion," said Blume with a jerk of his thumb in the direction of the door. "Take a hike, Sovrintendente. Come back when you're calm."

Grattapaglia marched straight through them, sending Rospo dancing away behind a desk, and stormed out of the room.

Blume went over to Caterina.

"I'm mapping out the muggings," she told him. She pointed to Rospo. "The Assistente Capo here has been offering constructive criticism."

"I already told her we did all that shit," said Rospo. "All they show is that the muggings took place in Trastevere, and that the convergence is in Trastevere, and there is nothing we can do with that data. For some reason she took all the pins out and then stuck them all back in, exactly where they were to begin with."

"It's a good way of getting a feel for the pattern," said Caterina, sticking another pin in the map. "There. That's more or less it."

Blume looked at the pins, which seemed to form the beginning of a spiral.

"How many are there?"

"Thirty-seven muggings. Today's makes thirty-eight," said Caterina. "These date back to twenty months ago." She pointed to a group of seven pins near Trastevere train station. "Those occurred within the time frame, but we have the perpetrator for two of them and we're pretty sure they are unconnected."

"We're totally sure," interrupted Rospo.

"OK," said Caterina with a nod at Rospo. "Those are not connected. Inside this spiral we may have two, three copy-cat, opportunist, or run-of-the mill muggings, but if we factor in that the victims were almost all foreigners, then the pattern . . ."

"We know that," said Blume.

"Wait," said Caterina, picking up a printout from the desk beside her.

"The victims were, let's see: Japanese, Spanish, Greek, German, Japanese again, French, another Japanese, Chinese, French again, Swiss, Austrian, Slovenian, Irish, Belgian, Japanese, Japanese ... and so on. But at number 23 we have an Italian, a businessman from Milan.

"It interrupted the pattern, but pointed to another one. Apart from being in that area at that time of night, the Milanese businessman, a certain Natale Rosa, was staying at the Hotel Noantri."

"We checked that, too," said Blume. "About two in three of the victims were in that hotel, which is by far the largest in the area, so it was not very surprising."

"Right," said Caterina. "And we looked into the possibility that someone in the hotel was involved."

"That was never discounted as a possibility," said Blume. "But the attacks seemed pretty random. The other main thing is that they were carried out by a single person, which is rare, and that a lot of the witnesses said he threatened them with a huge knife. If I remember, one or two even spoke of a sword or cutlass."

"I found another anomaly," said Caterina. "There is something not right in the balance of nationalities."

"Thirty-eight is a hell of a lot of muggings," said Blume. "But statistically it's negligible. You can't deduce too much from such a small number."

"I know ... but ..."

"But?"

"Where are all the Germans, Dutch, and English? I looked up the Rome Chamber of Commerce tourism figures. The Germans, Dutch, French, and English are the main visitors to the city; the Americans come a bit down the list, but they are still ahead of the Spanish and the Japanese. But we have no Dutch victims, no Americans, just one English but a preponderance of Japanese and a few Spaniards. Why?"

"Maybe because Japs are midgets," said Rospo and cackled.

"You're right," said Caterina. "That's exactly what I thought."

Rospo stopped laughing, sat up straight for a moment, and looked pleased with himself.

"Not anymore," said Blume. "The older generation is small, and so we think of them like that, but the young Japanese are as tall as anyone."

"The Dutch are the tallest people in the world," said Caterina. "When I saw there were no American victims, I looked it up, but it turns out the

Dutch are taller. That's more telling, since there are more Dutch than American tourists, but not one among the mugger's victims."

"Are you seriously building a theory out of this?" asked Blume.

"No, not really," said Caterina. "But it got me thinking about the size of the victims, and that got me thinking about their age. I checked out the age profiles. The average was over fifty-five. Which, for the Japanese, makes them small again."

"Basically, all you're saying is that the mugger picked on old people," said Rospo.

"Yes," said Caterina. "That's all I am saying. Small, old, frail people. It's not much, but it's a sort of pattern, and it hadn't been included in any of the reports."

"That's about as fucking useless a . . ." Rospo fell silent as he caught the look Blume was giving him.

"OK, now a mugger is usually a bully," said Blume. "And this one is no exception. He selects older and smaller people. Being tourists they are less sure of their surroundings and more likely to have valuables. I think we had got that far in our reasoning, Inspector, even if the pattern wasn't specifically mentioned."

"So you choose old people because they are easier to rob. Also, old people tend to have more stuff. So then I looked over the list of things stolen," said Caterina. "Mostly it's money but there was also three silver bracelets, pendants, a valuable necklace, an incredibly valuable watch, diamond earrings, a gold pen, cameras, video equipment, a silver cross, and so on. I want to get back to that last one in a minute, because there is something interesting about it. Once the pressure to catch the mugger became intense, we put a lot of effort into trying to trace where these things were going. Grattapaglia, you Rospo, patrolmen, the Vigili Urbani, Finance Police, and even the Carabinieri were keeping an eye open, yet not one of these items was spotted. Now we also know, almost for certain, that no one on the street even knows who this person is, right Davide?"

"It looks like—yeah, this person is a newcomer or an outsider of some sort," said Rospo, unhappy at having to agree. "And the Finance Police kept an eye on eBay small ads, Craigslist, and places like that and none of the merchandise came up for sale."

"So how is he getting rid of the stuff?" said Caterina. "He hasn't been fencing it to anyone. We could assume that he is fiendishly clever, but if he was, he would not be mugging for a living."

"So he's keeping the valuables," said Blume. "As trophies or something."

"Which means he's got some other reason for mugging tourists."

"Someone who just hates tourists?" said Rospo. "Like me." This time he missed the look from Blume and allowed himself a long laugh.

"Hates tourists," said Caterina. "Has no previous, is unknown, has no need of money, works alone, and is possibly small himself. Atypical."

"The investigating magistrate should have figured this shit out," said Rospo.

"It's not a priority for him," said Blume. "It is for us. Go on, Inspector."

"OK. Now I checked the police statements of the victims. Let's just say that a better job might have been done in asking them for details, getting basics like full names, time of robbery, home address—and we do have interpreters in the police, you know."

"You're confusing us with your previous job in immigration control, Inspector. I have never managed to find translators or interpreters. But go on."

"We've still got seventeen decent descriptions of the attacks. None of them mentions anything about the mugger seeming older or smaller than usual, but they all say his face was hard to see behind the hooded tracksuit and in the dark. Four mention that he was small, the rest say nothing at all," said Caterina. "Those who were asked the question say he was working alone, though one woman, a Swiss, wasn't sure."

"Not much help there," said Rospo.

"What were you saying about the silver cross stolen from one of the victims?" asked Blume.

"Yes. That is interesting. Around a year ago, a Spaniard called José Maria Carvalho was mugged and reported losing a highly valuable silver cross 'of extremely profound religious and symbolic value.' Carvalho had been visiting the hotel for a conference, but actually lives in Trastevere. He works as a diplomat to the Holy See."

"That Carvalho? The guy Grattapaglia thumped?" said Blume.

Caterina nodded. "So he was already poorly disposed to the police, seeing as we didn't find his silver cross. Now this," Caterina picked up a poorly-printed newsletter, "is the *Pigna*, a local newsletter that comes out now and again."

Blume nodded. He always read it, too. Local news was always interesting, the more local the better.

"If you read the letters page, there are three more contributions to the debate about the new hotel, the one at the center of the spiral on the board there, the place where twenty-two of our thirty-eight victims were staying. The debate has something to do with ruining historic quayside buildings, disrespecting the architecture of the area."

Rospo looked blank, but Blume had been following the matter. The hotel chain was accused of failing to respect the architectural exceptionalism of a series of eighteenth-century buildings, knocking down old walls, and, worst of all, creating a new upper floor that blocked the light of neighboring buildings. The letter writers seemed to know a lot about planning permission laws, and municipal directives, and nothing about concision.

"If you read these letters or follow the debate in the local news section of *Il Messaggero*, you'll soon come across the name of the chief campaigner: Alfonso Corsi. He's a bitter man. A nobleman in decline, whose family has been selling off property in the area since after the war."

"You think he's the mugger?" asked Rospo, the skepticism in his voice giving way to scorn.

"He's eighty-two years old," said Caterina, "but I still think he might be worth talking to."

"It's a long shot," said Blume.

"There is another thing," said Caterina. "Leporelli and Scariglia."

"Those two fuckers handed themselves in this morning," said Rospo. "Let's hope they get what's coming to them in Rebibbia."

"They will," said Blume. "Inspector, what's their connection to the mugger?"

"None that I can see," said Caterina. "But their file contains a list, sadly a short one, of the names of people who came forward to protest at their racketeering efforts. There was one case in particular that merits attention. Three years ago, a certain Corsi Hotel opened in Trastevere. It was a private aristocratic villa, and the occupants decided to open a guest house. They didn't get the necessary permits, or not all of them, but they went into business anyhow, and soon after those two vultures arrived demanding protection money. The Corsis, father and son, came straight to us and denounced the would-be racketeers. Nothing was done."

"Yeah, well ..." said Rospo.

"Then two months after that, there was a mysterious fire at the Corsi Hotel. It was a minor thing—basically a perimeter wall was blackened—but the Vigili Urbani and the Fire Department inspected the premises, found around eighty health and safety violations, and closed down the hotel directly afterwards. It never reopened. I followed this up, and Agnolo Corsi ..."

"*Agnolo?*" said Rospo. "That's the gayest name I've ever heard."

Caterina smiled. "Apparently that's the poor man's name. Agnolo filed a complaint in which he alleges that Leporelli and Scariglia were working for the Hudson & Martinetti Hotel chain, owners of the Noantri Hotel, which is where most of the mugging victims were resident. The Hudson & Martinetti Hotel chain sued for defamation, and the case is pending. The investigating magistrate appointed to look into the accusation wrote off Corsi's claim as 'highly improbable' and 'delusional,' which it is. A few months later, the first mugging, perpetrated against a guest from the Noantri Hotel, occurred."

"It's bullshit that Leporelli and Scariglia were working for the Hudson & Martinetti Hotel," said Rospo.

"Of course it is," said Caterina. "But it's interesting Corsi should make this claim."

"That's a strange ..." began Blume. He stopped as his cell phone rang. He excused himself and answered, walking away from Caterina and Rospo toward his office. The caller was Paoloni, who sounded very pleased with himself.

"I thought you'd like to know," he said. "Two men have just broken into your apartment."

# 32

W HEN BLUME CLAPPED a phone to his ear and wandered off to his office while she was in mid-sentence, and Rospo, already annoyed at being upstaged by her that morning, returned to his desk with a shrug, Caterina had to work hard to keep the disappointment and anger from her face.

She decided to wait for Blume to emerge from his office and advise on her next step. But when he did reappear it was only for the time it took him to walk quickly out of his office, through the operations room, and down the corridor.

She started mapping out an investigative approach, trying to find something for Rospo that he would not find demeaning and might possibly do well, when she got a call from downstairs to say that a certain Emma and Angela Solazzi were looking for her.

Blume had specifically removed her from the case, yet the arrival of these two was something she knew he would be interested in. Her hand hovered over her phone, but she made no call. Seeing as he saw fit to leave without saying where, and they had asked for her, not him, Caterina had them sent to the interview room.

Mother and daughter, alike in the shape of their noses and in their posture, but little else, sat side by side at the far end of the table when Caterina entered.

Emma Solazzi said, "I thought it would be like killing two birds with one stone, interviewing us together."

"Are we allowed to smoke in here?" asked Angela. "I'm nervous."

"No one asked you to come here," said Caterina. "And, no, you're not allowed to smoke."

"Smoking gave me these crow's feet around my eyes. I probably have cancer of the something, too. But I like my husky voice." And continuing in her husky voice, she said, "I wanted to clear up a few things about John Nightingale. And about Henry Treacy, too."

Caterina shifted her gaze to Emma. "And you?"

"I'm here to hear what she has to say."

Caterina glanced at her watch to make a point. "OK, but let's make this quick. I have other business. What sort of person is John Nightingale, Emma?"

Her asking Emma the question caught both visitors by surprise for a moment. Emma shrugged and said, "He is decent enough, I guess. Gentlemanly. Generous. Kind of ... boring? I hardly know him. Ask her: she's the one who slept with him."

"She's right," her mother said, nodding at Caterina. "John is very dull. Mostly in a good way. I have come to appreciate dullness in people. They are safer, more dependable, less violent. That's essentially why I am here. I want you to know that John Nightingale is not violent. It is not possible that he had anything to do with Henry Treacy's death."

"Who told you that he did?"

"No one," said Angela. "But I know that if you're investigating, this is certain to come up as a possible line of inquiry. John would not hurt a fly. If there was a dangerous one, it was Henry."

"Did you have a relationship with Henry, too?"

"Oh, yes. I thought that was clear." Angela looked taken aback and her daughter looked embarrassed. "Haven't you been investigating? I worked for them, just as Emma does now. Henry was my ... Emma, if you lean any further away from me, you risk falling off the chair."

"I am not very comfortable with this sort of thing. It's only natural," said Emma.

"Of course, darling. But Henry was my lover. There, it's not so bad a word now that I have said it. Henry came long before Nightingale, and was, well, he was Henry and John is just John. But I had to leave Henry."

"Was he violent?" asked Caterina.

"He was a raging fire who burned people up. Literally. Look."

Angela rolled up the left sleeve of her black cashmere cardigan, revealing a long white scar that curved up her forearm, branching as it went. "It reaches up to my clavicle, down to my breast. It doesn't look too bad now. But for years when I tanned, it would remain stubbornly pale, like a white snake."

"Treacy did that?"

"Accidentally. A splash of boiling linseed oil. He whipped it out of a pot with a ladle when I was standing behind him. I held my arm up to protect my face. He was drunk."

"Please, mother," said Emma.

"What? He was."

"It's obvious you were naked at the time, which is why it burned your breast. I can do without that picture in my head."

"That was accidental," said Caterina. "He seems to have managed to burn himself as well. Did he ever hurt you deliberately?"

"Oh, yes. Henry hit me in the mouth twice. Once he punched my shoulder so hard I couldn't lift my arm for weeks. He apologized for hitting me in the mouth, but he never took that shoulder punch seriously . . . He threw a bottle at me once, aiming to miss, I like to think."

"How much of that did you go through before leaving him?"

"I had already left him for Nightingale when he threw the bottle. It's why he threw it."

"When did you meet Henry Treacy for the first time?"

"In 1974," said Angela.

"No, sorry. I was talking to Emma here," said Caterina.

"Me? When I went to Galleria Orpiment. Three years ago."

"And you knew these stories?"

"Well, more or less."

"I warned her," said Angela. "I warned her not to put up with anything, and I mean anything, from Henry. I told her some of the stories, though not in full detail. I didn't want to be too prejudicial. Even so, I told her to keep her identity secret and her wits about her, and never, never to go drinking with him."

"So what did you think when you saw this man who had hurt your mother like that?"

"I don't know. He wasn't what I expected. He was far older. I knew he would be, but when I saw him, I couldn't make the connection. My image of him was from a photograph my mother showed me a few times over the years. He was young then. Handsome, too. Like that self-portrait in his room in the gallery. I'd see this old guy sitting there, with this blond Adonis painting above him, and it was like the young man had gone away, and Henry was his father, sitting there, ageing, waiting for the boy in the picture to come back. I half expected him to walk in the door one day."

"And how did he behave himself with you?"

"Oh, he was charming," said Emma, shaking her shoulder in an involuntary shudder.

"Wait, what do you mean by charming?"

"Theatrically charming. He used a lot of words. He was always saying things that . . . like he was saying something else. Not double entendres. Opposites. Constant irony. Like he'd say I was an ugly little bat that would 'scare the horses,' which is a weird phrase he used, and I knew it was a compliment. I'd have a new dress, he'd ask me what garbage dump I found it in, what was wrong with my hair, why I was born cross-eyed, stumpy-legged. But you could tell he meant the opposite, and if I was feeling a bit sad, he'd pick it up immediately and not make any jokes that day. He could be really funny."

"And he never guessed whose daughter you were? Never made any reference to your mother here, or to Nightingale?"

"No. He knew nothing."

"Emma, are you sure that Henry Treacy did not know who you were? Can you be one hundred percent positive about that?"

Out of the corner of her eye, she could see Angela fingering her scar.

"I don't see why this is so important," said Emma.

"Frankly," said Caterina, shifting her gaze to include Angela, "I don't either, but you two are the ones who contrived to hide the fact from Henry Treacy, by now an elderly man, and not your partner, Angela, for, what, decades? You're the ones who did all the hiding. You're the ones who decided it was so important to do, and now you feel it's important to tell me."

"It wasn't as if I had a strong paternal bond with Nightingale," said Emma. "He is more like a godfather or a great-uncle. It wasn't hard to pretend I didn't know him, because I wasn't really pretending."

Caterina turned to Angela. "You asked if you could smoke. Well, here is your chance. There is a coffee machine on the second floor at the end of the corridor, then a small balcony that gives you a nice view of the Galleria Pamphili. If anyone questions your right to be there, tell them I sent you."

"Is my daughter in trouble?"

"Why do you say that?"

"Because you want to talk with her alone. Is she?"

"Have two cigarettes, with a pause of about five minutes between one and the next, and then come back here."

Angela fished a packet of cigarettes from her purse, pulled out an elegant silver lighter. "I'll leave my bag here?"

"Fine."

When Angela left the room, Caterina turned to Emma. "You said Treacy could be funny. When was he funny?"

"When he began drinking. Before he got drunk."

"Did he drink at work?"

"No. He was hardly ever there."

"So when did you see him drinking?"

Emma hesitated before seeming to dismiss the possibility of a denial. "I went out a few times with him in the evenings."

"Exactly as your mother told you not to."

"My mother is extremely protective. She still thinks I'm a baby."

"Whereas you are not, of course," said Caterina. "Just you and Treacy?"

"No, no. With Pietro. He's like a boyfriend."

"Like a boyfriend? Whose?"

"OK. He's my boyfriend."

"What did he call you?"

"That's kind of embarrassing . . . Sometimes he'd call me his little . . ."

"Not in that sense! What name did he call you by?"

"Oh," she blushed. "Manuela. I was really getting used to it."

"You must have despised him a bit if you never even told him your real name."

"I didn't despise him."

"You must have felt he was someone you couldn't trust with a secret."

Emma bit her lip. "Well, I think he liked me. He still does, by the way. A lot."

"When you were out with Treacy, was Pietro always there?"

"Almost always. Not that we went out all that often together. When we did, it was to the Bar San Callisto. We'd have a drink or two, and then we'd leave and Treacy would stay. Treacy was entertaining. The thing about Treacy was he knew so much and he seemed to have met a lot of famous people: Woody Allen, de Chirico, Francis Bacon, Samuel Beckett, Mitterrand, Gore Vidal, Mick Jagger, Harold Pinter, Charles Saatchi, Van

Morrison, Damien Hirst, Gigi Proietti, Christian De Sica, the whole Pamphili family, Patricia Highsmith, and George Clooney. Who's probably the only one of them who isn't dead."

"So you enjoyed his company?"

"He was cool. For an old man. I admired him."

"You know he wasn't that old. You keep saying how old Treacy was. Maybe it was because he was sick."

Emma looked at her without comprehension.

"Forget it. Were you with him on the night he got killed?"

"On the night he died, you mean? No. But I knew you would be the person to ask me that."

"Why did you think that?"

"You don't like me."

"That is absolutely not true, but it's not my concern to persuade you. Where were you that night?"

"At home with Pietro."

"So he's your alibi?"

"Yes."

"Do you mind giving me his telephone number?"

Emma shrugged, with what Caterina gauged to be exaggerated nonchalance. "Sure," she said.

"Now," said Caterina.

"I don't know it by heart."

"It's in your phone, I imagine."

"Oh, right."

Emma pulled out her phone, slid it open, and tapped on the buttons with her clear polished nail. She read out the number, which Caterina wrote down.

"Thank you," said Caterina.

"You're welcome."

"May I have your phone a minute?"

"What for?"

"I just need to check the number."

Emma slid the phone across the table, giving it a sharp spin as she did so, but Caterina caught it. "Under Pietro, or under his surname—what is his surname, by the way?"

"Quaglia."

"Here we go." Caterina pursed her lips, checked her notebook, and then the phone. "You seem to have reversed the last digits. It ends in 37, not 73," she said.

"Or you wrote it down wrong."

"I am pretty sure I wrote it down exactly as you dictated it," said Caterina.

"Well, I am borderline dyslexic," said Emma. "I sometimes do that. You can ask my mother."

"I'm going to call this Pietro, you know."

"I know you are."

"What's he like?"

"You'll see," said Emma. "Pietro worships the ground I walk on."

"You're not the sort of woman who lets men walk all over her," said Caterina. "Like your mother does."

"Like she used to, but she learned from her mistakes. No man is going to hurt her again. She has taught me to strike first, told me if she ever got a second chance, that is what she would do. Strike first."

"Does she have any photos of Treacy?"

"A few photos, yes. Out of sight of John. Not because she was afraid of John, but just so as not to hurt his feelings."

"Any other mementoes?"

"Well, there are some Treacy Old Master imitations on the walls. They are signed, so they are not pretending to be the real thing. They've always been there. And then there is the one Mother keeps in her bedroom. It's by far the worst."

"How do you know it's his?"

"Because when it arrived, first she told me, and was all happy about it, but then she panicked and asked me not to mention it to anyone, like it was a big secret. If she hadn't said anything, I would have forgotten all about it."

"No mention of it to Nightingale."

"I suppose not. But it was not like Nightingale was always visiting us. I saw him in our house about six times in twenty years. I know they met at his place in Rome a few times, but that, too, was extremely rare."

"What's in Treacy's picture?"

"It's just a picture of a vista in a park. A fountain, a few trees. It's pretty unimpressive. Like a Sunday artist's effort. It's hard to imagine that he even painted it. It must have taken him five minutes."

"And yet your mother keeps it in her bedroom?"

"Yes. She admits it's no good either. Says it's the thought that counts. He sent it once with a letter saying he was sorry, and he wouldn't touch her again."

"Did he touch her again?"

"I don't know! I don't think so."

There was a soft knock on the door, and Angela poked her head in.

"That was just one cigarette," said Caterina. "But that's all right. I think we've finished here. For now."

# 33

As she walked out of the interview room, Caterina phoned Emma's boyfriend. They had probably worked things out already, but there was no point in giving Emma another chance at fixing up her alibi. The voice that answered reminded her immediately of Elia. It tried to be gruff and it was certainly deeper than her son's, but it still had the note of interest and expectancy of a young person. She said who she was and told him to come in immediately, and, before he could ask why or even think of refusing, she demanded to know how long it would take him.

He hesitated and said he had a lecture.

"Skip it," she told him. "Are you at the university now?"

"Yes, engineering department."

"Then it will take you no more than half an hour. Don't keep me waiting. Give my name at the desk downstairs, they'll send you up. Inspector Mattiola. Mattiola, yes. I'll tell you that when you get here."

She pressed the button for the elevator, and found herself standing beside Grattapaglia.

"Enjoy your walk?"

"It helped. I didn't go for a drink, though. Alcohol's not good for my mood. Even a Campari makes me aggressive."

"Have you ever tried anger management?"

"Yes. And it doesn't work."

They stepped out of the elevator and went into the operations room, which was empty. Rospo's absence was normal and welcome, but she was surprised Panebianco wasn't there. Grattapaglia shuffled across the floor toward his desk.

She tried to think of some encouraging words. "Don't clear out your desk. Maybe they won't suspend you."

"A ten-day suspension is automatic from the day I have my first meeting with the investigator, and that's today. The difference is whether it will be with or without pay and what happens afterwards."

"Oh." She should have realized that. "Maybe you'll be back in ten days' time."

"Sure." Grattapaglia pulled open a drawer and emptied hundreds of staples and colored rubber bands into his bag.

"You're filling the bag with rubber bands."

"So report me."

"I may have a lead on the mugger," said Caterina. "Though it's a long shot."

"Yeah?" She could see as a vein in Grattapaglia's neck began to pulse and swell. Grattapaglia balled his hands into fists and pressed them on his desk. "Looks to me like I won't be helping you there. I'm going to get suspended, you know? All because a certain female Inspector didn't . . "

"What didn't I do, Sovrintendente? Change your personality? Stop your anger in time? Do you need me to look out for you, to mother you, is that it?"

Grattapaglia took a threatening step toward her, and she stepped in toward him.

"You know what the secret of not getting angry is?" she said, as he stepped back in surprise at her move. "It's not to get angry."

"That's useful. Did they teach you that in an anger management class?"

"I've never been to any such class, idiot. I'm self-taught. Look, half the time when you get angry, you probably have good cause and half the time you don't. Or pick any ratio you want. Let's say ninety-nine percent of the time you get angry, you're absolutely in the right. So then what happens? Well, usually you think you have not only a right but an obligation to get angry, like it was compulsory. But it's not. Next time, when something happens that fires a rage in you, just do nothing. Don't bother. Don't get angry. You're right, the world has wronged you, like it wrongs trapped miners and starving children, car-crash or bomb victims, people swept away in floods, burned alive in their beds, women raped by soldiers. Except it's probably wronged you a bit less than them. So fuck it. I'm not even asking you to drop the hate. Save it for later. Just don't wrong yourself again. It's not morality, it's simple practical advice. Getting angry is like trying to treat a burn by burning yourself again in the very same spot. Stupid."

"Are you calling me stupid?"

"I wasn't, but you're reminding me that maybe you are. Go into the interview. Hate the investigator, hate the questions, hate the unfairness, resent me, resent the Spaniard, Blume, the Questore—You are right. Fine. You feel the rage welling up, fine. But don't act on it, don't claim it as yours."

"And you're the great expert because?"

"Because I am a woman in law enforcement. Underpaid, underappreciated, overworked. Because I lost a husband to a criminally negligent driver who didn't even get his license suspended, and because I have a mother who disapproves of how I'm bringing up what she considers her grandchild rather than my son, because I'm getting old, getting blamed, getting tired. Noise, dirt, and ignorance when I'm on the street, violence, waste, and pettiness at work. Want me to go on?"

"No. I get what you're saying."

"So maybe you're not stupid, then."

Grattapaglia grinned. "No one in here has ever dared call me stupid. Except for the Commissioner, but sooner or later he says that to everyone. But you're right. I'm really fucking stupid."

"Anger makes us do dumb things. It takes over our actions before we even know that it's there."

"That's exactly what it's like!" said Grattapaglia. "You don't see it coming, then, suddenly wham!"

"And down goes a Spanish diplomat."

"It took four blows, actually."

"Don't go to the opposite extreme and make light of it either," said Caterina.

"No, I won't. Look, about you not warning me ..."

"You're right, I should have mentioned it."

"You weren't to know what I was going to do. Shit, *I* didn't know I was going to do that."

"I know."

A young man appeared at the far end of the room.

Grattapaglia pointed at him and said, "Who's he?"

Caterina looked across the room. "A witness. Probably a false alibi. I'd almost forgotten about him. I wanted to get out of here soon."

"So break his alibi quickly," said Grattapaglia. "I can give him a slap if you want. Nothing left to lose anyhow ... From the look on your face, I can tell you don't know when I'm joking. Women rarely do."

Caterina went over to the youth and led him to her desk. He looked to her like he was thirteen, not twenty-six. He looked like he was about to vomit from fear.

She sat him down in front of her. "You are Pietro Quaglia?"

The young man cleared his throat, cleared it again, but his voice still came out in a squeak. "Yes. Can I ask why—?"

"No. Just answer me this. Manuela Ludovisi. Do you know who she is?"

"She's my girlfriend."

"I see. Where were you last Friday night? Friday September 26."

"I was with her. All evening and all night."

"Really?"

"Yeah."

"No trips to the Bar San Callisto, out and about."

"No. We watched a video."

She could see he was ready to fire off the name of the movie, so she didn't bother asking. Instead, she leaned sideways to look behind him and addressed Grattapaglia. "Is that holding cell free?"

The youth turned awkwardly in his seat to see the policeman she was talking to.

Grattapaglia paused in the middle of moving piles of papers from the top of his desk to Rospo's trash can. "What holding cell?" he said. "We don't have any ..." He caught Caterina's eye. "We don't have any free. Shit, you know better than to ask me that. You'll have to put him in with those two ..." he made a clutching movement with both hands. "You know, the two who ..."

Pietro spun around and stared at Caterina.

"What two? Two whats?"

"Choo choo, chuff, chuff!" said Grattapaglia from behind, and laughed. "Looks to me like he'll like it."

"Jesus Christ, what is he talking about?" said Pietro. "I want a lawyer."

"Have you got a lawyer?" said Caterina.

Pietro glanced around the room, desperately looking for someone resembling a lawyer. But he was alone there with Caterina and Grattapaglia.

"No. But I have a right!"

"I'll go and get you one, Pietro. Maybe it'll take a few hours." She pulled out a pair of plastic handcuffs. "So if you don't mind I'll just slip these on you and leave you in the holding cell until . . ."

"No!"

"It's OK, Pietro," said Caterina gently. "Listen to the advice the Sovrintendente here gives you, and you'll be fine."

Grattapaglia came over. "Once you're in there, just talk to the small guy with the brown hairpiece. Don't look at his hairpiece though. Whatever you do, don't let him know you know. Then if he likes you, his friend won't hardly touch you."

"Why did you tell me about it? If you hadn't mentioned the hairpiece, maybe I wouldn't have noticed. Now he'll see me looking."

"*Managgia*. I should have thought of that," said Grattapaglia. "They don't teach criminal psychology to people of my rank."

"Wait!" said Pietro, glancing around at Caterina.

Caterina stood there twirling the plastic bracelets, a perplexed expression creasing her brow. "What?"

"Can't we just talk in here?"

"In here?" She looked confused. "You mean a voluntary witness statement? Sure. But we can only do that if there is full cooperation. Once it becomes antagonistic, we go from interview to interrogation, which means . . ." She spun the plastic cuffs absentmindedly on her finger.

"I get that."

"So when I start asking questions, you tell me what I need to know."

"Sure."

"Show me you're serious about cooperating," said Caterina. "Prove it."

"How can I prove it? What am I supposed to say?"

"I don't know. OK, let's start over. Manuela Ludovisi. Do you know who she is?"

"Like I said, she's my girlfriend."

"Good. And Emma Solazzi?"

"I don't know anyone by that name."

Caterina looked into his eyes which darted back and forth as he avoided her gaze.

"Are you sure?"

"Yes! You have to have the wrong person. I know Manuela, but not this Emma."

"OK, let's forget about Emma. You just said you were with Manuela on Friday night, all night. Was that true? Just say 'yes' if it is, 'no' if not."

"No."

"A second ago you said you were. Manuela told me you were. What's going on here?"

"I was doing her a favor. But I wasn't with her."

"Fine. But now I'm going to ask you another question that may put you in a difficult moral quandary. OK?"

"OK."

"Manuela is citing you as an alibi for that evening. Do you still say you weren't with her?"

"I was not with her."

"She'll get into trouble, you know. She's sort of depending on you to say yes."

"I can't say yes, you just told me to be honest!"

"Well then, she's in trouble."

Pietro looked at his feet under the table.

"So where were you?"

"I wasn't even in Rome that night. I was with friends in Terracina. I was there for the whole week."

"Can your friends corroborate?"

"Yes."

"Give me their names."

Pietro obliged and Caterina noted them down. Then she dismissed him.

"Where do I go now?"

"I don't care. Back to the reptile house or wherever it is you live."

Pietro made his way unsteadily out of the office, and Caterina picked up her bag. Grattapaglia was still standing at his desk, smiling.

"Thanks for helping out. That was quick and inspired thinking, Sovrintendente."

Grattapaglia looked at her. "That was pretty funny. I've never seen someone break down a suspect so fast."

"He was not a suspect, only a witness."

"Little shit. I wish we had thrown him into a holding cell. Who was he?"

"Emma's boyfriend," said Caterina. "I'd prefer to see my son wrongly jailed than turn out like that."

# 34

C ATERINA CALLED ROSPO on his cell, told him to meet her on Via Jandolo in twenty minutes, but thirty-five minutes passed and there was no sign of him, and he wasn't answering. She called dispatch, gave them the address, told them to refer it to Rospo when he called in.

Now she stood alone in front of an imposing but graffiti-scored door. There was just one buzzer, and it looked as if it had not been used in years. She pressed it anyhow. She waited for three full minutes, giving the buzzer the occasional dab of her finger, convinced now that it was out of order. Just as she was turning to go to find someone who could tell her how to contact the occupants, if there were any, the door scraped open and a tall old man stood framed in the darkness, blinking papery eyelids at her and the sun.

"Inspector Mattiola, Police," declared Caterina. "Are you Alfonso Corsi?"

"Conte Alfonso Corsi, and there is no need to raise your voice." He sighed and tutted his tongue, but surprised her by stepping aside and elegantly ushering her in, then closing the door behind her, enclosing her in a corridor that smelled of damp brick and rust. The long old man, his pace far quicker than she had expected, overtook her, and proceeded with sharp footfalls down a corridor of black and red hexagon tiles.

"Wait."

But Caterina was not sure she had spoken loud enough. She increased her pace to catch up, but already he had reached a flight of stairs at the end of the corridor, and ascended it with efficient, light, insect-like leaps, leaving her plodding and heavy below. As she rounded the first landing where the staircase doubled back on itself, she worried that he might leap out at her. But he was already at the top, and calling down.

"They have kept me fit all these years."

By the time she reached the second floor, Conte Corsi had entered a high-ceilinged room with yellowed windows and no furniture save for a writing desk and a few chairs at the end. Behind him, a double-leaved door stood slightly ajar, allowing in a thin bar of brighter light. She had the feeling that the room behind was just as large and just as empty. She came over and took a seat, glancing behind at the echoing room. The Count turned his bone-white smooth countenance toward her and said, "Not much left, is there? Someone will have to build up the family fortunes, but it won't be me. I am eighty years of age. I can trace my lineage back to Enea Silvio Piccolomini on one side and Jacopo Corsi on the other. Do you know who they were?"

Caterina shook her head. "I've heard of Piccolomini. Wasn't he an artist or something?"

The Count shook his head sadly and from his desk picked up a pair of reading glasses, held them up like a glittering fish in the light from the window, then perched them on his nose. "Let me see what you have, then."

He reached his hand across the desk.

"I just want to ask some questions," said Caterina.

"You have not brought warrants?"

"No," said Caterina. She drew in breath to disguise the thrill his question had caused her. "Not yet, but they'll be coming, if we need them." Her father had once told her the best way of keeping the tremor of excitement from the voice was to imagine you had coated your mouth and throat with honey, thick blobs of it, slowly sinking down your throat, smoothing the ripples in your voice. Speak slowly, deliberately, calmly. She could taste the honey now and concentrated on slowing her heartbeat, as the old man lowered his arm onto the desk and took off his glasses to observe her with disapproving coffee-colored eyes.

"What do you want?" he asked.

Good question. Sprightly though he was, this eighty-year-old man did not hold tourists up at knife-point. And yet he was expecting warrants.

She took a leap of faith.

"Well, first of all, we know the stolen goods were never marketed. Can they be returned to the tourists?"

"You think that might help?"

"Yes, definitely." Had she sounded too eager? She instilled greater formality and severity into her tone. "Cooperation is very important in these cases. What I write in my report will have an enormous effect on the judge's decisions. Even better would be direct evidence of cooperation on your part. Repentance. Regret."

"I have that in abundance," said the old man. "What will happen to him?"

"What do you mean?" The real question, the only question, was not what but who. He had invested her with knowledge she did not have, but was moments away from acquiring. It was vital not to break the spell. One mistimed comment and she would disclose the full extent of her ignorance, but the Count seemed more interested in asking his own questions, like a catastrophic lawyer demolishing his own case.

"How many years? Is it possible for him to avoid prison?"

And now she understood. What was going on began to take shape. She understood who the old man was talking about and trying to argue for. She knew who the mugger was and what it meant to the Count. As the realization came upon her, she noticed a darkening in the air around the old man. The bar of light from behind the door had dimmed and become shadow, and the shadow moved.

Caterina sprang out of her seat and moved behind it, just as the door swung open and a heavyset but short man with square shoulders and a smooth, well-fed face emerged from behind. He stood behind the Count on whose shoulder he placed a pudgy babyish hand. He seemed to be pushing the old man into his chair.

"You called the police, *Papà*," he said.

"It had to stop, Agnolo. Someone was going to get hurt. And I did not call them. They found out by themselves, as they were bound to in the end. Ask the policewoman here."

The younger man, perhaps in his mid-fifties, stared over his father's bald head at Caterina, but asked her nothing. Slowly, he moved to the side of the desk, and Caterina shifted her chair slightly to keep it between them. Then he put his palms outward to show he was not armed, and grinned.

"The Noantri's bookings are down seventy percent this year. It won't recover. Reputation is everything. Mark my words. We are a family not to be crossed."

"Move behind the desk, please, and keep your hands visible," she said.

There was no honey taste now, just a sensation of tomato skins and copper at the back of her throat. Her hand was trembling slightly. The man turned his back with what seemed a shrug, then whipped around again, a thin blade in his right hand. The metal caught the faint sunbeam streaming through the faraway window and seemed to harden and brighten it.

But Caterina was pointing her Beretta directly at him, her hands steady, her finger on the trigger, the bluish barrel pointing directly at his forehead. Slowly, slowly, breathing in through her nose and out through her mouth, she lowered the aim to the middle of his chest. Stopping power, greater surface area, easier target, no hesitation, squeeze trigger don't pull, beautiful Elia with his soft cheeks needs you alive.

"No!" The Count, unnoticed by either, had arisen from his chair and, with the same surprising agility, interposed himself between his son and Caterina.

"Drop your weapon," said Caterina. "Drop your weapon, drop your weapon! I will shoot, drop your weapon, I will shoot; drop your weapon now!" Caterina repeated the command and threat in another burst of three, allowing the barrel of the pistol to shift left and right while steadying against pitch and roll in her aim. She would not miss, and the Count was so thin and his son so broad that the odds were . . . but she did not want to shoot.

"You betrayed me."

"No, son," said the Count. "But you have so disappointed me."

"Drop your weapon. Signor Conte, stand aside. Stand aside now."

With a balletic movement, the Count bent his knee and slipped sideways and downwards out of the line of fire, and Caterina drew a bead on the son's broad chest. In his hand, he still held the thin knife, now glossy and sticky at its tip.

The Count lay on the dark floor and groaned, and a small gleaming pool ran from under him.

Caterina began to squeeze the trigger, but at that moment the man dropped his knife and fell to his knees on the floor beside his father.

"I'm sorry, *Papà*. I panicked."

Caterina followed his trajectory, pointing at the back of his bowed head, her finger easing its tension.

"It's very painful, Agnolo. Very painful."

"I just meant to push you away. I don't think it went in deep. I don't . . ."

He wiped his fingers on the floor. "Where is all this blood coming from?" He looked over at Caterina. "Help us. Please, help. *O Signore, perdonami.*"

She edged over. "Move away."

"He needs me."

"Move away from the knife. I'll take the knife, and you can go back to him. Understood?"

"Do as she says, Agnolo," whispered the old man. "I'll be fine in a moment. The pain is fading already."

Obediently, without standing up, Agnolo Corsi moved backwards on his knees. Caterina kicked at the knife with her foot, then retrieved it, and backed away. The son, now oblivious of her, leaned over his father, and buried his large head against the thin bird-like breast. Caterina took her left hand off the butt of the Beretta and used it to pull out her phone. She called an ambulance and backup, ordering them to break down the front door, because, against regulations, she had come in here alone and was trapped. For fifteen minutes she stood there in silence, her pistol loosely trained on the bunches of curly hair at the back of Agnolo Corsi's head as he wept over his bleeding father.

Half an hour later, Agnolo was led out like trussed lamb preceded by his chalk-white father on an orange stretcher. Caterina ignored the questions of the two patrolmen who had arrived on the scene, both of whom had immediately started asking where her male partner was. She ordered them to stay where they were and walked into the room from which Agnolo had emerged. It was brighter but smaller, and devoid of all furniture except for tissue-thin Persian carpets on the floor.

"That was his weapon?" asked the patrolman, pointing at the tapered stiletto that Caterina had placed on the desk. He reached out to touch it.

"No! Contamination of evidence," said Caterina.

"You said you picked it up. You've already held it."

"Even so," said Caterina. "Leave it." She looked at the thin knife. Its grip seemed to be made of dull silver. The blood on its tip had already coagulated and was beginning to brown. It was hard to resist the temptation to wipe it clean again.

"It's a lovely knife," said the patrolman, his hand still hovering nearby.

"You can bag it, if you want," said Caterina. "Once it's in plastic you can examine it."

"Thanks. See the markings on the handle, the lion on the hilt? It's an antique."

"A stiletto," said Caterina.

"It's called a *misericordia*," said the patrolman. "A weapon of mercy. It was used to kill off the mortally wounded after a battle. I have a replica at home, but this looks like the genuine article."

"Bag it carefully," said Caterina.

A low doorway on the right seemed to lead deeper into the house, and pulling on a pair of latex gloves, she turned the handle, and peered into darkness. She found a light switch, turned it on. A red and white porphyry font sat in the middle of the room, its bowl filled with a shining heap of watches, necklaces, chains, earrings, bangles. On the floor in a corner, like a pile of animal pelts, lay handbags, wallets, some of them flung open and showing off their gold, silver, and green credit cards. She began to pick her way through the pile, then pulled out and held aloft a silver crucifix on a chain. She dropped it into her pocket and called Grattapaglia.

"I think I've found a way for you to please a Spaniard," she said when he answered.

# 35

"As long as they don't enter my parents' study," said Blume. "And even then, I'm not sure it's a good idea."

"I think it is a good idea. I never thought my cousin had so much imagination. Maybe I'll promote him," said Paoloni.

Blume moved his phone into his left hand to change gear. "It's not responsible behavior."

"That's why it's fun," said Paoloni. "More to the point, it's unexpected and will throw the Colonel."

"I don't know. How long will it take them?"

"He says they can be in and out of there in fifteen minutes."

"They won't trash my parents' study?"

"My cousin will impress the importance of that upon them."

"And we're sure about what happened?" said Blume. "I think I might need to see for myself."

"That makes no sense. As soon as you go into your own place, he'll spring the trap," said Paoloni. "My cousin's idea is by far the best. Amazing, really when you think who his father is. Did I ever tell you about my uncle Filippo and the five-way parlay at the Appian hippodrome?"

"Not now, Beppe. I need to think."

According to Paoloni's cousin, Agent Sudoku, as Paoloni had taken to calling the Carabiniere watching Blume's apartment, was joined by a second man fifteen minutes after Paoloni's cousin started watching the watcher. Together, followed discreetly by the cousin, Captain Sudoku and the new arrival collected four cardboard tubes from the back of a Peugeot 305, then slipped into Blume's apartment building, taking advantage of a woman coming out to let themselves in. The cousin waited ten minutes before someone else coming out allowed him to get in, then took the stairs, and walked the hallways till he passed the apartment with Blume's name on it. Then he went halfway up the next flight of steps and waited. Two minutes later the two came out. The cousin heard them locking the door behind them. When he was sure they had gone, he examined the door carefully.

"They had keys, or they were very professional," Paoloni told Blume. "You just have an ordinary H-key deadlock, right? Not milled down the center or anything difficult?"

"No. But it's still easier to break in by lifting the door with a foot lever and wedge, and hitting the strike plate," said Blume. "So they did not want to leave a trace."

"Right," said Paoloni. "And my cousin says he saw the other man toss the tubes into a dumpster before getting into his car. Then he left, and Agent Sudoku resumed his post, watching your apartment. Whatever was in those tubes is now in your house waiting for you to find them. Or, since we know what we're dealing with, waiting for you to be found with them. You tell me they are the paintings from Treacy's flat, planted by the Colonel, I give you a fantastic idea, and you object."

"Your cousin's idea of breaking into my apartment is not flawless."

"But it is simple," said Paoloni. "In they go, they find whatever was planted there. Paintings, but who knows what else, and remove it."

"If your cousin's friends know how to break into an apartment, it means they're housebreakers," said Blume.

"Your powers of deduction never cease ..."

"Shut up, Beppe. And your cousin's connection with them is what, exactly?"

"I don't know. I think they're his cousins, or nephews or something. On the other side of the family. Nothing to do with me."

"Let me think," said Blume. "I'll call back."

He drove past the Ostiense station and into the empty parking lot next to the abandoned airport train terminal. Designed for the World Cup 1990, it opened years too late, then closed shortly afterwards, and was now a good place to park, drink, and pick up a transvestite.

Blume thought about gays and about Inspector Rosario Panebianco's admirable precision, the way he never smelled too bad, looked good in his uniform, stayed calm. He had very clean clipped fingernails. Blume had noticed that one day. Maybe Caterina would know. Women sensed these things. She'd laugh and say, of course how could you not have seen it. Or else, of course not, how could you ever have thought it. Something obvious to her, not to him.

Blume called Lieutenant Colonel Nicu Faedda at the Art Forgery and Heritage Division. Faedda and Panebianco, good friends. Soccer matches together.

"Commissioner Blume? You're going to speak to me after all."

"You were right about the Colonel trying to do something with those paintings," said Blume. "He's trying to compromise me with them. Put me on the back foot."

"How?"

"By putting me in possession of them." He waited. Faedda's tone would determine the next step.

"He put you in possession of them. Are you saying you received them against your will?"

It was a reasonable question, and Faedda has asked it without detectable undertones of skepticism. He still seemed disposed to accept Blume's claims at face value.

"He planted them on me," said Blume.

He paused again, listening for any sounds of disbelief, but all Faedda said was, "Where?"

"In my apartment."

"He must be using his old network of professionals," said Faedda. "Calling in some favors."

"I appreciate the way you're accepting my version," said Blume.

"If I have to challenge you on some points, I will do that later, but I know what sort of a man the Colonel is. So do you have the paintings now?"

"No. I had them removed in a staged burglery."

This time he heard a sharp intake of breath followed by a sigh. He could hear the forbearance and strain in Faedda's voice as he said, with admirable understatement, "That's extremely irregular."

"I know," said Blume. "But the important thing now is to make Farinelli want them back immediately. When he comes for them, that would be a good moment to get him."

"How are you going to make him want them straight back?"

"By telling him there is a Velázquez hidden beneath one of them."

"A Velázquez?" Faedda permitted himself another sigh. "Is there?"

"There might be," said Blume.

"You are going to have to explain this to me."

"Later. It's to do with something Treacy wrote. Obviously the Velázquez idea can't come directly from me. But we know someone in your department is reporting to the Colonel. Do you know who?"

"I have a damned good idea."

"If you disclose some confidential information, how long before it filters back to the Colonel through his informant?"

"Within an hour," said Faedda without hesitation. "And there's more than one of them."

"Good. So you've got to let slip the news that I am suddenly desperate to get the paintings back because I realized one of them might hide a priceless Old Master."

"And how did I get hold of this information—from you?"

"No. Through Panebianco. I confided to Panebianco and then he told you."

Either Faedda was deeply offended by the suggestion or thinking it over, or both, but the silence that followed was lengthy. Eventually he said, "Catching the Colonel in the act might not be enough."

"I know," said Blume. "But it's a start. Then there are some interesting notebooks that might help you build a deeper case and finally put an end to his superannuated career as puppet master."

"Even if all this works out," said Faedda, "and even if I get all I want— which I won't, but let's even say I emerge from this covered in glory, you'll still owe me. You realize that?"

"I know," said Blume. "Deal?"

"Deal."

Blume hung up and phoned Paoloni again.

"Did your cousin make contact with his housebreaker friends?"

"They're waiting. Just say the word. They'll need a few sweeteners, of course."

"Well, they won't find anything worth taking in my house. Their sweeteners can be that I will be a big fan of theirs the next time they get arrested."

"Plus 800 euros."

"They want 800 euros to rob my house?"

"I'll cover it," said Paoloni. "I know how hard it is on police pay."

"Fuck the pay, it's the principle," said Blume.

"Are we doing this or not?"

Blume drummed his fingers on the steering wheel, then said, "Why won't you tell me I'm making a mistake?"

"Because I don't think you are."

"I'm pretty sure this is going to be a bad move."

"But it's the move we're making?"

"I suppose so," said Blume.

"Great! It'll take them up to an hour from now, but probably less," said Paoloni. "Meet you afterwards?"

Blume's phone started beeping, indicating another incoming call. First he asked, "What about Captain Sudoku or whatever his name is?"

"He's still there solving number puzzles, waiting for you. No reason for him to see anything else. Be obvious about coming home or he might miss you."

"OK, I need to hang up." Blume looked at his phone to see which button he was supposed to press. He couldn't read a thing. He moved it a bit farther away, saw the message "accept call." He pressed the corresponding button and brought the phone back to his ear. Silence.

He shook the phone a bit, but it seemed to have no effect. He tried the other ear, pressed the green button. Cell phones had no dial tone. It was the first time he had noticed that. Whoever it was could call him again.

It rang again, and Blume was asked to hold the line because the Questore wished to speak to him. He imagined what it might be. Grattapaglia had murdered the internal affairs investigator. A mugging victim had died. The Carabinieri or Buoncompagno had issued another complaint. Leporelli and Scariglia were dead in their cell. He was being transferred to Gela, no, better, Locri. Blume glanced at his watch. 3:30 p.m.

As he held the line, the phone beeped and he looked to see who it was. Caterina. She could wait.

Finally, the Questore deigned to take the call he had placed.

"Commissioner! Good to speak to you. I must say that's a bit of news, isn't it?"

Blume made a non-committal sort of grunt, which he ended with an aspirated noise that could be interpreted as a weary sigh if that's what the news demanded.

The Questore seemed to be waiting for a more elaborate response. Blume proceeded warily. "Of course, nothing's definite, yet."

This did not seem to be what the Questore wanted to hear. The irritation in his voice was clear when he demanded, "Well, have we or have we not got a confession?"

Was he talking about Leporelli and Scariglia or . . .

"I know the stolen goods have been found, too," continued the Questore. "It looks like they are all going to be there. At least that's what your man Rospo told me. He's a good cop, this Rospo, a name I should be watching?"

Rospo had solved a case? Blume saw no other choice than to make another non-committal grunt.

"It will definitely be a propaganda coup," said the Questore. "Maybe we should invite the press, get some photos taken of you, Rospo, a few others standing over this hoard of recovered material."

"Definitely," said Blume. "Photos. Good idea." This had to do with the mugger.

The Questore said, "Sometimes you are a very dour man, Commissioner. Very dour. Enjoy your successes more. God knows, they're rare enough."

Blume was about to call Caterina back when his phone rang again.

"You won't guess where I am," said Grattapaglia, sounding considerably more cheerful than Blume had heard him in months. "Spanish Steps," he added quickly as if afraid Blume might pluck an inspired guess from the air and ruin the surprise.

"You have a disciplinary meeting in fifteen minutes," said Blume.

"No longer a problem," said Grattapaglia. "I'll make it in time. Aren't you going to ask me why I am here, or has Caterina already mentioned it?"

"You tell me," said Blume.

"I have just left the Spanish Embassy to the Holy See where I have had a very useful conversation with José Maria Carvalho, the diplomat from the other morning?"

"Oh," said Blume. This did not sound promising.

"He's not just dropping his complaint against me, he says he'll write a letter of recommendation if I need one. I've never seen a man so pleased to get a silver cross back." He dropped his voice as if in danger of being overheard. "He's still a little shit, and I was right to give him a thumping. I hate to admit it, but Mattiola's just saved my ass. She said she thought the guy was probably a member of Horus Deus."

"Opus Dei?"

"Yeah. What did I say?"

Blume asked Grattapaglia what he was talking about. Grattapaglia explained all he knew about the Corsi father and son, Caterina calling him over and giving him the cross. Blume's pleasure at things working out was tempered by his annoyance that he had not been there.

"You're going to be late for your appointment, Sovrintendente."

"I'm in the car now. Only a bit late, and it's not going to matter."

Blume held the phone at arm's length and scrolled through missed calls. He found Caterina, called her, and listened while she gave him a more coherent version of events.

"I'll get in as soon as I can," he said, "I have something to attend to here."

He swept his eye across the parking lot, his eye attracted by an electric blue latex dress worn by one of a group of five transvestites eyeing his car.

"One thing, Caterina. Panebianco. Is he . . . do you think he's . . ."

"No. He's out. He got a call."

"That's not what I meant. I was asking if you know, if you thought he might be in any way homosexual."

"In any way?"

"Or in all ways."

She laughed. "Are you really having to ask that now? How long have you been working with him?"

"Six years, seven," said Blume.

"Yes. I would say he most definitely is. What gave you this flash of insight?"

"I know who he plays soccer with."

"I've never heard it called that before."

"No. They really do play soccer together," said Blume. "Among other things."

Blume drove out of the parking lot and back toward his home in San Giovanni.

He double-parked in front of green dumpsters, and opened his door into the traffic flow, earning a few horn blasts from passing motorists. His watcher's car was fifty feet away. He called Paoloni. If this thing was spiraling out of control, any words he spoke in haste now would be listened to at leisure by a magistrate later.

"I'm outside my apartment. I was thinking of popping in, maybe having a shower. It would mean I'll be a little late for lunch. Is that OK?"

"Sure," said Paoloni. "So you're going in now to have this shower?"

"Yes, right now."

He chose the stairs rather than the elevator. On the third floor he encountered Mrs. Egidi, the porter, who glared at him with barely suppressed rage. She had just been told by a neighbor that his apartment door looked forced. She turned around and followed him.

"Nobody's safe," she said. "Gypsies, Albanians, niggers selling socks on the streets waiting for their chance. We need a night watchman. In Naples there are certain houses that nobody robs and you know why?"

"Yes. That's why they call it a protection racket. Now if you'll excuse me . . ." He reached his own floor and his reclusive next-door neighbor opened his reinforced apartment door and peered out.

"Just so you know," he said, "I heard nothing. Otherwise I would have called."

"I'm sure you would," said Blume. "Thank you. Everything OK with you?"

The neighbor opened his door a little wider. "These things. They make you lose faith, you know."

"I know," said Blume sympathetically. He pulled out his keys.

"I don't think you're going to need them," said the neighbor.

"No, you're right. No lock to put it in."

"You're a policeman," accused the porter. "So I don't suppose I need to call the police. You'll do that." She marched down the stairs, muttering about plumbing disasters, break-ins, and foreigners. Blume heard her exasperated replies to people from the lower apartments. Everyone knew something was up. The porter would not have ventured so far into the building otherwise.

Blume pushed his front door inwards, then gritted his teeth and the bent frame scraped across his floor inside. He edged his way in and contemplated the devastation of his home that he had just authorized.

Was it possible to do this much harm in a quarter of an hour? They had pulled down his books, kicked over his television. Every drawer in the house had been carried into the living room, overturned on the carpet, and then thrown aside. Knives, forks, pens, socks, underpants, candles, tools, tape, string, and hundreds of other items lay in a heap.

Most of the drawers looked damaged. His expensive amplifier was gone, but the other components of the stereo were left behind, and his CD collection was scattered everywhere. The wooden table in the dining area was scored, and the glass coffee table in the living room was cracked. His Kenwood coffeemaker had been knocked over, the Pyrex coffeepot lay smashed on the floor along with several plates and china. They had poured cornflakes, pasta, flour, and cocoa over everything.

The sofa cushions were slashed open, chairs overturned. In his bedroom, his clothes lay in a grubby pile, mixed up with dirty laundry. His favorite suitcase was missing. In his bedside table, there had been €120 in cash. The money was gone, but his passport was still there. He checked his wardrobe. Empty. They had pulled out everything. Thorough bastards whoever they were. And this had seemed like a good idea?

Fearfully, he entered the study, the room that contained all his parents' art books, lecture notes, his father's old typewriter, a large collection of LPs, and some of the furniture from when they were alive. All was intact. If they had been in here they had touched nothing.

He called up his own office and said there was no need to turn it into an emergency, since the thieves were long gone.

"Just send two patrolmen out here within the next half hour or so," he said.

He went back to the living room and found that with some effort he was able to push the front door of his apartment closed again. He put an exploded cushion back on the sofa and waited.

Less than ten minutes later someone rang the doorbell seven or eight times, while someone else hammered on the door. Blume walked over, called to the people outside to push, saying it was a bit stiff.

They pushed and kicked even, and Blume pulled to help. Eventually four Carabinieri were in the room, staring at the chaos, unsure what to do. They were soon followed by the Maresciallo and Investigating Magistrate Buoncompagno. Blume stood beside the door, half blocking the magistrate's entry. Buoncompagno stood back and showed Blume a piece of paper.

"Commissioner Blume, pursuant to Articles 259, 251, and 352 of the Code of Criminal Procedure, I am ordering a search of your place of domicile with reference to a well-sourced report . . . as the following . . . what the hell happened in here?"

"I appear to have been robbed. I hope the police don't waste too much time getting here." To the Carabinieri still in an immobile cluster at the end of his devastated living room, he said, "Help me pull the door open fully. The fat bastard will never fit through that crack."

They glared at him without moving, but thirty seconds later they were all heaving at his door to make a large enough space for Colonel Farinelli to walk through.

The Colonel stood there surveying the mess, his face awash with sweat from the exertion of getting in and out of the elevator. "Did you Carabinieri do all this while I was on my way up? I told you to respect the apartment. It belongs to a police commissioner."

He patted his heart, took a few deep breaths, pulled out a linen hand-kerchief, and dabbed his brow. "Something's not right." He looked in alarm at the overturned furniture. "Where can I sit?"

The Maresciallo grabbed an overturned chair with one hand, spun it around, and placed it against the back of the Colonel's thighs. As the Colonel lowered himself cautiously onto the seat, there was a slight com-motion behind and two policemen appeared. The first of them saluted Blume, saying, "Sir, we got a message that . . ." He stopped as he took in the scene and the presence of the others.

He looked in amazement at the assembled group. "You called the *Carabinieri*?"

"No, Agente. Don't worry about that. They have to execute a search warrant. God alone knows what they expect to find. But you two might want to follow them around a bit. I'm giving you an order as your com-mander and permission as homeowner."

Buoncompagno gave his long gray hair a decisive flick and pointed at the Carabinieri. "Search the whole place," he ordered. "Start in the bed-room. Rip down the walls if you have to. Anywhere that . . ."

"Wait!" called Blume. "Don't touch anything. This is a crime scene. Pursuant to Articles 354, 355, and 360 of the Code of Criminal Procedure, I ask all non-essential persons to clear the premises immediately to avoid contamination of the scene."

The magistrate waved his search warrant. "This has precedence."

"Oh, and pursuant to Article 254, paragraph 2, and . . . a few other articles I forget. I don't suppose you can remind me, Magistrate?"

"Don't try to get smart with me, Commissioner. No public prosecutor has received notification of this alleged crime, and therefore as the most authoritative person in this room ..."

The Colonel, still struggling to control his breath, spoke so quietly the magistrate was forced to come closer to hear. He said, "Magistrate Buoncompagno? Please, just be quiet." He looked sadly over at Blume, seeking fellowship of understanding between intelligent men.

He inclined his head slightly toward the nearest two Carabinieri. "You, accompany the magistrate back downstairs to his car. I am sure he has other urgent crimes to solve."

"They could still be here, Colonel," said Buoncompagno. "Let them look in the bedroom at least."

The Colonel plucked a crumb of something from his lip and flicked it in Buoncompagno's direction. "You never miss an opportunity to ruin the silence by speaking, do you?"

"Agenti," said Blume, looking at the very confused patrolmen, "I want this place dusted for prints."

"Now you're overdoing it, Blume," said the Colonel.

"Someone trashed my house. I intend to find out who."

"Carabinieri," barked the Colonel. "We are going."

When they had left, the first Agente came over. "You OK, sir? Did they do this?"

"Of course not. It was thieves. Really. Write up a report, take a few latents from the walls, give it the usual treatment. No special privileges for me."

"We need to do more than that, sir. We can't let them get away with robbing a Commissioner's house. If word gets around, it'll look bad."

"It can't be helped. I prefer this to blow over. I prefer it not to get within earshot of the Questore, though it's probably too late. Look, tell you what you can do for me, get someone to come around and fix that door. If they need to put in a new one, fine. Accept any price up to ... I don't know. How much is a new door?"

"Reinforced and all that, around two thousand euros," said the Agente.

"May as well hang a bead curtain for all the good it does. Call me if you need me. I can't stay here."

"Yes, sir."

# 36

"D O WE ALWAYS have to meet at McDonald's?"

"Do you prefer Burger King? I think their buns are too sweet. We could go for a kebab if you prefer."

"This food will kill you," said Blume. "Have you ever read ... ?"

"No," said Paoloni.

"Right. Dumb question."

Paoloni received his tray and turned from the counter. "You didn't order anything after all that time in line?" he said. "Let's get those two seats over there. Grab me some of those paper ... thanks. Anyway, it's air that kills you in the end. I saw a program on the Discovery Channel the other day. Oxygen, they say, gives you wrinkles and breaks down your ... something inside that you need not to die, basically. Turns out, oxygen is what makes us grow old."

"Not the passing of time?"

"Apparently not. So, how did it go?"

"They might have trashed the place a bit less," said Blume.

"You said you wanted it to look authentic."

"It was authentic. They took money I left beside the bed, and the paintings of course. At least I'm presuming they found them there."

"Yeah. They were hidden in your closet. All together. They used a suitcase to take them out."

"I noticed," said Blume.

"You want the suitcase back? I can arrange it."

"No. This needs to run its natural course. I don't want any contact with these guys. I want to know absolutely nothing about them. The only thing I want is a heads-up if they make a move to sell those paintings."

"You want, I can stop that, too."

"No. Let them do what they want. They'll keep Farinelli occupied for a while."

"Did they respect your parents' room?"

"Yes. They left it alone. Were they wearing gloves?"

"It's not like I was there," said Paoloni. "But these guys are professionals. You'd need a lot of forensic work and lab time to catch their fibers, hairs, and so on. It's just not worth it for a burglary. Oh yeah, almost forgot. The car watching your place did not register back to the Carabinieri, nor was it stolen, nor did it seem to belong to anyone. The *motorizzazione* de-lists vehicles for special uses so that's Farinelli using his spooky contacts. Anyhow, they walked up unnoticed and unremarked to your apartment, did what they did, walked out with a suitcase. Then you arrived and Captain Sudoku spotted you and alerted the Colonel."

Blume left Paoloni to his lunch, and drove back to the station, conscious that the Colonel and the Treacy case were distracting him from his proper duties. He was letting things slip badly, and it would be noticed, once the rewards and benefits of catching the muggers and seeing the two extortionists jailed had been distributed and absorbed.

As he stepped into the operations room, Rospo bobbed up. "Inspector Mattiola took it upon herself to take the initiative while I was . . ."

From behind him, Sovrintendente Grattapaglia, nodding pleasantly at Blume, came up, put his hand on Rospo's shoulder in what seemed like a friendly gesture, but he held his hand there.

"The meeting with the investigator went like a fucking dream, Commissioner. Eight minutes. I timed it. He told me we needed one more meeting for the sake of appearances, and then I would be back to work." Grattapaglia smiled. "I must say, I haven't felt this good for a while." His knuckles whitened as he tightened the grip and dug his fingers into the space below Rospo's clavicle, drawing a gasp of pain from the Assistente Capo. "You and me, Rospo, we're going to have a nice little talk about Inspector Mattiola and the recognition of merit. Come over here."

Rospo winced as Grattapaglia steered him away from Blume, who looked across the room to where Caterina was sitting, apparently unaware of his arrival. Her head was bent slightly forward as if she were reading a breviary, but her hands held nothing. Blume went over to her.

"I expected to see you flushed with victory. What's the matter?"

"He died," she said. "Old man Corsi died. I just heard from the hospital.

The stab wound was superficial, but they say he died from hypovolemic shock."

Blume abandoned his self-serving plan to reprimand her for disobeying procedures and entering a suspect's house alone and for not trying hard enough to keep him in the picture.

"Why are you so upset about Corsi?" asked Blume. "I mean, sure, it's a bad thing, but he was an old man and old men die easily. Besides, it's not as if you knew him."

"Come to that," said Caterina, "the few minutes I spent in his company were enough to tell me I didn't like him much either. It's not him; it's the son I feel for. I passed by Mariagrazia Gazzani, the magistrate who was in charge of the investigation into the Corsis' denunciation of Leporelli and Scariglia. It turns out the failed hotel was the son's venture, but the affidavit on the attempted extortion was made by the father. It's a stretch to say this, but I have a feeling the son would have paid off Leporelli and Scariglia just to stay in business. He was trapped and the hotel was his bid for freedom. When it all fell through, he took it out on the Noantri Hotel. I think he was trying to escape, and instead he's lost everything and killed his only family . . ."

"That'll do, Inspector," said Blume. "Don't waste your sympathy. He's a mugger, now he's a parricide. He made his choices."

"Do you believe that's all there is to it?"

"No," said Blume. "I don't. But if you feel like this for him, how are you going to deal with the devastation of the truly innocent?"

"I have seen dead children. I have seen murdered young women. They were Chinese, Nigerian, Kurdish. When I worked in immigration I saw things you wouldn't imagine. Well, the public wouldn't imagine, or couldn't be bothered to imagine, because they were foreign and illegal."

"Exactly," said Blume. "So don't waste your sympathy."

"He didn't mean to kill his father, I'm sure of it. I was there."

"Sometimes I think we should just get rid of this whole business of distinguishing between what people meant to do and what they actually did," said Blume. "Think how many lawyers we could get rid of. The ancient Romans didn't allow for intentionality, you know. They just looked at the result of an action. I think it is a sensible approach. Their punishment for parricide, by the way, was to whip the culprit raw, sew him into a leather bag with a dog, a viper, a cock, and, where available, a chimpanzee, then throw the bag into the Tiber. The *poena cullei*. That's the name of the punishment. It's not on the statute books any more, unfortunately."

"That's horrific . . . a chimpanzee?"

"Apparently," said Blume.

Caterina repressed a giggle.

"I'm not making this shit up," said Blume.

She straightened her shoulders and looked directly at him. "You have a weird way of cheering people up."

"You did great work, you know," said Blume. "And I heard what you did for Grattapaglia. That's great. A fantastic move. It will put us all in the clear."

Caterina nodded. "Thanks."

"You've also cleared the decks of work, and given us a bit of breathing space. Even if now you've got to write up the reports on this morning. Then I'm going to have to sign off on the paperwork."

"There's something else," said Caterina. "Angela and Emma came in this morning, after you had gone. And then Grattapaglia and I established that Emma's not telling the truth about her movements on the night Treacy died. Where were you this morning, by the way?"

"I was going to tell you that." He glanced around the room, saw Rospo sitting at his computer massaging his shoulder, his forehead a map of angry creases.

"Come into my office."

# 37

AFTER HAVING CATERINA set forth the details of her conversations with Emma and her mother, Blume was very complimentary. "And I know you're protecting Rospo by playing down the fact of his absence."

Caterina ignored all this and looked at him expectantly.

"Your turn," she said. "You answered the phone while I was talking, and left directly afterwards, what was that about?"

"I asked you for a report in my capacity as your commanding officer. It doesn't necessarily work the other way round."

"What are you talking about? You have no right to reticence. None. I'm directly involved in all this and so is my son. Jesus, you are an irritating bastard sometimes."

"You can't talk to me like that. Not when we're inside these walls. That's why there are rules to stop this sort of thing from developing."

"What sort of thing?"

"You know . . . the personal entering the workplace."

"No. Spell it out."

"You know exactly what I mean," said Blume.

Caterina laughed. "You should see the color of your face now. Tell you what, just tell me about what you've been doing. It'll be a cinch in comparison with this conversation."

"It's really better you don't know. For your sake."

"If it's for my sake, I give you permission to disturb my peace of mind," said Caterina.

"No. Not in this building," said Blume. "We can't speak like this in here."

"Where then?"

Blume stood up quickly from his desk. "Come on."

"Where?"

"Have you ever seen a Velázquez?"

"No, I haven't. Treacy spoke of the portrait of the pope, I can't remember his name."

"Innocent the tenth. Giambattista Pamphili, if you prefer." Blume went over to his window and pointed. "It's about twenty paces from where I am standing now."

They left the police station and turned right. A few steps past heavily grated ground-floor windows brought an impressive entrance with a green flag announcing Galleria Doria Pamphili over it.

"In here?" asked Caterina.

"No. That's the old entrance," said Blume. "We need to walk around to the Via del Corso."

"You've been in there recently? I don't think I've been in a gallery since I was on a school trip," said Caterina. "Do you visit them a lot?"

"A bit," said Blume.

"Did you study art or something?"

"I was brought up in it. My parents were art historians."

They turned on to Via del Corso, and Caterina got caught behind a group of tourists in bermuda and cargo shorts who had aggregated into a tortoise formation and were proceeding along with defensive care, determined not to be forced by the natives off the sidewalk and into the path of the deadly buses. By the time she had managed to navigate around them, Blume had disappeared. She was walking blithely past a massive arched entrance to what she had always assumed to be a bank, when he stepped out and gently pulled her into a peaceful courtyard. He flashed his police badge at a man in a glass box selling tickets, who shrugged and scowled, and led Caterina down a long quiet hall toward a flight of curving steps.

"My father is dying," said Caterina into the silence. "I don't know why I said that. Nor why it should feel like a confession."

"It feels like a confession because you're telling me you don't know how you'll manage without him," said Blume. "But you will. When they are alive, your parents are like two fires: the focus of comfort, warmth, and light but also of anger, rage, and heated battles. When they die, they leave a sort of after-smoke which keeps expanding until it seems to be every-where and in everything you do and drains the color from it. So you accept that for the rest of your life you'll be walking around in that smoke.

Then one day you notice the smoke is thinning out, which is good, but you feel bad about it, too."

They entered the gallery and found themselves standing in front of a bronze centaur, and Caterina almost pointed like a little kid to say: "Oh, look!"

"We're the only ones here," said Blume. "Not even a tourist. Wonderful."

A tall blond couple entered the room speaking Dutch.

Caterina stood feeling suddenly self-conscious in the middle of the room between lines of white statues with muscular bodies. The bright ceiling frescos showed scenes from stories she did not know. The walls were not just hung with paintings, but stacked with them. Lines of paintings one on top of the other, most of them too high to see. Those that were at eye level shone back the light as a black varnished sheen beneath which she could see almost nothing.

She followed Blume down to the end of a long corridor.

"Wait! Have you seen this!" Caterina pointed at a picture of six naked cherubims grappling and wrestling each other. "That's so sweet! I mean it's funny, too. Mainly it's funny. I can see you're giving me a look—I don't have any taste for these things. Don't make me feel ignorant."

"*Putti* in battle," said Blume. He peered at the nameplate next to the frame. "It says it's by someone called Andrea Podestà. Never heard of him. Funny, I thought . . . never mind. I've seen it before. Not here." He touched her on the arm and ushered her into a small square room just big enough for the two of them, and said, "There!"

Staring sideways daggers at them was a large portrait of Pope Innocent X.

"Doesn't he look really hassled at our intrusion?" said Blume. "I love that."

"He doesn't look pleased at all," said Caterina. She turned to examine a calmer white marble bust of the same man, his eyes blank, uninterested, who seemed to be avoiding looking at them. "Nor here."

"You can tell that Velázquez had status by the fact they allowed him to paint the pope like that and Pamphili himself didn't object," said Blume. "Not flattering, but therefore flattering. Like when someone picks up on your faults? It's annoying as hell, but since it means you're interesting enough for them to notice, you should eventually take it as a compliment."

He gazed at the picture, nodding at it with the utmost approval. "Also," he said, "imagine being able to give people a fuck-off look that lasts for centuries. Who could resist that?"

They left the portrait, and walked slowly through the next room. Blume halted before a painting of a woman raising her hands in despair over a dying warrior. "That's a Guercino," said Blume, tapping the identifying tag on the wall. "He was one of the artists Treacy liked to copy."

"*Erminia Finds the Wounded Tancredi*," read Caterina. "Who were Erminia and Tancredi?"

"I don't know," said Blume. "Wasn't Tancredi one of those Norman knights who conquered southern Italy? It's still a name used down there."

"There's a Tancredi in *Il Gattopardo*, too," said Caterina. "Not this guy, obviously."

As they stood there looking at the work, which, if truth be told, she did not like, Blume began to tell her about Faedda, the staged housebreak-in and his idea of tempting the Colonel into making a rash move to get back the paintings.

"Is Farinelli really going to believe that Treacy hid something beneath the paintings?"

"I asked Faedda to deliberately leak the idea into his department, and I must say it didn't take long for the Colonel's source to refer the message back to him. I think that will help Faedda identify who it is, if he doesn't know already."

"But will the Colonel believe there is something?" said Caterina.

"In the paintings, behind them, beneath them. He doesn't need to believe, he just has to doubt. The important thing is to confuse him, rob him of his power to make clear decisions. And it's working. The Colonel has paintings planted in my home, then a few hours later he wants them back. He should never have given me control, even temporarily. He's losing command of the situation and he's not thinking straight. That'll do me for now."

"You tread a thin line, Alec," said Caterina. "But the Colonel operates completely out of bounds. Be careful."

"Decades of impunity will do that to you. Even though he knows intellectually that he's lost most of his power, he has no sense of proportion anymore. He still acts as if there were no limits. That's why I think he'll make a rash move soon."

"I want harm to come to him," said Caterina. "And I'm angry with myself for feeling that."

"It's understandable. The Colonel damages people. It's what he has done all his life. But he's careful, too. The harm he intends for me is administrative, penal, and moral but not physical. Same goes for you and for Faedda. And he won't touch Elia, of course. Even he knows better than to try."

"What about the others?"

"Who's left?"

"Emma, her mother, Nightingale."

"He could harm them," admitted Blume. "But for the time being, the Colonel will be focusing his energy on me and trying to get the paintings back. Then, with any luck, Faedda will get him. That's the idea."

"You draw his fire, so to speak. Was it your idea?"

"Not as such."

"What do you make of Emma's failed alibi?"

"It wasn't much of an alibi to begin with. We have witnesses, she probably had her cell phone with her, so we could get a reading from that. You can be sure the Colonel has."

"It means she was there a few hours before Treacy died," said Caterina.

"It also means the Colonel will know this. But Treacy died of natural causes. She's not going to face an investigation. There's a Caravaggio over here that's worth seeing. *Rest During the Flight to Egypt.*"

She allowed him to steer her into the next room, glanced at the painting, which didn't look much like the few Caravaggio paintings she knew of. "I hate to say this, Alec, but the more I think about it, the dumber the house-breaking idea looks. For about ten reasons."

"I know."

"So why?"

"It seemed like a good idea at the time. I let Paoloni talk me into it. He's not even persuasive, it's just I always feel I owe him something."

"Do you want to hear one or two of the reasons I think it was not a good idea?"

"No. I already know them all. I've been thinking them over myself."

"Can I talk about one of them?"

"If you must."

"You think you've managed to send the Colonel off the track by suggesting the Velázquez is hidden under one of the paintings that disappeared from your house," began Caterina.

Blume interrupted. "Not necessarily one of the ones he put in my house. It could be any one of the paintings he took from Treacy's house. He'll have already started on the ones still in his possession, which will keep him busy for a while, and when he finds nothing, he'll come looking to get back the ones that I had stolen."

"Which, meanwhile, you don't have."

"I can get them back easily enough."

"You hope. But suppose you've got this wrong? That is to say, suppose you're accidentally right and the Velázquez really is hidden in one of those paintings?"

"It isn't. I'm not wrong."

"Have you ever said that and then it turns out you were?"

"Never," said Blume.

"Be serious."

"Treacy would not risk damaging the Velázquez."

"If it's so very unlikely, the Colonel will think so, too."

"Yes, but he will have to check first. Just to be sure. If Treacy reprimed the canvas carefully with gesso, it would preserve what's underneath."

"But you are certain that never happened."

"Yes, he did not do that."

"You sound so certain."

"Because I am right. It doesn't fit with the Treacy I know. He wouldn't use his forging techniques on the Velázquez."

"Why not?"

"It's in the tone of his text. He's sorry, he's repentant . . . it's all in there. The Colonel will never pick up on it. It represents truth, beauty, forgiveness. He would not have painted over it. It is hidden somewhere else. I am certain of it. Unless . . ."

"Unless?" asked Caterina.

"I've just had a disturbing thought," said Blume.

"What?"

"Come on, back to the office." He set off at a fast pace, forcing Caterina to run the next few steps to catch up with him. "By the way, I meant to say the Madonna in the Caravaggio looks a lot like you."

"Really?" Caterina tried to call up the image of the painting, but she had not been looking at it properly. Now she would have to go back to see it again.

It took just ten minutes to reach Blume's office again.

"I don't suppose you brought the photocopies of Treacy's manuscript in today?"

"Let's not go through that again," said Caterina. "Don't you have the originals?"

"I gave them to Paoloni. It doesn't matter. I noted down the phrase ... here it is." Blume pulled a notepad out of his drawer, flicked through several pages, then read:

*"I have already given you the most valuable thing I ever had. It is there before you, it is in these words, it is in our hearts and our memories ..."*

Blume put down the pad and looked at Caterina. "I didn't imagine he would be so straightforward. *It is there before you!*"

Caterina said, "Angela. He gave it to Angela!"

"But hidden. It *is* behind a painting after all. I was wrong. It's hidden behind a work he gave to Angela. It makes sense."

He snatched up the phone on his desk. "Phone her. Tell her to get any of Treacy's paintings she has on her walls down. Tell her to bring them to us."

"Why me?" asked Caterina, ignoring the heavy cream-colored receiver in Blume's hand and pulling out her cell instead.

"You know her. She'll listen to you."

She held up her hand as she waited for the connection and nodded as it arrived.

"Ringing ... Angela? Inspector Mattiola, yes. Caterina. Look this may sound a bit strange but ... you mean now? He was there. And what ...?" Caterina listened, made some half-hearted attempts to sound comforting, then hung up.

"Too late," she told Blume. "The Colonel and the Maresciallo went all the way up to Pistoia. They just left her house. They took seven paintings off the walls. Emma was there."

# 38

FIFTEEN MINUTES LATER, he was sitting alone in his office with a feeling of foolishness beginning to creep over him. Caterina's shift was over, and he had told her to go home. "All I have to do is wait for the Colonel to make his move," he said.

Before leaving, she had said, "It would be better if you knew what his next move would be."

"He is moving a bit quicker than I thought."

But she went home all the same. She had a son waiting for her, after all.

For all he knew the Colonel, probably accompanied by his silent Maresciallo, was right now driving across the Swiss border, a priceless painting in the trunk of their car.

His cell rang. Wearily, he drew it out of his pocket. Number withheld.

"My Maresciallo has left an important package for you downstairs," said the Colonel's voice. "I advise you to go down and get it immediately."

"A parcel bomb?" said Blume.

"On the contrary. An opening of negotiations."

"It's money, isn't it, Colonel?" said Blume. He was delighted with himself. The Colonel was still looking. "How much?"

The Colonel stayed silent.

"You've betrayed yourself already," said Blume. "All calls are recorded always."

"I am not afraid of a recording. I just want our conversation to move up to a higher level of intelligence," said the Colonel. "I shall call you back in ten minutes."

Blume did not even have to go downstairs. An enterprising Agente brought the envelope up to him, then stood around waiting to see what was in it. From the shape and feel of the thing, it could only be money, which is what the Agente wanted to confirm so he could tell his colleagues.

"Thank you, Agente, you may go," said Blume. When he was sure he was on his own, he opened it and looked inside, then counted it out, dropping the fifty- and hundred-euro bills into the top drawer of his desk as he did so. He noted no sequence of numbers or obvious markings on the bills. The feeling of confidence in his own judgment flowed back into him.

When the Colonel phoned back, Blume said, "Colonel Orazio Farinelli, you are a generous man to give me 5,000 euros, just like that."

"Have you stopped playing games, Blume? A police commissioner staging the burglary of his own apartment, operating without the orders of a magistrate in a case to which he has not been assigned, withholding vital evidence in the form of notebooks, conducting his own personal investigations in search of a prize worth millions, dealing with a former colleague dismissed for what everyone knows was attempted murder and now running a security firm that operates in a gray area between legality and crime. And I am the one supposed to be worried about who might be listening?"

"Speaking candidly, then, what is this money for?"

"Your advance payment."

"I don't have the paintings. You saw how my apartment was burgled."

"I know you don't have them. You let them out of your control."

"Just like you, Colonel."

"This is the reason that we need to join forces again. We both made the same mistake, and we both need to get those paintings back, take a look at what is in them. That money is for you to hand over to whoever has them. Promise more, get them back."

"I see you finished reading Treacy's life story. I think you must have planned to plant the paintings in my house before you got to the interesting bit about the Spanish painter. Awkward of him to put it so close to the end, wasn't it? And a terrible disadvantage for you that he wrote in English.

"If you would only be more cooperative, we could work together on this."

"The paintings you planted in my house got stolen. Well and truly stolen. Think of it as if I had put them in a blind trust. They are beyond my or your immediate control," said Blume.

"I have simply this to say," said the Colonel. "Act always in the best interests of your friends. Think of what would hurt them most and the lengths you would go to save them from that. That's the level of commitment I want."

The Colonel had hung up.

Blume phoned the switchboard from his desk and had them call Caterina at her home number.

"Caterina?"

"No, it's Elia. Do you want to speak to my mother?"

"So you're at home this evening. Good boy. Yes, give the phone to your mother."

"Who shall I say it is?"

"Don't you recognize ... I am the Commissioner. Blume. Her boss. Alec."

A few seconds passed, then Caterina asked, "Don't tell me I have to come in tonight."

"No. On the contrary. Stay at home."

"Is everything OK?"

"Sure. You're at home?"

"This is my home number you dialed. Are you sure you're OK?"

"I meant later. Are you at home later? I was thinking of coming over later. We could have a drink. Is Elia going to be there?"

"You don't drink, Commissioner. Yes, Elia is here. He just got back from a friend's house. Are you suggesting I send him to my mother's tonight because you are coming over?"

"No! No, keep him there. Were you planning to go out?"

"Not if you're coming over."

"Good. Stay in. Both of you. Keep the door locked."

"Alec, what the hell is going on? Is it Colonel Farinelli? It is, isn't it? If he's threatening Elia again, I'm going to need to find a way of getting rid of the threat for good."

"He won't try anything," said Blume. "But stay in."

"You will come round?"

"I might be late."

"Come round at any time. I could do with the company. The backup."

"You'll get it," said Blume.

He hung up, then flung open his office door, and looked out. Panebianco was not there. He'd been gone for a while now. Blume roared at Rospo to come in.

"I have a chance for you to make up for being a useless little shit this morning—and every morning, and every day. Plus you get double overtime," he said as Rospo arrived. "I want you to guard a place. In a marked car."

Rospo made a face.

"Choose someone you get on with, if such a person exists, take a car, sit outside this address until I come and relieve you. Challenge anyone who looks suspicious going into the building."

"Is this an order from a magistrate?"

"No. It's from me."

"No magistrate?" said Rospo and puffed out his cheeks as he considered the information. "Is this even a case, sir?"

"Rospo, I'm warning you . . ."

"Of course I'll do it. What sort of person will I be looking out for?"

"Military, police, criminal, capable of violence. Probably a pair of males, aged between eighteen and fifty. Armed challenge. Don't hesitate."

"Who's the target?"

"Your target is anyone suspicious. You challenge, your partner covers."

"Not *my* target," said Rospo. "Their target. Who am I guarding?"

"A child."

"Whose?"

"Inspector Mattiola's. Now do you understand what I mean about redeeming yourself?"

Blume turned on his heel, then called Paoloni.

There was a problem.

# 39

"YOU KNOW WHEN they say the best lies are based on the truth?" said Paoloni as Blume entered his apartment. "Well, that's bullshit. The best lies are based on lies."

"Has something gone wrong, Beppe?"

"It's got a bit complicated. My cousin's mates . . ."

"The thieves," said Blume. "What do they want, money? Here." He put down the five thousand in cash from the Colonel.

Paoloni picked it up, handed it back to Blume. "Keep that. At least while I explain. The problem is the two who entered your apartment are beginning to feel nervous. They were hauled in by the Carabinieri a few hours ago and questioned about something totally unrelated that went down last week in Centocelle, then released. They think they were followed."

"Can't you help them get rid of a tail and reassure them?"

"I already did. They feel a bit more relaxed now, but, here's the thing, they don't want to sell the paintings to someone from law enforcement."

"OK, Beppe, tell them to choose anywhere they want to meet and I'll go there."

"They're a bit freaked. They don't want to sell the paintings to anyone from law enforcement. One of them said they were thinking of burning them."

"How would they know I was police, Beppe?"

"You? What else could you be?"

"I could be a foreign buyer."

"A foreign buyer . . . Come off it, Alec. They probably saw your picture when they were robbing your house. I didn't tell them, but I'd be surprised if they didn't work out that you're a cop. My cousin probably told them."

"I don't have pictures of myself in my house."

"Of your parents then. You probably look like them. Think it through, Alec."

Blume had an image in his head of his passport sitting on his bed, pulled out of a drawer along with the stolen cash.

Blume called Faedda on his phone. "There are a few complications on this side. I'll call you back once I get the paintings."

Blume snapped shut his phone.

"Give me that money back," said Paoloni.

Blume fished inside his pocket, pulled out an envelope, and tossed it to Paoloni.

"How much is in there?"

"Five grand."

"I'll add another three. They'll probably start at fifteen. Getting them down to eight shouldn't be hard. They're not so good at this sort of thing."

"So you think you should be the one to get the paintings from them."

"Can you think of a better person?" said Paoloni. "It's the only ..." He stopped as the phone in the apartment trilled and the dog started growling.

"He hates the sound of that phone," said Paoloni. "The only person who still uses that number is my ex-wife." He pointed at the growling dog. "Dog says what I think."

Paoloni reached for the phone on the sideboard, and picked up, rolling his eyes, then turning away so Blume would not have to listen.

The dog ambled over, yawned, stuck his head between Blume's legs, and snuffled contentedly at his genitals. With one bite, thought Blume, the beast could castrate him in revenge for being abandoned to Paoloni's care.

"I didn't think it was possible, but Filomena is worse as a mother than she was as a wife," said Paoloni, putting down the phone. "Fabio didn't come home after school and she immediately assumes he's here with me playing with the PlayStation. That's the worst she could come up with: video games. If she had any idea what he really gets up to."

Blume couldn't call Fabio's face to mind. What age was the child now—fifteen, sixteen? He asked the only thing he remembered. "Does he still play soccer?"

Paoloni nodded eagerly, pleased to be asked. "He does. As a matter of fact, he's captain. Not a complete loss, then. And I exaggerate about his behavior. He's got his act together this year. Gets sevens and eights instead of fours and fives at school. He even said he liked, what was it? Math or science or something improbable." He hoisted the bag onto his lap. "No point in delaying this thing. You need the paintings back, I can get them. Let's do it."

"I'm not sure, Beppe."

"If you had a better idea you'd have said it by now."

Blume glanced at his watch. Almost eight. Should he go to Caterina now, or wait for Paoloni to come back with the paintings? Paoloni could take hours.

"Where are you going to get the cash you were talking about?"

"I've got some stored away. Don't you worry about that."

"Then you call me, soon as you get it done?"

"It could take some time. Also, I don't want to be caught with you directly afterwards. Wouldn't do my credibility much—*cazzo*!" The phone was ringing again. "That woman has no patience."

Paoloni spoke, alternating hushed tones with raised voice. He made some comforting sounds, then got annoyed, and slammed down the receiver.

"Fabio's not at any of his friends' houses, according to his unbalanced mother," he said. "He doesn't usually pull this kind of stunt. Like I said, he's been doing better recently. I'll kill the little bastard when I get him. Puts his mother through this sort of worry, then she takes it out on me. It's not what he usually does."

"He never goes off without telling anyone? I thought all teenagers did that."

"No," said Paoloni. "He's done plenty of shit, but not that. No need, since we always let him go. Personally, I think having friends is better than being good at school. No point in ending up smart and alone, is there? But after this, I'm going to ground him." He slid an uncharacteristically apologetic note into his tone. "Look, would you just call in and see if there have been any, you know, accidents or incidents in this area?"

Blume took out his phone too quickly, fumbled, and dropped it. "No problem."

"You look almost as worried as his mother sounds," said Paoloni.

"Go and get those paintings, Beppe."

"Maybe I should wait till I get news of Fabio."

"Go get them now, Beppe. I mean it. The sooner you get them . . ."

"What? The sooner I get them, the sooner what?"

"The sooner all this is over. I'll find Fabio for you. I'll call you when I've found him. I've got nothing else to do."

Paoloni stood up, pushed the envelope under his arm, and walked out the room. Minutes later he was back. "You don't have to worry about paying back the difference."

"Thanks. I appreciate this. But I'll get the money back to you."

"Another thing." He handed Blume the three notebooks. "No point in keeping these here. If they come looking for them, this will be the second place they'll look. If I were you, I'd just burn them."

Blume took the notebooks back without any great pleasure. "Thanks, Beppe."

"Yeah. Listen, just now you said you would find Fabio . . . that was a strange way of putting it."

"What was strange about it? If I find him, you know, maybe a patrol car will spot him on a corner. If I don't find him, it means he's back with his mother."

"Just let me know," said Paoloni.

They left together. As Paoloni climbed into his car, he said, "I don't know how long this will take. I'll call you when I've got something." He paused. "It's the *motorini* that scare me most. Death traps. Let me know immediately if there's been an accident."

"He'll be fine," said Blume.

"Yeah. But let me know, eh?"

# 40

WHILE CATERINA WAS washing the dishes, wondering about Blume's weird self-invitation and dark warnings about staying in, Elia appeared at the doorway and informed her, with wonderment in his voice, that AS Roma had as good a goal average as Inter Milan, even though Inter was eight points ahead in the Championship. Did that strike her as in any way fair?

She feigned interest in this, and was rewarded with a series of statistics demonstrating beyond argument that AS Roma, despite frequent losses, seemed to be just as good as any other team in the Championship or, indeed, Europe.

Warming to his theme, Elia wondered who she thought they should use as the center-forward for the game against Palermo on Wednesday night? She frowned, thinking hard, until he offered a few names and thoughts of his own. She picked a name. Baptista. Elia was amazed. It was exactly the name he had been thinking of. Clearly she was not so completely out of the loop as all that. Now, as regards the defense, was Mexes better than ...

When he had finally finished, she told him to go to bed. She went into her bedroom, took her pistol from its hiding place in the closet, loaded it. By the front door she unhooked a framed poster from the wall to reveal a cavity in the wall that housed the electricity meter. She placed the pistol there, and hung up the poster, looking at it for the first time in years. It was an impressionist's work, showing a beautiful garden. She checked the name of the artist. Camille Pissarro. Probably Italian in origin. All the best artists were Italian.

Caterina looked at her watch. It was a quarter to ten already. Elia had to be in bed by nine-thirty and was usually asleep within twenty minutes or less. They had by unspoken mutual consent abandoned her attempts to read him bedtime stories. Instead, she listened to more soccer facts, while she helped him undress, brush his teeth, and climb into bed. She sat there for a while stroking his head until he told her to stop. She picked up his trainers and carried them to the shoe cupboard in the hall. They were like two dirty white barges. Size 35. One size smaller than hers.

At a quarter past ten, she went into her son's room, kissed him on the forehead, noting again how much he sweated in his sleep. Usually she left his door ajar, in case he called out. They liked to remind each other of their company in the apartment. He called out less often now. Tonight she would close it.

She undressed and put on a green sweatshirt, gray soft cotton pants, a pair of red woolen socks. It was not the most alluring getup, but it was her house and this is what she wore indoors. Besides, she was far from certain she wanted to allure anyone. Blume was coming round because her child had been threatened. Hardly a reason to put on makeup and high heels.

While she was in the bathroom removing her makeup, the buzzer to her apartment rang. She stopped in mid movement, a blackened cotton ball pinched between her fingers, staring into the mirror at her tense face staring back. Then she said aloud to herself, "That will be him. Early."

She let the cotton fall into the sink and walked toward the front door. The buzzer rasped again, and she unhooked the Pissarro, touched her Beretta, then answered the intercom.

"Inspector Mattiola?"

Not Blume. A woman. A girl. "Emma?"

"Yes, can I come up?"

"Are you on your own?"

"Yes."

Caterina paused, her finger hovering over the button.

"I really need to talk," said Emma. "And I have something I want to show you."

"Is there no one down there with you?"

"No. What do you mean? There's a police car across the street, two policemen in it, if that's what you mean."

"Police or Carabinieri?"

"Police."

"How did you get my address?"

"You're in the book. You are the only Mattiola, C. in Rome."

She waited, listening to Emma's breathing and the background sound of traffic.

She watched the corridor through the peephole in her door, and just as Emma, who was carrying something, stretched out her hand to knock, she swung the door open, catching the girl by surprise and leaving her with a slightly guilty look.

Caterina led Emma into the living room, and watched as she cast around looking for a place to sit. She finally chose the armchair, and placed the object she had been carrying flat on the floor, face up. It was a framed picture. Caterina looked down at it. It was filled with dark greens, blues, and a muddy brown. It seemed unfocused, or like someone had smudged it while it was drying. A garden again, maybe before a storm. The garden of a big house, or maybe a public garden. She preferred her Pissarro.

Caterina sat down on the sofa.

"Are we alone?" Emma asked quietly.

"My son is in bed asleep."

"I'm sorry about this," said Emma.

Caterina nodded. "Tell me what it is before apologizing for it."

"As you know, the Colonel and that Maresciallo turned up at my mother's house today," said Emma. "I've been staying there, in Pistoia. The Colonel said they were looking for paintings that Treacy had sent or she had taken, and my mother, looking him straight in the eye, said Treacy had sent her a painting once and she had sent it back. I never knew she could lie like that. But the Colonel did not believe her, and they just started looking around."

"You could have called the police."

"The two of them are pretty intimidating, and maybe they had a magistrate's warrant. It's easier to imagine all the things you should have done afterwards," said Emma. "After a bit the Colonel comes back. Behind him is the Maresciallo, seven framed paintings under his arms. Four of them are works by Treacy, 'in the style of Old Masters,' as he used to put it in his dishonest way. The fifth—I can't remember what it was. I think it was an original painting by some seventeenth-century Dutchman. I can't even think of a name, now. Ter Borch, maybe—probably another Treacy fake. And the last two were nothing to do with Treacy. He left us all the modern-style works, making sure he damaged them and my mother's feelings first. He says, 'These modern works here are obviously yours,' and starts circling the room, unhooking the paintings, breaking open the backing boards as if this was the most natural thing in the world, then checking out the canvas, smelling it. At one stage I think he even licked his finger, smiling all the time and shaking his head to show how pathetic he thought they all were."

Emma sat back with a sigh, and said, "Have you got a drink?"

"Only bottles of sweet stuff that I take out and put away again at Christmas without opening. Do you want some of that?"

"No vodka?"

"No."

"All right," said Emma. She half slipped a stockinged foot from her shoe. Caterina looked down at her own spreading thighs, her cotton running pants.

"I'm waiting," said Caterina.

Emma resumed. "Then he sits down. The Maresciallo comes up, hands him a file folder and a tin. He puts the tin in the middle of the table, opens it, picks out a round brown ball wrapped in crinkled plastic, unwraps it, pops it into his mouth.

"'Give me your hand,' he says, plucking another ball from the tin. I refused. 'From England. Uncle Joe's Mint Balls. Very hard to find here.' Then he pulls out pages of numbers with the TIM logo on it and fans them out on the table. He explains it showed the connections my BlackBerry had made with cell masts and the GPS satellites during the day on which Treacy was killed. It showed, he says, that I was with Treacy until late. So I asked him how he knew Treacy was with me all that time, and for a moment he stopped sucking the candies, then he smiles, and says, 'Good point. I like that. We'll have to get witnesses, too, won't we?' Then he asks if I had accompanied Treacy to the place where he was found dead, and I told him I had accompanied him part of the way.

"'So you do not deny you were with him moments before his death,' said the Colonel. And I sort of shrugged at that. I expected more questions, but then he announced, 'None of that matters, the case is being filed away since we do not suspect foul play.'"

Emma stopped talking and looked down at the picture. "The painting he was looking for is this one here."

Caterina looked at it again. It still seemed unremarkable. "Was it hidden somewhere?"

"No. It was in plain sight," said Emma. "He held it in his hands, looked it over, smirked, and put it back on the wall. It was one of the works he treated with most contempt, telling my mother she was a deluded incompetent. He didn't even seem to notice that of all the paintings in the house, it was the one that had the most space to itself. I looked at my mother to see what effect his insults were having. She was keeping a neutral expression, but I could see that inside she was happy."

"Happy?"

"Happy—triumphant. It was in her eyes. But he didn't see it, because he was squinting at the painting with exaggerated distaste. Now I suddenly remembered the way she looked at it, tilting her head to the side, sometimes frowning, sometimes smiling. She even touched it sometimes. She never did that with any of the others."

"What's special about it?" asked Caterina.

"I've no idea. Except it was the only one he sent. I remember its arrival, even though I was only a little girl."

"Your mother allowed you to take it after they had left?"

"She didn't try to stop me, if that's what you mean. But I didn't ask her permission. She doesn't deserve it."

"A moment ago, it sounded like you were admiring her."

"I don't think she's a good mother. She's not responsible enough. I paid for her artistic self-indulgence."

"You seem OK."

"Well, I'm not."

"She's the only mother you're going to get," said Caterina. "You're young. Maybe when you're a bit older you'll forgive her. She is human and humans are deluded. She probably thinks she was a good mother."

"She doesn't think about it. All she thinks about is herself."

In the pause that followed, Caterina listened for Elia's breathing, but he was too far away.

"Treacy only ever sent one painting," said Emma. She touched it with her foot. "And that's it there. I remember it coming to the house, just before we left for Pistoia. The others, the ones the Colonel took, were always there. As I was leaving, my mother gave me this, as if it would justify things. I balled it up and threw it away. But it has to do with me, too, so I picked it up again."

She pulled out a piece of crinkly blue writing paper of the sort Caterina had not seen in years and handed it to her. She recognized Treacy's handwriting at once. On this occasion, he wrote in Italian.

*Dear Angela,*

*I am keeping my promise and my distance. Some time ago, I found myself trying to copy some de Chirico works, and it turned out to be harder than it looked. I had more success in painting originals after de Chirico, and I am sending you the best result of my efforts. It was not until I tried to paint him that I realized what you were trying to achieve in your work. You were seeking expressiveness and therefore a truth that I stopped looking for too many years ago, and this is why I derided you. I never should have done so. And I also know that deriding your work was not even the worst thing I did to you. I am glad you found Nightingale, though I wish you had found someone better than him.*

*I should not have written that, but I won't score it out either, because it's right that you should hear echoes of the sort of person I used to be. I have always tried to tell you what was best for you, when all I really meant was that I was best for you. And I wasn't. That's not news to you, of course. I am glad you realized it long ago. Please destroy the various insulting notes and eliminate from your mind the punches, slaps, and moments of exquisite torture based on neglect and denigration. I don't know why I did those things. I shall never know why. Not everything has its reason, not everyone has his place in the world.*

*I have failed. I am still the best draftsman you will ever know, perhaps the best of my generation, and I have a good eye for color, but I have never found my own voice. I am a mere copyist, a plagiarist, a forger, and a cheat. I still say today's artists are no good, and the true greats belong to the distant past, but if I were less of a coward, perhaps I might have tried to create my own style.*

*This is my bequest to you. If you look at it carefully, you will see a thousand second thoughts, a thousand regrets, and a thousand "pentimenti" in it. Take them as referring to all the harm I ever did to you. If you forgive me, you will keep this painting, and perhaps hang it on a wall where it should sit happily with your own original works.*

*Someday, you will understand even better why I have sent this to you. Imagine ourselves in the foreground, sitting on a stone bench. I take a berry from a yew tree, and you tell me that a yew is pure poison from the leaves to the fruit. Your mother had warned you not to touch it. Then I put it in my mouth and eat it, and you panic, and I allow you to panic to see how much I mean to you. It was just one of a thousand cruel gestures, one of a thousand regrets. Yew trees last a thousand years. They will still be there, exactly where we left them. Go back there someday and think of me.*

*Your art was wonderful. The yew leaf and its seed are poisonous, but not its fruit.*

*Yours with love,*
*Henry*


Caterina folded up the letter and handed it back to Emma who took it, making tongs of her fingers and dropping it on the floor at her feet. "I am the fruit, you see? His fruit. It's so creepy that 'poetic' way of talking and thinking. My mother does it, too. Hippies, isn't that what they were called? But he was wrong about the fruit. The fruit is pure poison, too."

"I am not following you, Emma."

"I killed him," said Emma. "I killed Henry Treacy."

# 41

As EMMA PRONOUNCED the words, Caterina sat back, only now realizing that she had been leaning forwards and waiting for this confession. She had essentially known it since Emma's craven boyfriend withdrew his alibi.

Emma continued: "It was an accident. I didn't even mean to hurt him. He was drunk."

Caterina believed her at once. She tried to suppress the immediacy of the belief as unbecoming for a police officer, but it simply felt true. The incongruity of Emma killing someone was too great. But it wasn't just that. Emma's main concern now did not seem to be to claim innocence for herself, but to confess the reasons for her actions. The girl was telling the truth. She was reliving the moment.

"Henry tried to hug me, and he tried to kiss me, and then he started weeping like a child. It was revolting. The folds in his skin, the bristles, and the smell of beer, wine, urine, and old man's breath."

"He tried to assault you?"

"No. Not like that. All evening I had stayed with him waiting for him to reveal this really important thing he said he needed to tell me, but all he did was go on about how beautiful I was. How intelligent, how elegant and perfect until I thought I could take no more. It was so much better when he was sober and ironic, making jokes at my expense. Then we got to that piazza, and he started talking about the self-portrait in his office and asking me what I saw in it. And suddenly he grabbed me and pulled me toward him and he tried to kiss me, not on the mouth, but on the face, on my forehead. I struggled and pushed at him, but he kept begging me to listen to him for a moment, so I told him I would if only he would let me go, which he did.

"'Nightingale thinks I don't know about you. He thinks he has me fooled and blinded and that I'm no better than a bewildered wreck, which may be true. But I knew who you were even before Nightingale brought you to the gallery with his false provenance stories, pretending he had just happened to find a treasure like you lying about. And he thought I would not see the way he treated you and looked proudly at you, the way his breast puffed up like a pigeon every time he was watching you. Anyone would have noticed how he behaved toward you. His cover story was pathetic.'

" 'Is that what you needed to tell me?' I asked him. 'Why didn't you confront Nightingale first? I never saw the need for all the deception.'

"Then Treacy, he gives me a look which . . . I can't describe it. Proud and sad at the same time. Partly a leer, partly a look of pity, and he says, 'John Nightingale is an English cuckold. Three months after he took Angela from me, I went back and took Angela from him, only he never knew it. And I took her back time and time again. Ask her. Ask your mother. John Nightingale is not your father. I am.'

"I think I screamed," continued Emma. "I pushed him hard. Really hard, in the chest with the heel of my hand. I hit him there three times, and he fell backwards. I heard his head crack against the cobbles, only I didn't believe then that sound could have been made by his head. I only heard the crack afterwards, thinking back. I hear it now. But at the time I didn't hear it and Treacy wasn't even unconscious, because he kept calling my name as I ran away."

Emma sat with her hands folded in her lap as she spoke, her voice calm. She even gave a deeper and heavier intonation when repeating Treacy's words, and she would have been a model of perfect composure had it not been for the tears on the sides of her face.

Caterina thought of the handsome fair-haired youth that sat above Treacy's desk in the gallery, and wondered how neither Emma nor Nightingale had ever seen the likeness. She wondered how Emma's mother could have hidden the story from her daughter all these years, and why.

Emma asked for the bathroom and when she came back she had washed her face clean. She went back to the chair, picked up her purse, and pulled out her BlackBerry and showed it to Caterina, saying, "Look. It's switched off. That way she can't call me and the Colonel can't find me."

"So your mother can't call you?" said Caterina. She did not bother mentioning that Emma would need to remove the batteries, too, if she didn't want to be traced.

"I need to find a place to stay," said Emma. "But where? With my lying mother, my pathetic boyfriend Pietro ..."

"What about your own place?" said Caterina.

"The apartment paid for by the gallery? In other words, by my dead father and my ex-father or whatever I am supposed to call them. I'm not going there."

"Sooner or later you are going to have to talk to them about it."

"Why should I? My mother didn't tell Nightingale, Nightingale thought he was fooling Treacy. I kill Treacy, and now it's up to me to stage some sort of family reconciliation? Nightingale, Treacy. I don't even use their first names."

"Emma, if you say once more that you killed him, if you indicate to me that what you did was deliberate, I will arrest you now and have you taken to the station to be charged."

Emma looked at Caterina in shock.

"So, tell me, did you deliberately kill Treacy?"

Emma shook her head. "No. I ... no. I was just clearing space between us ... no."

"Did you think he was badly hurt when you ran away?"

"I didn't care."

"I repeat: Did it occur to you that he might be badly hurt?"

Emma closed her eyes and let out a long breath. "No. It did not. I have never hurt anyone physically in my life. I had no idea it could be so easy."

"People are frail," said Caterina. "Even so, you withheld vital information from us when we arrived the following day, and that is an offense with which you will be charged. But we can do that tomorrow some time."

"Can I stay here?" said Emma.

"What? No. Of course not."

"Just for tonight?"

"There are two bedrooms. My son is in one. I'm in the other."

"I could sleep on the sofa you're sitting on."

"Out of the question," said Caterina. "Apart from everything else, there's the legal aspect. I am a police inspector. You have just admitted to what could be construed as involuntary manslaughter ..."

"Oh. You just said ..."

"Forget what I just said. I'm sure there is a hotel you could check into. I don't think money is much of a problem for you, is it?"

"No. That's not my problem. It's just I get this feeling I'm being followed. The Colonel frightens me. You can't send me out there."

"I am expecting Commissioner Blume to arrive soon. He can accompany you somewhere. You'll be safe with him."

"Will he arrest me?"

"I don't know, Emma. He might have to."

Caterina's cell, set to silent, began to vibrate against the glass coffee table between them, and rotated around till it faced Emma who leaned over to look at the name on the display. "That's your Commissioner now."

Caterina wondered how Blume would react to her proposed change of plans for the evening, and was anxious about what he would say to her having Emma in her apartment like this. But she need not have worried. As soon as she answered, he announced, "Can't make it. Something else has come up."

Then he hung up without waiting for a response, without asking her whether she and Elia were OK.

Bastard.

Half an hour later, as she applied cold cream to her face and massaged the tense area around her eyes with her fingers, she thought of the almost elegant movement with which old Corsi had knelt down before stretching out on the floor of his dilapidated palace, stabbed in the back by his clumsy, unhappy child. She wiped the sink shiny with the towel she had just used and set out a fresh towel over the edge of the bathtub.

Passing the living room on her way to her bedroom, whispering so as not to wake Elia, she said, "The bathroom's free now, Emma."

# 42

WOULD IT BE by phone or face-to-face? Blume opened his car door, threw in the accursed notebooks, and pulled out his phone and looked at it in case it had rung on silent. Nothing. He walked back toward Paoloni's house, back down the sidewalk covered in dogshit and trash. A dark car came the wrong way up the one-way street.

Face-to-face, then, thought Blume.

The car stopped beside him. The Colonel rolled down his window and spoke out of the dark. "Where's your friend going?"

"Aren't you people following him?"

"My resources are a little stretched," said the Colonel. "Where is he going?"

"To look for his son," said Blume.

The Colonel considered this. "His son is fine," he said after a while.

"He'd better be," said Blume.

"I didn't want to worry the poor man," said the Colonel. "The idea was that you would see what was at stake."

"I see what is at stake," said Blume. "Where is Fabio?"

"The son? Torvaianica, I believe. We used your name to pick him up. Now he thinks he's being recruited for something exciting, and has been sworn to secrecy. Apparently the hardest thing was to keep a straight face as they told the kid to check for people following and to search out a certain face in a bar. It's been an evening of entertainment for everyone."

"When is he coming home?"

"When are you going to get my paintings back?"

"Tomorrow afternoon," said Blume. "That's the earliest I can do it."

"Then that's when your friend's son is coming home," said the Colonel. "Simple enough."

The Colonel's words disappeared into the blackness of the car, and then reappeared inside Blume's head. It would not do, but he had to keep calm.

A blue flare turning yellow lit up the Colonel's cheeks and nose. Blume watched and waited as the Colonel set his cigar aglow, and took comfort that the ritual suggested the Colonel was prepared to negotiate. He moved closer, picking up a scent of sweet wood and orange peel from inside the vehicle. The Maresciallo was in the driver's seat.

"Beppe Paoloni is my dear friend. The first thing he will do if he thinks his son is missing is enlist my help and demand my constant presence," said Blume. "As long as he does that, I cannot move to get the paintings, and as long as he is looking for his child, he cannot help me."

"Do you need his help?"

"The people who took the canvases don't want to deal with law enforcement. They'll do a deal with Paoloni, though. As long as the son is missing, everyone is wasting time."

A puff of smoke came out the window, and the Colonel said, "That sounds like a valid argument. And I really don't want to waste time. Here." His plump hand emerged and offered Blume a chunky Nokia with too many buttons.

"I don't know how to use that."

"It's already ringing. Connected by now, I should say," said the Colonel.

Blume brought the phone up to his ear, and noticed that the Colonel had a second phone and was talking into it.

"Yes?" A young man on the other end of the line. Blume realized he didn't even know Fabio's voice.

"Fabio?"

"Commissioner Blume?" The kid's voice wavered between disappointment and relief.

"The test is over. Can you call your parents? Call your father. He's looking for you." This was going to take some explaining to Paoloni afterwards.

"Yes. I was going to."

"Where are you now?"

"On the Via del Mare. On our way back in. They said I did well."

Blume heard a man in the background say something and Fabio's voice, uncertain, nervous, saying thank you.

"They're going to drop me off at the Line B underground. I'm not to mention this test to anyone except you. I'll just say I was with friends and my phone was dead."

"No," said Blume. "Say it was off, not dead. You need to use it now to call your parents."

"I'll just tell them I recharged it at a friend's house."

Maybe the kid would make a good agent after all. The lie came easily to him.

"Good," said Blume.

"Satisfied?" asked the Colonel as Blume handed back the phone. But now his own was ringing, and he answered.

It was Paoloni wondering if he had heard anything.

"No, Beppe. I called in. No accidents or anything. I'm sure Fabio will be OK. Maybe his phone is out of credit or something."

"Definitely something like that," said Paoloni. "It's his mother. She's very anxious. She's phoned me twice. Listen, things are moving faster than I thought here, which is good. It turns out these two guys . . ."

But Blume did not want Paoloni to talk about this now, as he stood there in front of the Colonel. He pretended to scratch his ear with his thumb and surreptitiously hit disconnect, then made a few grunts of assent, and pretended to finish up the conversation. He switched the phone off completely as he slipped it back into his pocket in case Paoloni called straight back.

"Colonel, this abducting and threatening children, for all that you do it so subtly and gently, and make sure the victims don't even realize it . . . someday you will get burned. You know that? Eventually something will go wrong, someone will find out, and you will be killed."

"I have been in this line of business since you were a child, Blume. I have not been caught yet."

"You have not been punished, you mean. But you have been caught. People know who you are, what you do. The American Embassy has a file on you. Older Carabinieri, police, criminals, and politicians remember you, some younger Carabinieri want rid of you."

"Lieutenant Colonel Faedda, for instance? Do you think I would allow a queer Sard kid to control me? You're tricky, Blume, I'll give you that. I want you to contact me tomorrow. We meet, exchange the paintings, maybe hammer out a new deal of some sort, and then that will be that. We won't have to meet again. If the truth be told, I didn't even want to get involved in this case. I was semi-retired, you know. This will be the last case. And as such, Velázquez or no Velázquez, money or no money, the ending will be dictated by me. I will decide your fate; I will decide who deserves favor, which gets punished. That's how it will be."

He closed the window and the Maresciallo drove away, flashing his lights as he sped the wrong way up the street.

Blume switched his phone back on. It rang almost immediately.

It was Paoloni. "We got cut off earlier," he said. "Anyhow, got them. It was that easy. Oh, by the way, Fabio called. He's on his way home. Thanks for your help there. Little bastard had his mother worried sick." Blume smiled as he heard Paoloni trying to keep an offhand tone. "Shall we meet back at my place?"

"No," said Blume. "I need to get home. Remember, Beppe, the front door to my apartment is broken. It closes, but anyone could get in. I'd prefer not to leave it unguarded."

"I could bring the paintings around to your place. Then tomorrow, you sell them on to the Colonel. You ask five times what I paid for them, we split the difference, and I get a nice quick return on this evening's investment. Everyone is happy, except maybe the Colonel, but fuck him."

"I think the Colonel's men may be watching my place," said Blume.

"If they are, I'll spot them."

"They're better at surveillance than we thought."

"Let's leave it, then. I'll see you tomorrow."

# 43

THE DEVASTATION OF his apartment looked worse at one o'clock in the morning. For a moment he thought he had been burgled all over again, and his chest trembled with incipient rage, at himself for allowing this to happen. They had polluted his apartment. Nothing felt clean. A strange smell, pungent like fermenting piss, permeated the apartment. Piss and salt. What had they done to his home? Beneath the ammoniac stink of the piss was something worse. Something that smelled of corruption, death.

It was strongest in the kitchen. Moving with a hunter's careful steps, he searched the cupboards. He opened the refrigerator. On the middle shelf, a gray sea bass lay shimmering in a pool of its own liquefaction.

The trip downstairs with the stinking fish cleared his mind of all thought. Back in the kitchen, he opened a package of bicarbonate of soda and tossed fistfuls of it into his fridge, raising a storm of white which he shut inside by slamming the door closed.

He washed and washed his hands. Now the idea of picking up things from the living-room floor was overwhelming. Even the thought of preparing for bed was exhausting.

Propped against the cracked spine of Volume one of Lotz's *Architecture in Italy*, his mother looked out of a silver-framed photograph. She looked like someone else. Unfamiliar, and younger than him. More than twenty years had passed since they died together, leaving him here. Now his memory struggled to retrieve clear images of both together. Was forgetting a sign of things getting better or worse?

There was a fabric conditioner called Chanteclair Marsiglia that brought back his mother. He wished it was something less synthetic—and it was probably poisonous—but nothing worked better. He kept a bottle under the sink and occasionally, but not too often, would add it to his washing.

He undressed. In the bathroom, he eyed his toothbrush with suspicion and decided not to use it. He would get a new one in the morning. He rotated the mattress back into place, pulled up the sheet, and dropped the duvet on top of himself.

The quickest route to remembering his father was a whiff of eucalyptus between the marshlands of Maccarese and the sea, or someone in the office unwrapping a medicinal mint, and there he was, Professor James Blume, standing beneath a balsam-scented tree in Seattle, his face still shining with sweat from the race he had just lost to the fastest ten-year-old in America.

As fast as the wind, Alec, all I could see was the dust behind you, he said, before slapping the white-lined bark with his hand. Black cottonwood makes your mother sneeze. Standing in the shade cast by the trunk, his father fingered the fissures in the bark. The triangular leaves above rotated in the wind and splintered the sunlight into bright shards and dark shadows, so that Blume could hardly make out his face at all.


During the night, Blume's cell phone died. In the morning, as he stood in the ransacked kitchen, Blume realized the thieves had stolen his recharger, too.

He cleaned up his house a bit, and as he was doing so, the buzzer sounded. Blume allowed a man to come up and measure the door frame. They haggled a bit over the price and vehemently disagreed over the utility of expensive anti-theft features. Blume said he didn't want them, the man pointed to his apartment and expressed surprise that Blume had not learned from bitter experience.

"They'd have got in anyhow," said Blume.

"Not with the anti-thrust, kick-stop, reinforced frame with anti-intrusion ..."

"No," said Blume.

"The police recommend that you have a door with these features."

"The police know nothing," said Blume.

The man looked offended. Then he had another idea. "They won't insure you unless you have ..."

"No!" said Blume. "Look, I'm sorry. I can't afford it. How long will it take to get the door replaced?"

"Seeing as you are not interested in extras, and it's a standard frame, we could do it today. If the warehouse has one in stock. This afternoon?"

"Great. Someone will be here for you."

He saluted the disgruntled workman, then hunted around for his telephone book. He had not used it in years, but Paoloni's number had to be in there somewhere. He decided to clear up the scattered books and papers as he looked for it, and for a while forgot the original reason for his cleanup. He hunted with more purpose, but it was nowhere to be found. Using his home phone, he called directory inquiries, but Paoloni was not listed.

Eventually, he decided to go directly to Paoloni's house. Typical of Paoloni not to bother phoning him at home.

Blume plugged his phone into the recharger in the car and tried to use it immediately, but the battery symbol flashed and the phone would not even switch itself on.

He circled for a while below Paoloni's apartment building before finding a narrow space three streets away into which he slotted his car. All the buildings in the area were part of the same massive development from the early 1980s. Pale yellow brick facades, square windows with brown roll-down shutters, cement gray cornices. The place looked better at night.

He walked back one hundred and fifty meters to Paoloni's building. He caught the front door as it swung shut behind a woman with a shopping bag, blocking the door with his hand before it hit his face and sweeping away the woman's apology with his other hand. Still smiling politely, while absently filing away aspects and curves of the woman's body in memory for later contemplation and evaluation, he stepped into the elevator, which took him to the third floor. As he stepped out, a door at the far end of the hall clicked softly closed, as if he were not the person they had been waiting for.

The air held a scent of something volatile, pleasant but alarming. It was the smell of someone cleaning brass with pink rubbing alcohol, of a dentist's waiting room, of a blue flame hovering over brandy. It was pungent and slightly sweet. It was the after-smell of gunfire.

Blume quickened his pace with the idea of smashing into Paoloni's door at speed and bursting it open, but the apartment was in the middle, not at the end of the corridor, and the best he could do was to check his pace and not overshoot the entrance.

Only as he slid to a sudden stop did he think to ring the doorbell. It rang like a firebell, but nobody answered. He pressed the button till his finger was bent back and whitening. Finally, he let go, stood back, pressed himself against the opposite wall behind, and focused on the point below the keyhole where he wanted his foot to land. He put out of his mind the certain knowledge that he had never seen anyone kick in a door of this type and, for a moment, he was certain it would burst open. He visualized himself crashing into Paoloni's dark living room. He kicked hard, heel first, and managed to hit the very point he was aiming for. It was enough to make the strike plate shudder. The door seemed to rock on its hinges, but didn't give. He drew back to deliver another kick, but stopped himself.

He pulled out his badge and marched down the corridor to an apartment door, from behind which he was sure he was being watched. The neighbor opened before he got there.

"Are you the police?"

"Yes."

"They only sent one?"

"What?"

"I called when I heard gunshots. I knew they were gunshots. There was shouting too. Then the door slammed."

"Stay there," ordered Blume, pulling out his phone.

"I was not planning on going anywhere," said the neighbor. He was a balding man in his sixties, and he seemed calm. Calmer than Blume.

The wailing sound inside his head resolved itself into real-life sirens, and he heard the police arrive. Four of them, from the sound of it. The elevator whirred and disappeared down the shaft, heavy footsteps came banging up the stairs.

Both policemen had their Berettas drawn, down by their sides. Blume held his badge up, pointed at the door. The elevator stopped and two more, a Sovrintendente in charge, emerged, one holding a long cloth bag, which they unzipped immediately to reveal a two-handled blue battering ram. On the second blow the deadlatch burst out of the strikehole and the door swung open and hit something on the floor. Blume was the third man in.

Everything and more than he needed to see lay there in front of him, but for some reason, his eye was drawn first to the bullet hole in Paoloni's flat-screen TV. It was a neat puncture in the upper left. It looked like the

TV might work even now, if he turned it on. Lying before the screen, face up, arms thrown forward like he was doing the back crawl, was Paoloni. The mess of gunshots to the head seemed nowhere in evidence, which did not make sense for a moment, until he lowered his eyes and saw the splashed table legs, the glistening skirting boards, and darkening sofa cushions. The final shot had been delivered to his upturned face. Paoloni's weapon was on the floor, just out of his reach.

The heavy black object that had been blocking the door was as lifeless a lump of anything as Blume had ever seen. The Sovrintendente was kneeling down looking at it.

"Poor thing," he said. "Looks to me like it took three bullets in its haunch before it let go. It's a Cane Corso. Or was."

"I know," said Blume.

The policeman snapped on latex gloves, then he bent down and pulled the dog's mouth back. "Some pressure in those jaws." He peeled back the black lips some more. "I was right. Look there. That's cloth and blood. It looks to me like this dog attacked the killer before he got shot. He may even have done some real harm to him. We'll certainly get a good DNA sample from this."

The Sovrintendente stroked the dog's face. "Good boy," he said.

One of the young officers came over, his face first-timer white.

"I know who that is. That's Chief Inspector Paoloni. And I know who you are, sir. You're Commissioner Alec Blume. I worked in Collegio Romano three years ago."

The policeman's face was familiar.

Blume said, "He's dead, right?"

The young policeman looked at him in astonishment, the older one with pity.

No matter how bad the crime scene, even one that included a child, Blume knew that if he waited, something would click in his mind and his thoughts could detach themselves from his emotions and float into a state of forensic serenity. But for now the feeling would not come. He could not bear to look at Paoloni, nor even at the dead black beast by the door. He checked an impulse to run, battled down a rebellion in his gut and stomach and a heaving in his chest.

After ten minutes, he began to reassert control. He still could not look at Paoloni, but he was able to start checking the apartment, making plans for his next moves, deciding on how he would deal with colleagues as they arrived.

He conducted a search of the kitchen, bedroom, bathroom, followed by the Sovrintendente, who was trying to be casual about making sure the Commissioner did not compromise the scene.

"What are we looking for, sir?"

"Anything," said Blume.

Paintings, which would not be here, he thought to himself. Paintings that, if he had left them alone in the wardrobe of his own house, would not have led to this. Paintings that were cursed.

"Sovrintendente, start calling all the hospitals in the city now, find out if anyone is being treated for dog bites. But this is not my crime scene. Seal it. Call in the forensics, the PM, medical examiner—the usual." He walked toward the door.

"Are you leaving?"

"Yes. I arrived outside the door approximately five minutes before you, I'll write up a report and respond to questions later. OK?"

The Sovrintendente deftly interposed himself between Blume and the front door, saying, "Don't you think it would be better to stay here, Commissioner?"

"No," said Blume and barged past.

# 44

WHEN HE REACHED his car, he delivered several hard kicks to the body and dented the door so badly that it was hard to open, which gave him an excuse to pummel it with his fists.

Blume phoned Caterina to get her to look up the Colonel's home address. She answered with what sounded to him like the epitome of irrelevance.

"Have you seen Emma? She was supposed to get back to me, tell me about how her talk with her mother went."

"Get me the Colonel's address and phone straight back," said Blume and hung up. He started driving back toward the city center, heading in the direction of his station until someone told him where to find the Colonel.

Then, clear as if a voice had spoken from the backseat, so clear that Blume checked his mirror, half expecting to see Paoloni there, grinning, whispering secrets, he realized where he was going. With a jerk of the clutch and a sharp pull on the steering wheel, he pushed the car into the left lane and accelerated hard, switching on his siren as he came racing up to within a centimeter of the car in front. He gunned the motor, wobbled the steering wheel side-to-side looking for a way around, and hit the whoop function on the siren. Reluctantly it moved away, and he went roaring up behind the next car.

On the seat next to him, his phone was ringing. He brought it up to his ear.

"We have been informed of Paoloni's death." It took Blume a moment to realize it was Lieutenant Colonel Faedda who was speaking. Faedda paused, and his voice took on a less official tone. "I am sorry. I understand you two were close. I have already sent two patrol cars to the Colonel's house, but he is not there."

"What about the Maresciallo who is always with him? Maresciallo . . ." Blume could not remember the name. Had he ever heard it?

"Maresciallo Farinelli," said Faedda. "His house is under observation, too. We have put out a call to all units. We're watching the airport, too."

"And the hospitals?"

"Yes. I see you ordered the Polizia to do the same. We've divided the task up between us. I think it's most likely that's where we'll pick them up."

"It's where you'll pick up the Maresciallo," said Blume. "He's the shooter . . . Wait, what did you say the Maresciallo's name was?"

"Farinelli. I thought you knew that."

Blume could not believe he was learning this only now. "He's the Colonel's son?"

"Not his son. His nephew. Not even that. Great-nephew. The Colonel's older brother's son's son."

"Let me know when you find him," said Blume. His phone was beeping to indicate another incoming call. He switched to it.

"Alec, I'm so sorry." It was Caterina. He said nothing and she continued, "The Colonel lives on Via Boccea, or nearby, his address is . . ."

"That's OK. I don't need that now. He's not there."

"Do you . . ." But Blume hung up on her, and, putting both hands on the wheel, drove hard and fast on the wrong side of the road past San Giovanni in Laterano, the car rumbling and sliding over the cobblestones. Above, the sky was blue, but in the background it was black. Outside the gates of the Irish College, a silver rain seemed to be falling sideways without reaching the ground.

As he descended toward the Colosseum, it almost became night as the clouds billowed and darkened. The background sky grew inkier. When the rain came, it would flood the streets in seconds, grease the cobbles, hollow out potholes in the asphalt, and cause three hundred or so accidents, of which five or six would be fatal. Romans can't drive in the rain. He did not turn off the siren until he had arrived in Trastevere. He parked his car on the corner of Via Corsini and Via Lungara and started walking. Twenty meters on, sitting there in broad daylight, was the Colonel's *auto blu*. Blume tried the door, but it was locked. He pulled out his pistol and rapped the side window hard. On the fourth blow, it disintegrated into thousands of glass squares. Without bothering to open the door, Blume poked his head in. There was blood still visible on the dashboard and seat fabric.

His cell phone rang.

"We got him."

"Great. Who is this?"

"Sovrintendente Branca." When Blume failed to acknowledge him, he added, "I'm the Sovrintendente from the crime scene. You told us to check hospitals, and you were right. A Maresciallo of the Carabiniere was transferred to Sant'Andrea for an emergency operation. He had lost a lot of blood. They radioed in the news just now. He can't be questioned yet, the doctors say."

"Good," he said. But nothing felt good. He hung up and switched off his cell phone. Why wasn't the driver's seat pushed as far back as possible to accommodate the Colonel's bulk? Who had driven him here?

The green door set into the high wall appeared shut, but almost collapsed as he touched it. He made a grab for it, catching it before it fell in and made too much noise. He moved slowly and quietly down the passage between the high walls on either side. The damp in the air and the heavy green of the creepers and ivy made his lungs feel waterlogged. He reached the door to the greenhouse, and eased down the handle, pausing each time it made a small click. When he had it all the way down, he pushed softly at the door, which opened with a slight creak of its hinges and scrape of its baseboard against the tiles of Treacy's greenhouse. He stepped inside, and gently closed the door behind him.

The room was filled with a heady reek of solvents, turps, paints, paraffin, and gasoline. They were smells that always elated him, though the gasoline sounded a nostalgic note, too. He could hear voices. A woman's voice and that of a man, not the Colonel. He drew his weapon, feeling the dry polymer grip slide a little before it found the ridges of his palm; he walked past the old-fashioned stove, and gently parted the bead curtain that led into the kitchen. The hollow beads clacked very slightly as he edged his way through the parting he had scooped out. He swept silently across the kitchen to the door leading into the living room, ready to pause and take stock. Framed there, looking straight at him, face flushed, blouse unbuttoned down to her breast, and hair askew stood a middle-aged woman he had never seen before, but who was somehow familiar. Behind her, beside the large portrait of Henry Treacy that he had last seen in the gallery, was John Nightingale, shaking his head at Blume as if . . .

The scene vibrated and faded as something seemed to cleave his head in two. The pain, too intense to remain in the one spot, rushed down his body, first as a boiling, then as a freezing sensation, as if the blood in his neck, spine, coccyx had turned to ice slush. He noticed his feet planted firmly on the ground, and felt pleased, especially as the ground seemed to be swinging upwards.

Another catastrophic and savage blow came racing out of nowhere, and this one frightened him, because it was the penultimate. He would not survive a third like this. He moved his hands, just for the sake of it, and felt millions of tiny spheres that tickled and jabbed his palms, like pins and needles, only more pleasant, like lying on a white sand beach, and he realized he must be on the floor already.

After what might have been several months, and certainly a good many hours, Blume was reluctant and tearful at the idea of returning. As he left the warm darkness and was dragged back into the present where unwanted light pressed hard against his eyeballs, he began to shiver. He kept his eyes shut and groaned. Distant voices gave commands, but he refused to hear them. A less distant foot gave him a kick, and he could smell the leather, the sock below. It was touch and go about weeping.

"Don't do anything. Anything at all. I will shoot this woman straight through the forehead. Did you call any backup?"

Blume opened his mouth to reply, not sure what he intended to say. It made no difference since the words that came out were incomprehensible even to him.

"Speak in Italian," ordered the Colonel. "But I've got your phone. Last call you made was almost an hour ago. Last one you received was twenty minutes ago. It looks like no one else is coming."

Blume said something else, and lay there wondering what it was. Water, perhaps. He may have asked for water.

The Colonel ordered him into an armchair. For a while he failed to understand the idea, since he could not see any armchair, then the Colonel's foot showed it to him. When he finally located it, cracked, leathery, and inviting, he was moved to great gratitude and crawled over, and heaved himself into a sitting position.

Reality continued to impinge upon his senses. A deep pain began not where he had been hit, but in a fold in the center of his brain, and pulsed outwards.

This is going to be some motherfucking headache.

"If you don't stop bleeding soon, you won't feel it for long," said a voice with an accent.

"Speak in Italian you two," ordered the Colonel.

Blume frowned. He was speaking his thoughts. He peered across the room. Nightingale was still there, so was the woman. They were still framed in the same taut, expectant pose they had had when he came into the room all that time ago. He put his hand to the back of his head and dabbed it in his soaking wet hair. If he had been bald like the Colonel, maybe all the blood would have flowed away and he would be dead.

Thank God for hair. He felt tears of joy.

"I seem to have knocked you stupid, Commissioner," said the Colonel, who was holding his pistol upwards, almost as if he intended to put it into his own mouth. "Try to talk sense. Why are you here alone? You always need at least one other person to help you. I'm without my Maresciallo, and it's almost impossible. Luckily, these two were together when I found them at Nightingale's apartment. Then we traveled over to the gallery to pick up Treacy's flattering portrait of himself. Nightingale was kind enough to do all the driving."

Blume looked at the portrait again. The face had been scrubbed and dissolved away, the blond hair remained. He looked at another painting, lying discarded on the floor, a colorless smudge running diagonally across its surface. There was another and another. Paintings from the gallery, from Angela's house, from here. Beside them, in an ignored pile, were the charcoal cartoons, pen and wash sketches, and drawings. Simple, direct, to the point and without layers. They were incapable of hiding anything beneath, and Blume felt a rush of affection for them. In the end, they were better than all the paintings. These preparatory sketches showed hope, potential, freedom.

The Colonel walked into the middle of the room and raised his pistol and pointed it directly at the woman. "I gather you two have never met. Alec, this is Angela, Emma's mother, the failed artist and woman of easy virtue. I found her with John cuckold Nightingale here at his house. It's funny that we know more about Treacy and Angela fucking than anyone else, except for Angela, of course. John here, his eyes have been opened to the ways of the world. We have just a few more of these to get through. Though I am not hopeful."

It had turned dark. Angela was working in a pool of light cast by two standing lamps. She took a wad of cotton balls from the table. From the floor in front of her she picked up a bottle of solvent and drenched the cotton and her hands in it, filling the room with a sharp scent, then made a swipe at the picture on the easel. On the first pass, the canvas merely glistened as if another coat of varnish was being applied, on the second it dulled, and on the third she left a messy streak. She concentrated on the lightest part, rubbing at it. Outside the thunder rumbled, and Blume remembered why it should be so dark.

"See, she's as keen as I am," said the Colonel. "OK. Switch to kerosene now, sweetie."

Blume planned ahead, making sure what he was going to say would come out right. "You really think you'll find a Velázquez under one of those paintings?" he asked.

"I said my hopes were fading on that front," said the Colonel. "But if not, I am going to talk to you about it after we're done here." He gestured at Angela. "Look at that woman. She used to look like she stepped out of Filippo Lippi's *Annunciation*. Her daughter does not resemble her. Her daughter was the spitting image of Treacy, whose youthful face I just allowed Nightingale here to cancel. Very symbolic that." He looked over at Angela. "Or do you object to being objectified?"

"You're the one with the gun," said Angela.

"Well observed. Dear God, these fumes are going to my head. Commissioner, aren't you going to try to rush me or something heroic? You need to make up for that pathetic entrance. Nightingale, John, throw that piece of shit aside, we can see nothing lies below. Try that one there, the over-darkened portrait of a woman. It looks suspicious. It also looks highly glossed and hardened. Start with sandpaper, then the solvent."

"Why are you here, Colonel?" said Blume. "Why didn't you take the paintings and flee to somewhere safe, check them at your leisure?"

"I cannot abandon my Maresciallo. What do you take me for? Also, you seem to be laboring under the illusion that I need to flee, Commissioner."

"Oh, trust me on this. You need to," said Blume. He was thinking straight and remembering now. The dribbling at the back of his head had stopped, the throbbing was waiting for another time, and the image of Paoloni was pin sharp.

"Remember Craxi?"

"I remember Craxi," said Blume.

"What was his big mistake?"

"It's hard to know where to begin," said Blume.

"Cowardice," said the Colonel. "He fled the country to hide in Tunisia and spent the next few pathetic years of his life threatening his former political allies. He died with a whimper. The politicians he was threatening, people like Andreotti, Cossiga, Berlusconi, Forlani, Amato, they stayed behind. Within a few years they were all back in power, and he was dead. He did carry out his threat to tell all, by the way, but we simply made sure no one was listening."

"What's your point, Colonel?" Blume figured he could reach the pistol in three moves. If he saw a way of reducing it to two moves, he'd try. Then, with a shock, he recognized the pistol the Colonel held was his own. That decided him.

"My point is as long as I stay here, I'll triumph. If I flee, I fail. Once I leave the country, I lose leverage and power. I am not even sure any painting is so valuable as to compensate for that loss."

"You killed a former policeman."

"Paoloni. An ex-bank guard, a criminal facilitator, a shady character. Not nearly as good at throwing off a tail as he thought he was. He brought the paintings back to his own house, which shows he had no imagination. I was there, waiting outside in the car. I didn't kill him. That was my dear, loyal, and, for once, careless Maresciallo, who met with surprising and uncalled-for violence when all he was doing was trying to prepare the ground for negotiations."

"If you want something done well, you'd best do it yourself," said Blume.

"I'm still not sure of that. My Maresciallo has always served me perfectly. But you may have a point." The Colonel looked over to the painting and moved closer to it. "Angela, use a light touch, there's a good girl. I have a good feeling about this portrait. John, make yourself useful and stop standing there like a pointless cuckold. Give her some kerosene."

Blume shifted his weight in his chair. If the Colonel took another step to the right, he could push himself over the arm of the chair.

He tried to move, but the Colonel leaned in toward him at the same moment and slapped him in the forehead with the side of the pistol.

The Colonel stood back, still pointing the pistol at him, his hand steady, and saying something, his voice booming but muffled and far away. Blume braced himself to receive a bullet, but the Colonel was now sitting down and wiping his forehead with the back of the hand that held the weapon. There was no question of rushing him now. No question of standing up out of this chair. The fumes in the room were choking him.

"I can read thoughts, Commissioner," the Colonel was saying. "Your intent was in your eyes. I expected you to be more phlegmatic, even a little disinterested in the justice or the injustice of all this, instead you get whipped with your own pistol. More worrying now, isn't it? If I'm waving yours about, maybe it's because I am planning on using it, then ducking the blame."

"The painting you are looking for is not there," said Blume.

"Well now, you would say that, wouldn't you?" said the Colonel. "Buy time. Always buy time. In this case, I believe you."

"It's not there." Blume wanted to save his breath and not speak, but he needed to speak to save his life. He closed his eyes and focused on getting the right words out. "We can sit here and watch. I can't do much else. When she has wiped the last canvas down, you'll see I'm right. I may have bled to death by then."

"Lean forward," ordered the Colonel. "And a little to your left. Do it."
Blume did.

"Not that much blood behind you. Where is the hidden painting?"

"Hidden."

"Yes, yes. Predictable to the end, Commissioner. Hey, cuckold, where's the Velázquez?"

"What Velázquez?" said Nightingale. "I have no idea what you mean."

"John," said the Colonel. "You and I go way back. Mid-seventies. You know I am capable of killing this woman. Perhaps that would please you, now that you're finding out what sort of person she is. She came around to your place this morning to confess, didn't she?"

Nightingale nodded.

"Do you want me to shoot her dead now?"

"No!"

"Weak. You always were weak. You're not a father. You're not a husband or a lover or an artist. You're not a man. Treacy was strong, honest. No, I exaggerate, no point in sentimentalizing his memory. He was not in the slightest bit honest, but if he was here now, he would be lying there dead, or I would be lying there dead. One of us, because he would not have allowed me to talk to him or his woman in this way. I forgot that there is no reason you would know of the Velázquez, but Henry found one. He didn't tell you that either. Work out where it is. I give you three minutes."

"A Velázquez, Harry? Look, Harry and I, we used to come across a lot of really stupid stuff. There is so much bad art, you know? Old and black and cracked with a whitish face of some unknown, bourgeois non-entity painted by a talentless hack, and people think it's an heirloom worth millions. Just because it's old, doesn't mean—Trees are older. Rocks are older. No, sorry, I must organize my thoughts."

"I'll point the pistol at the dazed Commissioner, if that calms you a little," said the Colonel.

"Colonel, you remember how we did the double-bluff stings? Harry would do a fine forgery using original paper, careful signatures. Then, when it was quite done, he would paint over it. To make sure we were caught, he had to allow the new paint to be too soft, or he'd use an anachronistic color. But the forgery underneath would be of a relatively important painter only. Or a *scuola*. We never stretched credibility. It is unthinkable he would hide a Velázquez in this way."

"John, John, you're not following. This time he would be hiding it to hide it, not to have it discovered."

"No, I'm not following. Harry would never have painted over a work by Velázquez."

"So where would one be, if he had it?"

"Here?" said Nightingale. "Or in a bank vault. I really have no idea."

With a soft sigh, the Colonel stood up, glancing down affectionately at Blume as he passed by. "Come here, John," he said, making a coaxing motion with his left hand, keeping the pistol trained loosely on Blume.

Nightingale came over, an uncertain smile on his lips as he continued to explain. "So the dealer thinks he's discovered an authentic painting, you see, and accepts my suspiciously low asking price for the alleged Bronzino or—?"

"Yes, yes. I know all this stuff. It has nothing to do with this. Now I want you to think about three things I know. Put your hands down by your side, and close your eyes while I tell them to you."

Nightingale closed his eyes, but they flickered open immediately.

"No, relax and listen. Henry Treacy continued to fuck Angela and neither of them told you until Angela decided to confess this morning, when she had no choice. No, no. Keep your eyes closed. The daughter you thought was yours is his, and he knew who she was from the moment she arrived in the gallery. Now please, don't open your eyes in surprise when I say she is in some way responsible for his death. Good. And the last thing is that Treacy discovered an original painting by Velázquez, and had you buy it, then hid it from you for years. Can you remember the time he asked you to bid for a painting?"

Nightingale nodded.

"Can you remember how big it was?"

Nightingale stretched out his arms, drew a rectangle in the air. "Not so big. About 170 by 90 centimeters." He widened his arms, "Maybe a bit more. 200 by 100."

"Excellent." The Colonel took a step closer. "Now are you still thinking about what I have just told you?"

"Yes."

"Including the cuckolding and the deception?"

Nightingale nodded.

"Good. Keep thinking of that."

The Colonel, standing about half a meter away now, raised his pistol, and shot Nightingale through the ear.

# 45

THE CRACK WAS loud but the room absorbed it quickly. Nightingale fell to the floor with a soft thump, and the thunder outside rolled and rain began to patter loudly on the panes. Blume expected Angela to scream. But the only one who had shouted out was himself, and his voice was drowned by the shot, the thunder, and the rain. Angela already held Nightingale's head in her arms, but was dry-eyed.

"I never liked him," said the Colonel, almost as a casual aside to Blume.

"And he's the only other person who knew you sold forgeries to the Mafia," said Blume.

"Except you," said the Colonel, "and maybe Angela."

Angela was standing upright, her foot planted in the half-moon pool that had leaked from under Nightingale's head. In her hands, she held three paintings of similar size.

"Those are about the right size," said the Colonel. "Smart girl. We'll start with the top one. Put the other two on the table, on the drawings."

Beneath a treacle veneer and thick ridges of poorly applied paint, the face of a bearded man stared out in anguish. Two doves, or angels, or clouds, or billows of mold and mildew appeared in the background.

"It's not going to be there, Colonel," said Blume. "He's hidden it somewhere else. You need to read the text of his memoirs more carefully."

"I reckon there is an eighty percent chance of your being right," said the Colonel. "But it is a hundred percent chance that you would say anything to regain some control, prolong your life. So let's just see, shall we?"

Blume turned his head in the direction of Angela to communicate some sort of apology for his failure, but her gaze was fixed on the Colonel. Not on the pistol, but on the Colonel's face. In her hand she held a retro-chic silver Dunhill lighter, its top flipped back, her thumb on the roller switch, the corner of the painting a centimeter distant.

"Don't even think . . ." began the Colonel.

Still watching the Colonel, she flicked her thumb, and the lighter spat out a wispy orange flame. It licked at the corner of the canvas, then seemed to die. But just as it gave up, a ghostly blue wave of flame rolled diagonally across the face, then left the canvas, and continued up Angela's arm. She let out a cry and threw the painting away from her. She successfully slapped away the blue flame which seemed to carry no heat. The discarded painting, looking none the worse, wafted down to the table, and landed on top of the other paintings. The Colonel seemed to relax. Lazily, the blue flame followed its descent, and then swam back and forth over the glistening painted surface of the canvas, puttering and almost on the point of going out.

Blume now noticed that a sputtering offshoot of the original flame was hovering around the bottles of solvent and turps at Angela's feet, and yet another flame, this one yellow, had wound itself around the leg of the easel. The Colonel, moving faster than Blume had ever seen, was advancing toward the table with the sketches. He pushed them aside to get to Angela. They tumbled and glided, creating an up-current of air. Finally the shining solvent and kerosene on the face of the man with the unhappy eyes exploded, and the flame immediately caught hold of the edges of the others in the pile. Angela leaped out of the way, and kicked over the bottle of turps and the can of kerosene. Blume jerked himself out of his armchair, the surge of power in his legs and the left side of his upper body easily overriding the dizziness and pain in his head.

Angela reached him as he got to a standing position. The last blue flames rose upwards and with a sudden outward pulse of air, the entire area where Angela had been standing burst into yellow and orange fire. The Colonel stood in the middle of it roaring. He fired two shots at them, one of which whined like a mosquito as it passed. Nothing followed. Now he seemed to be hurling fireballs, as he tried to throw the burning sketches out of the circle of flame. He seemed to be dancing, too, in a rage or in fear as the flames caught the lower half of his legs.

Without so much as a preliminary smoldering, the bookshelf and all the books behind flashed yellow and joined in the blaze, filling the room in seconds with heavy sooty smoke. The back of the chair on which Blume had been sitting was burning in sympathy. Angela seemed to be moving not away from the Colonel, but toward him. Small conflagrations started dropping from the ceiling, even though it did not seem to be on fire.

With pain and difficulty, Blume grabbed Angela with his left arm and pulled her away, his intention being to help, but he found it was he who was leaning on her. The Colonel continued to roar. They made it through the door into the kitchen, but somehow it too had filled with smoke. They stumbled onwards, sweeping away the bead curtain, and found themselves in the glass-covered greenhouse. Both of them suddenly stopped in amazement as they felt the coolness and heard the rain drumming away on the glass above. Blume breathed in deeply.

The doorway through which they came was blowing out masses of black smoke, and the bead curtain rattled and clicked wildly as the billow of smoke flapped it from behind. The lower beads were on fire now, crackling and then exploding like popcorn. It seemed impossible that they had been in there. Without warning, the curtain became a series of fiery pillars, and then suddenly was gone, and they could see a great ball of rage was coming toward them. Blume watched the object with a sense of detachment, dimly aware that it was the Colonel hurtling toward them, trying to escape.

What Angela did next was to fix itself in Blume's mind for many years to come. She reached over to the stove, and with extraordinary strength, grabbed the large copper pot on top. She glanced into it, where she may have seen her own face reflected back at her. It was full of liquid, and as the Colonel staggered to the doorway, she hurled it on him.

Perhaps she saw water in the pot, and if so, her intentions were merciful. But the pot contained not water but stand-oil. Linseed oil that had been boiled for several hours under pressure, as Treacy himself explained in his never-to-be-published book.

Even before it hit the Colonel, the oil ignited. With a strangely dry-sounding thud that shook the floor, the smoky orange flames enveloping him flashed yellow and then white. The Colonel vanished behind a hot sheet of flame, leaving a scream behind.

Angela ran directly through the greenhouse to the door communicating with the outside, and yanked it open, then vanished into safety. The freshly opened door sent a blast of delicious wet and cool air into the room, which reversed the direction of the swirls of smoke coming out of the burning room, and now seemed to be sucking back in all that it had belched out a moment before. Blume's vision suddenly cleared. It looked as if the fire had decided to spare Treacy's greenhouse.

Calmly, feeling sorrowful at all that was happening, Blume went over to the granite sink and slowly filled a terra-cotta pitcher with fresh water. He picked it up, stepped through the smoking gap where the beads had been, traversed the blasted kitchen, noting with regret that it, too, was burning on high, and reached the white blaze that marked the doorway into the living room. A massive dark shape was rolling on the ground, and Blume, full of pity, cast the contents of his pitcher at it. But the water droplets turned to steam and the steam exploded with almost as much force as the oil had, sending the Colonel crawling madly away from his new tormentor, back towards the living room where the fine shoes of a smaller, silent body were also beginning to burn.

Blume gagged as an overwhelmingly sweet and burnt fast-food smell rushed out of the room. He ran back through the kitchen and into the cool greenhouse. From above his head came a cracking and squeaking sound like thousands of ice cubes being thrown into hot water. He looked up and then down again quickly, as a shower of glass exploded overhead and came crashing down, with the rain following. The fire was sparing nothing.

The flames had insinuated themselves across the lattice of wooden frames holding the sloping glass roof, and were crisscrossing the timber beam holding up the glazing. The glass was blackening and shimmering and breaking everywhere, some shattering as it dropped in full panes to the floor. The Colonel made a final bellow like a distant bull, and from the other side Blume heard Angela calling. He ran toward her and the coolness of the night air, glass, sparks, and burning wood falling about him.

# 46

T HE FIRE CREW parked their engines on a bed of cream narcissus flowers in the garden and attacked the fire from there, leaving the street outside free. It soon filled with Carabinieri from the neighboring barracks, some of them under umbrellas, and a crowd of American students from John Cabot. The crowd was becoming quite festive as the fire raged on and the rumors of what had happened started circulating. In the middle, unnoticed and unexamined, sat the Colonel's car.

One of the first to arrive on the scene was Rosario Panebianco, solicitous, gentle, and persuasive. He had Angela in an ambulance and under escort within minutes. When Blume told him to fuck off, he nodded with understanding and was soon back with a blue waterproof jacket with "Polizia" written on the back in reflective letters, and a colorful golf umbrella. He ordered an Agente to stand close to Blume and hold it.

"Commissioner," she said, "you are shivering and there is blood on your collar and back. Put on the jacket."

Blume decided to comply.

Caterina arrived as the medics were on the point of asking his colleagues to force him into the ambulance. Blume called her over, told the Agente with the umbrella to get lost, and nodded in the direction of the Colonel's car.

"Treacy's manuscript is on the backseat. Get it. Then hold it or destroy it. It's just a copy."

"I know," said Caterina. "I was there when he made the copy, remember?"

Blume looked at her in confusion. "We need to get rid of them all, originals, copies, the lot."

"I'll see to it." She pointed at the flames and smoke shooting up from behind the wall. "Is it true what they're saying about the Colonel being in there?"

"Yes. Nightingale, too."

"Oh no," said Caterina. "Any chance he made it out?"

"None," said Blume.

She stepped over a puddle on the cobbles, and turned around. "When I left the house this morning, Rospo was asleep in a car opposite. He wasn't in a great mood, says you were supposed to relieve him. I began to worry about you then. Then you called and immediately after I heard about Paoloni, and then you disappeared again. I should have guessed it would be here. Sorry."

Blume tried to wave a forgiving hand, but he couldn't feel his arm or quite remember which muscles to tense.

"Alec, will you please stop sitting out here shivering and bleeding in the rain. You look so bad people are frightened to come over and tell you to get into the ambulance."

Blume allowed himself to be taken to San Camillo Hospital. He was left languishing for an indeterminate amount of time in a small white-and-green room, which smelled of tuna, then a doctor came in, examined him, shone a light in his pupils, and went jogging out, returning five minutes later in the company of three male nurses and a trolley. Half an hour later, Blume was undergoing emergency surgery to relieve a build-up of pressure in his skull.

Then he slept.

When he awoke, the nausea and headaches has decreased to a manageable level, and Blume announced himself fit and ready to leave. He made the announcement several times without drawing any response. They had shaved the back of his head and placed an oversized white bandage on it, but it did not hurt in the slightest. Not even to the touch. He thought he might make it home, clear up his apartment, and have some supper. He left the room and outlined his plans to a nurse in the corridor, who led him back to bed.

Blume protested in authoritative tones, but was hushed.

"You'll wake the other patients up."

"What time is it?"

"Half past four in the morning."

He slept fifteen more hours and found himself groggily agreeing to spend one more night in hospital. The following morning, he thanked them all for the excellent treatment. Even the doctor. If he had one complaint, he said, it was the excessive hygiene and the constant smell of bleach from the lime-colored wall.

The doctor actually went over to the wall and smelled it, then came back and announced Blume would have to stay for another battery of tests.

"What for?"

"Phantosmia."

"What's that?"

"Olfactory hallucinations. Could be serious."

The following morning, he learned that the results of the test would be ready in two more days. He announced he was discharging himself anyhow.

"You shouldn't drive. Can someone pick you up?"

Blume called Caterina.

"I'm on duty."

"Is that a no?"

"Just that I need to let the others know where I'm going."

"As long as you're not ashamed," said Blume.

As she drove him back to his house, she filled him in on some of the developments. "Angela Solazzi was discharged from the hospital immediately. She's staying with Emma now. She's been in contact twice, says she'll cooperate as much as we want."

"Good." Blume pictured her as she lifted the copper pot, looked into it, and threw the contents into the blazing doorway. He could see her face as she lifted the pot, the look in her eyes, the same as the look she had when she started the fire.

"I don't think she has much to answer for," he said.

"Some good news, too," said Caterina. "The Maresciallo has developed septicemia from the dog bites."

"Fatal?"

"No. But he seems to have slipped into a state of stupor. But we're not getting that many details. The Carabinieri are dealing with him."

"He's probably putting it on," said Blume. "It's the beginning of his defense."

Caterina's phone rang. She answered and Blume noticed the slight tremor of subordination in her voice, and knew who she was talking

343

to . . . She handed him the phone. "The Questore. He wants to speak to you."

That was quick, thought Blume. The Questore had probably asked to be informed as soon as Blume was out of hospital. Someone in the office had wasted no time in telling him.

He took it, and, with an extra layer of gruffness for her benefit, said, "Blume here."

"What the fuck was that, Blume?"

"It's a long story, sir."

"A long story can be told in a long report, and with four weeks' sick leave, to be reviewed at the end of the period and probably converted into a three-month suspension, you will have plenty of time to give me all the details."

"No need for the suspension, sir," said Blume.

"This morning I got news that the dead British national, John Nightingale, was shot point-blank with *your* pistol, also found at the scene. That has rather overshadowed our little propaganda success at capturing the tourist mugger. A Carabiniere colonel with an impossibly dense web of important contacts was burned to death while an internal investigation into his activities was being conducted. A former policeman, recently removed from duty under highly suspicious circumstances, was killed hours before that, and, in a minor development, I hear a search warrant was issued by a magistrate for your apartment which, it turns out, was also the scene of a burglary that was not properly reported. Did I say three months: how about thirty-three years?"

"One investigation fused into another, and things . . . I lost control for a while."

"And another thing. Where was the investigating magistrate overseeing all this? Did we even have one?"

"Not as such. Buoncompagno and the Colonel . . ."

"Buoncompagno has been hauled before the disciplinary section of the Magistrates' Council for his handling of this and other cases. Basically, his immunity disappeared along with the Colonel and a garden villa owned, it turns out, by a branch of the Pamphili family."

"I could come up with a summary version. One in which any unregulated actions are seen to be natural developments of a rolling, highly complex investigation in which, perhaps, there was insufficient liaison with the judicial authorities, but, in compensation, in which the police and Carabinieri worked closely together," said Blume.

"I see the knock on the head left you pretty much the same devious bastard as before, Blume. If you write that report, I want you to write a longer version, too. Just in case, God forbid, your version is viewed as not fully credible."

"I also think the American Embassy might put in a word on our behalf with the Ministry," said Blume.

"You think so? Well, that would be unaccountably nice of them."

"I have a favor I can do them. All I shall ask in return is that the Ministry recognizes the skill with which the Questore of Rome has handled a very difficult and complex case. I think what's-his-name the ugly little Minister from the Northern League would be chuffed to receive a pat on the head and a tickle under the chin from the Americans."

"Don't make promises you can't keep, Blume."

He handed the phone back to Caterina.

"I think it was probably Rospo who told the Questore to use my number to contact you," said Caterina. "In case you were wondering."

When they arrived outside his building, she opened her bag, took out a set of keys, and handed them to him.

"These are yours," she said. "Your apartment has a new door, remember? I picked them up for you."

"Right. Thanks." He fingered the three long new keys. "I don't suppose . . ."

"I need to get back to Elia," said Caterina.

"Right."

"But call me."

When he reached his apartment, he was shocked, then overcome with emotion, to see it pristine clean. She had picked everything up. The slashed cushions sat in a corner waiting to be stitched back up. The sink gleamed. On the kitchen table sat the three notebooks, looking a little dusty and tired now. He took them into the study, filed them away.

He passed across the hallway into his bedroom. The bed was freshly made, his clothes were folded in a pile on the polished dresser.

# 47

THE FOLLOWING MORNING he called the American Embassy and asked to be connected to Kristin Holmquist.

"Alec! Lovely to hear you. I'll phone you back."

She kept her word, but leisurely. Three hours passed before she finally rang his cell phone.

"I hear you were in the hospital again."

"Just a checkup, really. Home now."

"Great, I was beginning to feel really bad about not visiting."

"I picked up the anguish in your voice right away," said Blume.

"Yeah, well, you sound fine to me," said Kristin. "Were you making a personal call or is this business?"

"Business. I can talk on this line, right?"

"Sure. Not that I would vouch for your phone but shoot. Maybe be a bit oblique if you're going to supply me with more of that vital intelligence info you've been feeding us."

"Actually, I do have something you might be interested in." He paused, waiting for her response. "Kristin? Are you still there?"

"Don't you know the sound of bated breath when you hear it? Give me what you got, Alec. I'm busy."

"It's old stuff, not current or all that sensitive any more, but of some diplomatic value. The relationship between the US Embassy and the Christian Democrats back in the day. The hostage negotiator flown in— the guy who writes the books? We spoke about it after a pleasant Mexican chili in my house?"

"Got you," said Kristin.

"I'm pretty sure the manuscript won't go into the public domain unless I allow it."

"It would be nice if you didn't allow it. Can you do that?"

"Well," said Blume, "getting rid of it would be one way, giving it to you would be another."

"I prefer the second option," said Kristin. "Mainly because I am curious. You'll really hand it over this time?"

"Yes. The thing is, I have a very complicated police report to prepare, and I am going to find it hard not to refer to Treacy's memoirs to explain certain actions. That could kick-start an inquiry, get a magistrate interested, and then it gets all messy and public. See the problem?"

"You can't keep Treacy's memoirs out of your report?"

"I could write a report with minimal references, but to do that I would need the Questore to be backing me."

"I know your Questore," said Kristin. "He's a good guy."

"Adorable though he is," said Blume, "he answers to other people."

"I see," said Kristin. "Well, it is possible that at the next scheduled meeting—that's in about three weeks—one of my colleagues might be able to bring his sterling efforts to the direct attention of the Minister. Would that help, do you think?"

"Almost certainly," said Blume.

"It would be nice if we could meet," said Kristin. "Rather than you coming to the embassy or me sending someone over to pick up a copy of the manuscript. Are you planning on keeping a copy, by the way?"

"No," said Blume.

"How about we meet in the next few days? I'll call you."

"Great," said Blume.


He watched daytime TV incredulously. He had not done so in twenty years. He was scandalized. Nobody seemed to want to have any personal secrets any more. He switched over to a station called K2 and watched cartoons instead. He watched one called *The Fairly Odd Parents*, and thought it was great.

His landline rang, and he answered to a woman whose voice was very slightly familiar.

"Alec, it's Filomena," she said.

Such a horrible name, he had heard it recently . . .

"Remember? Beppe's wife. Widow."

"I'm sorry," said Blume.

"I am cremating him."

"He'd have liked that," said Blume.

"He'd have enjoyed being cremated?"

"As long as he was dead first, obviously."

"Jesus. I can see why he considered you his friend."

"I'm sorry," said Blume. "It's how we used to talk to each other."

"Will you be there? It's tomorrow morning. In Viterbo."

"Of course I'll be there," said Blume.

"Some people think I'm wrong to cremate him," she said. "It's not popular."

"People," said Blume.

"Yeah. Listen . . . the thing that got him killed—it was his own fault as usual, wasn't it?"

"It was the fault of the person who killed him," said Blume.

"But he put himself in harm's way, didn't he?"

She seemed to want to think this, but he did not want to exonerate himself.

"No. I put him in harm's way."

"If you think that, then I bet you want to make things right, don't you?"

"I can't do that."

"No, you can't. You were his best friend. He always said that. He was a violent man, too. It's what lost him his job."

"He was a good man."

She continued as if she had not heard him. "Our son, Fabio, is going the same way. He has the same vengeful mindset as his father. Now I have to pick up the pieces, all over again."

"If I can help . . ." said Blume.

"You can," she said. "You know who killed Beppe, don't you?"

"Yes."

"I want you to leave him alone. I do not want you or anyone else to do him physical harm."

"But . . ."

"You said you would help. Promise me."

Blume stayed silent.

"Promise me. I know you don't know me that well, but I knew Beppe and underneath it all . . . to save his son he would have renounced all vengeance. He wanted Fabio to be better than him. He always said so."

"OK."

"And promise no one else under your orders will harm the bastard?"

"That, too."

"There is one more thing you have to do. Not immediately, but soon. You have to talk to Fabio."

"I'll try," said Blume. "But I don't have kids, so I'm not going to be much good."

"You'll do fine. And I want you to explain why you decided not to revenge his father's murder with violence, and why he should not either."

"He won't listen. If I was him, I wouldn't listen."

"He might. He might not. Maybe he'll get it in a few years. But you can try. It's your duty."

"I haven't a clue what to tell him. The justice system in this country . . . it doesn't work. Nothing fucking works. That Carabiniere will walk. Maybe he'll lose his job, if they decide to be harsh. There's no comfort for your son."

"I didn't ask you to comfort him. That's my job. Talk, stay honest. Can you do that?"

"I don't know," said Blume.

"Good. Like that," she said. "You don't know, but you'll try. The crematorium is at Via dei Monti Cimini, number 36. Ten o'clock tomorrow morning. There won't be many of us there."

Shortly before dinner, he phoned Caterina.

"Who paid for my door?"

"I did. You owe me €2,600."

"Can I come around to pay? I've got a checkbook."

"There's no rush."

"Not to pay, maybe. But can I come around?"

# 48

"I T's JUST PESTO from a jar, I'm afraid," said Caterina.

"Pesto's fine," said Blume. He meant to be more gracious, but he was feeling uncomfortable at the kitchen table, Elia's big brown eyes on him, then off him every time he turned around to smile.

After dinner, Blume sat in the living room watching TV while Caterina did whatever it was mothers did to get children to bed. It took a long time, and Blume was beginning to get into a Bruce Willis film when Caterina finally came in. To the side of the television was a pile of bedcovers and a sheet.

Caterina sat down near him and watched a few minutes of explosions, then said, "I need to explain about those bed clothes. I had a visitor the other night."

"No, no. Nothing to do with me," said Blume. "You don't need to tell me anything, really."

"The visitor was Emma Solazzi," said Caterina.

"Ah," said Blume. He switched off Bruce Willis in mid-leap. "I think maybe I do want to hear about it."

When she came to tell him about Emma's confession, Caterina was both relieved and disappointed that he seemed to take the news in his stride. He seemed far keener on seeing the painting she had brought.

She thought he might have something to say about her harboring a suspect, but he hadn't. Instead, he began to tell her about the mistakes he had made from when he allowed Paoloni to talk him into staging a burglary in his own apartment.

"That was the point I stopped being a proper policeman and began playing a game that led to my friend's death. That was the point when I should have called up Faedda, and tried to set the Colonel up. That was when I should have called in an investigating magistrate, drawn up a report, put the facts in order. Everything I did from then on was illegal. A fatal game. And if you ended up with a suspect sleeping on your sofa and a rogue Carabiniere threatening your child, I'm responsible for that, too."

"It's a thin line between self-accusation and self-pity, Alec," said Caterina. "So shut up now before you cross it."

He looked at her in amazement.

"Seriously," she said. "Shut up. What's done is done. I'm sorry about Paoloni, and I'm sorry about Nightingale. But you didn't kill them. As for what Emma did and what you think her mother may have done . . . it's not for us to say. Now do you want to see that painting?"

Blume nodded.

"Good. I'll get it then. Meanwhile, there's a letter over there, on the desk next to my laptop. It's what Treacy wrote to Angela, if you're interested."

Blume went over and read the letter.

"He wrote better in English," he said as she returned. "All these yew berries and kisses, fruits and *pentimenti*. Awful stuff. He wrote mush in Italian."

"Maybe it's not because of the language but because of the person and his feelings of regret," said Caterina.

Blume was looking at the painting. "Jesus, this is one lousy piece of work."

"I like it now," said Caterina. "I didn't at first, but I do now. I like that he did it in the style of the woman he loved."

"The woman he bullied, you mean. And this is hardly a flattering homage to her art. It's a parody of bad painting. Or a parody of de Chirico. That's what he was on about in the letter."

"Is it?" said Caterina. "I don't know anything about painting. I can see that maybe this isn't great, but I don't see parody in it."

Blume propped the picture on the sofa and stood back. "Maybe not. It looks . . . it looks like a lot of correction effort went into it, which I suppose is not consistent with parody."

"Also, you can tell from his letter that he meant this sincerely. He wanted to be forgiven."

"You mean all that stuff about *pentimenti*?" said Blume. "It's not just another way of saying sorry. It's a technical term in painting. It means correction or second thoughts. When a painter starts drawing an open hand, then decides to turn it into a fist, or gets rid of a dog in the background, something like that, you can often see the traces of where the original was. That's a *pentimento*. Come here."

He led her closer to the painting and pointed to the center of the frame. "See, here? This, what is it, an empty grotto? It's the focal point of the picture, and it is set at the center of the curving walls, only he made a real mess of the proportions here. The *pentimenti* are crowded around the focal point of the picture. It's part of what makes it look so bad."

"Do you suppose the Velázquez went up in flames in that house or is it hidden somewhere else?"

"I was wondering the same thing myself," said Blume. "I think it was hidden somewhere, and he tells us where in his notebooks. And if that's the case, then I think some American is going to find it in the end, since I have promised to give the notebooks to the embassy."

"You're an American. You find it," said Caterina.

"Here," said Blume. "This is made out for €2,600. I didn't put your name or the date or anything. Just signed it." He handed her the check.

Caterina took it, went into the kitchen, and put it in a drawer, then returned to Blume in the living room.

"Tomorrow afternoon Elia is going on a school trip to Venice and Padua, then down to Rimini. I am a bit worried about all that water."

"He'll be fine. How many days?"

"Four days. Three nights."

# 49

THE CREMATORIUM IN Viterbo was not signposted, and Blume had to ask a local traffic cop for directions. He was told to follow the signs for McDonald's, then for the Coop supermarket, and finally for the sports center.

He arrived with minutes to spare, and found he was one of a tiny group of mourners. There was Fabio, shuddering as much with rage as grief, his arm in the tight grip of his mother. She now had a Botox face, yellow hair, and strange leggings under her too-short skirt. She had aged, and without any grace. He raised his hand in greeting, but she did not seem to recognize him. Perhaps he, too, had aged without grace.

A very old couple—Paoloni's parents? his ex-wife's?—three middle-aged couples, and about eight others, three of whom Blume recognized as being former policemen.

Blume did not fancy himself a religious man, but the civic cremation of his friend was the most dismal and meaningless event he had ever witnessed. Within five minutes of the coffin being sent on a conveyer belt out of sight, everyone had left except for Fabio and his mother, but they were nowhere to be seen. Presumably they were waiting for the ashes. When he got into his car, the upholstery smelled of nickel and asphalt and made his head swim.

After ten minutes circling the city walls, Blume parked, got out of his car, and walked into the historical center looking for a bar. He found a pleasant one near the papal palace, had two cappuccinos and several pastries, and sat staring out the window at the zebra-striped bell tower of the city cathedral.

After his coffee, he lingered in front of the city cathedral, trying to remember its name but it wouldn't come. He ambled around the side, and found a tourist information sign tucked against the wall. San Lorenzo. That was it. He had been here before, long ago, on a school trip or with his parents. He could not recall. What sense was there in being cremated next to a vandalized sports ground on the edge of town when a magnificent cathedral such as this stood empty and waiting? For some people, architecture like this was worth leaving all that was familiar and coming halfway across the globe to see.

Blume went up the flight of steps and into the cathedral, and found he was the only one there that morning.

He sat staring down the arcaded nave at the blank apse with the crucifix, and thought about Paoloni. It was a severe interior, with faded frescos and a few paintings. On impulse, he lit a candle for Paoloni. Then he lit one for his own father and mother, and fumbled in his pocket for change and found none. The smallest he had was a 20-euro note.

He toyed with the idea of dropping the full 20 euros into the collection box, but dismissed it as ridiculous. But he did not want to leave without contributing the one fifty he owed for the candles, and blowing them out seemed out of the question. He stood there in a paralysis of indecision.

Fuck it. He dropped in the twenty, and wandered over to look at the paintings. A guidebook at an unattended desk was on sale for fifteen euros. Great. He grabbed it, took it to a bench, and flicked idly through it. The painting in front of him showed the Holy Family and some saint, painted by Giovanni Francesco Romanelli, a native of Viterbo.

Blume looked at the painting, and heard his father's voice saying "mannerist." That had always been a term of abuse for him. He even had grave doubts about Michelangelo, and was generally dismissive of most of the three hundred years until the modernists arrived. Maybe someday, Blume thought, he would develop his own ideas about what was good. But the guidebook seemed to be on his father's side. This was not the best of his works, it noted regretfully. Most of Romanelli's important works were to be found in France not, for once, because the marauding Napoleonic armies had stolen them during their rape of this beautiful and incomparably more cultured country (Blume checked the name of the polemical art historian and found it was a priest), but because Romanelli had lost all his commissions in Rome after Pope Urban VIII, a Barberini prince, died and the throne was taken over by the pro-Spanish and violently anti-French Pope Innocent X, the great Pamphili Pope, immortalized in the famous portrait by Velázquez and the bust by Barberini. The art historian priest seemed to approve of the irascible Pamphili, even if his election to the papacy did mean that Viterbo's best artist had to leave town.

Blume stood up, pulled out a 50-euro note from his wallet, and stuffed it in the collection box. He would have said a prayer of thanks if he had been a believer. Or maybe this was the beginning of faith.

He had just worked out where Treacy had hidden the Velázquez.

# 50

B LUME CLEARED SPACE in his living room, turned on his laptop, and fetched a series of art books from his parents' study.

But he knew he was right even before he had finished opening the art books and Web pages. He called Caterina at the station.

"I need you to get a tactical bag. We're going to need a battering ram, a set of chain cutters, maybe a hammer, crowbar, screwdriver, and flashlight. When you have all that, go home, pick up that painting Emma left, and come here."

"They wanted to know why I wanted a tactical bag," she said when she arrived forty minutes later.

"Did you tell them?"

"How could I?" She handed him the painting.

"OK," said Blume. "Now I want you to look at this." He gave her an Editalia art book.

"That's Treacy's painting!" said Caterina. Immediately. "No, wait . . ." She looked more carefully at the picture, then at Treacy's painting. "Well, except the trees are in a different place, and the wall and arch aren't the same either, and . . . I think I'm going to stop now before I come across as a complete idiot."

"No, you're right. The colors are similar. You can't tell properly because this is a reproduction, but you can still see they are muddy, green, gray, beige, and depressing, same as this painting. The theme, too, the mood, the size even. You saw the likeness before the differences, same as me."

Caterina looked at the cover of the book she was holding. "Giorgio de Chirico," she said. "I thought he only did surreal paintings."

"What you're looking at is a view of Villa Falconieri," said Blume.

"Which?"

"The one in the book. De Chirico's," said Blume. "Now, listen to this," he pulled over a battered old blue hardback and read:

*"During his second visit to the Eternal City, Diego Velázquez was an honored guest at the graceful Villa Medici, where it was only natural that a mind of refined artistic temperament and an innate sense of the aesthetic . . ."*

"God." He tossed the book aside. "I can't stand that sort of drivel. The point is when Velázquez was in Rome and painted the portrait of Pope Innocent X which we saw a few days ago, he was staying at the Villa Medici. Where the French Academy now is."

She nodded.

"And when Velázquez was there, he did a painting, of the gardens. It's not as well-known as his portrait works. Now listen: In 1946, Giorgio de Chirico painted two landscapes, one of Villa Falconieri, which I've just shown you, and one of Villa Medici. Both of them reference Velázquez's painting. If you take the two de Chirico paintings and merge them, you get a sort of reproduction of Velázquez's painting. It was de Chirico paying homage to but also copying the master. Treacy went on about it in his notes.

"Now, we also know from his notebooks that Treacy was a great fan of de Chirico, he talks about a sense of affinity. More to the point, he turned down a chance to pass off forged de Chirico works to de Chirico's niece when they were stolen.

"Now that ugly painting there is not just homage to Angela, it's a message, too. Personal and professional. It is also a variation on the de Chirico painting."

"Which is a variation on Velázquez's."

"Right. But Treacy's painting isn't a casual variation. It's a landscape of a specific place. A park, in which he used to live as a guest. A park that is now open to the public, but belonged to the Pamphili family for centuries. The park where he and Angela kissed and were interrupted by an Englishwoman with dogs."

"Villa Pamphili," said Caterina.

"That is where we're going now. Bring the painting and the tactical bag."

# 51

BLUME DROVE ACROSS town, struggling to keep a light foot on the accelerator. At the San Pancrazio entrance he drove into the park. "Nice and slowly. Don't want to kill any joggers," he said. "Though those cyclists weaving in and out among people trying to walk are fair game."

He drove slowly up the pebbled path toward the Quattro Venti triumphal arch.

"We're going to go as far as the palace itself," said Blume.

Blume stopped talking and they listened to the crunch of pebbles under the tires. "Looks like we've been spotted."

A Municipal Police car had stopped in front of them, and the two occupants were getting out.

"Is this some sort of mix-up?" asked the Vigile. "As far as I know we're patrolling the grounds this week, next week it's the Carabinieri, and the week after it's you guys."

Blume took his hands off the wheel and noticed for the first time he was in a squad car with all the markings.

"No. It's not a mix-up. We're here for an investigation," said Blume. "We were going to park over there by the chapel."

"Fine, I'll get out of your way then," said the Vigile.

Blume allowed the car to roll a few more meters and then pulled onto the grass underneath a rotting holm oak. They sat side by side looking over the grounds, half-heartedly landscaped and lazily vandalized.

"You know who has a lot of *pentimenti* in his paintings?"

"Velázquez?" said Caterina.

"Yes."

Blume climbed out of the car, looked across the lawn. He popped the trunk, took out the painting. "I've been thinking about the letter Treacy sent Angela where he talks about poisonous yew berries and them sitting together. Grab the bag of tools and follow me."

He led Caterina across the lawn onto a pebble path and then followed a wall until it curved inward and then out again making a large U-shape, like the apse of a church. Vandalized bas-reliefs and niches were spaced at regular intervals, separated from the pathway by a small moat. In the center of the concave area was an enclosed rectangular chamber, which was closed off with a padlocked gate.

"This is called the 'theater,'" said Blume. "I don't know if it was ever used to stage outdoor plays, but if it was, the audience would have sat over there." He pointed to a circular area with patches of grass and scree surrounded by dark green trees with orange berries.

"Are those yew trees?" asked Caterina.

"Yes, they are," said Blume. "Let's go over and sit there, shall we?"

Caterina hefted the bag over and sat down on the remains of a cracked stone bench defaced by graffiti. Blume sat beside her. A jogger went puffing past, and then they were alone.

"This is where Henry Treacy and Angela sat together in 1974, when Henry lived at the porter's lodge, and they had all this park land to themselves. They sat on this bench and, according to his memoirs, they kissed for the first time."

Caterina put the palm of her hand on Blume's cheek and, hooking her finger over his ear, pulled his face toward hers. His lips were dry and his neck was tense, but it still felt good, and she liked his breath. But then he turned away.

"I still need you to look in front of you. Look at the scene in front of us now."

Caterina examined the concave area, the pine trees in the background, the embankment that formed a proscenium, the white marble wall curving away from them, the niches, the masonry. It was the scene in Treacy's picture.

"Give me the picture."

"Here," said Blume.

She held it in front of her.

"It's here. It's the view from where we are now. That tree is a little taller now, and there seems to be an extra—no, wait ..." She stood up and walked a few paces to her right. "From here it's perfect. Like he was standing here. Come and see."

Blume came up behind her and they looked at the painting. "Treacy knew this park like no one else. He walked through it undisturbed. He would have explored its hidden nooks and crannies and hiding places. The *pentimenti* converge in the middle of the painting, which corresponds to the chamber there."

"Do you think Henry Treacy hid his Velázquez in that grotto? What about damp?"

"The oldest paintings in the world are in caves," said Blume. "Rock often creates very dry environments."

"Why did he not just give the painting to Angela?" said Caterina. "Wouldn't that have been easiest?"

"Who says he wanted it to be easy? If she kept the painting and if she also read his notebooks or autobiography or whatever it was intended to be, all the clues were there. He hid it where they fell in love."

"And if she hadn't kept the painting or the letter or read his autobiography?" asked Caterina.

"Then it would mean she had not forgiven him, and his *pentimenti* would mean nothing, and in exchange, she would have got nothing from him."

"So it was repentance with a 'but' built in."

Caterina lifted up the bag and together they approached the grotto. When they reached it, Blume peered in and said, "It would be easy to climb over this gate without removing the padlock. There's another door in there, which must open into a cavity under the embankment behind. So, now, tell me what you think: Is there going to be a Velázquez hidden in there, or have I read this all wrong?"

Caterina watched him peering through the bars like a child at a zoo. In her hand she held a heavy pair of bolt cutters, far too powerful for the flimsy padlock holding the gate shut, and waited for him to get over his self-doubt and out of the way. Then she cut through the chain like it was made from paper clips, and they walked into the empty hollow. The sunlight from outside slanted in so that the central area was bright and the walls to the side dark. They were white and smooth, plastered without so much as a rose, flute, or scroll, but filthy and covered in graffiti. People had evidently scaled the gate to come in here simply to spray-can the place. Every building in Rome was "tagged" already, so this must have made a tempting target.

"You know," he said, looking at the black, purple, and red squiggles of paint all over the walls, "my apartment block is covered in this shit, too."

"Every building in Rome is. The Vigili Urbani aren't so good at catching the kids," said Caterina.

"You know what the message scrawled on my building is?"

"*W la fica, Fuck The Police, Debora ti amo, Lazio Merda*?" asked Caterina.

"No. It's 'impossible is nothing.' That's an advertisement for a watch or a soda or something. These kids are spouting corporate messages. They aren't rebels; they've no philosophy, no message, and no courage. Look, there are your *putti*."

Caterina looked. Carved into a niche was a bas-relief of little boys with angel wings intent on beating each other up, same as the painting in the Pamphili Gallery. But here they had been spray-painted and their features chipped off.

In front of the entrance was a second door, warped by damp and age. There was no padlock or chain, and though closed it was not locked. The space behind was a narrower, darker version of the first chamber, and Caterina took out the flashlight and shone it around.

The room was airless and lifeless, almost without insects. A few withered leaves on the ground made an unpleasant scratching noise as they moved in the slight breeze.

"More graffiti, and an old blanket," she said, shining the flashlight along the walls and concrete floor. "Cigarette butts and an old Rizla packet."

"This is mostly old-style graffiti," said Blume. "Less spray-paint, more penknife cuts and indelible pens."

"The graffiti archaeologist," said Caterina. "There's an erect penis, there's another, and, oh, look, there's another."

"Pair of tits over there," said Blume. "Not bad. Some soccer scores from bygone years. *Liverpool 4 Roma 2*. A gloating Lazio fan spent some time in here, in the early '80s."

"This one *Kossiga = Amerika* comes from the seventies or eighties," said Caterina. "*Juden Raus*, now there's an old favorite. Someone's done a sweet little bunny rabbit face."

"I got a Smurf over here," said Blume.

"What sort of person penetrates a hidden room to deface a piece of baroque architecture with a picture of a rabbit or a Smurf?" said Caterina. "Someone's done a picture of a dog fucking a cat. It's pretty good, actually.

So is this one. It's a rifle sight and there's the face of someone in the middle. Cossiga again, I think."

"I used to do that as a kid," said Blume. "In fact, I still do. I draw circles around faces and add in the crosshairs."

"Lots of Celtic crosses and anarchist 'A' symbols," said Caterina, waving her flashlight about, and looking up at the ceiling. "We can't reach the top of the wall without something to stand on."

Blume was running his left hand along the walls, stopping now and then to rub his fingertips clean on his jacket.

"Let's start by looking in areas that are easy to reach," he said. "Let's start at eye level. Now this entire back wall is very slightly dusty, so there is some damp coming from the embankment behind. I wouldn't put it there. But the wall between this chamber and the one in front is perfectly dry."

"It could be in the first chamber, too," said Caterina.

"It could," said Blume. "But if I were hiding something, I'd choose this room where there is no chance of being seen from outside rather than the first room. If it was daytime, the sunlight reaches into the first room, so that would have been a risk, and if it was night, then he definitely would not want to be in the first room because any light he used would be very visible from outside. Also, I think we need to remember that at this point, he's just concealing it in a safe place, not hiding it from anyone who is in here specifically looking for it. He wanted Angela to find it."

"The walls are smooth plaster. Could he have plastered over that well?"

"Sure. He made his own frames, paints, ink, boards, paper, solvents, I'm sure he had a go at fresco painting. He'd be an excellent plasterer."

"That meant he had to carry a bag of plaster in here."

"Yes," said Blume. "Maybe he left it in here the day before ... what are you doing?"

"This." Caterina had taken the crowbar from the bag and slammed it against a crude image of an ejaculating penis.

"Ouch," said Blume as he saw the shock travel up her wrists and arms. "Try stabbing it at the wall instead."

Caterina did so, but only left pockmarks and scrapes.

"We could try the battering ram," said Blume.

"Let me try your side first," she said.

Blume moved out of the way. "I was thinking," he said, "that knocking a hole into a solid wall and then refilling it is a lot of work. You would choose a place that already had an alcove or shelf, then cover it over. So we should tap the wall and listen for where it might be hollow."

Caterina shone the flashlight at the wall against which Blume had been leaning. "There's another of your telescopic sight things," she said.

"No," said Blume. "That's supposed to be the peace symbol."

"Right," said Caterina. "Someone's even put a peace dove next to it, and some wag has painted a rifle sight over it. All this clever irony going to waste in here."

But Blume did not reply. He took the flashlight from her. Then he turned it on the graffiti showing the dove caught in the crosshairs of the rifle sight.

"Do you know what the Pamphili symbol is?" he said.

"I would have said bees, but from the way you're staring at that dove . . . If that's what it is. A bird with backward wings like that could never fly."

"The Barberini family were the ones with the bees, the Pamphili are doves. But there is something you don't know, because I never thought of mentioning it until now. The third of Treacy's notebooks had a fore-edge drawing. You know, a picture drawn on the edges of the pages."

"I used to do that with school textbooks, while you were drawing sharpshooter sights and crosshairs," said Caterina.

"Right. Well, the image Treacy drew on the edge of the paper was a dove. It just seemed like a doodle, which is what it was. You would never have seen it because you only had a photocopy, and the Colonel, too, would never have seen it."

Caterina was standing beside him, crowbar in hand. "Shall I?" she said.

"Go for it."

She jabbed the sharp point of the crowbar at the eye of the dove, and drove a hole straight through the plaster.

# 52

M OVING THE CROWBAR back and forth she easily levered away pieces
of plaster. The aperture she had opened was arched, more or less
the same shape and size as the flap of a mailbox. The wall on either side
was made of tufa and every time she hit it, crumbles of orange and yellow
grit poured out at their feet, but she was not making much progress.

"Try striking downwards," said Blume.

"Shut up. And keep the light steady."

She raked away at the wall with the gooseneck. The plaster and loose
cement gave way easily, causing her to sneeze. Within a few minutes she
had hollowed out a keyhole-shaped aperture in the wall.

"It's a narrow niche, a bit like the ones on the outside. There is probably
one next to the other side of the door as well," said Blume. "But this has
to be the one we want."

Caterina hunkered down and clicked her fingers impatiently over her
shoulder until Blume handed her the flashlight, which she shone into the
narrow space. Then she stood up and made an attempt at dusting herself
down.

"It's there," she said.

"Are you sure?"

"There is a package wrapped in yellow cellophane and some sort of
masking tape."

"Can you reach it?"

"Sure."

"Why didn't you pull it out?"

"I thought you might want to do it," said Caterina.

"You do it," said Blume.

He held the light as she put both hands in and pulled out the heavily
wrapped package, small enough to fit under one arm.

Caterina propped it against the wall and they stood there in the semi-darkness. She allowed herself to lean against his shoulder a little, and felt him lean back into her.

"We can hardly see anything in here," said Caterina.

Without saying a word, Blume stooped down, picked up the package, and put it under his arm. "I am going to take this back to my house. I will wait for you. Go back to the station, sign in the squad car, collect your own, and come back out to my place," he said. "But off duty."

She drove him back in perfect silence. He sat there clutching the package, looking straight ahead.

"See you here in an hour," was all he said as he got out of the car.

She was back in thirty-five minutes. The package was intact, propped up against the slashed sofa cushions.

Blume sat on the floor of his living room, box-cutter in hand.

"It's in a carrying box, from the feel of it." He slashed the blue plastic, and started pulling away reams of bubble wrap, a silicon sheet, white cotton strips, and finally a backing board. Then he turned it around for her to see.

"It's brown," was all that came to her. The small work, no bigger than a folded newspaper, seemed to consist of three shades: coffee, tea, and piss. Her disappointment was as enormous as the picture was small.

But he was looking at it with reverence.

"I know you don't get it, yet, but wait . . ." He left the room and returned so quickly with a large art book, that it must have already been ready and open in the next room. "Look. The woman to the left pushing back the red curtain and looking down at the spinning wheel. Now look at the painting. No curtain, no spinning wheel, no color, but look at that pose. It's a study for the same thing. Look at the canvas, look at the line . . . I don't know. I'm not an art expert but I believe this. I believe Treacy. This is genuine."

"You trust the word of a dead forger?" She did not want to deflate him, but nor did she want to get carried away on a wave of misguided belief.

"I trust his story."

"Why?" asked Caterina.

"Because he did not write to deceive. He painted to deceive, but even then he left the real lies to Nightingale. I believe he was earnest in his writings. They allowed us to find this."

365

"It is all that valuable?"

"Oh God, yes, Caterina. Beyond reason. Once they prove that this is really by Velázquez, it will sell for—I don't know. Tens of millions of euros easily. It will take a lot of time for it to be proved that this really is his. Especially since Treacy is the source. The notebooks will help. That means I might have to go back on my word to Kristin."

"Who's Kristin?" said Caterina.

"A woman at the American Embassy—I'll tell you some other time."

"Tens of millions?" It did not seem right that a yellowing rectangle was worth lifetime after lifetime of work by her and her colleagues.

"Yes," said Blume. "Tens of millions. In a few years, perhaps, once it has been completely authenticated. But take this to the right people, make some promises, they'd spot you an advance of a few million. If you wanted, you could turn this into serious money in two days."

Caterina sat down. From this angle the picture looked black rather than brown. Blume's eyes were bright, as if he had a fever. She moved her head and the work seemed to change color again. Now it reminded her of dried old glue on the broken spine of an old dictionary. Blume had sat down beside it and was cradling his arm over the frame, glancing at it sideways, shifting it to catch different light angles.

She decided she did not like it.

"What are we going to do with it?"

"We could both become very rich," said Blume.

"Our ownership would be challenged. We're public servants. This belongs to the state. For now."

"If you find something like this, you get to keep it," said Blume. "That's how it works. Use the money to buy lawyers, then more lawyers. Unmanageable wealth in a few years. You're not into this, are you?"

"No. The Colonel had me convinced for half a day that you could be bought, and then you proved him and me wrong, and I was ashamed," she said. "But now ..."

"You are afraid."

"Yes," she said.

"Do you not find it tempting?"

"Yes. But it disgusts me and frightens me, too."

"Great art is for keeping the people down, you know," said Blume. "That's what it's all about. We can't help but think something is great if it fetches a great price, or if a lot of rich and educated people talk about it a lot. Treacy knew this, but I still think he really enjoyed this find. It's a sketch for something that came later, became part of the canon. What's exciting about this is the potential. The drawing in itself . . . Who knows how good it is?"

"I don't want to have anything to do with it," said Caterina.

"It's the size of the sums involved, isn't it?" said Blume. "Suppose you and I got, what, fifty million euros each. Think of all the Ikea furniture you bought, the making do with old things, slowly building up your collections of books, that nice carpet that was a big extravagance but you don't regret. All those years and years on the lowest-paid police force in Europe suddenly blown away. It would retroactively mock all that effort. You could buy a lifetime's possessions in a single afternoon, using less than one year's interest on the principal. That's what I don't like about the idea of sudden massive wealth. It would invalidate all your earlier struggles, make your life up to now seem pointless."

Caterina felt her chest relax as he said this. She had not realized how tense she had been. Hearing him say these words was a huge relief, and she was still nodding in happy agreement with his reasoning, when he said, "But sudden affluence, now that is a different matter."

"What do you mean?"

"I mean imagine getting enough money to buy a larger house, to send Elia to college abroad, go on vacations, have a home help, and not have to work as a policewoman any more. Not untold wealth, just a large amount of money that would make your life easy and would not humiliate your past efforts at making do or propel you into an alien social circle. That would be better, wouldn't it?"

"I suppose," said Caterina, looking at the black object squatting on the sofa beside Blume. "But . . ."

"Wait. Who does this painting really belong to?" asked Blume.

Ridiculous though it seemed, Caterina feared it was a trick question, and thought for some time before answering.

"The Republic of Italy, I suppose. Or Angela. If it was Treacy's to begin with, then he definitely gave it to her," said Caterina.

"Exactly. So the beneficiary is Angela and, by extension, Emma. She'll inherit the wealth afterwards. The daughter who pushed her father dead on the ground," said Blume. "Maybe, after a fifteen-year legal battle, they will show their gratitude. Even if they gave you half a percent of the probable value of this, you could probably quit the force."

"What about you?"

"I don't want to quit the force. I would not know what to do with myself or where to go."

"Neither do I," said Caterina.

"Think about it. Think about your son. You're on your own. It's a dangerous job, poorly paid, bad hours, and you carry the violence you see every day inside you. Maybe someday the violence will hit you and your son will be left to fend for himself. Richer people live longer. Don't just say no to the idea. Think about it."

"While I think about it, what happens?"

"I think I'll carry out my plan anyhow, give this back to its rightful owner. Then if she offers you a reward, as I think she will, you can decide then."

"But you're not taking anything?"

"I don't need to. I've no one depending on me. I've no children, relations, or debts."

"Always on your own."

"Yes," said Blume.

Caterina went over to the sofa, removed the painting from beside him, and sat down in its place.

# 53

S HE PULLED THE sheet over her shoulders, shivered a little, and said, "It will never get published, will it?"

Blume pushed the sheet off himself and contemplated light burn marks on his forearm. "I doubt it. He never got to finish it. And Treacy doesn't get to live happily ever after, does he?"

"You mean he is not eternal like you are?" said Caterina. She reached out and yanked his ear. "Up close like this, I can see your wrinkles, and did you know you're going gray at the sides?"

"Silver hair, not gray," said Blume. "He got killed by his own daughter. I hope to do better than that."

"Maybe you should beget yourself a daughter first before you jump to optimistic conclusions. I think it's sad that no one will read Treacy. I didn't even get to read it in the end. Just the beginning bit with you, and then I went ahead on my own for a while before I had to give up. How does it end?"

"With the narrator lying dead on a cold Trastevere street and an Inspector called Mattiola feeling the base of his skull for evidence of a countercoup blow," said Blume.

Caterina shook her head. "That's not nice. How does it end, really?"

"I can't remember exactly," said Blume. "He was not always chrono-logical; some of it is cryptic, sometimes impenetrable. And we do know the ending. We know it better than he does."

"What about his version, how does it end?"

"It becomes disjointed, breaks down into notes, half sentences, cryptic phrases, scrawls. He was dying."

"I liked when you were reading it to me. He was in London when we stopped. What happened then?"

"He went back to Ireland, got fed up, and decided to walk down to Rome."

"Very funny," said Caterina. She turned her back on him and pulled the sheet tighter around her shoulders. "I'm interested in finding out how he came to be in Italy, what it was like for him to spend his life here, a stranger in a strange land. I want to know what happened to his parents, whether he saw them again. I want to see how he started off and ended up alone."

Blume pulled up the bedcover and wrapped it over the sheet and around her shoulders. "No, really," he said. "He did. He walked through France into Italy."

"That's the next bit?"

"Yes," said Blume. He left the room and came back carrying the first notebook, climbed back into the warmth beside her. He opened it at the beginning, and started turning the pages until he found the place he wanted.

"This is where we were."

Caterina closed her eyes. "Read it, Alec. Out loud and slowly."

*"After London, I went back to Ireland for a few months, but it did not work out. There was nobody there for me, and all I did was spend the little I had saved drinking pints of plain in Sinnotts pub. It was one golden afternoon there, when I was on my fourth pint, that I conceived of the idea of walking away from it all. Literally walking away.*

*"No one believes me when I tell them I walked to Paris and then Rome, but, with the help of one ferry boat, that is just what I did. The walking started in Normandy, but the beginning of my journey was a freezing cold morning of drizzle as I left Killiney Hill Station for Bray to catch the mid-morning train down to Rosslare in Country Wexford, where that evening I boarded the ferry that would bring me to Cherbourg. It was June, but the Atlantic was still in a swollen and wintry mood, and rolled me back and forth across the lounge bench inside where I tried to sleep, without success, and doused me in icy spray when I went up on deck to vomit, with great success.*

*"We docked in Cherbourg at lunchtime, and having completely emptied my stomach of all content during the night, I was ravenous. Every time I go to France now, I search for a croissant as buttery, savory, and perfect as the one I had that morning in a bar in Cherbourg. I had to mime my wishes and point to what I wanted to eat like a well-trained monkey, and I was aware of seamen smelling of diesel oil and surrounded in black tobacco smoke laughing at my expense, but*

*hunger swept away all embarrassment. It also swept away four days' of the allowance I had given myself. It was not until my third day in France that I realized how much they had overcharged me.*

"*I had travelers' checks in British pounds and some francs. The travelers' checks were a parting gift from my stepfather on the night before I left. He pulled them out of his jacket pocket with a jocular expression on his face, as if someone had put them there unbeknownst to him and he was just discovering them, like a kindly uncle might discover candies and thruppenny bits in his pocket. Ho-ho-ho, what are these? My inheritance, you bastard. Enough to live on for one frugal month.*

"*To be fair to my mother and stepfather, they were probably expecting me back soon, but I never saw either of them again. My stepfather died suddenly of heart failure a few weeks before I reached Rome. My mother had sent a telegram followed by several letters to a poste restante address at the main post office in Piazza San Silvestro, but I arrived several weeks later and did not bother checking for letters until several weeks after that. By the time I had read through the letters, my stepfather was dead almost two months and my mother was so hurt she had decided not to speak to me again. Nor did she, though I do not think she ever intended permanent silence. But eight months later, when I finally had an address of my own in Rome and wrote to the post office asking them to divert the mail to it, I received a letter from a lawyer telling me that she, too, was dead of a stroke. The funeral was over. He assured me it had been a dignified affair, and he had looked after the funeral costs and would forward the 'remaining' inheritance, which he did. The last trace of him was his signature on a check for a scandalously modest amount that arrived just in time for my first Italian Christmas.*

"*But that morning in Cherbourg, with the sea wind stabbing my ears and the strap of my army surplus backpack already rubbing my shoulders raw, I set off on the first stage of what was to become a six-month two-thousand-mile meandering walk.*

"*It is hard to say now why I decided to walk. Part of the idea was to arrive in Rome, the inevitable destination in 1969 for an aspiring painter who preferred the classical style, with a certain sophistication of manner. I thought I would learn French by walking through France—and I was not entirely mistaken, though I learned far less than I hoped. I had read Baudelaire, Rimbaud, and Leonard Cohen. I wore my hair long and heeded the spiritual advice of psychedelic rock stars. And I wanted to take a long, slow walk away from Monica, Ireland, and my old self.*

371

"I had a small tent. The tent had a small hole. It did not rain that night, but the wind whistled. I started walking in the wrong direction on a minor road that skirted the coast. I set up my tent in a plowed field, near a place named Cosqueville. All the villages there were named something-ville. I slept between the ridges of two furrows, and woke up half dead from cold, damp, and lumbago and raging with thirst. I had filled a water bottle in the toilets at the Cherbourg docks, and thought it would do me.

"I found the farmhouse. Or, better, as I drew near the farmhouse I was chased, caught, crowded, and cowed by a pack of dogs. I think I was crying when the farmer finally came out to shoot me dead with a very military-looking rifle.

"He looked at me, paying particular attention to my hair, then deciding that I was obviously some sort of bewildered half woman and posed no threat, sent me in to his wife. 'Eau, eau,' I kept saying. The farmer and his wife thought this was very funny. But they gave me water and milk and rolled-up buckwheat pancakes, and pointed me in the direction of Saint Lô, which they seemed to imagine was my ultimate destination, for who could go farther than that? Or maybe that's what they thought I meant with my pathetic cries of 'eau, eau?'.

"But night fell before I had even reached Carenten and I turned left by mistake and started heading back toward the sea. I had to pitch my leaky tent in another field, and lie there listening to the sea turning in its sleep, the slap and drag of rocks on a beach nearby, trying to imagine what warmth and Italy would be like. The rain came in slantways, and in the morning, the frost was so sharp and hard, I thought it would pierce my boots. It may have been the hunger, the cold or just the age I was, but that morning, in which I could have died from exposure, I felt brighter, more alive, and bristling with hope than I ever have since. I turned my back on the Atlantic and finally started walking inland, toward my future in Paris, Provence, Florence, and finally Rome with its ochre architecture, crumbling decay, and endless days of heat and sun.

"All this beautiful life lay before me."

Caterina slept, her breathing regular, her mouth open in a tiny "o."
He closed the book.

# ACKNOWLEDGMENTS

I owe a particular debt of gratitude to Cormac Deane for his structural and creative assistance, and to Ciaran Deane for psychological support, constructive criticism and encouragement. I could not have finished or even begun this without the love and patience of my family here in Rome. Thank you, Marion, for the regular phone calls and for hearing me out as I complained and updated in equal measure. My thanks also to Sarah Ballard, Michael Fishwick and Ben Adams.

I am indebted for certain technical aspects to Giuseppe De Rosa, whose website is to be found at www.ilcollezionista.it, as well as to Ispettore "Beppe", Sovrintendente "Mimmo" and the excellent journalist Luca Pietrafesa.

# ALSO AVAILABLE BY CONOR FITZGERALD

## THE DOGS OF ROME

'A powerful and hugely compelling thriller. Dark, worldly and written with tremendous style and assurance . . . Conor Fitzgerald is a class act' William Boyd

On a hot summer morning, Arturo Clemente is brutally murdered in his Roman apartment. Clemente is no ordinary victim. His widow is an elected member of the Senate, and Chief Inspector Alec Blume arrives at the scene to find enquiries well underway. The murder case seems clear-cut and a prime suspect is quickly identified, but Blume must fight to regain control of the investigation, aware from bitter experience that in Rome even a murder enquiry must bow to the rules of politics. The complex and uncomfortable truth he will unravel will shock even him, and his struggle for justice may yet cost more innocent lives . . .

'Blume is an engaging hero who might just have to potential to fill the gap left when Michael Dibdin's death ended his Italian detective Aurelio Zen's investigations'
*Sunday Times*

# A NOTE ON THE TYPE

The text of this book is set in Bembo. This type was first used in 1495 by the Venetian printer Aldus Manutius for Cardinal Bembo's *De Aetna*, and was cut for Manutius by Francesco Griffo. It was one of the types used by Claude Garamond (1480–1561) as a model for his Romain de L'Université, and so it was the forerunner of what became standard European type for the following two centuries. Its modern form follows the original types and was designed for Monotype in 1929.